Nicola Gill lives in London with her husband and two sons. At the age of five, when all of the other little girls wanted to be ballet dancers, she decided she wanted to be an author. Her ballet teacher was very relieved.

The Neighbours

NICOLA GILL

avon.

Published by AVON
A division of HarperCollins*Publishers* Ltd
1 London Bridge Street
London SE1 9GF

www.harpercollins.co.uk

A Paperback Original 2020

A catalogue copy of this book is available from the British Library.

ISBN: 978-0-00-835539-5

Typeset in Bembo Std by Palimpsest Book Production Limited, Falkirk, Stirlingshire
Printed and bound in UK by CPI Group (UK) Ltd, Croydon CR0 4YY

For Stuart, and Charlie and Max

Chapter One

Today. Has. Been. One. Of. Those. Days.

So, of course, there on the Northern line platform is Clare Hayes, aka Little Miss Perfect from school. I haven't seen her for over a decade but today here she is.

I rummage in my bag, let my hair fall over my face and pray she hasn't seen me.

'Ginny!'

Short of throwing myself on the track, there is no escape.

'Clare. Hi.'

She looks as if she has just stepped off the pages of *Vogue*. I, on the other hand, look like someone who put on the last clean(ish) items she could find regardless of the fact they in no way constituted an outfit. Someone who decided their hair could 'definitely do another day' when it definitely couldn't. Oh, and I have a spot the size of Africa on my nose.

A packed train pulls into the station and people surge towards the doors.

'I'll wait for the next one,' I say.

Clare shakes her head and pulls me on. I am squished against a large man with a bulging backpack.

Clare works as a film producer now. She lives half the year in LA. Nightmare! The backpack nudges me in the back of the head. She's doing a movie with Meryl right now.

We stop at a station. Angry people on the platform tell people to 'move down, please'. Angry people on the train mutter 'move down where?' People squeeze on. I am shoved even closer to backpack man, who glares at me furiously.

Meryl is a *total* sweetheart!

The backpack hits me on the back of the head.

They are shooting the movie on location in Bali. Bloody hard work but such a fabulous place. Wonderful, welcoming people.

More stations, more people, more whacks in the face and more about Clare. What the hell did I do in a former life?

My mind drifts to the presentation I so spectacularly messed up this morning.

Clare, or Clare-Bear as her (many) friends used to call her, doesn't look like she messes up. Ever. She looks like the sort of person who makes herself hot water with lemon in the morning, puts her gym sessions in her diary and buys her Christmas presents in October.

'What about you, Ginny? What are you up to work-wise?'

I breathe a sigh of relief. For one God-awful minute I thought she was going to ask me if I was married. I have already spotted the diamond the size of a golf ball on her left hand. My job sounds okay. It's a dream job, in fact. Not my dream, but Clare's not to know that. She won't remember me gobbing off about how I was going to become a great novelist.

'I'm in PR.'

'PR? Great. You didn't become a writer then?'

Damn her perfect bloody memory! No wonder she got a string of A stars. 'Oh, I do a bit of writing on the side.' Why did I say that? I feel the sweat beading on my upper lip.

The backpack whacks me in the face.

'That's fabulous. Novels? Screenplays? Telly?'

2

Emails, the odd letter. 'Err . . . This is my stop. Lovely to see you.'

When I get home Nancy is on her knees ironing a dress on the coffee table.

'We've really got to get an ironing board,' I say. 'Functional adults own ironing boards!'

Nancy laughs. 'How was your day?'

I groan.

'That good?' She unplugs the iron.

'I bumped into Clare Hayes on the tube.'

'Our esteemed Head Girl. Tell me she's doing some dead-end job she can't stand.'

I shake my head. 'She's a Hollywood film producer.' Nancy groans. 'And – AND! – she asked me if we were *still* friends.'

'The cow!'

'I got off the tube two stops early just to get away from her!'

'You walked further than you actually had to? That is bad! Lucky I got us wine.'

'Aww, Nance, you really are the perfect flatmate. I can't believe you're moving out. I'm going to miss you so much.'

'I'll miss you too.'

'No, you won't. You'll be too busy swanning around in your fancypants new job in New York.'

She laughs. 'Well, that is true.' She pours two large glasses of wine. 'Marielle seems lovely.'

I nod. Marielle does seem nice, although if I'm honest I had thought my days of sharing a bathroom with a complete stranger were over after uni. I just keep telling myself that she won't be a stranger for long. And it's not like we didn't interview heaps of potential flatmates before settling on her. Nancy was particularly fussy on my behalf. One guy didn't make the cut because she 'could just tell' he would be the writer of passive aggressive notes. I take a sip of wine. 'Hey, at least I've got the training course to cheer me up.'

She laughs. 'It won't be that bad, will it?'

'Three days locked in Premium Inn, Swindon. With Annabel. Assault courses for "fun". Being forced to chant "YES WE CAN" every three minutes.'

She holds her hands up laughing. 'Okay, okay. Let's get drunk.'

We clink glasses.

She gestures towards the Xbox. 'I see you've bought yourself something to fill the gap in your life once I've gone to New York.'

'Very funny. It's Jack's. I reckon it's a big step forward from just keeping a pair of socks and underpants here.'

'Yay!' Nancy says in a very un-yay voice. She recently bought me a book called *Stop Kissing Frogs*.

'Nance! On Saturday, he said he cares about me lots.'

'Here,' she says, rummaging around in her handbag, 'I got us some Twirl Bites.'

'I really shouldn't,' I say, opening the packet and popping three into my mouth at once. 'Did you hear what I just said? About Jack.'

'Yes.'

'Well it's a good sign, isn't it?'

'A good sign of what? You've been going out with him for two years. Well, two years minus the periods of time he decided he couldn't handle being in a relationship at all. And the best that he can manage is that he cares about you.'

'*Lots.*'

'Forgive me if I'm not exactly punching the air.'

'I know you don't like him.'

'It's not that I don't like him, it's that I don't like the way he treats you.'

I pick at my cuticles. 'He's had a very troubled past.'

'Who hasn't?'

'Seriously. His parents' divorce sounds really bloody. And his father was just never there for him. Too busy shagging around.'

'Proving the apple doesn't fall far from the tree.'

'Nance! Just give him a chance will you? For me?'

She pauses, and I realize I'm going to get the Best Friend speech. The one where she tells me I can do better. It will be peppered with Nancyisms like, 'Give and take doesn't mean he takes and you give.' She has a glug of wine. 'Shall we open another bottle?'

List your biggest achievements to date. I stare at the piece of paper in front of me, my mind going completely blank. I don't think winning the Kindness Cup at Primary School is going to cut it here.

I look over at Charlotte, who is scribbling furiously. No doubt her achievements will require a supplementary sheet.

The woman running the training course is a groomed-to-within-an-inch-of-her-life American whose shoes I can't stop staring at. I realize that if I spent less time focusing on such things, I might have more achievements to list, but they are extraordinary (the shoes, not the achievements). The heels are clear Perspex balls! They'd be even cooler – although probably a little dangerous – if they rolled around when she walked.

'Don't get too hung up on your answers, people,' says Ms Perspex Heels. 'This is just a starting point for discussion. And remember to think not just about what you want out of your career at Splash PR, but about what you want out of life.'

I have to stifle a snigger here as, for the majority of people in the room, life and Splash PR are one and the same. I'd rather fallen into working there. I left university and got a job waitressing to tide me over while I decided what I really wanted to do. And although there were bad bits – the stag nights and the mothers who lectured their kids in front of me about trying harder at school so as not to end up like me – there were also great bits: masses of fun, zero responsibility and great tips. And then I looked around, and all my friends had miraculously got themselves proper grown-up jobs. The thing with bumbling around is that it's a lot like singing. Fine when there's lots of you doing it, but deeply embarrassing when it's suddenly just you. I answered the first job ad I saw which was for a receptionist at Splash.

My boss, Annabel, is staring at me. Annabel is the one who promoted me to PR Manager in the first place and now she is DISAPPOINTED in me. She doesn't actually come right out and say this of course, but she goes around with it written all over her face (even though she's had so much Botox, she finds it hard to make any sort of expression at all). Annabel likes to bounce around lots of ideas and doesn't like people who never quite catch them.

We have been at the Premium Inn for three days, and I am longing to get home, even though it's weird to think Nancy won't be there when I get back. I am desperate to see Jack though, and hoping he's missed me. A couple of nights before I came here, we were supposed to be going for supper at Julia and Adam's. When I called Jack to remind him, he said he'd completely forgotten Jed's leaving drinks. And of course there were all sorts of things I wanted to say. But I didn't say any of them because I don't want to be Natalie. Natalie is Jack's ex and the ghost of nagging past. I didn't nag, and Jack didn't come. Which was fine. As long as I pretended not to notice that Julia hugged me a little too hard. And kept flashing Adam thank-God-I've-got-you looks.

I force my mind back to the present and the piece of paper

in front of me. *What do you think are your weaknesses?* How long have you got? I glance across at Kieron whose brow is furrowed. Kieron is about seven, but already a PR Executive.

He's the type to list strengths dressed up as weaknesses here. 'Sometimes I just care too much about a project', 'I have ridiculously high standards'. I suspect that he's not really a human being, but some sort of PR robot from another planet. I have become more convinced of this during the intensive 'down-time' we have 'enjoyed' over the last few days. For me this has been easily the most exhausting part of the trip. Kieron, however, is the Duracell bunny of Work Appropriate Fun. He gets drunk but not too drunk – on the lager whose PR account Splash handles – and chats in a way that seems casual but is actually one long advert for Kieron. All his conversations lead back to PR. It's in his blood, you see. Or it would be if robots had blood.

List your goals. I did have goals once. At the age of fifteen, when thirty-four seemed forever away, nothing seemed impossible. Hell, I could have been an astronaut or nuclear physicist by now. But somehow the years just got sucked into the vortex of day-to-day living. The truth is, I don't really know what I've done with the time. Get up, go to work, come home and do it all over again.

At lunchtime, as she is avoiding the evils of carbs by carefully peeling the bread off her turkey sandwich, Annabel beckons me over. She wants me to make a speech at Inspirational Women next month. It will be held at Grosvenor House.

The (bread included) cheese and pickle sandwich I am eating turns to stone in my mouth. 'I . . . I . . .' Why has she asked me to do this when we both know she finds me about as inspirational as a sweaty sock? Why isn't she doing it herself when she feeds on such things like a rattlesnake does on rodents? 'I . . .'

She puts a sliver of turkey into her mouth. 'I'd do it myself but I'm in Milan.'

One thousand five hundred people. Watching me. I think of my first experience of public speaking, aged eleven. Mrs Gozney, my history teacher, was so pleased with my model of the Coliseum that she asked me to give a talk in assembly about how I'd made it. I wrote and re-wrote my speech, practised it in front of the bedroom mirror – 'I have some tips . . .' The day dawns and my legs shake as I walk up to the stage. I take a deep breath. 'I have some tits . . .' (Did I mention that I am the only girl in my class to already wear a bra, and it's a D cup at that?)

Annabel's head is cocked to the side and her black patent pump is drumming on the floor.

'I . . . I know Charlotte really wanted to do it . . .'

Annabel's eyes widen. She was expecting me to be kissing her feet in gratitude by now. 'Charlotte's in Milan with me. And Jess can't do it. Or Sarah. Or Hayley.'

I'm last choice. Well, unless you count the blokes on the team and you can't really send one of them to talk at Inspirational Women. Though I'm pretty sure Kieron would dress up in full drag if necessary.

Annabel pops a cherry tomato into her mouth. I watch her throat to see if she swallows it whole. I am thinking back to my friend Jenny's wedding. Jenny insisted that as chief bridesmaid, I simply had to make a toast. I spent the weeks beforehand having nightmares about standing up in front of everyone in the nude (in the event it was only marginally less embarrassing as I was wearing a Little Bo Peep style dress complete with a bonnet). It's only a toast, I tell myself on the day. I can do it. And I can. My voice is loud, clear and only slightly shaky as I ask everyone to raise their glasses 'to Jenny and Robert'. And that would have been fine if Jenny hadn't been marrying Brendan. And Robert hadn't been her ex.

Annabel's foot is tapping so much now it's a wonder she hasn't rubbed a hole in the blue carpet. 'So?'

'I'd love to,' I say, my voice cracking.

I look out of the window and see that it's pouring with rain. This afternoon we are team-building. It's hard to see what twenty highly educated grown-ups can learn from clambering around on a series of elaborate bouncy castles, but perhaps I will have the scales lifted from my eyes.

Chapter Two

I know that the whole New Year, New Me shtick isn't traditionally something one tackles in November, but I sit on the tube deciding I can't possibly wait another two months. I must have faith that Jack and I will work out. All the wasted energy I spend worrying can be channelled constructively, so that I can be more impressive at work, make a great speech at Inspirational Women (another thing I must stop worrying about), and go to the gym for something other than the jacuzzi or sauna.

The man next to me is looking at me out of the corner of his eye whilst pretending to read the *Metro*, and I realize that I am actually muttering some of my resolutions out loud.

Not stressing about my relationship with Jack is going to be easy-peasy after last night. We went to a party together. Normally when we go to parties, I hardly see him. But, last night, it was me he was flirting with, me he was making laugh. When we got home, he was solicitous: was I cold? Should he have let me go out when I wasn't quite over my chest infection? Oh, you of little faith, Nancy!

Now I need to be a whole new me at work. In this economic climate I'm lucky to have a job at all. It's time to stop dreaming of living on the beach writing novels and buckle down. My last performance appraisal was both lacklustre and completely fair. But, all that's set to change. I'm going to make a fabulous speech at Inspirational Women (I can see Shirley Williams and Judi Dench congratulating me now). I'm going to dream up stunts that get hundreds of thousands of YouTube hits within days, create product launches that make even the most jaded journalists sit up. I'll be a *PRWeek* 'one to watch'. Someone that every client insists they have on their account. Annabel will put her Blackberry down when she talks to me. In brainstorms, she'll underline my ideas with lots of red pen on her flip charts.

I'll be turning into the new me tomorrow. Or at least later today. I forgot all the concept boards for a presentation so am having to go back home to collect them, which will make me very late. By some miracle Annabel is out of the office this morning so I should be okay. Especially since I phoned my mate Jess and gave her a Code Red. (Code Red equals leave jacket on back of chair and place warm coffee on desk.)

I come out of Camden Town tube station and realize that I'm humming to myself. I cannot stop replaying a conversation I had with Jack last night. We talked about Rosie and Jake who were about to have a baby. And then Jack said that our babies would be terrible at bowling because we'd both completely sucked at it at when he came with me to the Splash Christmas party. And I struggled to stay nonchalant, whilst all the time my brain was screaming: OUR BABIES! OUR BABIES! He kissed me, and then pulled away, telling me I'd been poorly and ought to get some sleep. I undid his belt and he made love to me. Gently, as if I might break.

I'm nearly back at the flat now. A cat darts in front of me. Isn't a black cat crossing your path supposed to be good luck?

A little girl of about two is splashing in a puddle. She is wearing ladybird wellie boots and a green woolly hat under which peep bright red curls. Her face is full of wonder. She reminds me of Simon's little girl, Evie, who he bought into the office yesterday because her childminder was sick. Simon was up against a deadline, and somehow it was me who got to show Evie the photocopier and coo over her drawings. When they went home, Simon thanked me profusely and told me how great I am with kids, but none of that mattered in comparison to the fact that Evie gave me a sticky Ribena hug and insisted I keep her drawing of the Princess's castle (masquerading as a pink splodge).

I open the front door, thinking how I must pop in on Mr Holden in the basement flat later to see if he's managing to get out and do his shopping since his operation.

I tear up the stairs. The door to the flat isn't double-locked. Jack mustn't have left yet. How odd! I hope he hasn't succumbed to my bug.

I walk into the living room. Sunlight is streaming through the window. There, in its spotlight, stands Jack, his jeans around his ankles, his head tipped back, his eyes closed and a low moaning escaping from his lips. Kneeling between his legs, with her back to the doorway, is a semi-clad woman, her blonde curls bouncing up and down.

Neither of them are aware of me, and I stand, rooted to the spot, my head spinning and vomit welling up in my throat. Finally, after what must only be a matter of seconds, but takes on the quality of slow-motion, I hear a strangled sort of cry escape from what I presume to be my own throat. Jack's eyes spring open and the woman spins around. It's Annabel.

My first thought is: Oh God, now she'll realize I'm not in the office. What can I say? The mind works strangely at certain moments.

I run out of the door, not bothering to close it behind me. I take the stairs two at a time and hurtle out of the front door and down the street. I hear voices behind me but carry on. I don't even know where I'm running, just that I have to run. I run until my heart feels as if it's going to burst through my chest and my breath is ragged. I slip and hear a sickening thud as I hit the pavement. A woman in a passing car stops to ask if I'm okay and I nod even though I feel slightly unsteady on my feet. My shoulder and knee hurt and I've taken the skin off my hands. A dustbin man stares at me. I start running again.

I find myself in Regent's Park, where I collapse on a bench, my heart pounding. I wipe away the tears with the back of my hand, which is bleeding. Jack and Annabel! The image of the two of them is horribly vivid. Annabel's bright pink underwear (on anyone else, cheap; on her, fabulous), the expression on his face. My mind flashes back to our love-making the night before. What had seemed tender now seems vanilla. I cry great big hiccupy sobs.

A jogger goes past, looks at me, and then speeds up as if the unhappiness might be contagious. It starts to rain, lightly at first but then more insistently.

Why the hell were they in *my* flat? (Presumably because the post-coital commute was slightly more convenient than from his?) When had it started? Had it been going on when Annabel gave me that appraisal? How many times had they done it? How many lies had they told? Had they been laughing at me behind my back? Poor, stupid little Ginny. Could do better. At work and at home.

An old lady with a Scottie dog stops to ask if I'm okay. I am obviously very far from okay. Okay people don't sit sobbing on park benches in the teeming rain. Okay people attend to cuts on their hands, wipe the snot and tears from their faces. But I nod and the woman walks away, shaking her head. 'I daresay he's not worth it, love,' she mutters.

I am suddenly aware that my teeth are chattering. All I can

think about is that image. The bright pink underwear, the look on his face.

Eventually I heave myself off the bench. My shoulder is sore. And I have a feeling the pain is only going to get worse.

Chapter Three

Bright pink underwear. The look on his face.

It's three days since I walked in on Jack and Annabel. I sit on the kitchen floor shovelling Shredded Wheat Bitesize into my mouth straight from the box. They aren't very nice without milk. Jack's Coco Pops would have been better but they went in the bin on that first day along with his Yorkshire Tea and multivitamins. What kind of a grown man eats Coco Pops anyway? I should have known then. I use the sleeve of my dressing gown to wipe away the tears that are rolling down my cheeks. The Shredded Wheat are sticking in my throat. There are no clean glasses left so I fill a mug with water. Jack's keys are sitting on the counter next to Nancy's.

My new flatmate Marielle was supposed to have moved in by now but she called me to say there's been a family emergency in France and she won't be able to move in for a week. It's a horrible thing to admit to but, although I felt sorry for her, I was also relieved for me. The thought of trying to act normal around someone right now isn't good.

I'm appalled by my appearance in the bathroom mirror. My hair seems to have gone into shock and is sticking up in little tufts. Red, swollen eyes stare back from a doughy white face, and my lips are cracked and bloody.

The phone rings. Perhaps it's Jack or Annabel (perhaps

both of them together, phoning from bed)? They've each left countless messages. Because there's so much to say.

Bright pink underwear. The look on his face.

I turn the bath taps on full, steam swirling up in my face. I undress gingerly. My shoulder is still sore from the fall, but it's more than that; my whole body aches. It seems it's not just my heart that's broken.

I lie in the bath, letting the tears roll down my cheeks and into the bathwater. So much for bloody karma. I've been a 'good girl' all my life: sleeping through the night as a baby, handing in my homework on time at school, growing up to pay my bills on time and saying No to drugs. I've never dished out the kind of hurt I'm experiencing now. The kind of hurt that makes you feel as if your skin has been peeled off and you're just a gelatinous heap of raw nerves.

The worst part of the day is when I first wake up. For a nanosecond – just a nanosecond – I don't remember. And then it hits me; hits me like a two-tonne truck. I lie there, wanting to scream and trying to breathe.

I slump on the bed, exhausted. When I got back that first day, I ripped off the sheets and put them through a boil wash. If I could have done, I'd have thrown out the bed. Not that I knew if Jack and Annabel had ever had sex in it. In fact, the evidence of my own eyes suggested their sex was much too hot and exciting to even make it to a bed. How many times had they done it? Had Annabel been better than me? The sound he'd been making certainly suggested she might have been.

The phone rings again. Go away! I don't want to speak to either of you! But it's my mother's voice talking to the answering machine. I run into the sitting room, my hand hovering. I want to pick up. To tell her to come to get me.

18

To take me back to my parents' slightly too warm house where she'll tuck me up in the single bed I used to lie in looking at my Take That posters. My mum will bring me a tray with a bowl of Heinz tomato soup on it and white bread cut into triangles. She'll make me eat it. But I don't want to hear that my mother had never liked Jack. And I don't want to be asked what I'm going to do about work.

I replay Mum's voicemail. 'Hello, darling. Haven't heard from you in a couple of days. Expect you're very busy. Talk soon.'

Bright pink underwear. The look on his face.

Maybe relationships are going to be like backwards somersaults; something I will never get the hang of despite trying over and over again and making myself sick and giddy in the process. I've always been bad at them, right from when Jamie Robb stuck his tongue down my thirteen-year-old throat and I started wondering if he was The One.

I keep the curtains closed night and day. I remember once going to see a friend who'd just had a baby. She said the boundaries between day and night had become blurred, that it no longer seemed to matter if it was three in the morning or three in the afternoon. I'm like that now. I sleep when I'm overcome with exhaustion, eat when I remember (from a diet that would appal Annabel, who always eats her five a day). I am a feral cat.

I start to cry again. Can you run out of tears? I'll never have a baby of my own now. I'll die alone. Annabel will have Jack's baby shortly after their fairy-tale wedding. Mr Can't Commit and Miss Work Is Everything live happily ever after.

My romantic history consists of a series of Jacks. A Jack called Mike. A Jack called Ed. A Jack called Raif (stupid name!). Nancy always says it's 'them not me', but surely there must

19

come a point when there are too many 'thems' for it not to be me? What a fool I've been! But that's all going to change from now on. I am going to be a cold, hard bitch.

Yesterday, Jack's tickets for Manchester United/Tottenham arrived in the post. At least I can stop trying to make myself like football now. Ditto R&B. (Could have been worse. The Jack called Ed was a *Star Wars* nut. I actually spent a day of my life at a convention where every other woman there had Princess Leia Danish Pastry hair.) I looked at the tickets, which said 'North Lower BLK 5', and ripped them to teeny tiny shreds. I felt a euphoric high before coming crashing back to earth. Cold, hard bitch is one thing, but I don't want to edge into bunny-boiler territory.

I rub my pounding head. The birds singing in the trees outside the window are driving me insane! I snort. This is the sort of dried-up, miserable old cow they've turned me into. Someone who is irritated by one of nature's most beautiful sounds.

I pick up my phone and start scrolling through Facebook.

Lulu Jordan
I said yes! 💍
Isn't my fiancé just the cutest? Last night the love of my life asked me to marry me and I said yes! #engaged #Ilovehim #fiance

Great! Great, great, great. Congrats, I write. Oh God, have I become *that* person? I add an exclamation mark and a few emojis before casting my phone aside.

Next time I meet someone – assuming there is a next time – I am going to have a list. Apparently, this is what normal people do. I only discovered this by accident fairly recently when I was chatting to Julia and she told me that she couldn't really mind that Adam didn't like camping and outdoorsy things because he ticked most of the boxes on her list. Apparently, it's just like when you're buying a flat – you can't expect to tick all the boxes. (I am just thinking: who can actually afford to buy a flat nowadays? Especially on their own. And I am probably going to be on my own forever.)

I haven't told Julia what's happened yet. It's hard not to notice that since we first met waitressing thirteen years ago, Julia has become a Global Head of Marketing and managed to find herself in a relationship that looks like the last few scenes of a rom-com without any of the 'will they, won't they' lead-up. I, by (stark) contrast, seem to have endlessly cried on her shoulder about my failing career and relationships. So is it any wonder that I'm slightly embarrassed about rocking a Britney 'oops, I did it again'?

I haven't told Nancy either. This job is a huge promotion for her – she's editing the American *Elle* – and I don't want her to have the distraction of worrying about me. She sends me messages about people keeping shoes in their ovens because their flats are so tiny and they eat out all the time anyway, and I reply trying to sound chirpy and normal. I keep pretending to be in meetings when she tries to FaceTime me. I know as soon as she sees me the jig is up.

The couple upstairs are shouting at each other. They're always shouting at each other. I don't know why they stay together. Why anyone bothers to stay together. It's all going to go wrong at some point, so why not just cut to the chase?

Chapter Four

'What a class–A bitch!'

I am sitting in my sister's kitchen. It's now a week since I walked in on Jack and Annabel and self-pity, despite my virtuoso performance, is getting a bit samey, so I've popped round for tea, biscuits and a serving of How Could Theys? Rachel is delivering as best she can, though is severely hindered by my twin nephews who, naked from the waist down, are in the throes of potty training. Apparently, they're quite old to still be in nappies. I feel a bit sorry for them really – I know what it's like to be stuck in the slow lane sometimes, but they're not even three and they're already lagging behind.

'Do you need a poo, Felix?'

Felix shakes his blond curls and carries on pushing his brick trolley through his brother's train track.

'Be sure to tell Mummy, won't you? Wees and poos in the potty get a Smartie.'

'Want Smartie!'

'When you do a wee in your potty.'

The kitchen, which was once a gleaming white example of minimalism, is strewn with brightly coloured plastic. The remains of the boiled eggs and soldiers are still on the table from breakfast and I can't help noticing that my socks kind of stick to the wooden floor.

'So,' Rachel says, 'you just walked in on them?'

'It was awful. Like some—'

'Wee wee!' shouts George.

Rachel leaps up and flings George onto one of the two bright green pottys sitting in the middle of the kitchen. Everyone waits hopefully. George gets up. The potty is bone dry.

'Smartie?' he says.

Rachel shakes her head and comes back to the table. 'Sorry. You were saying?'

'Oh yeah. I found them. It was awful. I'd rather not think about it actually.'

Felix has got out some pink playdough and is feeding it to the Blu-ray player.

'No!' Rachel says. Felix's brow furrows. He rubs the play-dough in his hair. 'Felix!'

'Smartie!' Felix says.

'Smartie! Smartie!' George adds, sensing blood.

Rachel sighs. 'All right. Just one each though.' My sister was once a person who never took orders from anyone. Then she had children. 'Let's put *In the Night Garden* on.' She picks up one of the DVDs that is lying on the floor out of its box and wipes a piece of smushed banana off it. 'Don't forget to tell me if you need the potty though.' She sits back down. 'Sorry.'

'Like I said on the phone, nothing like this is going to ever happen to me again.'

'Right. You're rebranding?'

'Yup. Ginny The Mug is replaced by Ginny The Bitch.'

'Except you don't really want to become a bitch?'

'Why not? It certainly beats—'

'Poo!' George yells.

Rachel jumps up from the table and grabs the potty.

'Felix done poo!' George says.

Sure enough, there is a small, brown pile in the centre of

24

the cowhide rug. Rachel pins a rictus smile to her face. 'Next time in the potty?'

She gets to work on cleaning up first Felix and then the rug, and I sit at the table trying not to cry. This isn't helped by the fact that it occurs to me how funny Jack would have found it that Felix chose to poo in the middle of the cowhide rug rather than anywhere on the vast expanse of wipe-clean wooden flooring surrounding it.

Rachel slumps back down in the chair. 'Lovely!' she mouths, making a face. Then she launches into a diatribe about how awful Jack and Annabel are.

'Do you think I've missed my chance of having kids?' I say.

Rachel puts her hand on my arm. 'Of course not. You're—'

'Wee wee,' Felix says.

'Sure?' Rachel says, not moving from her seat.

Felix nods and clambers on the potty.

Rachel gets up. 'Sorry, Gin. They go to bed at seven. In nappies! Why don't you stay and have supper with Paul and me? Then we can talk properly.'

I can't face the thought of playing gooseberry. Nor can I deal with my brother-in-law who, despite being a really lovely guy, has a sense of humour that requires some forbearance on my part. (He thinks whoopee cushions the apogee of a sophisticated evening. Ditto a food fight.)

There is a sound of liquid hitting plastic. Everyone – Felix included – looks amazed. 'Wee wee!'

Rachel erupts into whoops and cheers. I try my best to join in.

If there is another poo on the floor, do I have to clear it up? Rachel has nipped out (with what seemed like slightly unseemly haste) after going to make another cup of tea and discovering they had run out of milk. Perhaps I can leave any bodily fluids where they land until she gets back. I love my nephews to bits, really I do, but scraping poo off upholstery?

The boys are both playing trains, burbling away happily about Fat Controllers and Very Useful Engines. I envy them their carefree existence. If only one red Smartie could make my day. If only my shattered self-esteem could be repaired by a single well-aimed wee.

'Chugga, chugga, chugga,' Felix says, taking the little blue train over the bridge.

'Want Thomas!' George says.

Felix snatches the blue train away from its perilous position on open ground and clutches it to his chest.

'Want Thomas!' George says.

I hold my breath. Please don't fight! Not until Mummy gets back. I'd prefer a poo on the rug to a fight. I kneel down beside George on the floor and offer him a blue train that looks identical to the one Felix is holding. 'How about this train?'

George looks at me like I'm insane. 'Not want Edward!' He lunges over to Felix and snatches the train out of his hands. I gasp. Felix stares at his brother. A counter-attack is surely on the way. But then he picks up a red train and carries on playing.

'No!' I say, ignoring the voice inside my head screaming at me to leave well alone. 'You had that train, Felix!' Both boys stare at me. I take the train from George and give it to Felix. 'Do NOT –' my voice seems to be going quite screechy now '– DO NOT LET ANYONE TAKE ADVANTAGE OF YOU! THAT TRAIN WAS YOURS.'

Rachel walks into the kitchen just as both of the twins burst into tears.

Chapter Five

I have become the sort of person who spends all day looking forward to *I'm a Celebrity . . . Get Me Out of Here!*, though I do have a slight vested interest as my downstairs neighbour, Cassie Frost, is on it this year. I don't really know Cassie – this is London, for goodness' sake, where it's practically against the law to talk to your neighbours – but she has thrown me the most cursory of nods when we've passed each other. She always seems to be dressed in expensive-looking gym gear, carrying a yoga mat, and sporting huge sunglasses indoors as well as out. (Nancy used to joke she imagined her struggling to keep them on whilst doing a downward facing dog.)

I have now been off work for over a week and, despite increasingly irate 'we have to talk' voicemail messages from Annabel, I'm willing to put money on the fact she'll stop short of actually firing me, which is lucky as I am effectively putting quite a lot of money on that. My whole livelihood in fact.

Things are really hotting up in the jungle. The hypnotist had a big row with the page three girl and told her she'd better start pulling her weight around the place because people – I think he meant him – were fed up of getting water and sorting out the camp while she was topping up her tan. Then there's the boyband guy who's flirting with the girl from *Emmerdale*. But the real car-crash viewing is Cassie. She has been voted to do the challenges on the last four nights by the public, and tonight will be buried in what is to all intents and purposes a coffin underground for as long as she can stand it whilst rats and bugs crawl over her. I had little idea of Cassie's career before the programme – hers is one of those names you sort of know, but you're not sure why – but to watch the way she carries on, you'd think she was Madonna or something. Diva doesn't really cover it.

The ad for a supermarket reminds me I'm hungry. I should keep a stock of frozen desserts on hand like the ones they show. I could have Black Forest cheesecake for my breakfast and not feel a shred of guilt since I am officially miserable. As it is, my freezer compartment is bare and my fridge offers up the exciting possibilities of one small piece of mouldy Cheddar, a jar of curry paste and three yoghurts that are two weeks past their sell by date. I am willing to bet that Annabel's fridge is a nutritionist's wet dream. She is the kind of woman whose 'indulgence' is one small square of the best dark chocolate after her superfood salad. I cut the mould off the cheddar – people buy mouldy cheeses on purpose, so what harm can it do – and take it back to the sofa.

Marielle called me to say her grandmother is better and she'll be moving in at the weekend. Which means I won't be able to sit around the living room gnawing lumps of suspect cheese in my fluffy chimp slippers (a gift chosen by my nephews). I'll have to stop crying all the time. Smile and make conversation.

I think I remember how.

It turns out being miserable and weepy gets a bit boring after a while. I have moved to anger.

On the plus side, anger is much more energetic. This morning I cleaned the flat, imagining Jack as the soap scum on the bath.

I am now in Sainsbury's buying the ingredients to make supper for Marielle and me the night she moves in. She seemed pleased when I offered, and I am trying to squash down the little voice that screams that it's the very last thing I feel like doing. None of this is her fault. Nor can she help the fact she's not Nancy.

I throw two steaks in the trolley. They're hideously expensive but somehow it feels like you have to make an effort with a capital 'E' when you're cooking for a French person. It also helps to alleviate my guilt for not feeling more enthusiastic about the whole thing.

In the fruit and vegetables section, I load up on blueberries and broccoli. I'll show you, Annabel Baxter! I will be stick-thin and glowing. And I will still be two years and four months younger than you!

My stupid trolley keeps veering to the left. I confront the first person I can see in a Sainsbury's uniform. Would it be too much to ask to provide trolleys that actually work? Especially since I had to dig around for ages in the bottom of my bag to find a pound coin to get one in the first place. Chanelle runs her tongue over her teeth. Would I like her to get me another trolley? She has a golden tropical beach painted at the tip of each long fingernail, complete with swaying palm trees and a shimmering ocean. The work that must have gone into them! There are even tiny birds flying above the trees. She is being very patient with me. Not telling me there is no need to be rude. I feel the anger starting to drain out of me like I have sprung some sort of a leak. Yes, please, I say.

I mooch around by the newspapers. Cassie Frost is all over the front pages. Queen of the Jungle Moaners one headline calls her, which seems a pretty fair cop if you saw last night's show. (Naturally, I did, since I have no life.) Her sleeping bag was leaky, she was frightened of the spiders, all the other campmates were ganging up on her. For goodness' sake, woman, you're on a reality show, not in Sarajevo! You're getting paid a lot of money to do this.

29

I find myself in the confectionery aisle where I throw two packets of Twirl Bites into my trolley, telling myself that chocolate is a great source of antioxidants. I must phone Nancy later. I finally told her yesterday, and I really snapped at her when she dared to suggest I ought to be thinking about going back to work.

Today is the day I would have been making the speech at Inspirational Women. Given both the inevitable outfit crisis that would have ensued (a whole roomful of Annabels!), and the fact my palms begin to get clammy at the mere thought of going up on that stage, I am unbelievably relieved not to be there. The only downside is my chances of ever becoming an Inspirational Woman are looking fairly slim. Who am I kidding? They're looking make-Victoria-Beckham-look-like-a-chubba slim.

A father is negotiating over chocolate buttons with his daughter, who is dressed in a swimming costume and wellie boots. I don't think my father ever took me to a supermarket. He's a paediatric cardiac surgeon and he spent most of mine and my sister's childhoods at the hospital. He missed me playing Mary in the nativity play. There was always some other kid who needed him more than us.

'Mummy would let me!'

'That's not true.' The dad looks over at me and gives me a rueful smile. He's actually rather handsome in a battered kind of way. His wife is probably a horrible corporate bitch who takes him for granted and moans that he always forgets to pick up her dry-cleaning.

'But I'm so huuuuuungry!'

'Well, why don't we get you a banana?'

They disappear, the little girl moaning about how she doesn't want a banana, doesn't even like bananas. Her voice fades out like the end of a record.

His wife is probably lovely. I've got to stop being like this.

A woman I don't even know, Sainsbury's trolleys, Cassie Frost, Nancy, my father (a real low ebb, that one, since my father saves children's lives). I am turning into the Incredible Hulk.

Marielle and her boyfriend Jean arrive with her suitcases and boxes, and the three of us stand in the sitting room smiling hard. I offer them a cup of tea, which they decline. Us English people and our tea, I say, even though I barely drink tea. They laugh politely.

We talk about how cold it is outside, how they got here, and how you don't know how much stuff you have until you move.

After what seems like an eternity but is probably only about ten minutes, I tell them I'll leave them to get Marielle settled in and disappear to my bedroom.

As soon as I'm alone lying on my bed, I start going over the thoughts my mind plays on an endless loop.

I think about how when Nancy told me she was moving out, I actually thought that Jack might suggest he moved in. I was convinced he was finally falling in love with me at a time he was screwing my boss behind my back. Talk about seeing what you want to see.

I think about how I'll be thirty-five on my next birthday and everyone knows that means my fertility is about to drop off a cliff. Yesterday I went swimming and a hugely pregnant woman in a pink spotty one-piece lowered herself into the lane next to me. All of a sudden I was filled with a sadness that almost made me feel as if I couldn't stay afloat. What if I never have what she has?

I think about having to go back into work. To wonder who knows and who doesn't. To sit there in meetings with Annabel talking about how to rehabilitate the reputation of some Z-list celebrity who's been caught shoplifting or how to launch a new jewellery brand. Act normal! Come up with ideas! (Kill Annabel?)

Fat tears roll onto my pillow. How did I let all this happen? Everyone else I know seems to have their shit together. Careers, marriage, babies, flats where they're allowed to hang pictures.

I must doze off because I wake up to the sound of bed springs creaking in the other room.

I put the pillow over my head.

A low moaning starts up. Then some quick-fire French. Jeez, these guys are loud! I lived with Nancy for three years and her sex life was something I heard about but never heard. I scrabble around for my noise-cancelling headphones.

By the time I dare take them out, it's nearly 7 p.m. and I realize I'd better get on with making dinner. Despite my nap, I feel exhausted. All I want to do is mope in front of the telly. It's so much easier to concentrate on whether Cassie Frost is going to get forced to do yet another challenge than focus on my own trial of trying to get through a couple of hours making small talk with my new flatmate without bursting into tears and blurting out that my life has gone to shit.

I go into the kitchen and start peeling potatoes. Marielle and Jean appear and I find myself blushing a little.

'See you later, Ginny,' Jean says putting his leather jacket on.

'Bye,' I say, marvelling at his perfect English. I mean it's one thing to be fluent, quite another to use 'see you later' as a goodbye like that. You'd think the guy was brought up in Deptford.

'Still on for dinner?' I say to Marielle when Jean's gone.

She nods. 'It will be fun.'

Yes! Fun, fun, fun! 'Excellent. I'll aim to have it ready for eight?'

'Perfect. Can I help?'

'No, I've got this.' I force a smile. It's not her fault she's not Nancy.

I concentrate on the food. I make a big tray of garlicky roast potatoes and a peppercorn sauce for the steak. Then a

32

simple green salad, no funny turns. The concentration takes my mind off things and I feel my mood lifting a little. This will be good for me.

At 8 p.m. on the dot, Marielle appears.

'Red or white?'

She looks thoughtful. 'What are we eating?'

I'm about to tell her when the doorbell goes. I bet it's those people selling dusters again. I bought some ludicrously expensive e-cloths off them once and now they ring my doorbell all the time.

Marielle goes to answer it and then reappears with Jean, who is carrying a large B&Q bag.

What? I thought he was long gone. Dinner was supposed to be the two of us. I've bought two steaks, for goodness' sake.

'Red or white wine?' she says to him.

'Red.'

Can I say something? There seems to have been a bit of a misunderstanding. I'd love to get to know Jean better another time (once I can see the two of them together without thinking about their decibel-busting copulation), but this was supposed to be a girly night and I've only got enough food for two.

Jean rubs his hands together. 'Thanks for this, Ginny. I'm starving!'

I guess he's worked up an appetite.

I lose half a stone, get a fabulous new outfit, march back into the office and publicly dress down Annabel. She crumbles and resigns, saying that the least she can do is give me her job.

Okay, no. I limp back into the office looking reasonably okay, but certainly no thinner (and why would I be, given that the blueberries were easily equalled by Twirl Bites).

Ronaldo and Van Percy have both pulled out of next week's launch party for a football boot, so the atmosphere is one of crisis, and most people barely look up when I walk in, let alone ask if I am better from my week-and-a-half-long mystery illness. Jess, who's the only person at work that knows the truth, gives me a big hug and says we must grab a coffee later, but then even she has got to get back to 'Give other boots the boot'. So I sit down at my desk, not really knowing what to do next. At that point Annabel comes out, smooths her skirt over what I now know to be her perfectly toned bottom, and flashes me one of her most hostile smiles. 'Do you have a minute, Ginny?'

Do I have a minute? I look at my switched-off computer. Boyfriend, self-esteem, waistline? No. Minutes, yes.

I close the door behind me. Her office looks like offices look in movies.

'Sit,' she says. I feel like a puppy. Perhaps I will piss on the floor. 'This is obviously going to be hard for both of us.' Hard for both of us? Cheeky, stupid, boyfriend-stealing, traitorous-to-the-sisterhood cow! I want to vault over her smearless glass desk and punch her in the immaculately glossed mouth I keep picturing around Jack's penis! I want to put my hands down the back of her Prada pencil skirt and give her a wedgie with her bright pink pants! 'I think the way forward is to be completely professional—'

I don't really remember what happened after that. I know I was laughing – a sort of insane cackle – and then I started crying and screaming. And then I threw her orchid at her. And that suddenly everybody else didn't seem to be so taken up with the football-boot launch after all, and they were all staring. Did I mention that Annabel's office has glass walls?

Jess helps me pack my personal belongings. Then I walk out as slowly as I can possibly bear, making sure I smile and say goodbye to people. I think it's important to keep your dignity in these situations.

Chapter Six

I feel kind of bad for Cassie Frost. I know, I know – she is definitely an out-and-out madam, and I don't even know her. You might think I've got bigger things to worry about right now, what with my life kind of down the toilet . . . but I can't help but feel for her. Because her life's down the toilet too.

I am in my local newsagent's. This takes care of at least half an hour every morning and delays the awful moment when I have to start that day's job-hunting: phoning recruitment consultants and sounding chrirrupy and upbeat while I tell them what unique things I have to offer. (Excellent at hurling orchids?)

I pick up a bar of chocolate. Christmas is coming and Ginny's getting fat, please to put a penny in the old man's hat . . .

The final of *I'm A Celebrity* was a week ago, and the weepy girl from *The X Factor* was crowned Queen. But Cassie Frost is still all over the front pages. There has been a barrage of abuse on social media with people criticizing everything from her fake boobs, to her attitude, to the way she separated her rice and beans. 'They're really gunning for her, aren't they?' I say to Mr Sharma.

'Oh yes.'

A man purchasing cough sweets pipes up. 'Deserves it though, don't she?'

I'm suddenly not so sure. Don't get me wrong, I hated her on the programme. But no one deserves this, do they?

I pay for my paper and chocolate.

'Stupid old has been!' cough–sweet man says. 'Someone ought to put her up against a wall and shoot her.' He has a thick neck which is almost purple in colour and has folds in it like the face of a pug.

'She comes in here to buy her papers and magazines, has done for years,' Mr Sharma says.

'Is she nice?'

Mr Sharma shrugs. 'She's okay. Shouts if we run out of sugar-free gum.'

So it turns out that I've been on Cassie Frost's mind too. Well, not actually me, but she thinks it's me.

I get back from the newsagent's to find a note has been shoved under my door.

Is there someone being tortured up there? If so, please do call 999 as a matter of urgency.

If you're not being tortured, please might I ask you to tone down the 3 a.m. moaning a notch? Oh, and maybe fix your headboard?

Your (sleep-deprived) neighbour

Apart from the fact it's very weird to be on the receiving end of the blame about someone else's noisy sex life, I'm not completely sure how I feel about Cassie's note. I can absolutely see why she's written it – with the benefit of hindsight, Marielle and Jean's moving in day shag turns out to be one of their quieter, less athletic performances. And they are at it *all* the time. Seriously, no wonder they eat a lot.

But it's also hard to shake the feeling that Cassie has been *very* quick to complain, especially since she's hardly the perfect

36

neighbour herself. She burns this hideously strong incense every morning that wafts through the floorboards and puts me right off my breakfast and she has a VERY loud visitor who arrives at 8 a.m. EVERY Saturday morning. Goodness knows who he is and what he's doing there, all I know is that the two of them chat and laugh very loudly whilst blasting out 80s pop. Suffice to say, the only time in ages I've enjoyed a Saturday morning lie-in was when Cassie was in the Australian jungle on *I'm A Celeb*.

But have I ever complained to her? I have not. Instead, I have gone out of my way to be a considerate neighbour, taking my shoes off the minute I get through my front door and never putting the washing machine on after 9 p.m. even if I'm out of clean pants.

So it does seem a little rich that Cassie was so quick to put pen to paper. Also, why did she write a note (admittedly quite a funny one) instead of talking to me? Although, to be fair, I can't even imagine having *that* conversation in person.

I open my bag and get out the Twirl Bites. I had promised myself I wouldn't eat any until after lunch but I think this situation overrides that. Because it is a situation, frankly. Presumably I don't have to write a note back? *Dear neighbour, thanks for your helpful feedback. I am not actually the moaner but will be passing on your comments to the person in question.*

And that's the other thing: how the hell am I going to bring this up with Marielle? So, new flatmate I barely know, let's talk about your sex life.

I pop a Twirl Bite in my mouth. I will just leave Cassie's note out on the kitchen worktop and hope Marielle and Jean see it and take the hint.

As for Cassie, well, I'll just have to hope that if the sex noise calms down a bit, so will she.

That's the last time I let myself start feeling sorry for her though.

I am putting out the rubbish when Jack appears from nowhere.

'Sorry,' he says, seeing me jump, 'didn't mean to frighten you.'

'Well maybe you shouldn't hide behind parked cars!'

'What else am I supposed to do? You don't let me in when I come round, you don't return my calls . . .'

'Have you considered that I might not want to talk to you?'

He has the good grace to look sheepish. 'I just want to tell you how sorry I am—'

'Spare me!'

He holds up his hands. 'Look, I did a terrible thing. But it was a mistake—'

'Oh well, that's okay then. As long as it was a mistake.' I am quite pleased with my tone. My dignity is slightly compromised by the fact I have a bulging black bin bag in my hand, but you can't have everything. 'You slept with my boss.'

'Yeah. That wasn't good—'

'Y'think?' It's all I can do not to whack him with the bin bag until its smelly contents ooze all over his expensive suit. Jack cares a lot about his suits. He never left them lying on the floor, even in the throes of passion. (Although thinking about it now, maybe I just didn't arouse enough passion. I bet his suits got hurled all over the place when he was with Annabel.) My bin bag swings from my fingers, and I imagine bits of bloated Weetabix and soggy potato peelings all over the charcoal fabric. A sort of modern-day equivalent of putting someone in the stocks.

'I know what I did was unforgivable—'

'But you want me to forgive you?'

'No. Yes. It doesn't matter. I just want you to know that I'm sorry. Really sorry. And that you deserve so much better.'

He's going to ask me back. My heart is beating so hard and fast, it feels like it might burst out of my chest. 'Let's stick entirely to clichés here, shall we?'

'Gin, this isn't like you!'

'Not like me? Not *like* me?' I hear my own voice getting louder and louder.

The front door opens behind us, and Marielle and Jean emerge and walk down the front steps. (It's always Marielle AND Jean, I don't think I've seen her without him since she's moved in.) They look rather embarrassed to have stumbled into a row. And, oh God, the protocol! Am I supposed to introduce them all to each other now? *This is Jack who's just broken my heart. These are my new flatmates. I only thought one of them was moving in with me but turns out — lucky me — I seem to have got them both. They have a penchant for noisy sex.* I settle for a cursory nod.

As they disappear, Jack's eyes fix on mine. 'Ginny—'

'How's work?' I say, cutting him off. I'm buying myself thinking time. A brief oasis of small talk in which to catch my breath.

His brow crumples. 'Fine.' There's a pause. 'Simon got promoted.'

Simon is Jack's best mate, and the two of them have what one would politely describe as a slightly competitive relation-ship (Nancy refers to them as 'a couple of chest-banging chimps'). So, a reflex here makes me want to remind Jack, as he often has me, that Simon does a money-shifting job he loathes. But then I remember that soothing Jack's ego is no longer my concern.

It starts to rain.

'Let's go inside,' he says.

'No.' If we go inside, I have no chance of telling him he can stick his big reconciliation. He will charm and wheedle and do that thing he does so well. If I don't let him into the flat, I have some chance of not letting him back into my life.

He puts his hand on my arm, and I shake it off. 'I know I screwed up, Ginny. Not just with . . .' he pauses '. . . her. But generally. I took you for granted. I didn't realize how special what we had was.'

I choke back the tears. I am not going to let him see me cry. 'Yeah. Well "had" is past tense, isn't it?' The tears roll down my cheeks despite me, and I sink down to sit on the step. Jack puts his arm around my shoulders, and I let it rest there. I can smell the Johnson's baby soap he uses.

'I'm so sorry, Ginny.'

I look up at his face. He looks gratifying terrible with dark purple rings under his eyes. Maybe he has really changed this time? Maybe we could have a future together? It has started raining more heavily now, and we are both getting soaked through, but we sit there on the steps in silence. 'You should go,' I say. He stands up, and I want to shout that I didn't mean it, and that I want him to argue, for goodness' sake. To fight for me.

'Ginny . . .'

I stare at him. This is it. The moment of truth. And I have no idea how I will respond, because my head is telling me one thing, but the idea of him taking me in his arms right now is hard to resist.

'May I take my Xbox?'

'What?'

'My Xbox. I left it here by mistake. Because I packed in such a hurry.'

The rain plasters my hair to my face.

★   ★   ★

I am lying having the plaque scraped off my teeth by the dental hygienist. They are talking about Cassie Frost on the radio. Apparently, there have now been death threats made against her.

'The actress has been at the centre of a social media storm since her appearance on the reality show *I'm a Celebrity . . . Get Me Out of Here!* A spokesman for the show issued the following statement this morning: We are all deeply shocked and saddened by this news. Our thoughts tonight are with Cassie Frost and her family.'

Danielle is new to The Bridge Lane Dental practice and from the pain she is inflicting inside my mouth, quite possibly new to being a dental hygienist too. 'Have you been flossing daily?' she says, sounding cross.

I answer as best I can for someone who has a human hand and several pieces of equipment inside their mouth.

'There's considerable build-up here.'

'Police are said to be taking the death threats seriously.'

I feel sick, and not just because of Danielle – who I am half expecting to climb on top of my chest at any minute.

She hands me the aspirator whilst she does the machine scaling. I seem unable to hold it in the right place, so not only am I constantly in her way with it – something she reacts to with loud tuts – but I have drool running out of the corners of my mouth.

'Just a polish now. They're very stained.'

Even the polishing hurts. I find it hard to imagine ever being able to eat solid food again. Finally, she finishes and I sit up and pick up the plastic cup of mouthwash. It has turned from pale pink to deep red when I spit it out.

'Your gums are bleeding,' Danielle says, stating the obvious. I nod and hand her back my yellow plastic glasses. 'It's because you're not flossing.'

'I am flossing.'

'Not daily.'

I feel like I am back in primary school and haven't handed in my homework. 'Most days.'

Danielle snorts.

'I Wish It Could Be Christmas Everyday' is blaring out now. I wish the radio stations could play something else.

'It's terrible about Cassie Frost, isn't it?'

Danielle looks at me strangely. I don't know why I said that. I mean, I know why I said it: it is terrible. But why did I say it to her, the Butcher of Bridge Lane? 'Poor woman!' It seems I'm on a roll now. 'The story was trending globally for three days, you know. And the things people said – things they'd never have said to her face, or if they'd had to put their name to it. Terrible things like they wished she'd got malaria in the jungle; that they hoped her breast implants ruptured and gave her cancer—'

'I recommend the satin floss. It glides between teeth more easily.'

Chapter Seven

Maybe there's something about being in the house you grew up in that makes you behave like a child.

It starts with the tinsel. I like tinsel. It may not be very *Elle Deco* but we always have it. You have to have tinsel at Christmas. Just like you have to have Christmas Pudding even though no one really likes it. It's Christmas Eve, and Mum and I decorate the tree together. We laugh at the cotton wool snowman I proudly brought home from nursery thirty years ago. Mum makes me hang him up, even though his hat is crushed and he's missing one eye. *Oh Come All Ye Faithful* is playing on the radio, and suddenly, singing along, I feel engulfed by the Christmas spirit that's been eluding me. And then Rachel whirls in with all her bags and boxes and people, and just whips the tinsel off the tree with one disgusted 'eeurgh'.

Later, when she's putting the boys to bed, I put the tinsel back on. She may have got married and had kids before me (even though she is younger so technically should have let me go first), and she may be a teacher, but she is not the Boss of The Tree.

We bicker about the stuffing for tomorrow. She wants to make some Nigella thing with gingerbread that she had at Paul's parents' last year. I want the sage and onion stuffing we have every year. Mum says we'll have both.

Over supper, Dad is at the table but not present, which is

something we've come to expect when he gets home from work. It's as if all his emotions have been used up by other families. We are drinking a very expensive red wine that's a gift from one such family. Dad gets lots of presents from patients.

Paul, who is wearing flashing reindeer antlers, asks me how the job-hunting is going, and I try to ignore the little subtitle I see that says: Shouldn't you have sorted something out by now? Four weeks since Orchid-gate! I have just put a large piece of sausage in my mouth. He waits patiently for me to chew, and I try to think how to say IT IS NOT A GOOD TIME OF YEAR FOR JOB-HUNTING without actually screaming.

We are clearing the table, when Mum tells Rachel to go and sit down because she looks very tired. I know looking after twins and holding down a job (part-time, mind you) is hard work but still I bristle. Rachel always seemed to get out of her fair share of the chores. She always had too much homework. Or gymnastics club. Or something. I dry the glasses so hard that one of them cracks in my hand. 'Sorry,' I say to my mum when what I really mean is: It's your fault.

When we go into the sitting room, Dad is already snoozing on one sofa. He looks older and smaller than I remember him, and I suddenly feel guilty I don't visit more often. Mum sits down next to him, which leaves me the choice of squeezing onto the other sofa with Rachel and Paul or sitting alone in the uncomfortable armchair. I settle for the armchair, feeling martyred and irritable.

Rachel offers me a Quality Street, but all the good ones have gone.

I wonder if I'm a disappointment to Mum and Dad. They were never pushy parents, never nudged me towards medicine or said anything bad about any of my boyfriends (even when there was so much to say), but I can't help thinking they must be worrying about me. It's ironic that Rachel, who was always the naughty one when we were growing up, has ended up doing everything 'right'.

A movie is playing, but I can't be bothered to try to work out what's going on. Instead I think about what Jack will be doing. We both used to spend Christmas Day with our own families but Christmas Eve was 'ours'. Last year, I lit every candle in the flat and made us rib eye steaks and béarnaise with chips (Jack's 'death row' supper). We exchanged our presents in bed at midnight. It seems so romantic in comparison to tonight, and when I find tears welling up in my eyes I have to remind myself how fraught I'd got trying to buy him a gift that was nice but not over-the-top in any way.

I root myself back to the present. Rach is asleep too now, her head resting on Paul's shoulder. She really was exhausted, poor thing. I resolve to be nicer. And then my eyes drift across to the Christmas tree. The tinsel-less Christmas tree.

The diary is candy pink (like Annabel's knickers) and locked (unlike Annabel's knickers). I sit in my pyjamas on the edge of the single bed I used to sleep in as a child and run my fingers over the smooth cover. I remember my journal writing phase. It suddenly seemed important to record every thought and emotion, perhaps because I was making the classic teenage error of confusing quantity with quality. The diary lives with a collection of photos and school books and records in a cardboard box at the bottom of the wardrobe. The forgotten treasures of my past. I wonder briefly if my mother ever read the diary but know even as the thought flashes through my mind, it's a preposterous one. My mum is a great one for privacy. She hasn't even asked me exactly what happened with Jack.

It's late and I should probably get some sleep. This is the first Christmas that George and Felix have been old enough to be excited about and they are bound to wake the household before dawn demanding presents. My mind flashes back to Rachel and me creeping into our parents' bedroom in the pitch black. 'You wake them.' 'No, you.' 'Happy Christmas,' we eventually chorus. 'Good Lord, what time is it?' my father says, sitting up in bed, a lifetime of bleeps from the hospital having trained him to be instantly alert. 'It's not morning yet.' But my mother is already putting her slippers on. 'Don't be so mean – it's Christmas!'

I fiddle with the small padlock. I have no idea where the key is – I assume it was lost a long time ago – but I know the padlock could be forced open easily. Do I really want to do it, though? I don't remember anything I wrote in here but it's bound to be excruciating.

The lock snaps open with one sharp tug. My first thought is how neat my handwriting looks. Big, earnest loops. Each entry is written in a different colour. I remember that set of gel pens. Mum made me lend them to Rachel one day. And then she left the lid off the yellow.

Got 89% in English!!!!!!! Miss Pinchbeck says if I keep this up, I could take my GCSE a year early!!!!!!

Harry Baker told Nancy he was going to ask me to McDonalds!!!!!!!! Hope it's soon, but not so soon the spot on my nose hasn't gone!!!!!!!

I smile. Harry Baker never did buy me a Big Mac. Turns out he was the original Jack.

Dad missed my recorder solo at the Music Concert. I know he was operating on a very sick baby, but it still made me sad when I came out and saw the empty seat next to Mum.

Notes for my novel!!!!!! A fourteen-year-old girl goes to boarding school in the country. She teaches the other kids her sophisticated London ways.

I smile. I'd completely forgotten about *Boarding School Bedlam*. My first foray into writing. I didn't finish it. I wonder what happened to the manuscript. It must have got lost. Along with the dream.

Everyone wants to know what I'm doing for New Year's Eve. Not in a genuinely interested I-wonder-what-she's-doing-because-she's-insanely-popular type of way, but more in a better-make-sure-she-doesn't-chuck-herself-off-a-tall-building kind of way. Rachel wants me to spend it at her house – 'We haven't had New Year together for years' – with her, Paul and a few of their mates. Paul's organized a few party games (of course he has).

I picture the scene: me and three married couples, them all worrying their kids won't settle in their travel cots, me worrying I'm never going to have anything to put in a travel cot. Rachel will have briefed them before arrival on my 'situation', so as we work our way through the antipasti and osso bucco, no one will ask what I do for a living or utter the word 'single'. This will make for the kind of easy, flowing conversation in which how Rachel got the parma ham sliced so thinly is the most animated and entertaining topic. (Next: the chorizo!)

I will guzzle the champagne, and someone will tell me I'm so lucky that I haven't got a toddler who'll clamber over me demanding I do 'The Wheels On The Bus' at 5 a.m. Rachel will glare and cut them a very small slice of tarte au citron. She will say, 'Cream?' as if it's an expletive.

At midnight, Paul will kiss me before he kisses Rachel because that's what she has told him to do. Then I will kiss Rachel and then the four strangers I have shared the last fragments of the year with. We will link hands for 'Auld Lang Syne', and it will be more 'hmm, hmm, hmms' than words. Lots of us will be desperate to go to bed – me in particular, so I can cry in private.

Julia and Adam are going to Trafalgar Square, and apparently

I should go with them because it's going to be amazing. *Just think of the fireworks!* I don't know how to tell her that I might not be able to avoid feeling miserable, but I can certainly avoid being freezing cold as well, or how to say that I am resigned to feeling lonely but that I can't bear being lonely when I'm surrounded by thousands of people.

I call Nancy who, of course, completely gets it. 'It's a horrible night anyway. All that forced fun. The feeling you may be arrested if you're not racing around the streets in a stupid party hat vaulting over dustbins and squirting people with silly string.'

I laugh. 'And then you're expected to make resolutions!'

'Yeah, the trouble with them is that you're supposed to make them for yourself. If you could make resolutions for other people that would be kind of fun. My boss wouldn't be allowed to say the words "you English girls" ever again. Like, just because we don't have perfectly straight teeth, immaculate manicures and twice weekly blow dries, we're from another planet.'

'I'd like to make some resolutions for Annabel. First, she has to stop going to the gym—'

'Bit of a reverse on the normal resolution. I like it.'

'Then she has to start eating doughnuts and cake and biscuits. If it's carby and over-processed, then it's perfect.'

Nancy laughs.

'I wish I could come to New York for New Year's Eve.'

'Me too. At least we'd be together.'

'We could have an embargo on silly hats. And vaulting over rubbish bins.' My mind goes back to last New Year's Eve. 'Lizzy and Mike's party was quite fun.' I was ecstatic because Jack and I had only been back together for a few weeks after one of our breaks. I knew that him being the first person I kissed as Big Ben struck twelve had to be a good omen for the year ahead.

'Ginny, you spent the whole evening on edge because Jack was flirting with Lizzie's little sister.'

Sometimes I hate Nancy's memory. There's not nearly enough blurring.

We go back to planning our fantasy New Year's Eve. PJs, wine, an insane amount of cheese.

After I hang up the phone to Nancy, I dial Rachel. I tell her I've decided to go to Trafalgar Square with Julia and Adam. She tells me she's sure it'll be a blast and that she was worried it might all be too boring for me at her place.

Then I phone Julia and tell her that it was so nice of her to invite me, but I'll be spending the evening at my sister's.

Chapter Eight

Although the banner on the shelf boasts 'Cards for every occasion', there doesn't seem to be a sorry-you-humiliated-yourself-on-national-TV option.

In my old life, I'd be at my desk by now busily trying to catch up on all the emails Annabel had been sending since she finished with her personal trainer at 6.45 a.m. Now, I've got into the habit of popping to Mr Sharma's every morning, ostensibly to buy the newspaper, but also to stock up on chocolate and, even more importantly, delay the phoning headhunters and networking part of the day. (If there's a word I dislike as much as networking in the English language, I'm hard-pressed to think of it, although moist and gusset come close. Especially when put together.)

I settle on a nondescript pattern involving butterflies and flowers, which is 'blank for your own message'. My own message doesn't come easily. In fact, it takes me so long to write three lines in the card, I have to laugh at the thought I'd ever be able to write a book. I seal up the envelope. Perhaps this is a mistake — something designed to make me feel better rather than the recipient? I put the card into my handbag and head for home. Then I remember my aunt Rosa, whose son was killed in a car accident. People used to cross the street to avoid her. She knew it was because they didn't know what to say, but she wished they'd say the wrong thing rather than nothing at all.

The door to Cassie's flat looks tired close up, like it needs a lick of paint. I get my card out of my bag and ease it under the door. The card is halfway under when the door is flung open. I look up and get a faceful of freezing cold water.

'I thought you were that nosey bitch journalist again.' She adopts a shrill little-girl voice: '"I want to tell your side of the story, Miss Frost." She's been going through my bins, you know.'

I dab at my face with the towel I've just been handed. Cassie Frost is clearly a nut-job. Well, hello! It's not like there weren't any warning signs.

'What did you say you were doing here again? Putting a card under the door?' She manages to sound cross, as if it is her who has just had a bucket of icy cold water thrown at her.

'I was just wishing you well. A "sorry" might be nice.'

'Sorry,' she says, sounding anything but.

I pass her back the towel.

'You're one of my neighbours, aren't you?' Her expression is hard to read. 'Do you want a cup of coffee?'

I assume this must be an olive branch, or at least an olive twig. Still, the obvious answer is no. A saner woman would be halfway up the stairs by now. But after watching Cassie night after night on *I'm a Celebrity*, I can't help but be slightly intrigued. I guess I want to see if she's as bad as she seemed.

We are talking about Cassie's foray into pop music. 'That was quite a video, wasn't it?' I say.

She laughs. 'It sure was! Wait, how come you've seen it though? I mean, I was ridiculously young, you can't even have been born.'

'Someone posted the clip from *Top of the Pops*.' I don't add they made a comment that Cassie was a talentless slag then and she's a talentless slag now.

'Oh. The video was so cheesy! Me walking along a school corridor with a pile of school books, Shane bouncing along behind me in yellow dungarees and a back-to-front baseball cap. And then I drop the pile of books and Shane picks them up for me. And that smile of his, shy but not too shy: it made every teenage girl in the country long to be in my shoes!'

'He was very pretty.'

'Yup, that's why I married him.' She takes a sip of her coffee. 'Eeeurgh, that's disgusting!' She picks up both our mugs and throws the contents down the sink. 'Serves me right for trying to make fresh coffee! I'm not much cop in the kitchen, I'm afraid.' She puts a teaspoonful of instant coffee into each mug.

The newspapers put Cassie's age at fifty-five, which makes her old enough to be my mother. But she doesn't look like anyone's mother. She is incredibly glamorous with fine delicate features and big brown eyes that make her look a lot kinder than she probably is. She is tiny and very thin – it's true what people say about the telly putting ten pounds on people – albeit with unfeasibly large breasts.

'We were only married five months.' She shakes her head. 'Crazy. It's weird looking back on me and Shane. It doesn't seem like something that ever happened to me; it's like something that I watched in a movie. The Vegas wedding, the scarlet mini-dress, the hash brownies as wedding cake. We thought we were so bloody cool! Then we got home and we were like two little kids playing house.' She takes a sip of her coffee. 'What about you? Are you married?'

'No. Not yet.' I regret the 'not yet' as soon as it's out of my mouth. I sound desperate; like the sort of woman who may hang around strangers' weddings just hoping to catch the bouquet.

'I've walked up the aisle three times.'

'Weren't you married to that Chelsea footballer?'

'Lee Pearson. Yup that was me. *Hello!* called it a "fairy-tale wedding". Not sure the Prince in the fairy tale is usually too off his face to get through his vows without slurring. Or that he's doing the wedding planner, but hey ho.'

Cassie's flat may be in the same converted house as mine but that's where the similarities end. Her white, light-filled living room is not only decorated to within an inch of its tasteful life, but it's also bigger than my entire flat.

She yawns. 'Sorry. Didn't sleep well last night.'

The mention of her not sleeping suddenly brings the mortifying revelation to my mind that she must still think I'm the moaner. 'Oh, by the way, sorry about the . . . umm . . . noise recently. It was actually my new flatmate.'

She bats the air. 'It wasn't anybody else keeping me awake last night. I just couldn't sleep.'

I wait for her to say sorry about the grumpy note but she doesn't mention it.

Framed photographs are littered on every surface: Cassie with Tony Blair; Cassie on the red carpet with Jonathan Ross; Cassie accepting an award. There's even one of her looking relaxed and suntanned with a flower in her hair next to Sean Connery.

'Sean Connery,' I yelp in a way that's uncool even by my own gold-standard-setting uncoolness.

She laughs. 'We were in a movie together. I've had all the best leading men. And when I say "had" . . .' She winks. 'That photo was taken on a three-day-long party on some sultan's yacht. I can't even remember his name now, which is pretty shabby considering he once sent me an eight-carat diamond ring as a "little present". I do remember the boat though. It was 240-foot long with three decks, six ensuite bedrooms, a swimming pool, a gym and a helipad. It even had its own dry cleaners! EVERYONE was at that party. Sean, Andy Warhol, Catherine Deneuve – God she was beautiful! – the Stones . . .'

'It's a tough job . . .'

She laughs. 'Yup. And actors say their life is hard work! My mum worked in a biscuit factory all her life. Eight hours a day on a production line for Jammy Dodgers. That's what I call hard work.'

There's a picture of Cassie looking slightly older and wearing scrubs. 'You were Dr Lisa in *Casualty*.'

She nods. 'For seven years. That was my comeback. I'd buggered up my film career. Too busy being young and wild long after I was young enough to get away with it. Ended up in drug rehab. This God-awful place in Arizona, filled with Yanks who were "reaching out to me" and "sharing my pain". I'd never felt so proud to be British in my whole life. I wanted to plaster my room with pictures of the Queen and make them all stop for tea and cucumber sandwiches every day at four. The only saving grace was there was a Hollywood actor in there at the time being treated for sex addiction. I won't tell you his name – but let's just say it was a household one – and he and I had a few VERY nice afternoons.'

'But he was being treated for sex addiction!'

She shrugs. 'Cold turkey doesn't suit everyone.' She yawns. 'When I got back to London, I wasn't exactly deluged with offers. *Casualty* brought me back out of the wilderness.'

The phone rings and Cassie picks up. 'Hi Barry . . . Barry . . . Barry . . .?' She hangs up. 'My agent. He can't work his hands-free. He's the only person in the world who has embraced modern technology less than me. He's still trying to work out where you put the stamp on an email.'

I laugh. 'Yeah, well talking of emails, I'd better send a few.' I pick up my coat.

'Did you watch the show?'

'*Casualty*?'

She makes a face. '*I'm a Celebrity.*'

'Yeah.'

'Hateful, wasn't I?'

'I . . . well . . . you were very brave to eat the kangaroo's anus.'

She puts her head back and laughs. Not a small laugh, but a big throaty guffaw that makes me want to laugh as well. 'Yup. I'm a hell of an arse kisser!'

Chapter Nine

'No one in the PR world mourned the death of Amelia Baker, who'd been a much-hated figure.'

The flashing cursor blinks accusingly. I've been in The Tea Room for nearly three hours and written the sum total of one line. At this rate, I'll have finished chapter one about a year from now. And that's if I don't get an actual job. (Which doesn't look terribly likely. The headhunters all keep telling me that nobody is 'properly' back at work yet. Really – in the second week of January? And the only 'interview' I've got lined up at the moment is with my friend Julia's brother and she's made him see me.)

'I'll have a skinny latte. No chocolate sprinkles.' The voice is familiar. I look up to see Cassie Frost. It's pouring with rain outside, and everyone else bears splatters of muddy water up the back of their legs, but Cassie, who is wearing a long white fur-trimmed coat, looks immaculate. I assume the gods don't dare incur her wrath.

'Hello,' she says, just as a couple of yoga mums with designer buggies commandeer the only free table.

'Would you like to sit down?' I say, moving my bag off the other chair at my table.

She sits down. 'You're a writer?'

'No!' There's an uncomfortable pause. 'I work in PR. But I'm out of a job at the moment . . . I'm just fiddling around really. Wouldn't call it writing . . .'

She shrugs. 'Those who write are writers. Those who wait are waiters.' I smile. 'Good, isn't it? Not mine, I'm afraid.'

I shut my laptop.

'I don't want to disturb your work.'

'I just wish there was some work to disturb.'

'Tell me about it. Do you remember when you were a teenager and you were waiting for a boy to call and the phone used to be so silent that you started to think it couldn't be working, so you got your mate to call you just to check? That's my phone now.'

'I'd have thought you'd be pleased that all the brouhaha has calmed down.'

'I guess. A happy medium might be good. It would be nice if my bloody agent called now and again. He and his wife Shirley keep delivering food.' I screw up my face in confusion. 'They're Jewish. But it's parts I want, not smoked salmon. Wait, did you say you were in PR? What kind of PR? Do you do image management?'

'Yeah, among other types. I represent – sorry, used to represent – Lean Machine and Mama Bear.'

'Who?'

'They're influencers.'

Cassie's face scrunches. 'I hate influencers. Like celebs but with even less talent. Did you represent any proper people?'

'Influencers are proper people. But I also worked for Bob Jacobs, Marina Piper, Hayley Wiseman—'

'Now there's a woman who's slept her way to the middle.'

'She speaks well of you too.'

Cassie laughs. 'I've been looking to hire a PR firm. Y'know because my image could do with a little *help*. Barry has sent me to see a few people but . . . well, what I'm really saying is, even though I don't know you very well, you do just seem to be slightly less of an arsehole.'

'Err thanks?'

'So maybe you could do a trial stint as my PR?'

Oh, my goodness, I thought Cassie was making chit-chat about my work but she was actually interviewing me. 'I don't think so. As I said, I'm not working at the moment. You need a PR company.'

'Couldn't you do it on a freelance basis?'

'No.' I'm keen to change the subject as quickly as possible so gesture towards a toddler with thick dark lashes who's table-hopping. 'Isn't he gorgeous?'

Cassie raises her eyebrows. 'If you say so. Is that a definite no to representing me?'

'It's a definite no.' The little boy has reached our table now. It's fair to say Cassie doesn't look entirely charmed. 'Don't you like kids?' I say as he moves on to the next table.

'Sure. As long as they're someone else's. Oh, and not on stage with me. I once did Oliver with twenty-seven stage school horrors. Never again! Apart from that I'm fine with kids. Oh, unless I have to pretend to be interested in them. I was in the hairdressers the other day, and this woman I barely know pulls out her iPhone and says, "Want to see pictures of my grandchildren?" and I'm thinking, "Sure. Forget the mega comeback, being the toast of Hollywood, winning an Oscar, shagging Damian Lewis. What I dream of – live for – is sitting here looking at photo after photo of the grandchildren of someone whose name I can't be bothered to remember!'

She catches sight of herself in the mirror and pulls a face. 'I don't like what's happened to my neck. I never even thought about my neck before I hit a certain age. It was just the thing that held my head on. But my God, I wish I hadn't taken it for granted; that smooth and beautiful thing. Now I spend hours on websites looking for polo neck pyjamas.'

Her neck – now she's drawn my attention to it – does look kind of older than the rest of her. Chickeny. 'There's nothing wrong with your neck.'

Cassie is too intent on scrutinizing herself in the mirror to notice a woman walk into the café and appear at our table. She has mousey hair and a tired, worn look like she's been faded in the wash. 'I'm Meg,' she says, extending her hand in my direction. 'Cassie's sister. Much younger sister, I should say.' She lets out a forced laugh to signal that this is a joke.

Cassie stops pulling at her flesh and mutters a hello.

'So, Cassie, how have you been?' Meg says, sitting down.

'Well, no death threats so far today. So pretty peachy really.'

'I'm sure no one really wants to kill you.'

'Except the people who know me that is!'

Meg gives a tight little smile. 'I'm glad you can still laugh.' She turns to me. 'How do you two know each other?'

Cassie answers before I have a chance. 'This is Ginny. I threw a bucket of water on her.'

'You and your jokes,' Meg says.

'It's true.'

'We're neighbours,' I interject.

Cassie hums the *Neighbours* theme tune.

Meg gestures towards a large chocolate cake sitting on the counter. 'Oooh, look at that! They do the most delicious cakes here. They're all homemade. Well café-made, but you know what I mean! I think I might have to have a small piece. Are either of you hungry?'

'I've been hungry since 1983,' Cassie mutters.

'Ginny?' Meg says.

'I'd better not. I've already had two flapjacks.'

As she ploughs through her chocolate cake, Meg tells us that it's been all go and that her boys have had a stomach bug. All those sheets to wash! When will they ever reach an age where they know they're going to throw up before they throw up?

Cassie may be an actress, but she doesn't seem to have mastered acting interested. At one point she actually yawns. Meg shoots her a look. 'Sorry. I haven't been sleeping well. I keep waking up at 3.15 for some reason. Always exactly 3.15 . . .'

'Poor you,' Meg says, her tone cool. 'Right. Well, I'd better be off.'

When she's gone, Cassie rolls her eyes heavenwards. 'My sister is officially the most boring woman in the world. One of those people with the complete inability to edit. The idea of having a point or a punchline seems to have completely passed her by. Seriously, I'd rather be back trapped underground in the Australian jungle with rats crawling over me than spend half an hour in her company.'

'Close family, are you?'

She smiles. 'I'm not kidding. The only person more boring than her is her husband David. I imagine the two of them have boring, obligatory sex – Fifty Shades of Beige. You can't have hot sex with someone you call Pumpkin. It's not possible.'

'She's your *sister*!' I say, raising my eyebrows.

'I know,' Cassie says, laughing. 'You can see why people call me a bitch.'

Julia's little brother is six foot two and film-star handsome.

'So my sister told me I just –' he adopts a stern voice '– HAD to see you.'

'Argh, I'm sorry.'

Nick laughs. 'S'all right. You know we're not looking to hire at the moment though, don't you?'

'Nobody's looking to hire.'

He smiles at me. He has very kind eyes. According to Julia, his wife left him last year. Call me shallow, but I am wondering what woman in her right mind would walk out on a husband who looks like Nick. He must be a really horrible person. With poor personal hygiene.

'Your old boss gave you an excellent reference.'

'Really?' I say, before I can stop myself.

He gives me a funny look.

We carry on with the work talk and, for once in my life, I think I do pretty well. It's helped by the fact that Nick is charming and funny and extremely easy to talk to. His major personality flaws are obviously well hidden. Anyone can appear nice. We've all read the interviews with the friends and neighbours of a serial killer saying he'd always seemed like such a lovely guy.

He explains that whilst MediaMaster don't have any jobs at the moment, they're pitching for several big accounts, and may be able to offer me something in couple of months.

'You know,' he says, as he walks me to the lift, 'my heart sank when Jules asked me to see you. I never imagined you'd actually be someone I'd want to hire. She's full of surprises, my sister!'

'She is. She's the last person I thought would ever get me a job. Not that you're giving me a job yet, but . . .' Oh God, now I sound really smug; as if I'm taking a job offer as a done deal. Why didn't I just say nice to meet you? 'And when I said she was the last person, I didn't mean she was horri—'

'Stop!' he says, laughing. 'I'll be in touch.'

Chapter Ten

I keep crying over nothing.

Right now, I am sitting in the hairdressers bawling because I spilt coffee all over my newish white blouse. Yesterday I burst into tears when I got a note from Mr Holden saying I'd left my wheelie bin in the wrong place (seriously, two notes from two different people in my building within a matter of weeks! I am a GOOD NEIGHBOUR!). The other day I had to reach for the tissues while watching a nappy ad.

Except, of course, I wasn't really crying over any of those things. I was crying because I miss Jack. And I know everyone hated him, and even I hated the way he behaved, but I do miss him.

'Aww, don't get so upset,' Lisa my hair stylist says. She's being incredibly kind to me, which is making me ten times worse. 'I expect the stain will come right out with a good soak.'

I miss the way Jack used to tease me about the cushions on my bed. *What is the point of having cushions you take off every night and put back every morning?* I miss his laugh, the warmth of his body that fitted so well next to mine.

'Shall we get you some magazines?' Lisa says. 'A nice bit of celebrity gossip will cheer you up.' I manage a nod and Lisa dispatches an insanely young girl with lots of piercings to bring me this week's *Hello!* and *Grazia*.

I thought Jack and I were going to get back together that day he turned up on my doorstep. I thought he was there because he couldn't live without me, but actually, it was just his Xbox he was missing.

The woman next to me with the foils in her hair keeps glancing in my direction. I really need to stop snivelling.

The girl with the piercings comes back and says there are no copies of *Hello!* but she's found *Grazia*. She says this extremely tentatively, as if it might set off a fresh wave of sobbing. Which is crazy because I don't even like *Hello!* that much.

I feel like I *should* be better by now though. I know that it's perfectly acceptable to wallow straight after a break-up and live off a diet of pizza, wine and recriminations but now, all this time later, I ought to have moved on. There's a statute of limitations on self-pity and I am failing to observe this.

I flick open the magazine, try to concentrate on the style editor's Lust List.

When people ask me how I am, I say I'm fine because that's what you say. (I once worked with a woman who gave you chapter and verse *whenever* you asked how she was and no one could stand her. It's a social nicety, I felt like shouting!) Normally I'd be more honest with people like Nancy and my mum and sister but I'm holding back because I know they all have such a low opinion of Jack, which makes it embarrassing to admit that I'm still such a mess. What, over *him*? They'd never say this, of course, but I bet that's what they'd be thinking.

'Okay?' Lisa says, catching my eye in the mirror.

I give her a wobbly smile and look back down at the magazine. I need to distract myself by reading about the ten best foundations on the high street. But all it does is remind me of yet another time I started crying recently, which was when I was at a beauty counter and the assistant commented on me having 'quite a few fine lines around my eyes'. That was a double-blub day actually. I'd already got upset in the post office queue when a man spoke sharply to me saying I'd pushed in front of him.

Lisa is tentatively snipping at my hair. I told her I was happy for her to take a couple of inches off but she looks as if she's going for the most cautious of trims. She probably doesn't consider me emotionally stable enough for a proper haircut.

What makes this break-up even worse than previous ones is the visceral fear that, as well as losing Jack, I've lost my chance to have a baby.

I hate him for the fact that next time I meet someone – a thought I have little enthusiasm for as it is – I'm going to have to start playing relationship maths. How long do you date someone before asking if they want kids? How long do you leave it before trying for kids? How many months, or even years, would it take to get pregnant? How does this all square up with the big number: my age?

These fears are probably what makes sense of me crying over the nappy ad (with 'sense' being a word I use loosely).

'There,' Lisa says. 'Now let's give you a nice blow dry, shall we?'

I keep wondering if there's anything I could have done differently with Jack to have stopped this happening. What if I'd been tougher with him, given him an ultimatum maybe? What if I'd played a bit more hard-to-get? (Or, let's be honest, at all hard to get.)

Perhaps we will get back together? That's how this would end if it was a Hollywood movie.

But life isn't a Hollywood movie.

Lisa is showing me the back of my hair in a mirror and asking me what I think.

I tell her it's great and tip her ridiculously generously (by way of making up for my behaviour).

'I'm sorry about your top,' she says, putting her hand on my arm. 'Hopefully it will come out in the wash.'

I nod. I just want to get out of here as quickly as I can now. And I'd like to say that's because I'm desperate to get on with all the things I should be doing – sending out CVs, chasing headhunters, writing the novel I've always said I'd write if only I had the time. But really it's because I know I'm about to start crying again.

When I hear a knock at the door, I am lying on the sofa feeling sorry for myself as I scroll through my Instagram feed, which is awash with weddings and babies. And to think I only went onto it because I was fed up looking at people crowing about promotions or new jobs on LinkedIn.

'Cassie,' I say, opening the door. 'This is a surprise.' I am suddenly acutely conscious of my appearance. I may have freshly blow-dried hair for once but I also have puffy, red eyes, kneed tracksuit bottoms and a stained sweatshirt. Oh and the fluffy chimp slippers for that extra dash of sophistication.

'Do you have a minute?' she asks.

'Sure. Come in.' The flat looks about as glossy as I do, and there's a distinct waft of bin. But hey ho, it'll be a chance for her to see how the other half lives.

'Oh,' she says, 'you've got hard floors.'

What's that supposed to mean? There are lots of big rugs! Also, it's not me that has Kylie Minogue blaring out first thing every Saturday morning (I should be so lucky to get a lie-in).

And even Marielle and Jean have been much more considerate lovers recently (I don't mean to each other – eww.).

I decide to let Cassie's comment go. I'm just not up to a neighbour-spat today. 'Tea? Coffee?'

'I'm fine, thanks.'

She probably doesn't trust the cleanliness of the mugs.

'I've just been to see another PR. Ophelia she was called – I kid you not. My God she was awful, Ginny.' She shakes her head like she's trying to make the memory fall out of it.

'Awful! So I just thought I'd have one more go at persuading you to work for me.'

'Look, I'm flattered . . .' Not to mention tempted by the idea of earning some money. 'But I really don't think it's a good idea. I think you need the weight of a big firm behind you.' To be honest, with the way her reputation stands at the moment, she needs a miracle, but why be unkind?

'Are you sure? Because the other thing about Ophelia is she was just ridiculously young. I mean practically a foetus. At least you're quite old.'

'Is this your idea of a charm offensive?'

'Hey, I'm managing one out of two,' she says, laughing. 'Sure I can't talk you into it?' I nod. 'Okay.' She gets up to leave, smoothing a non-existent wrinkle from her expensive-looking silk shirt. As she gets to the door she suddenly turns back. 'I don't suppose you fancy coming to the cinema with me this afternoon?'

'Umm . . .' I am thrown, to be honest. Am I the sort of person who goes to the cinema on a weekday afternoon now? And why is Cassie asking me to join her anyway? Is she lonely? She doesn't look like the sort of person you think would be lonely but then neither do I and, even though I hate admitting it, I think I kind of am at the moment. I may be lucky enough to have great friends and family, but everyone (except me) is just so busy all the time, and it's actually pretty easy to go a whole day where I don't really talk to another human being. I don't suppose it helps that I seem to be constantly making myself supper for one while Marielle and Jean sit entwined on the sofa (I have christened them Jarielle, but of course haven't shared that with them).

'Don't worry,' she says. 'You're busy.'

'No,' I say, because suddenly I realize that I really want to get out of this flat. I don't care that I don't know Cassie that well or even what film we see. I don't want to job-hunt and I don't want to try and fail to write. Oh, and I'm sick to bloody death of looking at tiny fingers and toes on Instagram.

'I'll just change quickly.'

Cassie looks pleased and I'm not sure if it's because I've agreed to go with her or because for a second she wondered if I might have been thinking of leaving the house in the chimp slippers.

We are standing in the queue at the Swiss Cottage Odeon but we still haven't decided what we're going to watch. It's a toss-up between one I don't want to see because I've read the book and the movie won't be as good, and one Cassie doesn't want to see because she should be playing Glenn Close's part.

'Can you believe Meg invited me to her book group?' Cassie says as we wait. If loneliness is what made Cassie ask me — can you be a lonely household name or is that an oxymoron? — it hasn't made her desperate enough to hang out with Meg. 'When I said no, she asked if it's because I don't read! My sister is one of those people who thinks she's "deep" because she has a bad haircut and a penchant for dodgy knitwear!'

'I'm sure she speaks highly of you too!'

'The truth is, I can't think of anything worse than sitting around with a bunch of middle-aged, middle-class women acting like they're in an English lesson. She forced me to go once before, and they all banged on about schools and kids all evening. Have you ever noticed that people with kids spend their whole time telling you how hard their lives are, and what worry their darlings cause them, but at the same time they act like anyone childless is holding onto a winning lottery ticket that they just haven't bothered to cash in?'

The two women in front of us in the queue are chatting away loudly in Spanish. I can't understand what they're saying except that one of them just mentioned the name of a famous Hollywood actor who was all over the papers today sunbathing naked.

'Did you see the pictures?' I ask Cassie.

She nods. 'He's not what he was.'

'You know him?'

'Used to. Rather well, actually. Well enough to tell you that the newspaper were rather generous with those pixels!'

I laugh. 'Did you sleep with absolutely everyone in Hollywood?'

'Only the ones who asked nicely.'

A group of girls who look like models go into the Ambar bar. 'This cinema has changed so much since I was a kid. Apparently, they spent three million on the makeover.'

'That's what I need.'

'You do not.' I shake my head, smiling.

'Do too. Getting older sucks. I'm not any wiser, I've just got batwing sleeves when I'm naked.'

'Too much info, Cassie!'

She laughs for a moment, before she starts scowling at the people coming in and shaking their umbrellas. It's obviously started to rain outside, and the couple that have joined the queue behind us smell of damp dog.

'Anyway, how's your job-hunting going?'

I shrug. 'One big lesson in rejection.'

'Sounds like the life of an actress. Hang in there and remember that although "we'll call you" might be baloney nine times out of ten, sometimes they actually do. You've got to keep positive.' She laughs. 'And this coming from me, as Barry would say.'

'You're pretty positive.'

She raises her eyebrows. 'I'm a mess.'

69

An elderly couple are staring at Cassie from across the foyer. They glide towards us, the woman a little ahead. 'Didn't you used to be Cassie Frost?'

I stare at the swirly carpet.

'Yes,' Cassie says, more gracious in her tone than I would ever have imagined.

'Still a good-looking woman,' the man says.

Cassie smiles. 'And in that one word!'

'We loved you in that beef burger ad!' the woman says. 'Mmm, juicy!'

'Thank you.'

The woman secures an autograph and then goes away.

'Beef burger ad?'

'I was six. Like I said, my best times are rather behind me!'

Chapter Eleven

My mother is talking about her first date with my dad. 'I was so jittery and excited that day, I got one of the other nurses to check all the meds before I gave them out to the patients,' she says, her eyes shining.

'We went to that little Italian place just off Goodge Street,' Dad says.

'That's right! I was afraid to order spaghetti in case I got it all over my pale blue top!'

My dad laughs. 'I'd have still married you!'

We are celebrating their thirty-fifth wedding anniversary. At the moment, I can barely imagine being in a relationship that lasts thirty-five days let alone thirty-five years. The table was set for six people when we arrived, despite the fact my mum was adamant she had only booked for five. It's as if I'm haunted by the husband I don't have.

'Where on earth are Rachel and Paul?' Dad says, looking at his watch. 'Wasn't it her who got you to change the restaurant reservation from eight thirty to eight so it wasn't a late night?'

My sister never has the ability to just 'fit in' if an arrange-ment doesn't suit her. I am irritated by and admiring of this in equal measure.

'I expect she's having trouble getting the twins settled with the babysitter,' Mum says.

'We should start without them,' Dad says.

Mum smooths her hair back off her face. 'They'll be here any minute.'

Mon Plaisir is London's oldest French restaurant, a place which transports you to the 5th arrondissement the minute you walk through the door and treats the whims of culinary fashion with classic French disdain. Here is a place to come for garlicky escargots and coq au vin that bears little relation to its bastardized dinner party cousin. The bistro's interior is casually elegant; crammed with souvenirs, posters and flea market bric-a-brac.

Dad tells us a funny story about one of the nurse's writing 'only feed patient when awake' on a chart. 'As if she was going to be chomping through chicken pie and broccoli in her sleep!' He is on full, sparkly form tonight, probably more by coincidence than because it's his wedding anniversary. His moods cannot be ordered up in advance.

Rachel and Paul arrive. He is wearing his grey work suit and a large, bright green Afro wig. This is classic Paul. I know such zany antics (and surely this is the correct term here?) are supposed to make me fall about laughing, but my funny bone always remains resolutely untickled. He makes me feel uptight and humourless, although, in my defence, my parents' laughs are hollow and their smiles do not reach their eyes.

'Phew, I'm shattered,' Paul says, sitting down.

'Don't talk to me about tired!' Rachel says. 'The boys had me up three times last night!' Rachel has the monopoly on tired.

'Well, I was in surgery all night,' Dad says.

Whoa! Dad, two points; Rachel, one. She scowls and picks up the menu.

We start chatting about the first flat my parents bought together. 'Do you remember we didn't have any money left to buy furniture?' Mum says to Dad.

'That's right,' Dad says. 'We used an upturned bookcase to eat at.'

'Typical Mum that you still "ate at the table" even when you didn't have a table!' Rachel says, laughing.

'Oh yeah,' Dad says. 'She set it properly too. Flowers, candles, linen napkins folded into swans!'

Mum laughs. 'I've never made napkins into swans!'

Later, after Paul has finished a series of jokes that make him – but only him – cry with laughter, Dad asks me how my job-hunting is going. I wonder if he's thinking I should have got a proper job like him and my sister. I babble nervously about the headhunters all saying what a bad time it is at the moment, but that I've got a few interviews lined up. 'Oh, and I'm going to try to do some writing,' I say, regretting the words as soon as they come out of my mouth.

'That's nice,' Dad says. As if I've taken up knitting or softball.

I try to steer us back onto safer ground. 'I had an interview the other day that went really well. They can't offer me a job at the moment but they might if they win some new business. I don't think he was just saying it either. Anyway, as Cassie says, you've got to stay positive . . .' I always babble when I'm nervous.

'Cassie?' Mum says.

'Cassie Frost. She's my neighbour. And friend.'

'She's hideous!' Rachel says.

I bristle even though I'd have said the same myself up until very recently.

'Actually, she's not really like she comes across on the telly . . .' I launch into a speech about how she's actually very funny and self-deprecating.

A woman with a round, careworn face has appeared at our table soundlessly. 'I'm so sorry to interrupt your dinner, Dr Taylor,' she says, 'but I just had to come to say hello. I'm Sarah Holmes, Katy's mother.'

'Oh yes, I remember,' Dad says, although I know he'd say that even if he didn't. She gushes about what a wonderful man my father is. How he saved her daughter's life. How there isn't a day goes by when they don't remember him in their prayers.

'And lo, he walked on water!' Rachel says, when the woman is out of earshot.

'Rachel!' Mum admonishes. 'I think it's lovely that people feel that way about your father.' Then she farts very loudly.

Rachel, Dad and I all stare at her. To say that this is out of character doesn't really cover it. My mother looks totally bewildered. Then Paul starts guffawing. 'It's my fart machine,' he says, brandishing a remote control. 'I popped it in Helen's pocket when I kissed her hello.' He presses the button and another loud fart is emitted. What can I say? My sister has married an eight-year-old boy.

Respite comes in the form of the arrival of our food. My father and Rachel are sharing the poulet rôti which Dad pronounces 'nearly as good' as my mother's.

'Did you tell your mum and dad about yesterday?' Paul says to Rachel.

Rachel shoots him a look. 'Don't make such a big deal of everything.'

'George bit Felix,' Paul says. 'Really hard. Teeth marks and everything. I read online that a three-year-old can bite with the same force as a dog.'

'Oh, they all go through phases,' Mum says.

'Exactly,' Rachel says glaring at Paul. She turns to me. 'Did you ask Dad what he thought about the fertility MOT?'

I nearly spit out my mouthful of pommes dauphinoise. 'No!'

'What fertility MOT?' Dad says.

I shoot Rachel a look.

'What?' she says. 'You may as well get his advice.'

Oh yes, and what better time to get it? Perhaps he could check my AMH levels before dessert? 'I was just thinking of going for a fertility check, that's all.'

'Really?' Mum says. 'Have you got any reason to worry?'

I shrug. 'I hope not. But I'm thirty-five next birthday and, well, as you know I'm not with anyone. So I thought maybe it made sense to find out if I'm running out of time.' I look at Dad waiting for him to say that of course I'm not, that such an idea is preposterous.

But he doesn't say that. 'The trouble is those tests are a complete waste of time for women in your position.'

'That's what I told her,' Rachel says.

'Umm, last time I checked you had precisely NO medical knowledge,' I say.

'No,' Dad agrees. 'But she happens to be right about this. Those tests only give you a snapshot of your ovarian reserve at one point in time. They're not a reliable indicator of how quickly you will or won't get pregnant. They were designed for subfertility and assisted conception management and the way they're marketed as a fertility "check" is a bit of scam.'

Bam goes my 'knowledge is power' plan.

'I really don't think you have any reason to worry, darling,' Mum says, putting her hand over mine.

'No,' I snap, 'but you don't know that, do you? Now can we please stop discussing my ovarian reserve over the dinner table.'

'Yes,' Paul says, 'it's egg-ceptionally rude!'

Christ.

There are a few seconds of strained smiles before Dad breaks the silence to launch into a story about the first time he took Mum home to meet his family. 'She even managed to charm my formidable grandma, who took me aside and told me I'd better not let this one go.'

Later, when the bill is paid, everyone is stifling yawns and

Rachel is wondering how many times the boys will get her up that night, Dad raises his champagne glass. 'I'd like to propose a toast. To my beautiful wife, who is a better person than I'll ever be. And who I learn something new and wonderful about every single day.'

I feel happy and sad all at the same time. Will I ever have what my parents have?

'Thank you,' Mum says, her eyes filling with tears.

'Here's a question,' Dad says. 'If you knew thirty-five years ago, what you know now, would you still marry me?'

Mum cocks her head to one side and affects an air of thoughtfulness. Her eyes twinkle. 'Are you kidding?'

We all, including Dad, roar with laughter.

Chapter Twelve

'I am *never* getting another job,' I say to Nancy.

'Don't be silly,' she says, rummaging through her wardrobe.

We try to FaceTime each other at least once a week. Nancy usually calls me when she's got a moment because, let's face it, my schedule is pretty flexible right now. Today, she phones me at 7 a.m. New York time and I make a guilty mental note that it's been a while since I was up at 7 a.m.

'It's true,' I say. 'The headhunter called about the job at Razor this morning. They've given it to someone else but wanted me to know I was a very impressive candidate. Yeah, right.'

'I'm sorry,' Nancy says. 'Nothing from Julia's hot brother?'

'No . . . he seemed pretty genuine but I'm beginning to suspect he was just fobbing me off.'

She holds up a blue jacket. 'Do you think I should wear this to the meeting with my boss? Or is it a bit too "grown up"?'

'I think technically we are actually supposed to be grown-ups. And the jacket is great.'

'Cool,' she says, putting it on.

'Also, I'm going to die old and alone.'

'Don't be silly. You've got me.'

'You're right. Let's get married.'

She laughs and holds up two necklaces. 'Which one?'

'The one on the right.'

'The worst thing is that, initially, the headhunter wasn't even going to put me forward for the job at Razor because she thought I was overqualified for it. Then I persuade her to let me go for an interview and they give it to someone else.'

'You'll get something soon.'

'Hmmm. How's everything with you? How was the date?'

'Indescribably awful. Imagine the most socially awkward, misogynistic guy with zero sense of humour and even less sex appeal.'

'So you're seeing him again then?'

'Absolutely. Arranged a date for next week. I'm hoping he might grow on me. Especially since he's such a rare breed.'

'Hot, single man in New York?'

'Hot, single, *straight* man in New York. Listen, I've got to go to work.'

'Oh, rub it in, why don't you?'

She laughs. 'Hang in there. Things will get better.'

Nancy is gone and I wander into the kitchen to help myself to a biscuit. Tomorrow, I'm going to start eating really healthily. I'm also getting properly dressed first thing instead of slobbing around in my PJs. You shouldn't be calling headhunters in your PJs. They can probably tell somehow. 'Put that candidate to the bottom of the pile, Jen. She can't even be bothered to get dressed.'

I consider the afternoon ahead. I've got to pop over to see my mum, return some books to the library and then maybe tidy the flat. I had promised myself I'd go for a run too but the weather is grim with a capital 'G'.

Yesterday wasn't quite so grim weather-wise (cold, grey, miserable, just not actually raining) but I didn't run then either because it was a Monday and on Mondays I look after my nephews. It's a temporary arrangement, and one that's made my sister more grateful than I've seen her since I lent her my Rimmel Chestnut Whip lipgloss when she was twelve. In fact, I really look forward to Mondays and think I enjoy playing with the Playdough even more than the boys (the smell!). I particularly enjoy using one little device, a bit like a cross between a citrus press and a sieve, which makes the Playdough come out in squiggly worms.

What if I never have children of my own to make squiggly Playdough worms with?

Stop it!

The cuddles I get from the boys when they're tired and watching *Tweenies* at the end of the day take some beating too. It crossed my mind on the way back from the swings the other day that I should apply for the position as their nanny. But imagine if I got rejected for that! I think I am what the headhunters describe as a fairly marketable candidate. I may lack experience – Rachel still has to give me a detailed list every morning with foods and nap times (although detailed lists are *very* my sister) – but I do make my team seem motivated and engaged, particularly if I throw a few Smarties into the equation. I am a little worried about how I should handle it if George tries to bite anyone – apparently he's now something of a serial sabre-tooth – but so far this hasn't happened on my watch.

I glance at the clock and realize that it is later than I thought and I'd better hurry up and get to my mum's. I open my wardrobe where my work clothes stare back at me reproachfully. I pull out a pair of jeans.

The phrases I'm most sick of hearing are 'there's not much out there' and 'it's not a great time'. Most of the headhunters haven't even fixed me up with a single interview.

I glance in the mirror. My hair is also 'off work' and has decided to have a mind of its own. Today, it is wavy on one side and completely straight on the other. I could take the straighteners to the wavy side, but I decide I will rebrand as quirky. Besides, who's going to see me?

I lace up my Converse. Apart from the salary, here's what I miss about working: wearing proper shoes; office banter, even the kind that seemed inane at the time; a compelling reason not to still be in my PJs at lunchtime. But what I miss most is feeling like I'm useful – contributing to the world in some way – which is odd because my job is not like my father's or my sister's. I have never repaired a child's aortic valve or taught them to read. But it still gave me the feeling of being a fully paid-up member of adult society. Someone who deserved their glass of wine at the end of a hard day's work.

I shut my front door behind me. Mum is very good at not showing it, but I know she must be worried about my job situation. I wonder if she's concerned about my lack of a husband too. I know that all sounds a bit Jane Austen, but everybody else seems to be. Jarielle were asking me the other night if there was anyone special in my life. Yes, I felt like snapping, I just keep him hidden away in my wardrobe which is why you've never seen him. My friends keep oh-so-casually suggesting I give a few of the dating apps a go. What's to lose, they say. It'll be fun. Plus, Sara/Rebecca/Janey at work met The One like that.

I just want to swipe left on the whole conversation.

When I told Cassie there was nothing she could say to persuade me to work for her, I meant it. So why I am standing outside her front door, I do not know. I could – probably should – just walk away, but somehow I find myself knocking.

'Ginny,' Cassie says. She looks impossibly glamorous for 9 a.m. I wonder if she goes to bed in full make-up.

'I've had an idea. The sort of thing I might suggest *if* I was your publicist. But I want to be absolutely clear that this isn't me changing my mind. If you like this idea, I can help you get it sorted but it's just a one-off.'

'Oh-kay.' She raises an eyebrow.

'Have you heard about Suki Norris?'

'The TV presenter?'

'Yeah. She's getting ripped to shreds on social media.'

'They were talking about it on the radio. She made some joke about a bit of sexual harassment in the workplace being a good thing. What's she got to do with me?'

'She's a big story right now. It's all anyone wants to talk about. And one angle the media will definitely be interested in is how it feels to suddenly find yourself as a national hate figure. Which you're ideally placed to talk about because you've been through a similar thing yourself recently. I've got contacts on *This Morning* and, while I can't promise anything, if you're up for it, I can definitely try to get you an interview.'

Cassie smiles. 'See, I knew you weren't one of the idiots.'

'This is just a one-off though. A favour to a neighbour, if you like.'

Cassie shrugs. 'If you insist. You must let me pay you, though.'

I think of the bank statement I opened this morning. Lots going out, nothing coming in. And Cassie can definitely afford to pay me. On the other hand, once you accept money from someone, it definitely changes everything. 'You can buy me lunch.'

'Don't be si—'

I hold up my hands to interrupt her. 'Let's see if I can even get you the gig first. One thing, if they are interested, they'll want you on tomorrow morning. This isn't a story that's going to hang around. Is that okay?'

Cassie nods. 'Oh wait, what day is tomorrow? Wednesday? No, that's no good. Wednesdays are Bruno's day off.'

'Bruno?'

'My hairdresser. He's been doing my hair for years. Comes every Saturday morning and then I go to him in between if I need him.'

Bruno is the Saturday-morning visitor whose loud laugh and penchant for Kylie puts paid to me ever having a lie-in. 'Don't worry, they have hairdressers there.'

Cassie looks at me like I'm insane.

This, I think, is why I definitely don't want to work for you. 'What, so you'd be prepared to turn down an interview on *This Morning* just because Bruno can't do your hair? Which looks immaculate, by the way.'

Cassie sighs. 'No, I suppose not . . .'

'Good. Now let me go and make some calls.'

I have to say, getting Cassie the slot on *This Morning* is just about the easiest thing I've ever done in my life, but when I tell her I think she's going to dance a little jig.

'That's incredible, Ginny,' she says, throwing her arms around me. 'Thank you so much. Come in and have a celebratory drink?'

I think about Jarielle, who were whispering together and giggling conspiratorially in the kitchen when I left. 'Sure. We should probably do a bit of prep too.'

'Oh, I've already been prepping just in case. I had one of those Venus Freeze facials earlier.'

'When I said prep, I was thinking more in terms of what you were actually going to say.'

'Oh yeah. Still the Venus Freeze wasn't a bad idea either. Although the time I end up spending on maintenance now just doesn't bear thinking about. Dyeing, plucking, waxing, electrolysis. Honestly, Ginny, enjoy being young because you have no idea.'

'Well, thanks for giving me so much to look forward to!'

She starts mixing us up two G&Ts, each of which seems

to be about four parts gin to one part tonic. 'Chin hairs sprout from nowhere overnight!'

'You're the last person I can imagine with chin hairs!'

'Well, I have them! And I seem to need my moustache waxed about every twenty-two seconds. The snotty South African girl at Beautyworks hates it when I call it that. *We call it the upper lip, Madam.* It's my tache and I'll call it what I like!'

I laugh. 'Listen, there is one small hitch about tomorrow. I'm afraid I won't be able to come to the studios with you. I've actually got an interview, and the headhunter made it very clear to me that trying to reschedule at such short notice would mean there was no point bothering to go at all.'

'It's fine, darling. I'll have Bruno there to hold my hand.'

'Bruno? I thought Wednesdays were his day off.'

'I managed to persuade him change is as good as a rest.' She reads my expression. 'I know, I'm a nightmare! But I'm a nightmare who's very grateful to you.'

I laugh. 'Now, I'm sure you know this, but the line you want to take is that, while you completely disagree with what Suki Norris said—'

'But a little sexual harassment *can* be lovely. It just depends who is doing it.'

Dear God. I take a big swig of my drink. 'Cassie. You cannot seem in any way to condone what Suki said. Sexual harassment in the workplace is not something to joke about.'

'Everything is so PC now,' she grumbles. But I can tell she'll toe the line.

'What you can say is that you feel very sorry for Suki as a person. That it's easy to make a bad joke and painful to then be vilified for it. You want to come across as brimming with compassion.'

'Gosh,' Cassie says. 'Lucky I can act!' She takes a sip of her drink, catches a glimpse of herself in the mirror above the fireplace and pulls the skin across her cheekbones taut with her fingertips. 'All this lack of sleep is really catching up with me. I'm going to have to go back to that nice Dr Lowe.'

'Oh, don't do that.'

She pulls the skin even tauter. 'I have to. Growing old gracefully isn't an option in my business. Well, not for women anyway. Harrison Ford can still be Indiana Jones, but where are the leading ladies of the same age? Closer to home, where's the female equivalent to David Dimbleby? I'll tell you where she is: sitting at home because she's considered too saggy and wrinkled for HD.'

'It just seems so sad – this eternal quest for youth.'

Cassie snorts. 'Yup. Pointless too. Gravity and time always triumph. Just look at that picture of Marcia Blake in *Heat*!' She drains the last of her drink. For a tiny person, she can certainly put away the booze. 'Another?'

I nod. Say what you like about Cassie but she's good company. Plus, Jarielle will probably be having sex on the kitchen floor by now.

'You never did tell me what happened to you and your boyfriend.'

'He shagged my boss,' I say, wondering if a strong gin and tonic on an empty stomach was really such a good idea.

'Ouch.'

'Yes ouch.'

'Men like that should come with a warning around their necks, shouldn't they? I was stupid enough to marry one of them.'

'Shane?'

'No, to the best of my knowledge Shane never cheated on me. We were only married five months, so I bloody well hope not! I think Lenny – he was my third husband; God, how does that make me sound? – was faithful too.'

'Was he the one who played Doctor Mike?'

'Yeah, that's him. He had his faults – y'know, drug addiction, all about him-itis – but I think he managed to keep it in his trousers, probably because no one else would have him. I was talking about Lee. Never failed to score, on or off the pitch. I always knew when he'd been up to no good because he bought me flowers. Say it with flowers! He actually bought me roses after shagging a girl called Rose once. I can only assume we had his subconscious to thank for that one. I suppose it could have been worse – she could have been a Daisy.'

'What about now? Are you seeing anyone?'

She shakes her head. 'No, not for ages, which is odd considering when I was younger I was always in a relationship. I'm great at the falling in love bit. Well, the clue's in the word "falling", isn't it? Not hard. But staying in love – when they fart in your bed and leave their toenail clippings on the bathroom floor – that's hard.'

'You make it sound so romantic!'

'Yeah. I'm probably just a grumpy old woman who's been on her own too long. I think even George Clooney would get on my nerves now.'

She pours us more drinks and we carry on chatting, and I'm struck not for the first time by how funny it is that women who barely know each other will have conversations about everything from their sex lives to their deepest insecurities, whereas two men who've known each other twenty-five years will probably share little more than banter about the football.

'Did it really hurt, the things people said about you?' I suddenly blurt out.

Cassie sits up a little straighter. 'Sorry,' I say. 'None of my business.'

'It's okay.' She pauses. 'And yes, it did. Mostly because I knew I deserved it.'

I feel a little knot in my stomach. 'No one deserves that.'

She shrugs. She looks sad and tiny. She also looks the age quoted in the papers for once. 'I guess it's better to be talked about than not talked about. Anyway, this interview on *This Morning* is going to be a new start for me.'

I smile and raise my glass. 'I'll drink to that.'

I'm taking the bus to my interview because then I can watch Cassie's appearance on my phone.

Gino D'Acampo is preparing pasta with meatballs. Phillip Schofield is teasing him about his very tight trousers and Gino says he can't even wear anything underneath.

The show breaks for commercials and I wonder if Cassie will have decided to wear the green top or the burgundy one. She was curiously passive about the outfit – 'you choose'. I am praying for everything to go well. I just want people at home to see the Cassie I see.

Holly Willoughby gives a quick rundown of the Suki Norris story (presumably for people who've been on Mars for the last couple of days) and introduces Cassie. She's wearing the green and looks fabulous. Good. 'Cassie, you've been through what Suki Norris is going through right now,' Holly says. 'What would your advice to her be?'

Cassie leans forward on her chair. 'Not to listen to them.' Her voice sounds a bit odd. I turn up the volume on my headphones.

'That can be difficult though, can't it?' Phillip says.

Cassie rests her chin on her hand but it slips slightly. 'Very difficult. But that's what you gotta do. Ignore them.' Her voice is slurry. I am desperate to try to pull the tiny figure out of the screen in front of me. Don't do this to yourself, Cassie!

The questions continue. The slurring continues. I watch through my fingers.

'Cassie,' Phillip asks, leaning forward on the sofa. 'Are you all right?'

I put my head in my hands, unable to watch.

'Of course I'm all right! Never better!' The slurring is aggressive now. A drunk told he can't have another whisky by the barman.

'It's just your speech is a bit slurred.'

'Is it?' Cassie's voice drips with fury and disdain.

'People in my ear are asking me if you're okay. If maybe you'd like to continue the interview another time?'

Cassie jabs at the air with a pointed finger. She looks grotesque. 'I tell ya what I wanna do. I wanna talk about Susie Norris—'

'Suki Norris.'

She swipes away the correction. 'Whatever. Her. I wanna say: Susie . . . Suki . . . don't let the bastards grind you down!'

By the time they cut away to an incontinence segment, I am almost at my interview and almost in tears.

I did this.

My interview goes about as well as Cassie's TV appearance. Well, okay, that's an exaggeration, but let's just say I'm not expecting a callback.

Cassie's clip is already on YouTube. I read the comments.

'LOL. She's scum. A filthy, attention-seeking whore.'

'That woman is a useless ugly moron.'

'Drunken slapper.'

I stop reading and dial Cassie's number. It goes straight to voicemail.

Chapter Thirteen

Cassie is insistent about two things: the slurring on *This Morning* was caused by a bad reaction to a sleeping pill she'd taken the night before, and she still owes me lunch.

We go to Lemonia, an insanely popular Greek restaurant where there is always a queue.

'Perhaps we should just go somewhere else?' Cassie says.

'We've only been waiting a few minutes.'

She is standing with her arms crossed, impatience seeping out of every pore. 'Excuse me,' she says to the harassed-looking Maître-d, 'have you any idea how long our table is going to be? You did say it wouldn't be long.'

I try to sink my head down into the collar of my jacket as if I'm a tortoise who can disappear into its shell.

'Not too long now, beautiful lady. I promise.'

The 'beautiful lady' appeases Cassie slightly, but she still clearly struggles with the whole concept of waiting. In an effort to distract her, I ask her something that crossed my mind about her brief foray into the world of music. 'You know when you recorded that single with Shane. Were you frightened? I mean, you were an actress, you weren't trained as a singer.'

Cassie looks at me as if it's only just occurred to her that fear was any kind of an option. 'Not really. What was the worst thing that could have happened? Well, apart from humiliating myself in front of millions and putting the kibosh on my whole career!'

'Excuse me,' says a middle-aged woman. She's the type who wears a Juicy Couture tracksuit with a full face of make-up and freshly blow-dried hair. 'I saw you on *This Morning* the other day.'

Dear God, I think, please let her have seen the grovelling apology and explanation I tweeted on Cassie's behalf from the account I set up for her. (Cassie, who was a Twitter virgin, was incredibly impressed. 'How fabulous to message the whole world from your phone!')

'Sleeping pills don't suit me either,' the woman says.

I let out a breath I didn't realize I'd been holding.

'May I have your autograph?'

Cassie flashes me an oh-what-a-frightful-bore look, whilst simultaneously seeming to puff up. 'Of course.'

The woman starts scrabbling around in her handbag. 'Now what have I got for you to write it on? I watched you in the jungle too. I know you weren't everyone's cup of PG, but I thought you were very good to eat the kangaroo's nasty bits. I wouldn't have fancied that myself!' She has a laugh like a creaky door. 'And I used to love you as Dr Lisa in *Casualty*. It's never been the same since you left.'

'Thank you.'

'Would you ever go back?'

'Oh well, you know, never say never,' says Cassie, who has confided to me she'd go back like a shot. 'I never thought I'd eat kangaroo bottom!'

Peal of creaky door laughter. 'I'm Jan,' says the woman, pulling a crumpled receipt out of her heavily monogrammed handbag. 'Oh dear, I can't have you sign this! And this is my husband, Alan.'

Alan and I exchange the polite smiles of the extras in this little scene.

'I'm going to ask Christos for a piece of paper,' Jan says.

'Ask him for a table for me at the same time,' Cassie says. I hope she's joking.

'Here we go,' Jan says, presenting Cassie with paper and a pen. Cassie writes her message, signs and hands it over.

'Would you mind having your photo taken with me?'

'Jan!' her husband admonishes.

'Don't worry, it's fine,' says Cassie, already getting herself into her side-on, one-hand-on-hip pose.

Alan fumbles around with the camera on his phone. For someone who's just been promoted to supporting cast, he doesn't look terribly happy about it.

Jan stands next to Cassie, grinning widely. The two of them actually look quite alike, although Cassie would be completely horrified if you said that to her. Both have very straight, very blonde hair, expensive all-year light tans and fairly fine features. However, although they're probably around the same age, Cassie looks a good fifteen years younger, and she's certainly fifteen pounds lighter.

'Ladies,' Christos says, 'I have a table ready for you.'

Cassie is all smiles as we bid goodbye to Jan and Alan but her face quickly changes when she sees our table. 'Don't you have one near the window?'

Christos raises his hands in a gesture of supplication. 'Only this.'

I can't help feeling sorry for the guy. I give Cassie a pleading look.

She looks mutinous but sits down. 'All that waiting and then he goes and sits us in Nowhere-ville. To think I used to get the best table wherever I went.'

'This table is fine,' I say. But I know my words will fall on deaf ears. The best table or seat or billing matter A LOT to Cassie. She probably rides on the coffin when she goes to a funeral.

'It's near the toilets!'

The waiter comes over and we order drinks. Cassie seems to inhale her first glass of wine.

'I bumped into Jeanie Marsh in the street the other day. She was my first agent. How I wish I'd stayed with her. I left her after we had some silly row about the commission on something. She's one of the biggest agents in town now. She represents Georgie Hurst, who's in absolutely everything, although goodness knows why. The only thing she seems to really excel at is carrying very tiny dogs in great big handbags. Anyway, Jeanie actually seemed quite pleased to see me – she gave me a big hug, took the time to chat. But then I called her and she hasn't called me back.'

'Perhaps she's just very busy?'

Cassie raises her eyebrows.

'Don't you like the agent you've got?'

'Barry? Yes, I like him. You can't really not like Barry. But he doesn't get me much work. Apart from *Celebrity*. And we know how that turned out.'

'Was it like you imagined it would be?'

'It was worse. First off, you know you're being beamed out in high definition looking just dreadful. I tried to sneak in my mascara in my knickers but they took it from me. Also, you're really hungry. And, believe me, I'm used to being hungry, but I'm talking two tiny spoons of rice and beans a day. And then there's all the insects and the challenges and stuff. But the worst of all is the other contestants. The rats were more intelligent than most of the people they put me with.'

'You weren't keen on that *X Factor* girl, were you?'

'No. I can't bear the way people just become famous overnight because of some stupid competition. In my day, you had to work at your craft. Anyway, she was Pond Life. And she had to be the centre of attention all the time.' I smile. 'Yes, I know. Pots and kettles!'

The waiter brings our food, and I eat while Cassie picks. We chat and laugh about everything from holidays to relationships and Cassie comes across as the smart, engaging person that I was desperate for her to be on *This Morning*.

'Nice of that woman to say *Casualty* hasn't been the same since I left. I mean, a crock obviously. Like someone telling you the lines on your face make your face look lived in, add character, when we all know the only lines worth having are the ones you put up your nose. But nice of her to say nonetheless.'

'She's obviously a big fan.'

'Yeah, it's good to know I've got one left.' She takes a glug of her wine. 'Do you know the whole sorry story about why I got fired from *Casualty*? Quite a spectacular downfall. Well worth googling if you're bored on a rainy day. I was back on the drugs again, often didn't even turn up for work. And when I did, I'd fall over on set or forget my lines. I wasn't exactly professional . . .'

'Ouch. So what happened after you were fired?'

'Oh, you know the usual stuff. I threw a stone Venus statue at a woman in a garden centre and was arrested for assault.'

'Cassie!'

'She deserved it.' I make a face. 'Really. She kept staring and pointing. Telling her mate how rough I looked in a very loud voice—'

'Did you hurt her?'

She shrugs. 'Three stitches on her shoulder. I've never been a very good shot.'

I stare at her, lost for words.

She laughs.

The waiter clears our plates.

'I'll tell you one thing about that time of my life. The old cliché about finding out who your real friends are is true. You also discover a lot about yourself, much of which isn't very pretty. It's so easy to be a "nice person" when you're at the top. You lead a totally charmed existence where everyone sucks up to you and you only have to offer a journalist a cup of tea for people to comment on how down to earth you are. But when everything's gone to shit . . . well, that's when you find out who you really are.'

'Well, I think you're nice.'

She laughs. 'Nice enough that I can persuade you to be my publicist? Just temporarily?'

'No, not *that* nice.'

She sighs. 'Ginny, I need the help and you need the money.'

'There are loads of PR companies out there. I'll help you shortlist some good ones.'

'But I want you.'

'Why? Because the *This Morning* appearance went so well?'

'Because I think you're smart and because I trust you.'

'I can't. I haven't got time for one thing. I've got interviews to go to . . .'

She screws up her face.

'I do go to *some*,' I say defensively. 'Anyway, job-hunting takes up hours.'

'But being my publicist – temporarily – wouldn't take up that much of your time, would it? How many clients did you look after at your old place? I'm only one little person.'

Something tells me that although Cassie is physically small, she could actually take up a hell of a lot of mental energy. 'What happens if I get offered a job?'

'Then you can dump me.'

'Look, it's just too weird. You're my neighbour.'

'Just for a month or two.'

I take a big sip of my wine. 'Do you always get what you want?'

She grins. 'Usually.'

Chapter Fourteen

Cassie and I are at The Groucho for our first work meeting. I must say it feels a little odd to have had to take a cab to chat to someone who lives in the same building as you, but Cassie was adamant it was good to make a clear line between work and home. Yes, I thought, which is why I should not be your publicist.

To say I've got cold feet about the whole thing doesn't really cover it. I can't think for the life of me why I said yes to Cassie in Lemonia. Too much wine? Guilt about the *This Morning* interview going so badly? Greed because she was offering me such a generous hourly rate? Probably all those things. But mostly I think I was just flattered that Cassie seemed to want me and only me. Let's face it, that's not a familiar feeling at the moment. Mind you, she hasn't seen any of my ideas yet.

As if on cue, Cassie says, 'Right, show me what you've got.'

I reach for my notebook, suddenly feeling nervous. 'Look, I need to be honest here.'

Cassie grimaces. 'Oh dear.'

'What we're talking about here is what PR people would refer to as crisis management. Public opinion wasn't kind to you after *Celebrity* and now with the *This Morning* debacle—'

Cassie interrupts me. 'Ginny. People think I'm an absolute

cow. A bitchy, lazy, stuck-up drunk. They think I'm slightly more of a diva than Beyoncé without any of the right to be.'

'Err . . .' Before I can even form a sentence, she interjects again.

'I know I badly need your help, Ginny. That's why I fought so hard to get you to say yes. Now, tell me how we're going to turn me into a national treasure.' She makes a face. 'Actually, scrub that, national treasure means O-L-D. How are we going to make me even more popular than Holly Willoughby?'

A waiter comes over with our tea. I'm pretty sure I see a flicker of amusement behind his eyes. 'I could try to get you a newspaper interview with one of my more simpatico journos. The trouble is, even nice journalists are still journalists, and if you said one thing that could be twisted . . .'

Cassie nods. 'I get it. And let's face it, I'm not exactly the most diplomatic person.'

I smile. 'If I could get us copy approval, I'd do it. But nobody will give us that. And even if they did, the subs could still give us the wrong sort of headline.'

'Hmm,' Cassie says, taking a sip of her tea. 'Always nice to be in the headlines though.'

'It's not always nice. You of all people should know that.'
She shrugs.

'It would be good to get some column inches about you doing worthwhile things. Do you work for any charities?'

'I give money to Cancer Research. Is that any good?'

I shake my head. 'We need you actually doing something. Working in a soup kitchen or something.'

'Ewww.'

I ignore her and make a note to organize some good deeds. 'A few pap pics that show you in a flattering light could work wonders. You know what they say about a picture painting a thousand words. I'm also keen to get you on telly again.'

'*Love Island*?' She sees my face. 'I'm joking, Ginny! *Strictly*?'

I'll never get her on *Strictly*. 'Maybe. But that's not until the autumn. I was thinking of *Celebrity Come Dine With Me*.'

Cassie almost spits out her Earl Grey. 'Err, you do remember I struggle to make a cup of instant coffee?'

How is the person sitting opposite me a functional adult? 'We can practise the dishes together. Plus, *Come Dine* isn't really about the food. It's about being a good laugh and getting on well with the other contestants.'

'Well, I can do one of those.'

'Cassie!'

She smiles. 'Okay, okay. I can play nicely in the sandpit. I only have to have a few dinners with the cretins after all. It's not like being stuck in the jungle with them.'

'Good. That's settled then. I'll look into it and let you know.'

'Excellent,' she says, signalling to the waiter for the bill. 'See, I told you working together would be fun.'

It's raining heavily outside and we're just putting up umbrellas when Cassie is tapped on the shoulder by a bloated-looking man with a bright red face. I don't know who he is but Cassie is visibly taken aback. 'Shane.'

'Cass! How are you babe?' He has the soft hint of an Irish accent. 'I was so upset to hear about all your problems recently. Did you get my note?'

'I did, thanks. It was kind of you.'

They chat for a few minutes in the doorway, and then Shane suggests a coffee.

The windows in Patisserie Valerie are all steamed up. There's a bit of a fuss because Cassie doesn't like the table we're shown to and insists on waiting while they clear the one in the window.

'You look fantastic, Cass!' Shane says when we sit down. 'You haven't changed a bit. Same as me really.' He pauses and then breaks into a guffaw, and Cassie and I laugh too.

'Are you in the business?' Shane asks me.

'Ginny is my PR,' Cassie says.

'I'm helping Cassie out a little,' I say. 'But really I'm between jobs.'

'Join the club,' he says, laughing.

'Aren't you at QVC?' Cassie says.

'Not anymore. I was the king of Diamonique, the prince of microfibre cloths. I sold more exercise bikes than any other presenter – which is a bit of a joke to look at me! Then I got canned. New producer.'

Shane orders a croque madame, french fries and a cappuccino, I opt for a smoked-salmon sandwich and Cassie asks for a black coffee.

'I watched you on *Celebrity*,' Shane says. 'Reckon they did a bit of hatchet job with the editing.'

'No,' Cassie says. 'I really was that much of an arsehole.'

Shane and I laugh.

'I thought you were bloody brave doing all those challenges,' he says. 'I was really proud of you.'

'Nice to know I had one fan. Anyway, what brings you to Soho today?'

'I was at a casting at The Green Room. Ad for an insurance company. I definitely haven't got it. They didn't say anything, but sometimes you just know, don't you? Some you win, some you lose.'

Cassie fiddles with a sachet of sugar. 'More losses than wins in my case. I am the very epitome of persona non grata.'

'Don't say that, Cass!'

'It's true. But Ginny will sort me out, won't you?' She winks at me, and my stomach knots. What on earth have I got myself into?

Shane and Cassie catch up on people they have in common. He tells her that Tommy Kent had just written his first novel, a story of a washed-up gameshow host who shags anything that moves. 'Can't think where he gets his material!' Johnny and Timmy, the brothers from Boyz, now run a pub in Kent, which has weekly karaoke nights they sometimes sing at. There had been some talk of the Boyz getting back together, but Derek, the other band member, lives in Singapore now. Angie Butler has confirmed what everyone has suspected for many years and has finally come out as gay. She's in love with her manager.

'Sorry, Ginny,' Shane says. 'This must be so boring for you!'

The waitress comes over with the food, and it occurs to me that I've never seen Cassie properly eat.

A toddler at the next table is screaming as chocolate ice cream and snot are wiped off his face.

'People shouldn't take children to restaurants unless they can behave!' Cassie whispers.

Shane laughs. 'I'd forgotten how much you love kids! Missed your vocation as a nursery school teacher, you did! Bethany's eighteen now. I love her to bits of course, but she's a right little madam.' He pats his head. 'I got her to thank for the grey hair! She's just got a job singing on a cruise ship and her mother and I couldn't help but feel a bit relieved to see the back of her for two months!'

'Are you still with Rochelle?' Cassie asked.

Shane shakes his head. 'Nah. It was an amicable split though.' He pops a chip in his mouth. 'How's your dad?'

'Still alive, but not great really. He's got Alzheimer's.'

'Oh Cass, I'm sorry to hear that. I always liked your dad.'

'I know you did. He liked you too. He still harps on about I should have stayed with you. Mind you, like I said, his mind's not all there!'

Shane laughs. 'Do you see a lot of him?'

'Not as much as I should. I make sure I get to the care home at least once a week.'

Another unexpected side to Cassie.

'Must be tough,' Shane says.

She shrugs. 'S'okay. It's not like those awful places you see on the news, they take brilliant care of him. I'm not keen on the smell of the place – I don't think Jo Malone are ever going to start making a pee and cabbage scented candle. But, on the plus side, it's one of the few places I feel young. Also, Dad's usually stuck in about 1987 which means he still thinks I'm a big movie star.'

A little later, we pay the bill.

'Nice to meet you, Ginny.' He turns to Cassie. 'And lovely to see you again. Give me your mobile number, and I'll give you a shout if I hear of any work going. I don't think we're going to be chasing the same roles!'

An old couple are at the counter arguing over whether he should have the chocolate cake.

'Don't come crying to me when you've got a belly ache later.'

The man raises a liver-spotted hand and bats the air with a hefty sigh. 'A little bit of what you fancy.'

'Fine,' the woman says, in a tone that makes it clear it's anything but fine. She adjusts her rain bonnet and stares straight ahead.

'Oh! Suck the joy out of everything, why don't you?'

Shane looks at Cassie and winks. 'Could have been us.'

'There's still a chemistry there!'

Cassie bursts out laughing. 'Oh yeah. It was all I could do not to jump on him right then and there! I don't think the phrase "let yourself go" really covers it! You should have seen him back in the day, Ginny. He was utterly beautiful. Now, well, let's just say I could have quite easily walked past him in the street and not recognized him.'

Dean Street is crowded, and all around us people are scuttling along in a hurry to be somewhere.

'I thought he was lovely.'

'He is lovely, but not in that way. Just because you've got an ex on your mind!'

'I have not got Jack on my mind.'

'Hmmm. Just don't go back for more of the same. Men like that rarely change.'

'You've never even met him properly.'

'No. But I've met a million like him.'

'So, Shane called me this morning, all casual. "Hi, Babe. Just wondered if you fancied grabbing a bite tonight." As if it's the most normal thing in the world for the two of us to share a mezze. Like the last thirty years and the decree absolute didn't happen.'

'Hmm.' I balance the phone between my ear and my shoulder and pull on my navy dress. 'Do you think I ought to wear the grey dress or the navy one for my interview?'

'I forgot it was today. Grey. Definitely.'

'What's wrong with the navy?' I say.

Cassie tssks.

I pull a pair of tights out of the drawer. 'Are you going to go?'

'I don't know. It was nice to see him the other day and catch up. But it seems a bit odd really. I wouldn't want to give him the wrong idea.'

I am trying on shoes now. The red ones look too take-me-to-bed but the black too boring. 'Is it the wrong idea?'

'Of course it is! I know you're an incurable romantic, Ginny, but there's not going to be any big reconciliation between me and Shane. C'mon, you've seen him.'

'Beauty is in the eye of the beholder.'

'Hmmm. Well, I'm not beholding.'

I feel a hard knot of tension in my belly. I really need this interview to go well.

The receptionist has a shiny black bob and the kind of alabaster skin that always makes me decide never to go out in the sun or use fake tan again. Which usually lasts until people start asking me if I'm okay because I look a little peaky. She is managing to look Nicole Kidman pale, rather than peaky pale. And I bet she doesn't have a hole in her tights she has had to repair with Sellotape.

'Richard will see you now,' she says, her vowels as crisp as her immaculate white shirt.

At first, I think Richard Moore is pacing around his office talking to himself, but then I notice the headset. 'I'd like to hammer this out with them,' he says, motioning for me to take a seat on the red sofa. 'We need to think outside the box. Yup. Yup. Okay, mate. Catch you later.' He takes the headset off and shakes my hand.

'Thought you were talking to yourself at first!'

He looks at me quizzically.

'You know, because of the headset.' There isn't even a flicker of a smile. Great. Perhaps I can run masterclasses in how not to behave in interviews?

'So,' he says, 'tell me why you want to work at Hill Knight?'

I've done quite a bit of research on the place so launch into my carefully prepared speech about how I can add value – a real Annabel expression that one – on specific accounts. Somewhat to my surprise, I reckon I'm doing quite well and there are lots of 'yups' from Richard (maybe even enough to make him forget my ill-received gag). I think of the pitiful amount of savings I've got left and up the ante a bit.

A girl with pink hair pokes her head round the door. 'Sorry to interrupt—'

'No worries. I was going to touch base with you in a bit anyway. Hit me with your ideas.'

'Stacey Solomon?'

He shakes his head.

'Coleen Nolan?'

He wrinkles his nose.

'Cassie Frost?'

'What, the crazy bitch who was in the jungle and everyone wants to take out? The one who was pissed as a fart on *This Morning* at 11 a.m.? Definitely not.' I sit quietly, clasping my hands tightly together in my lap.

'We're looking for celebs for a media event next week,' Richard explains to me, when the girl has left.

I can feel the blood rushing around my head. Let it go, I tell myself. The job at Julia's brother's agency may or may not ever happen and there are precisely zero other interviews lined up. One headhunter told me to enjoy some time off and get in touch again in three or four months' time, like paying the rent just wasn't an issue. 'Umm,' I say, without knowing exactly what's going to come out next.

Richard runs his tongue over his very white teeth.

'Cassie Frost is a friend of mine.' Is she? Yes, I suppose she is.

'Great. Now tell me what piece of work you're most proud of and why?'

'It's just I don't think it's very nice to talk about someone like that. Make a joke about them receiving death threats.'

Richard bares his teeth in a glacial smile. 'I don't think I made a joke.'

'Well, maybe joke is the wrong word. But it wasn't very nice – the way you talked about her.'

Richard gives a mirthless little laugh. 'Right. Sorry.'

I start to tell him about the work I did on MagiBra, but somehow I don't think I've got the job.

Chapter Fifteen

'My God,' I say watching Cassie attempt to chop an onion. 'You're supposed to dice it, not massacre it.'

'No need to be rude,' she says. 'You may remember I wanted to do smoked salmon as a starter.'

'And have people say you haven't made any effort?'

We are an hour into our practice meal for *Celebrity Come Dine With Me* and I am amazed at how even the simplest of cooking tasks seems to baffle Cassie. No wonder the woman is thin.

'Right,' Cassie says. 'What do I do with the onion now it's chopped?'

'You need to sweat it.' She looks confused, so I elaborate. 'Put it in a pan with a little olive oil and leave it on a low heat for five minutes or so.'

After days and days of debate and going through (my) recipe books, we settled on a menu of pea and mint soup, butterflied leg of lamb with roasted baby veg and a passion fruit pavlova for dessert.

'Cassie, that onion is catching! Give it a stir and turn the heat down.'

She pokes disinterestedly at the onion.

'By the way,' I say, 'I'm going to do some waitressing.'

'Oh, I don't think I need a waitress, darling. After all, we want people to think I'm down to earth.'

I laugh. 'Noooo, I mean I'm going to have to get a waitressing job to tide me over financially until I get another job in PR.'

'But you're my publicist now.'

I roll my eyes. 'Yes, but the work I do for you takes up about a day a week and that's not enough for me to live on.' I feel a bit awkward saying this. Cassie insisted on paying me a very generous hourly rate and I'd hate her to think I'm trying to get more money out of her.

'You could do more days a week for me? Two or even three? Let's face it, my reputation needs all the help it can get.'

I shake my head. 'You absolutely don't need more than a day a week of my time. And I'm fine about the waitressing.' The last part of that is sort of true. Going back to waitressing does kind of feel a bit like, well, going back. 'I've already been down to Pizza Napoli.'

'Will you still be around for the *Come Dine* shoot?'

I smile. 'I'll arrange my shifts around it, you self-obsessed monster! Now let's start getting our veggies sorted.'

'When are we going to talk about what I'm going to wear?'

'Later. When we've got all the food prepped.'

The pudding has been a particular bone of contention with Cassie. 'They won't eat pudding, darling. They're celebrities.'

'You have to make pudding,' I said firmly. 'And you have to eat it.' Cassie looked horrified. 'But I never eat pudding, darling!'

'You ate a kangaroo's anus,' I reminded her.

She pushes the onion around a bit. 'This is all so time-consuming!'

'We've only just started. Right, now, while the onion is doing its thing, you need to get on with the potatoes and mint. But check on your meringue first. It should be ready to come out of the oven.'

Miraculously, the meringue looks perfect. Though goodness

knows how it will turn out when Cassie has to separate the eggs herself while being filmed. She made me do it this morning so she 'could learn'. With all four eggs.

'You just don't want to touch the raw egg, do you?' She made a face but I could tell I was right. 'What on earth do you eat when you're on your own?'

She shrugged. 'Smoked salmon, salad, houmous . . .'

'Do you have napkins?' I ask her.

She looks at me like I'm mad. 'No.'

I add napkins to the list of things we need to get. I'll buy some for myself at the same time. I'm too old to be giving people sheets of kitchen roll when they come over to supper.

'Now,' I say, looking up from my notebook, 'what's the mantra we need to remember with all the other contestants?'

'Be nice,' Cassie says in a bored, sing-songy kind of voice.

'That's right. And that means BE NICE WHATEVER. Even if someone says your food is disgusting.'

Cassie shrugs. 'I couldn't care less what they say about the food.'

'You're right – bad example. Even if someone says you look older than they thought you would.' Cassie blanches. 'Even if they say Hayley Wiseman deserves a BAFTA. Even if—'

Cassie holds up her hands. 'I get it. Be nice. Whatever. Right, what's next with this soup?'

'You need to add the mint, sugar, lemon juice and cream.'

Cassie sighs. 'I still don't know why we couldn't get caterers to knock something up and then have me just fart about with a bit of garnishing at the end.'

'Yes, because that's exactly what you need right now: to get involved in a cheating scandal.'

Chapter Sixteen

Is a video of some cute kittens too much to ask, Facebook? Or baby pandas? Or puppies? I'm not fussy. But instead you serve me this:

Nicki G *Welcome to the world, little Brooklyn! #newbaby #blessed*

And this:

Sarah Jane *Looking back at one month of marriage like . . .♥ I've never loved so much, felt so much joy, or been more aware of the world's beauty. #love #blessed #marriedlife #joy*

You are supposed to be cheering me up, Facebook! Making up for the fact I didn't get the job at Pizza Napoli. Instead, you are reminding me that work is not the only area where I'm lagging behind. That everyone else's lives are *#BloodyPerfect*.

When he phoned, the manager at Pizza Napoli said he was very sorry that I hadn't got the position. *Position*, I felt like screaming. I hadn't even really thought of yesterday as an interview as such. Because, while I may not be able to get a job in PR, I thought I could at least land a part-time job serving up American Hots. I had a job doing that when I was sixteen and at sixteen I knew precisely nothing!

I take a deep breath and force myself to think positive. It's no good wallowing, and anyway, I haven't checked my emails in nearly an hour. Perhaps there will be one from a headhunter telling me they've found the perfect job for me. They'll have already sent over my CV and the person who is hiring will have phoned them instructing them to get me in for an interview as soon as possible.

I open my email and scan the senders and subject lines: *Don't miss our 50% off sale . . . An offer just for you, Ginny . . . Your new wardrobe must-haves.* Don't they realize I am already past my overdraft limit?

And then an email from Julia's brother! He's actually going to offer me a job. He wasn't just fobbing me off. Take that, Pizza Napoli! I didn't need your POSITION anyway. My heart beats fast as I open the email, but starts to sink as soon as I start reading. Julia told him I haven't found a new job yet. He wanted to get in touch to say he was very sorry but his agency didn't win either of the pitches he mentioned to me. But he wanted me to know that things change all the time (really?), that I'm still 'top of the list', but he's sure I'll be snapped up very soon anyway.

I guess it was nice of him to write, although I'm sure Julia nagged him into it. *Just send her a quick email, can you? She's so down at the moment.*

I sit there not knowing what to do next. I should phone some headhunters. Sound chirrupy and upbeat, make small talk and remind them of my existence.

I should check LinkedIn to see if there are any new opportunities other than the ones to 'say congrats' to yet another person. *James Anderson starts his new job as VP Operations at Blink Media! Katy Randall is celebrating two years at Found! Jo Jackson has started a new position as Senior Account Director at Marcom!*

I should call my bank who are looking forward to discussing my 'financial situation' at my 'earliest possible convenience'.

I should start looking for another waitressing job. Just because Pizza Napoli rejected me (still ouch) doesn't mean other restaurants will. I know the Mexican place on the high street are looking for people.

Yup, there are lots of things I SHOULD DO, but instead I find myself back on Facebook. Because they still owe me a video of some cute kittens.

Chapter Seventeen

I throw myself face down on my bed. I don't think I can be bothered to take my make-up off tonight. Or even take my clothes off. Despite the fact they stink of sweat and fried food. I'd forgotten how exhausting waitressing is. One minute I was being introduced to the rest of the staff, trying to not to notice that they barely looked older than my nephews, the next I was donning my sombrero (yes, really) and starting my shift.

After that, everything is one big blur.

'Welcome to Carumba. My name is Ginny and I'm your server for tonight. Can I get you started with any drinks?'

'One Mexican Platter, one Popcorn Peri-Peri Chicken and one side of Guacamole.'

'Ginny, table four are still waiting to order.'

'Welcome to Carumba. My name is Ginny and I'm your server for tonight. Can I get you started with any drinks?'

'Ginny, table seven!'

'I'm not sure if the Pollo A La Diabla contains gluten. Let me check with the kitchen.'

'Welcome to Carumba. My name is Ginny and I'm your server for tonight. Can I get you started with any drinks?'

'I'm so sorry about that, madam. I'll get you another one.'

'Let me get a cloth to wipe that up.'

'One Chilli Con Carne and one Sizzling Prawns?'

'GINNY. THE PEOPLE ON TABLE FOUR NEED THEIR MAINS.'

'Welcome to Carumba. My name is Ginny and I'm your server for tonight. Can I get you started with any drinks?'

'Happy Birthday to you, Happy Birthday to you, Happy Birthday dear . . . Happy Birthday to you.'

'Another bottle of that?'

'Just past the bar and on your left.'

People in offices don't know how easy they have it. They get to sit down. Drink cups of tea. Have conversations.

I message Nancy. *I am a rubbish waitress! And I think I might die of exhaustion.*

Then I feel a surge of guilt. I was so grateful to get the job at Carumba. I am so grateful.

Nancy messages back. *Don't die yet please. And send pic of you in sombrero.*

I feel a bit sorry for verging-on-human headhunter. It can't be nice phoning people to tell them they haven't got the job. Again.

The annoying thing is I actually thought I was in with a chance with this one. What's that famous quote about hope being the real cause of despair?

I've got the measure of interviews now. It's just a different person asking me exactly the same questions. *Would you say you're good with detail? What are your key strengths? Would you describe yourself as ambitious?*

I thought the Northern blokey-bloke who interviewed me this time had quite liked me (y'know, in so much as he could like anyone who knows nothing about football). He said my CV looked good, I was in there for nearly an hour, and when he asked me what attracted me to the role, I didn't burst out laughing and say, 'Err, it's a job.'

So it went pretty well really. But obviously not well enough.

★　　★　　★

My friends keep setting me up. They don't describe it as such, they just invite me over and there happens to be a spare man there. Usually this spare man comes with a set of instructions. 'The two of you will have so much in common' (yeah, because I'm passionate about medieval battle re-enactments). 'If I was single . . .' (you'd give him the swerve). Most of these Daves or Robs or Tonys are okay, but all of them make me feel that if Jack isn't the only fish in the sea, then he's certainly the only one I want to settle down and make little haddocky babies with. My friend Julia gets a little impatient with me. 'Give people a chance!' What she really means is: tick bloody tock, Ginny! Those eggs won't stay good forever!

Chapter Eighteen

I'm at Cassie's talking to her about what she should wear on *Celebrity Come Dine With Me* when the doorbell rings.

'It's my sister,' Cassie says staring at the entryphone and looking confused. She opens the door to her flat and there in the hallway is the washed-out looking woman I met in The Tea Room, accompanied by two super-cute-looking little boys of about four and six. The boys are brandishing large bright yellow guns.

'Can I . . . c . . .' Meg says, her voice breaking.

Cassie swiftly ushers the kids into the living room, telling them to watch whatever they want on telly while simultaneously getting Meg into the kitchen and sitting her down. Meg slumps in the chair and starts making a sound that isn't quite human; the desperate guttural sound of an animal that's mortally wounded but not yet dead.

'I should go,' I say.

Meg lifts her head. 'No, stay. I need to leave the kids with Cassie overnight and she's bound to want some help.' Cassie's face is a mask of shock as she tries to process the words 'children' and 'overnight'. 'David's left me. Just came home from work and said he didn't love me anymore. And then he packed a bag and went. And I was so shocked, I didn't even get a chance to ask him all the questions I want the answers to. So now I need to go after him. Talk to him. And I thought about leaving the kids with friends but I don't want anyone to know what's happened because this is all just a mistake . . .' She breaks off and starts sobbing again.

Cassie puts her hand on Meg's shoulder. 'Okay. Take a breath. You're not going to go after David tonight.'

Meg shakes her hand away. 'WHY NOT? HE'S MY HUSBAND! JUST BECAUSE YOU DON'T WANT TO LOOK AFTER THE KIDS!'

'You're in no fit state to go anywhere tonight. You can talk to David in the morning.'

'It's just so out of the blue!' Meg wails. 'We've been together for twelve years! Twelve happy years. We've had our bad patches. Who doesn't? But I never expected this.' She breaks into a fresh wave of sobs. 'We had a very healthy sex life!'

A brief look of 'really – with Pumpkin?' crosses Cassie's face.

'He says he doesn't know what he wants. That he needs space.' She blows her nose loudly. 'What should I tell the kids?'

'Nothing yet,' Cassie says.

A light comes back on in Meg's eyes. 'You think he'll come back?'

'N—'

I shoot Cassie a look. Sometimes false hope is better than no hope at all.

'What do I know about relationships?' Cassie says. 'My three marriages put together didn't last as long as yours has.'

One of the boys bursts into the kitchen in a hail of Nerf gun fire.

'Die, sucker!' shouts his assailant.

'Boys!' Meg says weakly.

A rubber bullet hits Cassie on the forehead. The boys erupt into high-pitched laughter.

'Thomas, Matthew. Go and play nicely,' Meg instructs.

She starts crying again the minute the boys leave the room. 'I just don't know what I did wrong!'

'Sssh.' I pat her shoulder and do my best to soothe her. 'This isn't about you.'

'That's what he said!'

'You surprise me,' Cassie mutters.

'At least he's not seeing anyone else,' Meg says.

I see the look on Cassie's face and will her not to say anything.

Meg picks up a stray orange rubber bullet from the floor. 'I just didn't see this coming.'

'No,' I say, 'none of us ever do.'

I am woken by the sound of the phone. 'I've become her bloody person,' Cassie says. 'My sister hates me, and yet I've become her person.'

'What?'

'Were you asleep?' she asks.

'No. Yes. What are you, my mother?'

'It's nearly midday. Aren't you supposed to be resuscitating my ailing career?'

'I only work for you eight hours a week. An arrangement you very much talked me into. Which could be terminated at any time.'

If Cassie notices the edge to my tone, she's completely unabashed. 'Well, what about your job-hunting then?'

'Not that it's any of your bloody business but I was working at the restaurant until 1 a.m. last night and I'm shattered. Anyway, I can't job hunt twenty-four hours a day.'

'If you ask me, you don't love PR.'

'No one did ask you,' I huff. 'Now, why did you call?'

'Meg. She's round here every second of the day weeping and gnashing her teeth. Asking me if it's a good sign that he's checked out of the Ramada.'

I yawn. 'Probably because you're such a naturally sympathetic person!'

'This is no time for jokes! I'm not sure I can cope with it anymore. I'm running out of things to say.'

'It's not about what you say – it's just about being there.'

'Well I don't want to be "there"! I'm supposed to be at yoga right now but instead I'm at her house because I had yet another hysterical bloody phone call from her telling me she can't cope. Surely she's got friends?'

'Maybe. But for whatever reason she's reaching out to you.'

There is a pause, and I can visualize Cassie tapping her tiny foot the way she does when she's agitated. 'Any chance you could come over here and give me a hand?'

'Why on earth would I do that?'

'Because you're a nice person?'

I laugh. 'You're going to have to do better than that.'

'Because if you do I'll pinkie promise that I'll be an absolute angel on *Come Dine With Me*. Not so much as a bitchy look, let alone remark.'

Meg's kitchen is as different from Cassie's as the two women are from each other. Where I'm willing to bet Cassie's gleaming stainless-steel oven is a virgin, Meg's dark green Aga looks like it's been up close and personal with many a roast and casserole. In Meg's kitchen, there are children's drawings plastered across every wall; in Cassie's, a wall of mirrors.

We're at Meg's making lunch for the boys while she takes a sob-induced nap.

'I wish she'd told us what to give them,' Cassie says, looking in the fridge. 'I don't know what children eat.'

'Food. They're human, y'know.'

She pulls out a packet of mince and holds it up.

'Perfect,' I say. 'We'll make spaghetti bolognese. Everybody likes that.'

'I don't.'

'Everybody except you.'

I get a pan out of the cupboard and start looking for an onion. Matthew comes into the room. 'When we were at your house the other day, we saw pictures of you without any clothes on!' he says, taking an apple out of the fruit bowl and disappearing.

'I posed for *Playboy* years ago,' Cassie says, answering my look.

'Great. Nothing like seeing your auntie's nunny at a young age. That'll give him something to talk about in therapy.'

'They're up on the wall in the bedroom. I can hardly be blamed for the kids going in there.'

I hand her an onion. 'Chop this, would you, please? I've witnessed your incredible knife skills before.' I start opening cupboards on the hunt for tinned tomatoes.

'I'm sure he's seeing someone else.' Cassie states, too loudly.

'Sssh!'

'I can't understand how she doesn't see it.'

'Because she doesn't want to. My God, that onion looks even worse than the one you chopped for the soup! I cannot believe that I've actively chosen to put you on *Come Dine With Me*! I must be mad.'

Cassie laughs. 'I'll pour us a drink.'

'Well, don't wear yourself out too much.' I start browning the sad-looking mess that was once an onion. 'You know what you said earlier about me not loving PR? If you don't think I'm doing a good job for you, we can always part ways.'

She laughs. 'I didn't say you weren't good at PR, I said you don't love it. Which is true, right?'

'No. Yes. Look, who does LOVE their job?'

'I loved mine.'

I want to say, *What, even when you were in the jungle?* But I bite my tongue. I add the mince to the pan and turn up the gas. 'I don't believe many people are leaping to get out of bed on a Monday morning. I bet even people with dream jobs have nightmare days. JK probably doesn't always want to put fingers to keyboard—'

'Interesting that you picked a novelist.'

I roll my eyes. 'Look, it's okay for you. We don't all have big, fat divorce settlements from footballers to live off.'

'Fair comment. Although I used to have a lot more money. You know, before I put so much of it up my nose. I lived in this incredible penthouse overlooking Hampstead Heath.'

'Your flat is lovely,' I say.

She nods. 'But it's a flat for norms.'

'Norms? You mean normal people?'

'Yes,' she says, flicking her hair over her shoulder.

'You're a monster, you know that?'

She shrugs. 'Anyway, back to the point I was making. I wasn't saying you shouldn't keep looking for another job in PR. Just that it doesn't hurt to be thinking about what you really dream of too. You could try that creative writing course I told you about, for example.'

'Thanks. Nothing like a few life tips from you.' I regret the words as soon as they're out of my mouth, and for a moment Cassie looks hurt, but then she laughs. 'You're sounding more and more like me every day.'

Chapter Nineteen

The local adult education centre is a very ugly building. I don't know how the people who run Introduction to Creative Writing can expect us to feel inspired in there. I take a deep breath. These are my reasons I don't want to go in:

1. The classroom will smell of BO and cheap air freshener.
2. The course will be rubbish.
3. The course will be good, but I will be rubbish.

After forcing myself to enter the building, I walk down the narrow grey corridor with all the enthusiasm of someone on their way to the electric chair. If I never go into that room I can always tell myself I could have written a great book if only I'd tried. I can tell myself I could have given Lorrie Moore and Anne Tyler a run for their money if only I'd got around to it.

The teacher is wearing huge gold hoop earrings that contain miniature parrots sitting on perches. Her earlobes are stretched so that they are impossibly long and thin. She is wearing a big, flowing crimson dress from under which peek jewelled sandals that her feet are spilling out of. She introduces herself as Judy and hands me a manila folder to read through 'before we get going'. I settle on one of the red plastic chairs, which are arranged in a circle, and skim the course notes. There is a fat man next to me who is dressed in head-to-toe black and sweating profusely.

'Boiling in here, isn't it? Perhaps we are being hot-housed?' I say.

He rewards me with the barest flicker of a smile and wipes his brow with a Starbucks napkin.

A woman on the other side of the circle is tapping away furiously on her Blackberry. *Time is money!* Her glossy chestnut hair is cut into a bob so immaculate, it could be fashioned out of plastic. She looks like Annabel's soul-sister. Or should that be souless-sister?

'Right,' says Judy, rubbing her hands together. She has rings on every finger including her thumbs. 'Let's get going, shall we?' And then she's off, talking about things we will cover over the coming months. She swoops through eight-point arcs and viewpoints and dialogue and all manner of scary stuff. I absolutely can't do this!

But it gets worse. We all have to say a little something about ourselves!

Man in black starts off, which means I will be last to speak. I don't know if this is good (gives me time to think of what the hell to say) or bad (by then I will be in a frenzy of nerves). Man in black's voice is booming, authoritative. He has lots of published work! I feel sick! It's just like when I signed up for beginners salsa and ended up in intermediate by mistake. (That didn't end well. More 'sorrys' than in a month of tube journeys.)

A guy that looks like a stereotypical surfer (mahogany tan, raw pink nose, beaded necklace with a shark tooth pendant) is talking now. He has no published work, thank goodness. He speaks in a monotone telling us about the travel diaries he plans to write. 'Most travel diaries just focus on the highlights and lowlights of the trip,' he says fiddling with his multiple friendship bracelets. 'But mine will be

124

different. I will write about every single mooooooment. I won't edit at all.'

I'm no expert, but surely this can't be good? I know 'Desiderata' instructed that even the dull and ignorant have their story, but surely no one wants to pay £7.99 for it?

A woman called Katia explains that she wants to write because she's just split up from her husband. Writing is her boob job basically.

The plump, mumsy lady who looks like she has an extensive collection of Tupperware tells us quietly she's always wanted to write but 'has left it rather late in life!' She giggles nervously. Her spectacles magnify her watery, pink-rimmed eyes so they look cartoon-huge.

'Thank you, Anne. Now, Ginny?' The parrot perches swing expectantly.

My palms are sweating and I know my voice is going to come out high-pitched and strangulated. I feel like I did when I had to speak in assembly aged eleven. And we all know how that went.

I blurt something out, and whilst it's not exactly a masterclass in oratory, for me, it's an achievement. Judy smiles. I expect she's hoping I'm more articulate on paper.

We do various exercises including free writing, which basically means writing whatever comes into your head, and writing for fifteen minutes about an object we can see in the room. Mercifully we don't have to read either of them out.

Over a tea break – or should I say Assam break – Judy counsels that writers should always be as specific as possible. Published Guy talks about how this course compares with other writing courses he has been on. 'Of course, she's hardly Bob McKee,' he says, talking about Judy. I wince as she's only a few feet away, but she either hasn't heard or doesn't care because she remains as perky as her parrots.

Tupperware Lady is confirming my prejudices by asking

Judy if she made the flapjacks herself, and Annabel's souless-sister is still tapping away on her Blackberry.

Mr Travelogue embarks on a long story. All around, smiles sag and eyelids droop. If this guy sent you an FYI email, there is no doubt the 'I' would be used loosely.

I am relieved when it's time to get back to work, although that joy is soon punctured by hearing that we are now going to write a short piece that we will read out to the group at the end.

Somehow, I get through it and, although what I write won't make any Booker lists and definitely isn't the best (Katia's is amazing, damn her!), it isn't the worst either (thank you, Mr Travelogue!). I'm starting to feel quite pleased I came.

And then Judy sums up. 'One of the best quotes I ever heard about writing was this: If there's anything I can say about writing to put you off – anything at all – then don't do it.'

Chapter Twenty

'I am *never* getting another job,' I say to Nancy. 'Well, not one I don't have to wear a sombrero for.'

These days, we often FaceTime when I get home from Carumba. Nancy is also just getting home from her (proper) job.

'You will,' she assures me.

'But, Nance. It's been nearly three months since I threw that orchid at Annabel!'

'These things take time. Oh, hold on a minute, that's my take-out.'

I am left staring at Nancy's empty sofa while she goes to the door.

'You said take-out!' I say when she comes back.

'I did not.'

'You did too.'

'Oh my God, it's happening – I am Americanizing.'

I nod. 'Show me your nails.'

She holds up her hands.

'No manicure. Good – there's still hope.'

She laughs. 'Mind if I eat?'

'As long as it's not Mexican, you're fine. I swear to God if I see another fajita . . .'

She holds up a little fish-shaped bottle of soy sauce and some chopsticks. 'Sushi.'

'Nice. So where were we?'

'I was telling you these things take time.'

I groan. 'Also—'

'You're going to die old and alone?'

'Yes. You know Jenny set me up with that bloke called Phil.'

'Yeah,' Nancy says, biting into a sushi roll.

'Well, he was nice – not my type, but nice – so I told myself that "not my type" was a good thing.'

'Riiight. Not sure I entirely agree with that. Although if by your type, you mean Jack . . .'

I absolutely can't defend Jack after what happened but I still bristle at other people slagging him off. He's kind of like family in the sense only I can be mean about him. Also, although I wouldn't dare admit this to Nancy, I still don't think I'm over him. The other day on the tube platform, I was convinced I saw him laughing and joking with another woman and I felt physically sick. Which would have made me feel pretty stupid if it had been Jack, but instead it made me feel patently ridiculous because, when I looked again, I realized it wasn't Jack. In fact, the guy didn't look much like him at all. My mind had just somehow conjured him up. 'Anyway, I told myself that I would give Phil a chance to grow on me. That when he called, I'd say yes to another date. And then he didn't call.'

'Bastard.' Nancy spears a piece of tuna.

'What about you? Have you been on any more dates?'

She shakes her head. 'It's true what they say after all – there really are no single, straight men in New York. Even if you would happily settle for one who's more lukewarm than hot.'

'Hmmm. I guess you'll have to come home then.'

She laughs, and her phone pings. 'Oh no, message from my boss saying he needs to talk to me asap. It's half past eight in the evening, for goodness' sake. I only left the office forty-five minutes ago.'

I tell her I hope it's not a big drama and that she's back to her sushi in no time. That we'll talk soon.

And then I hang up the phone feeling weird. Because it's not that I'm jealous exactly . . . First of all, this is Nancy we're talking about. And secondly, I don't want a boss calling me with urgent requests when I'm at home.

But I guess that is something that only happens to people who have a career.

I was struggling with this week's writing homework so I decided to take a walk on Primrose Hill to 'unblock' myself. 'Sometimes your subconscious has all the answers,' Judy says.

Hmmm, not sure about that. I am delighted to be away from that reproachful blank page though. And it's nice to get out of the flat, especially since Jarielle have the week off work and seem to be really putting the stay into staycationing.

It's a gorgeous spring day. Blue sky, sunshine, blossom . . . I'm half expecting to see gambolling lambs.

My life seems to have settled into a kind of routine: five shifts a week at Carumba, a smattering of work for Cassie, Mondays looking after my nephews, writing school on a Thursday. And in between all that, I go to the occasional interview, see family and friends and try to fend off any questions about either my career or my love life.

I take a deep breath. Sometimes you just have to take each day as it comes.

Cassie and I sit down together to watch *Celebrity Come Dine With Me*. 'I feel really nervous,' she says, pouring us two large G&Ts.

'Don't be daft,' I say, even though I feel exactly the same. Cassie was good as gold on the shoot. She didn't go bananas when the ex-*Love Island* girl asked her if she'd ever made a movie with Clark Gable, laughed gamely when the ageing rocker told her that her soup looked like snot and – perhaps most surprisingly – didn't make a single tactless remark about the comedian's size. So I don't really see how they could edit the programme to make her look anything less than delightful. And yet I won't be able to fully relax until I've seen the finished result on air.

The first dinner is at Nicki the girl from *Love Island*'s place.

'God, she was stupid.' Cassie says to me. 'And so much Botox! I mean, this coming from me, but she's twenty-three!'

I laugh as I watch Cassie tucking into stuffed mushrooms and pronouncing them delicious. 'Were they?'

Cassie makes a face.

Nicki is getting into a spat with Jane the comedian about *Love Island*. Jane says it's ridiculous to only feature young, thin, beautiful people.

'That's what people want to see though,' Nicki says. 'No offence.'

Jane takes offence (and why wouldn't she?) but somehow Cassie manages to step in and smooth things over so that suddenly everyone is back to talking about the best party they've ever been to.

'Look at you playing the peacemaker!'

Cassie smiles and flutters her eyelashes. 'Polish my halo.'

On screen, everyone is in the back of the taxis scoring Nicki's night. She gets a five and a six from the others and a seven from Cassie.

'See,' Cassie says to me. 'I was generous with the scoring, just like you told me to be.'

The next scene shows the beginning of Cassie's night hosting. She is seen shopping in the local greengrocer's while Dave Lamb describes her as an actress and TV personality.

'God, I look old,' Cassie says.

'You look great.'

On screen, Cassie is marinating the lamb and then whisking eggs for her pavlova.

'You also look verging on competent,' I say.

'And they say the camera never lies.'

Cassie's night goes smoothly and she gets good scores from everyone.

'Thanks for getting me this,' she says as she turns to me suddenly. 'I think it will help a bit, don't you? I mean, you don't go from Cruella de Vil to Cinderella overnight, but it's a start.'

'Absolutely,' I say and I really mean it.

We watch the rest of the show and even though I was there throughout the shoot, I can't help but be a little surprised by just how well behaved Cassie is. She flirts just the right amount with the ageing rocker, neatly sidesteps getting involved in the underlying tension between Nicki and Jane, and eats everything that's put in front of her. 'I think I had my normal calorific intake for a year.'

All this means the Cassie people see on screen is the witty, fun Cassie I see – but minus any bitchiness whatsoever. And she couldn't have come across as less of a diva. When Jane is pronounced the winner, Cassie looks genuinely delighted for her.

'Well done,' I say as the final credits roll. 'That really couldn't have gone any better.'

I wake up late the next morning and reach groggily for my phone.

There's a tweet from Cassie that's trending. I blink – Cassie doesn't even use the Twitter account I set up for her.

Delighted to see @janebetts win @celebritycomedinewithme. Now there's a girl who really cares about her food!

No! No, no, no!

I scroll down to see the reaction but I already know the sort of thing I'm going to see.

> @**ThisIsGemz** *So depressing to see a woman taking a cheap pop at another woman because of her size.*
> @**Gina_FabNewsUK** *In the week we learned that 1.6 million people in the UK are struggling with an eating disorder, we have @cassiefrost making this kind of idiotic remark.*
> @**Davina.H.84** *@janebetts is one of our most gifted comedians, but all @cassiefrost can talk about is how she's not a size 10!*

I need to get a press release out as quickly as possible but I am numb with shock.

What was Cassie thinking? Then again I'm the one who set up a Twitter account for her. I may as well have handed a toddler a loaded gun.

What was *I* thinking?

I don't feel good about eating a whole Easter egg in one go. Especially as it's one of the Easter eggs I bought for the twins. But sometimes needs bloody must.

Not only am I still feeling fed up about Cassie's defeat-from-the-jaws-of-victory tweet, but the interview at Sharp PR did not go well. I was in and out of there in twenty-six minutes.

I'm pretty sure the woman who was interviewing me took a dislike to me within about three seconds of meeting me. She had improbably glossy hair. Perhaps I can sue her for being 'hair-ist'?

I have stopped tasting the chocolate some time ago but still I keep shovelling it in.

I don't think I did anything wrong as such.

I didn't greet my interviewer with the words, 'I'm Ginny and I'm your server for tonight.'

I made a reasonable fist of explaining why I left my last job and did not say anything about my boss being a traitorous, boyfriend-stealing bitch.

When Ms Glossy-Locks asked me how good I thought I would be at disciplining my team, I didn't guffaw and say, 'Are you kidding? I just want everyone to like me!'

So I know I didn't do anything wrong, but I also just know they'll say I'm not right for the position and I won't have got the job. Again.

Chapter Twenty-One

I am getting slightly less rubbish at waitressing. Today, for example, my station is full and I'm just about managing to keep on top of things.

I take yet another bottle of Prosecco over to table seven, trying not to fall over their children Jasper and Elsie who are running feral around the restaurant. I know their names because every now and again one or the other parent will say, 'Stop it, Elsie' or 'Don't hit your sister, Jasper' half-heartedly while pouring themselves another glass of Prosecco. They have a baby with them too. He woke up as they were in the middle of their lunch and the parents had an extended stand-off about whose turn it was while the rest of the restaurant shot them STOP-THAT-GODDAMN-THING-MAKING-THAT-NOISE looks. Eventually the father gave in and bounced the baby around a bit on his lap while spilling refried beans on top of its head.

From the other side of the room, the man at table eleven gestures for my attention. He and his wife have been locked in an intense row since they arrived.

When I get to their table, they abruptly stop spitting insults at each other and are all tight smiles. She'd like the Sizzling Prawns but with the chilli sauce on the side if that's possible, please.

He'd like the Chicken Barbacoa if he may, please. His tone

is even more oleaginous. It's like they're trying to out-nice each other. Whoever wins the waitress wins the war!

'Jasper! *No!*'

My main courses for table six are out. I race across the room so I can get to them before Greta has to rescue me yet again. Greta has been working here for twelve years and is always talking about how in some countries, like France or Australia, being a waiter is a really respected profession. 'They never have an optional service charge,' she says.

I load myself up with all five plates and offer up a prayer to the God of waiting staff that Elsie and Jasper are enjoying a brief cessation in their activities and won't career into me.

'Who's having the Enchiladas?'

Everyone carries on talking.

'The Enchiladas?'

Nothing. Plates are getting heavy, guys. And also kind of burning my arm. 'The Enchiladas?' I say, a little louder.

Five heads swivel round and look at me as if it's very odd that I've suddenly appeared at their table with food.

'Err me,' the guy with the beard says eventually.

'Hottie alert, hottie alert!' Pete whispered to me when the man first came in. I make a mental note to tell Pete later that he may be good-looking but he is definitely not his intellectual equal.

Pete and I quite often have a beer and a bitching session after a shift. Did I see that big table who left him a pile of loose change as a tip? Bastards, I'll say, before telling him about the woman who demanded a full refund for her 'inedible meal' which she'd just eaten.

'Hi,' I say, greeting a young couple who have just sat down at table four. 'I'm Ginny and I'm your server today. Can I get you started with some drinks?'

They'll both have a Bloody Mary, please. She giggles and reaches across the table for his hand.

I really have to pee. I have needed one for nearly two hours now. We are supposed to have a fifteen-minute break mid-shift but no one ever takes it. You only stop to pee or smoke. During a bad shift, I've seriously wondered about taking up smoking. I ask Pete if he can keep an eye on my section while I dash to the loo.

It's a joy to sit down and, if it wasn't Pete covering for me, I might be tempted to string it out for a few minutes.

I spoke to a new headhunter earlier. He was called Gareth and he was very serious about everything. He did not find it as funny as me that he's set up an interview for me on 1 April.

'April Fool's Day,' I prompted.

Silence buzzed down the phone line.

I walk back out onto the restaurant floor. Only two more hours.

'ELSIE! WHAT DID MUMMY SAY ABOUT BITING?'

I take table eleven their mains and they stop hissing at each other just long enough to thank me effusively. The woman, who is immaculately dressed and makes me acutely conscious of my sweaty red face and sombrero, asks me if she may please have another glass of Pinot Grigio. She says it in a manner that suggests this will involve gargantuan effort on my part. Her husband looks on furiously.

'Excuse me,' says hottie as I walk past. 'I asked for some fries.'

'I'm so sorry.' I race towards the kitchen narrowly avoiding Jasper's fire truck.

Loved-up couple order next. They're going to have the sharing platter (of course they are), then salmon for her and steak fajitas for him. They are still holding hands. I wonder if they will uncouple briefly when it's time to eat?

Did Jack and I ever hold hands in a restaurant?

Pete is doing a rendition of 'Happy Birthday'. As always,

he throws himself into it completely, not only belting out the tune but treating everyone to an extended chorus of 'For She's A Jolly Good Fellow', breaking into a tap dance and then finishing the whole thing off with some stagey bowing. Pete really needs to get his big break as an actor.

The male half of loved-up couple approaches me. He looks sweaty and furtive. Could I hide this ring in his girlfriend's dessert, please? I push away unkind thoughts about Carumba being a very strange choice of place to get engaged in and tell him that it would be my pleasure. Even if the pair of them do only both look about twenty-four.

My drinks for table nine are on the bar and I rush to get them before Greta 'rescues' me.

'Don't get sucked into doing this forever,' she said to me randomly the other day when I was cleaning down my section. 'Just because you're getting a tiny bit better at it.'

I thought about what she said as I lay in bed that night. There are things I prefer about working at Carumba to my old job: not being shouted at by Annabel; not sitting in long boring meetings that seemed utterly devoid of a point; never hearing people talk about 'decision gates'.

But I'm not sure I can see myself still working here in five years' time, ten years' time . . . And not just because it would break my body either (seriously, I end every shift with my feet and back screaming at me). It's hard not to notice that all my friends seem to be getting promotions. I didn't think I cared about things like that. But it seems like maybe I do.

'I am *never* getting another job,' I say to Nancy. 'It's the middle of April, for goodness' sake – it's MONTHS since I left Splash.'

'The next one will be the one.'

'You said that last time,' I say, biting the skin around my nail.

'I know,' Nancy concedes. 'But this time it's true.'

138

'You know the worst thing? I wasn't even that upset when the dreadful Gareth told me I hadn't got the last one. Perhaps rejection is a thing you can become immune to? Wait, are you wearing running gear? Have you been running?'

'I'm living in New York, Gin. Sometimes, you've just got to give in to the inevitable.'

'Traitor.'

She laughs. 'Listen, I've got to go and jump in the shower. I've got that date with Todd.'

'Remind me again why you've agreed to go on a date with a Republican?'

'I don't know. Did I mention there really are very few single, straight men in New York? Listen, please don't be down about the job thing. The next one will be yours, I promise.'

I try to smile.

'I'm Ginny and I'm y—' I break off because there, sitting right in front of me, at one of my tables, is Annabel.

The restaurant is particularly manic tonight. Not only is the place heaving but a new girl called Sophie has started and she is not coping. She is racing around with a permanently shell-shocked expression: *I thought this would be an easy way to help me through uni.*

I wish I'd noticed Annabel coming in but it's just so busy tonight. It wouldn't have made that much difference I suppose. It's not like I could have hidden in the loo all night. At least I could have taken a deep breath though, composed myself just slightly before blurting out, 'Annabel.'

'Ginny. I didn't recognize you at first. You look so . . . different.'

I feel my face flame as I imagine myself from her point of view. Multi-coloured nylon shirt (supposed to evoke the mood of a poncho according to Greta), sombrero, purple face that's long since sweated off any make-up.

'So you work here now?'

'I . . . I . . . Well, sort of. I mean, I do, obviously.' I glance at the three people she's with, all of whom are staring at me expectantly. Then I look back at Annabel. She's immaculate as ever in a hot-pink silk blouse that makes my mind flash back to the underwear she was wearing when I walked in on her and Jack. 'I'm very close to getting to a big role in PR. I can't say where –' BECAUSE IT DOESN'T EXIST '– but it's very exciting. Anyway, in the meantime . . .' I drift off, not really knowing what to say next. If it was anyone else, I'd say I need to pay the sodding rent but I just don't want to give Annabel the satisfaction.

The temptation to pick up a frozen Margarita from the next table and chuck it in her horrible Botoxed face is enormous. Orchid-gate mark two! But the truth is, I need this job.

Annabel gives me her version of a smile. 'So if we could order?'

'Yeah. Be right back.'

Hot tears spring to my eyes and I walk towards the kitchen feeling like I'd like to drown myself in the pot-washing sink.

Chapter Twenty-Two

As soon as I see Fiona Carlton-Smith, I know I haven't got the job. Fiona is one of those frightfully posh English girls to whom insecurity is as alien as social security. She will have friends called things like Bear and Boo, a house in the country she decamps to at weekends and at least one minor member of the Royal Family on speed dial. Women like Fiona intimidate me. Which is bad because, according to the book Rachel bought me on interview techniques (I think she was being nice), it's important to create chemistry with your interviewer.

'Take a seat,' Fiona says. She has the biggest diamond studs in her ears I've ever seen on anyone. It's a wonder she doesn't need to be accompanied by someone from De Beers at all times. I expect the earrings have been in her family for generations and she wears them in the bath and to muck out her horse.

'So, tell me a bit about yourself.'

My mind goes blank even though I've answered this countless times in the last few months. For some reason, the first thing that comes into my head is to tell Fiona I know what a finger bowl is and that I'd never try to drink from one. (As I mentioned, women like her intimidate me.) I suddenly feel utterly exhausted – like I just want to curl up on Fiona's sofa and have a nice long nap. What was the fairy tale about the princess who slept for a hundred years? I bet she'd gone for a job interview after job interview and then been set up with a few disastrous blokes. I bet it was rejection upon rejection that wore that princess out.

'Excellent,' Fiona says when I've given whatever answer my brain managed to dredge up. I expect she's wondering what to tell the couple who look after everything for her at the country home to cook for the house party she's hosting this weekend. Fish pie or sausages and mash? Rupes loves a sausage. 'Would you say you're good at motivating people?'

Not really. I switch back to autopilot. 'Well, I led a team of six at Splash . . .'

'Splendid,' Fiona says. I bet she could ski before she could walk.

I quite enjoy the rest of the interview. I know I haven't got the job, so I may as well just relax, enjoy my cappuccino and coast through my stock answers. I even chuck in an unrehearsed bit about helping a celebrity friend of mine on a freelance basis, and it comes out sounding quite good even though the reality is I haven't exactly turned Cassie's reputation around. ('It's not you, it's me,' she said the other day. 'Oh God, I sound like one of those blokes!')

'It's been delightful to meet you,' Fiona says, standing up and smoothing her Boden skirt. 'I'll be in touch.'

I smile and shake her hand, confident in the knowledge I'll never hear from her again.

Chapter Twenty-Three

I am the ant with no bit of leaf to carry! I am at the Natural History Museum with George and Felix and we are looking at the big glass box full of leafcutter ants. Millions and millions of them are scuttling around with a purpose in life. Things to do, people to see. And they look so content with their business (in so far as one can judge an ant's level of contentment).

'Orange,' George says, pointing his chubby little digit at a piece of satsuma peel an ant is carrying. The satsuma peel is about fifty times bigger than the ant.

The boys are transfixed by the hardworking ants and we have been staring at the formicary for ages now. I have to say I'm kind of relieved about this since I was starting to wonder if bringing them to the Natural History Museum had been such a good idea after all. I only really decided to come because Rachel was so adamant the boys were 'way too young' (the Natural History Museum was NOT on her list for today). 'They'll love it,' I said, strapping them into the double-buggy. The journey was a nightmare. Who knew South Kensington tube station had so many stairs? Or that no one would offer to help you heave a double-buggy up them? I was sweaty and exhausted by the time we arrived. The boys didn't want an explorer backpack or hat even though they were free. The wildlife garden failed to impress and they were scared of the animatronic T-Rex. ('Let's not tell Mummy about the dinosaur.') I thought I was on to a hit when I took them to the supermarket where you can experience what an earthquake feels like, but then George spotted some chocolate-chip cookies on the shelf and couldn't understand why I wouldn't buy them for him.

We had our lunch at 11.15 and were the only people in the picnic hall. I was very excited about the sandwiches which I'd cut into dinosaur shapes (not that I'm trying too hard, you understand) but the boys wouldn't eat them. 'I thought you liked cheese.'

'Not *yellow* cheese,' they corrected me in unison.

'Swimming!' Felix says, his eyes big and round. Several of the leafcutter ants have made a leaf raft and are venturing across the water.

And then a section of leaf that several of the other ants have been working on falls to the ground and I almost want to let out a cheer.

By midday, when the blue whale got a kind of 'meh' from the kids (so tiny for teenagers!), it was only the thought of getting the double-buggy back down all the stairs in the tube that kept me from admitting defeat and going home. But that's when I remembered the leafcutter ants.

George is now following the progress of a particular ant who he has named after himself. George Ant is the very model of 'busy, busy' and is currently commuting across an aerial walkway. I also have an ant I identify with although I don't announce this to the boys since Ginny Ant is somewhat less than impressive. She's near the edge of the water and, unlike all the other ants, doesn't really seem to be doing very much at all. A little bit of PR work for a friend and some waitressing maybe?

My phone rings and I pick up expecting it to be Rach on her lunch hour checking up on us. I am looking forward to telling her what a triumph the whole outing has been. But it's a number I don't recognize. I pick up and hear a frightfully posh 'hello'. The line keeps breaking up and at first I still think it is Rachel – she's calling from the school office and putting on some kind of funny voice (except funny voices are normally more Paul's territory). But then I realize that it's Fiona Carlton-Smith and she is offering me a job. And I'm so stunned, I almost drop the phone and lose the ability to form coherent sentences. And Fiona starts to talk about packages and accounts and all other kinds of grown-up things, at which point the boys, who have had their noses pressed up against the glass box for ages, suddenly completely lose interest in it and start whining about ice cream. I make frantic shushing gestures. Fiona asks me if I'll be free to start in a month and I stifle the urge to laugh hysterically.

After saying goodbye to Fiona, I hang up the phone and retrieve the felt tip that Felix is about to draw on his brother's face with.

'Ice cream?' they chorus.

'Big ice cream!' And then I turn back to the leafcutter ants, thinking how very soon I too will have my bit of leaf.

Chapter Twenty-Four

I am cleaning the oven when the phone rings.

'Hi, is that Ginny? It's Nick Fraser here . . . Julia's brother.'

'Oh, yes, hello!' I love the fact that he adds the 'Julia's brother'. Because so many people have talked about the possibility of hiring me in the last few months. I hope he's not annoyed about me taking the job at Impact. Surely, he must understand I couldn't hold out for a job that may never have been on offer. 'Sorry, I just had my head in the oven. I wasn't trying to top myself, just cleaning it . . .' I trail off, realizing I've just made a joke that is beyond lame and in questionable taste.

He laughs politely. 'Julia told me about the job at Impact. I just wanted to say congratulations. I'm really pleased for you.'

'Oh. Well, thanks.'

There's rather an uncomfortable pause. 'I start there in a few weeks,' I say, as if he's asked.

'Great. They've got some good accounts.'

'Yeah.' I'm about to start telling him about some of the things I'll be working on but decide that seems a bit ungracious under the circumstances. The acrid smell of oven cleaner is making my eyes water.

'I wondered if you'd like to go out for a drink sometime. Or a coffee . . . or something else if you don't drink coffee. Blimey, this is sounding slick, isn't it?'

I realize I am suddenly grinning like an idiot. 'I'd love to.'

We arrange to meet next Tuesday evening, I witter on pointlessly about how I can't believe it will be May by then and we say our goodbyes. I put down the phone, my brain struggling to catch up. I think Julia's little brother has just asked me out. Julia's little brother with the eyes that are almost too pretty for a man and the seriously hot body. I force myself to remember that his wife walked out on him and there was probably a damn good reason. And that I have resolved to be a cold hard bitch when it comes to blokes.

I come out of Swiss Cottage swimming baths to see that there are fourteen missed calls from Cassie. I immediately worry. Has she sent another of her disastrous tweets? She promised faithfully after the last time that she'd stay off Twitter. I still worry about her though, and not just in terms of her upsetting people on social media. She's been odd recently. Nothing I can put my finger on – just a bit flat. 'Are you okay?'

'Yes. Well, no. She's left the children with me.'

I tip my head to the side to try to free some trapped water from my ear. 'Meg?'

'Yes, Meg. Who else?'

'I don't know why you're being so snappy. And FOURTEEN missed calls? I thought it was some kind of emergency, Cassie.'

'It is! This isn't what I do.'

Warm water gushes out of my ear. 'Just act like it's a part. You're playing Mummy.'

'Haha. They're like wild animals! Can you come over?'

'No. Look, how long has she left them with you for?'

There is a burst of loud discordant music, which signals that the boys have discovered the baby grand.

'What did you say?' Cassie shouts.

'How long have you got to look after the kids for?'

'I don't know. A couple of hours I think. She's going to Relate. Like that's going to help.'

The impromptu piano recital is really picking up pace now. 'You'll be fine.'

'No. Ouch. Stop shooting at me! Ginny, are you still there?'

'Yup. But I'm hanging up now.'

'Ouch!'

'I've never been so pleased to see you in my life!' Cassie says, opening the front door. 'Even if you do smell of council pool.'

'I think you'll find council pools smell like every other type of pool. Anyway, I've had a shower.'

'Doesn't matter. You'll smell like that for days. And your hair will go green.'

'Gee, thanks.'

'So, first a job and now a date?'

'Well, kind of,' I say hesitantly. I'm not feeling ready to be interrogated and rather regret telling Cassie about Nick's call. 'It's not really a DATE date.'

She raises her eyebrows at me.

'Can I have a drink?' I say, desperate to change the subject.

'Sure. Help yourself.'

'My goodness there's food in your fridge!'

'Haha! Yes, apparently fridges aren't just for keeping your nail varnish and eyeliner pencils at the optimum temperature! Shane bought the food over last night. He made us dinner, but he insisted on stocking my fridge with what he describes as "a few basics" as well.'

'He's so sweet!'

'Ginny!' Cassie says in her stern voice.

'He is though. And you have been seeing quite a lot of each other.'

'As *friends*. Listen, I know you think life should be like one big Mills & Boon plot, but, trust me, I have no romantic

149

inclinations towards Shane whatsoever. He's very useful for work because he knows absolutely everyone and makes it his business to know our business. And I like him. But that's it.'

'From your point of view. And you must have felt more than that once. Why did the two of you even break up, by the way?'

Cassie laughs and rolls her eyes. 'I don't know! Because we were about seven when we got married? Because we were just two little kids playing house? Now, stop!'

Thomas and Matthew hurtle into the room demanding snacks for their den.

'You were really pretty,' Matthew says, pointing to a picture of Cassie taken about twenty years ago.

I wince but Cassie just smiles and rolls her eyes. She gives them a satsuma and a biscuit each and tells them not to get crumbs on her bed. 'No crumbs!' they chorus, disappearing in the direction of the bedroom.

'Cassie,' I say. 'You know I'm starting my new job really soon?'

She looks confused for a second but then says, 'You're going to tell me you won't be able to work for me anymore?'

I nod. I feel kind of guilty even though that was always our agreement. It's just I had hoped Cassie's reputation would be in better shape by now. 'You know I talked to you before about a photo op? Getting some paparazzi pics in the papers that show you in a flattering light?'

'Ha. Good luck with that!'

'What about pictures of you going to visit your dad in the care home?'

She shakes her head. 'I don't want to use him like that.'

'Well, that makes me feel small.'

She laughs. 'Yeah, when I'm the bigger person, you know you're in trouble.'

'What if I could get you into bed with a charity? You could help out in a homeless shelter or something?'

'Maybe. But I'm pretty toxic right now. I don't think many charities would want me as a figurehead.'

'I could try.' I say, but I know she's right.

'Stop worrying about me, Ginny. You've done all you can and now you're about to start a new job. I'd better go and check on the boys. They've been quiet too long.'

She reappears laughing and saying I should see her bedroom.

'Who knew you'd be so good with kids?' I say.

She looks at me like I've just said she's put on a few pounds. 'I am NOT good with kids!'

'It was supposed to be a compliment!'

'Only because I get vicarious pleasure from letting them stuff their faces with biscuits! Oh, and because they find my Scary Lady face amusing.' She picks up some dirty glasses from the breakfast bar and puts them in the dishwasher. 'I'd have been a terrible mother.'

'No, you wouldn't,' I respond, even though she almost certainly would have been. I can't really imagine her as a mum. She'd probably have been the type who barely noticed when you won a race at Sports Day because she was too busy limbering up for the mothers' race. The kind who came to see you in hospital with the words 'what a day I've had'. She has surprised me in the role of Auntie Cassie though.

Something clanks into place in my brain. A devoted Auntie Cassie is just what we need for a photo op. All this time, I've been trying to think of something and the – cartoon-cute – solution has been right under my nose.

Chapter Twenty-Five

As first date stories for a wedding speech go, it's pretty good. Not that I think in those terms now I'm all cold and hard, but I'm just saying.

It's one of the first warm days of the year and Nick phoned and suggested that, instead of meeting at The Lansdowne as agreed, we have a picnic in Regent's Park. He'd bring all the stuff. I instantly gushed about how lovely that would be, and then put the phone down kicking myself for breaking the first rule of cold, hard bitchdom by being so easily pleased.

Getting ready takes some time. I am half tempted to ask Marielle for advice on what I should wear but she and Jean seem to be locked in a particularly intense conversation. In all fairness she'd probably interrupt it if I asked her, the pair of them positively gushed with enthusiasm when I said I had a date tonight. *Finally!* the look in their eyes said. *Come to the light side.*

I should be able to choose an outfit on my own though. I'm thirty-four, for goodness' sake. I put on jeans and a top that flashes just the right amount of bra strap every now and again. Then I decide I'm too hot – and I don't mean the good kind of hot – and change into a dress. But then I worry that I look like I'm a fascinator short of a summer wedding outfit and change back into the jeans. I am still hot – why wouldn't I be, it's only a few minutes later – so take them off again. No wonder people often stay in dead-end relationships. However bad it gets, there are no first dates.

I am properly sweaty now, so lie on my bed in my bra and pants to cool off a little. This will also help me be late. I've decided cold, hard bitches aren't punctual.

About five minutes before I'm supposed to be meeting Nick – a fifteen-minute walk away – I go out of the front door. (I'm not still just in my bra and pants, in case you're wondering. I've settled on a denim mini-skirt and the orangey T shirt Jack bought me. Ha! Wearing a T shirt he bought me to go on a date with someone else. That'll show him!)

Nick is sitting on a rug with his back to me and is watching some boys of about nine playing football. He jumps up to greet me.

There's a bottle of chilled white wine, some olives, a big wodge of cheese, some antipasti, a sourdough loaf and some really ripe-looking tomatoes. A pretty perfect picnic in fact. Not scarily Salmon in Aspic Too Much Fuss, but not a bag of cheese and onion and a can of warm lager either.

'Sorry I'm a little late,' I say as he kisses me on the cheek.

'No worries. Can I get you a glass of wine?'

Before I can answer, a dog – I'm not sure what type it is, but one of those ones that looks like it ought to be on wheels – bounds into the middle of the rug, knocks everything in its path flying, and starts digging into the chorizo and Parma ham.

'Tippy!' shouts a red-faced man, who is running towards us. 'Tippy!'

Tippy looks up briefly, a large slice of Parma ham hanging out of his mouth to provide a comedy tongue. 'Tippy, come!' Tippy does not come.

Nick and I try to coax the dog away, but we are no match for the chorizo in terms of appeal. The red-faced man arrives and pulls the dog off. 'Sorry.'

'It's okay,' Nick says, 'these things happen.'

'Only you shouldn't really lay food out like that. Asking for trouble.'

My mouth almost drops as open as Tippy's. Nick has been faultlessly gracious considering the man's dog has just run through our picnic and eaten about a tenner's worth of antipasti but still it is somehow his fault. But it gets better.

'I hope it's not spicy that sausage he was eating? Only it'll play havoc with his stomach if it is.'

When he walks away, the two of us dissolve into helpless laughter.

'Next time,' I say, 'make sure you bring dog-friendly food!'

The ice is well and truly broken after that, and we have a lovely picnic – albeit one that's a little light on food. (What Tippy didn't eat, he sniffed or walked through.) We talk about how we both love Nick Hornby, and although Nick's favourite book is *High Fidelity* and the best is obviously *About a Boy*, I'm prepared to forgive him. We both love Chinese food although only if it's Szechuan, and he even knows I'm referencing *Planes, Trains and Automobiles* when I tell him not everything in life is an anecdote. (I should probably point out I say this in a self-deprecating way about one of my own stories. I'm not rude enough to say it to him, and anyway, he's not boring.)

'I'm so glad you didn't come to work for me,' he says, when we're walking out of the park.

'Thanks,' I say, pretending to be offended.

He laughs, we stop walking, and I know what's about to happen, and I'm almost hoping he's going to be one of those awful 'snakey-tongue' kissers or slobber all over my face. Just to make it a bit easier to be cold and hard. But, of course, he kisses very nicely. Very nicely indeed.

Chapter Twenty-Six

I hit refresh for the gazillionth time. It's way after midnight and I'm waiting for tomorrow's edition of the *Sun* to come out online.

Getting to this point has been no mean feat. To get the photo op I had in mind meant begging a contact for tickets to the premiere of the hot new kids' movie, convincing Thomas and Matthew that said movie wasn't a 'girls' film', talking Meg into allowing her kids to be photographed and begging editor after editor to run the pictures.

But when I received the images earlier, all the effort seemed worthwhile. In every single one of them, Cassie looked loving, kind and affectionate. There she was crouching just before the red carpet to tie Matthew's shoe lace, giggling with Thomas as they spotted Mr Duckie-Duck, crouching down beside them with her arms protectively around their waists. Truly, I couldn't have asked for more.

But now I'm sick with nerves because, despite all the paper's assurances, there's still a possibility they won't run the Cassie shots after all. Anything could get in the way, from the whim of an editor to some big disaster.

I tell myself I can't hit refresh again until I've counted to sixty slowly in my head. Can I possibly hope for them to run more than one picture? At least online?

Finally, tomorrow's papers are up. Cassie is on page five,

but, oh God, it's not one of the pictures they sent me. Instead it's an image of her bending down to wipe Matthew's nose, her face scrunched up in utter disgust. The headline is: *Snot fun!*

I bang the bedside table with my fist. They had so many good pictures – pictures that showed Cassie as a loving, solicitous, fun auntie. But instead they chose to run one that makes her look she's physically repulsed by an angelic-looking four-year-old.

I suddenly think of the unflattering photo of Ed Miliband eating a bacon sandwich the papers couldn't get enough of. They will have had heaps of photos of him looking fine. But when they don't like you, they don't like you.

Snot fair!

Chapter Twenty-Seven

We go to restaurants and I hope Nick will be rude to the waitress or tip really meanly.

We talk about what happened with his wife and I hope he will confess he was cheating on her for years before she did the same to him.

(Okay, he has baggage but small consolation. Anyway, a guy in his mid-thirties with no baggage? That's baggage!)

We talk about politics and I pray for him to be a member of the BNP or something. But no.

Nick is not making it very easy for me to be a cold, hard bitch. In fact, he's the kind of guy I could fall for very hard. But then I remember that hard falls hurt very badly.

It doesn't help that all my friends and family seem to be rooting for him. 'He sounds lovely,' Nancy says. 'Why not bring him to Sunday lunch,' my mum suggests. 'I think you've found one of the few good ones,' Cassie says.

I feel like saying, *You don't even know the guy*. But they know he's not Jack.

Yesterday, I spent all morning not returning Nick's call. Returning his call would have taken a matter of minutes, but not returning his call proved very labour intensive. It meant I had to arrange all my books alphabetically and clean out my kitchen cupboards. I even took Jarielle's laundry out of the washing machine and hung it all out for them. Anything to keep my fingertips from dialling his number.

The rules are straightforward: I can't see Nick unless I've turned down at least one opportunity to do so already, I don't answer the phone when he rings, and take my time about calling back (same rules for texts, emails, etc.).

None of this stuff comes naturally to me but it's made a little easier by the fact I'm still working my five shifts a week at Carumba and won't finish there until just before I start at Impact (on account of trivial stuff like the need to pay the rent). It's easier to do Pretend Cool when you don't also have to do Pretend Busy (as this morning illustrated).

I struggle most when we actually see each other. Tonight has been particularly tricky. We went ice-skating. I used to go a bit as a kid, so whilst I'm no Jayne Torvill, I am at least able to stay upright. Nick, on the other hand, was a newborn foal and spent far more time on his bottom than he did his feet. Which shouldn't have been so attractive, but kind of was. (The idea that women like guys who are super-cool all the time being something of a myth.)

Now we are back at my flat and kissing and I know I'm in big, big trouble. I realize there are plenty of men who can be having sex with someone and still stay emotionally distant – hell, I've been out with them. I know there are even quite a few women who can do this, but I'm not one of them. So it can't really be a good thing when I end up in bed with Nick. Especially when it is such a good thing.

The next morning, I wake up feeling panicky and not just because I haven't had time to put some mascara on before he wakes up.

I force myself to say I have other plans when he asks me if I want to go out for brunch. (I don't kick him out first thing – I'm not trying to channel complete arsehole here.)

Later in the day, he sends me a text that is so sweet and

funny it brings a lump to my throat. I wait two hours and three minutes before answering (was going for two and a half hours but couldn't bear it) and make sure it's fairly neutral.

It's not easy this whole new Ginny thing, but I think I'm just about pulling it off.

Chapter Twenty-Eight

The morning I'm starting my job at Impact I wake up feeling sick with nerves. It's been over five months since I last worked in PR. Well, apart from the work I've done for Cassie, and we all know how that's gone. What if I've forgotten everything I knew? What if I never actually knew anything to forget?

'This is classic imposter syndrome,' Nancy said on FaceTime last night. 'I wrote an article about it once and you wouldn't believe how many truly successful people suffer from it, particularly women.'

'But I'm not truly successful.'

'Ginny!'

I recall this conversation as I lie in bed next to Nick trying not to wake him. It's not even 5 a.m. yet. Vivid mental images of me screwing up keep flashing through my mind. 'I'm frightfully sorry,' Fiona will say to me before the day is out. 'But it seems Annabel was right about you all along.'

I should never have given up my job at Carumba! I was good at that – well, passable. I wonder if they'd have me back? My last shift was only a couple of nights ago and they did say they were sorry to see me go.

I take a sip of the water that is beside the bed.

Nick reaches over and pulls me towards him. 'First day jitters?'

'Sorry, I didn't mean to wake you.'

He kisses the top of my head. 'S'okay. You're going to smash it, Ginny.'

'What if I'm introduced to a big client and I randomly ask them if they want guacamole or salsa?'

He laughs. 'You can do this. I promise.'

I must doze for a bit because suddenly it's 6.30 and the alarm is going off. I shower and get dressed in the outfit Nancy and I selected last night.

Nick makes me scrambled eggs on sourdough toast but I feel too sick to eat it. He squeezes my hand. 'You can do this.'

Then we get on the tube together and Nick insists on taking me all the way to my office even though it's completely out of his way.

'Remember,' he says, as we stand outside the building, 'they're lucky to have you. As am I.'

He kisses me goodbye and I go inside. Nick has made today seem a whole lot easier. Unfortunately, he's also made keeping my cool with him even harder.

I leave the office on a high.

As I'm walking to the tube, Nick calls. 'So I'm not going to tell you I told you so but I told you so.'

I laugh. 'Just because I said I'd done okay in my text.'

'Ginny, you saying you did "okay" means you did brilliantly. Do you want to grab some dinner tonight? I'd love to hear all about it.'

I am blindsided because Nick and I don't have an arrangement to see each other again until Thursday and I'm pretty sure agreeing to a spontaneous extra date is against the rules.

Before I have a chance to construct an answer, he fills the silence. 'I can cook for us if you're too tired to go out.'

I stop walking for a second trying to gather my thoughts. I really want to see him. To tell him that his words and his kindness were invaluable today and that I used them as a sort of metaphorical lucky charm every time I felt a bit shaky.

People are tutting and glaring at me as they dodge around me. I can't really blame them. I am standing still in the middle of Oxford Street in the rush hour and everyone knows that you can be whatever you want to be in London as long as that's not slow.

'I can't do tonight,' I blurt out.

'Oh . . . okay.'

I can hear the disappointment in his voice and it's all I can do not to change my mind. Or at the very least make up some kind of excuse about why I can't see him so my words don't seem quite so abrupt.

But then I think of the book I read called *Too Much Too Soon*. Never apologize, never explain.

I think about Jack and how if he rang on my doorbell at eleven o'clock at night after a boozy night out with the boys, I fixed my face and made him a bacon sandwich. With Jack, all the rules came from his side.

This time, I have to do things differently.

Chapter Twenty-Nine

What the hell happened to treat 'em mean, keep 'em keen? Here I am smug in the knowledge that I have finally got this relationship thing right and then Nick stops calling! It's been nearly a week now. 'You are not seeing Nick anymore?' Jean asked me last night. Marielle shot him a look.

In the same way I always think I can keep a houseplant alive in the first few weeks I have it, I have made the foolish mistake of thinking this time I could get it right. I look across at my Dracaena Marginata, its browning spikes glaring at me reproachfully. The man in the garden centre assured me it was easy to care for – foolproof! (Now what does that make me?) All I had to do was not let the compost dry out and give it some liquid feed every month or so. I thought his 'or so' very casual, so noted its feeds on the calendar. But still it wilts and sheds and browns.

I really thought I was getting things 'right' with Nick. Managing to stick to 'the rules' despite every fibre in my being not wanting to. I thought he might be a bit sulky with me after me flatly refusing to see him the night I started at Impact but of course he wasn't. Damn you for being so nice, I thought. Day after day I forced myself to keep being the new me.

I run my fingers down the plant's leaves. Tell me what to do! You will go the way of the Weeping Fig if you don't.

I think back to Julia and her contention that you need a list of what you want from a man, just like one you'd have if you were buying a flat. Then I meet her brother who has the equivalent of outside space AND a spare bedroom, and now he doesn't answer my calls. (Well, call in the singular. I'm not going to repeat the same mistakes.)

I pick up the plant and take it down to the bins. If it's going to die on me, I don't want to watch it.

'I thought it all sounded so good between you and Nick,' Cassie says. 'Still, what the hell do I know about good matches? I've had lipsticks that have lasted longer than most of my relationships.'

Hot tears prick the back of my eyes, and before I know it, they are rolling down my cheeks.

'Hey,' Cassie says.

I can't really say anything because I've started to cry properly now. I'm not a very pretty crier. It's not like the movies. My nose always runs for one thing. 'I figured I needed to be a bit hard to get,' I say, hiccupping loudly. 'I've never played games in the past . . . but then look where that's got me.'

Cassie hands me a tissue.

'I was just trying to be the new Ginny.'

Cassie sighs. 'Pity, because I think he really liked the old one.'

I blow my nose.

'When you say you've been "playing hard to get", what do you mean exactly?'

'You know,' I say shrugging. 'Not saying yes every time he wants to see me, not returning his messages and calls.'

'So,' she says, swiping one of her child-sized hands through the air, 'do you think it's possible he thinks you're not very keen?'

'That's the whole idea!'

'Yeah, up to a point. But if he thinks you're really not bothered, well he might just decide to walk away. Especially after what he went through with his ex.'

'Or he's just ghosting me.'

Cassie shrugs. 'Or he's just ghosting you. But you need to talk to him to find out. You need to RING HIM.'

I look at my mobile sitting on the breakfast bar. I know Cassie's advice makes sense.

But it doesn't make it any easier to pick up the phone.

Dating, it appears, is an activity I am better at vicariously. Antonia, who is Fiona's uber-gorgeous young assistant, spends much of the working day discussing her Tinder life. I have fallen into the role as her advisor, giving opinions on everything, from whether she should see Wild Jim again (definitely not), if it's okay to double-message (sometimes) and whether she should give Mark one more chance but stay sober this time (yes).

'You're so good at all this,' she says to me.

I think about how I still haven't managed to pluck up the courage to call Nick. About how one minute I'm convinced he's a nice guy who got the wrong signals from me and the next minute I'm sure he's just another Jack.

'I'm really not.'

Everyone on the course is better than me! Mr Published is talking about critical choices and reversals. He bandies these terms around with complete ease, and even Judy seems impressed by how many books he's read on writing ('Of course Dorothea Brande is THE authority), how many courses he's attended (even one in LA!). 'I recently discovered the joys of implied stasis,' he says, waving a pudgy finger in the air.

I don't even know what 'implied stasis' is. Published Guy is Chris Hoy, and I am yet to take off my stabilizers.

We start an exercise using the five senses. We are to make notes about things we have strong feelings about for each sense. 'Think about things you really love or really hate. Jot down any memories they trigger,' Judy says. She has even bigger earrings on today – I worry for her earlobes. These ones are like purple chandeliers and almost touch her shoulders.

I start to think about smells I love and am transported back to lying on Nick's bare chest and breathing in a mixture of him, us and something vaguely citrussy. I nearly called him earlier. But then I thought of all the times in the past where I've chased after guys only to end up feeling humiliated.

Annabel's soulless-sister is scribbling away furiously. Perhaps she is writing about how she loves the feel of her Blackberry. Its keyboard smooth against her fingertips.

I pull at my T shirt which is sticking to my back. Even though it's nearly 8 p.m., it's still baking. Apparently, the temperature today has been a record high for early June. The streets are packed with people with angry red noses and shoulders, and there are signs all over the tube stations telling you not to travel without a bottle of water.

Published Guy wants to know if he can take this exercise 'one stage further'. Any minute now I'm expecting him to tell Judy to put her feet up while he takes the class.

I can't believe I've messed it up with Nick already. 'What did I do wrong?' I wailed on the phone to Nancy. I'd been so careful to fight the Labrador puppy inside me who wanted to jump up and throw myself at him every time he walked through the door, my tail thumping around like crazy.

'Right,' Judy says, purple chandeliers swaying, 'let's see what we've got, shall we?'

What we've got? I've been sitting here mooning about Nick. The only sense I've thought about is smell, and I am not going to share that memory with the group.

Annabel's soul-sister talks about the smell of incense and

how it's instant guilt for her taking her back to her convent education.

Tupperware Lady talks about the sound of a telephone ringing too late at night or early in the morning. 'It always means bad news.' Her huge, pink-rimmed eyes water behind her spectacles.

I am desperately racking my brain for something to talk about. I know – I will talk about the feel of the sun on my skin when it is still wet from the sea. I scribble down a few notes.

We are on taste now. People talk about roast potatoes, crunchy outside and soft within; sherbet lemons; their mum's gravy. They 'eww' and 'yuck' over kidneys and uncooked egg white.

Katia has written a short piece on sight. It's about the empty patch of sofa when she turns around to look at her husband during a funny bit in *The Thick of It*. She describes how she can still see a faint groove where he used to sit, how the joke no longer seems funny when there's no one to share it with. By the time she finishes, many of us have tears in our eyes. I don't think I'll ever be able to write something so beautiful. So simple and so true.

Mr Travelogue stands up. I am shamefully relieved that at least his piece will make me feel that not everyone is better than me. 'I chose to explore a special memory from a trip to Ko Samui.' His voice is toneless, nasal. 'The sense I am describing is feel. It is the sensation of getting out of the cool sea and then feeling the very hot sun on my back.' He goes on. And on. And on. But I am not listening because all I can think about is that Mr Travelogue and I had exactly the same idea. That's the kind of writer I am.

I am still smarting about this as I get home. My basement neighbour, Mr Holden, is sorting through the post in the hall. I feel an instant rush of guilt. I always mean to look in on him. True, he can be a little on the dull side, but he is old and alone. 'Mr Holden, how are you? I'm so sorry I haven't seen you in ages. I've just been so busy . . .' Have I? 'I've started my new job. And this writing course which is taking up so much time.'

Mr Holden puts down the post and wrings his hands together as if he's washing them. 'Writing course? What is it you want to write? A screenplay? A novel?'

'A book, I guess.' I avoid the word 'novel'. It sounds too self-important somehow.

'I've always wanted to write a book. If only I had the time.'

I stare at him dumbfounded. Mr Holden's favourite subjects are wheelie bins and fox poo; he makes Mr Travelogue look fascinating. Why is it that EVERYONE thinks they can write a bloody book?

Chapter Thirty

The tap in Cassie's kitchen is dripping. 'Isn't that driving you mad?' I say. 'You should get a plumber round to look at it.'

She shrugs. She's odd this morning. It's as if she's not really here. She reminds me of my dad when he comes home from the hospital sometimes. 'How come you're not at your yoga class?'

'Didn't feel like it.'

Cassie never misses her yoga. It annoys her that Triyoga closes on Christmas Day.

She yawns. 'I was too tired.'

The phone rings. Cassie makes no move to answer it. The answerphone clicks on and Shane leaves a message. 'Aren't you going to pick up?' I ask. She shoots me a look, but I continue. 'Perhaps you ought to see the doctor about not sleeping?'

'To do what?' Her voice is aggressive.

The tap drips.

'It's just it's been going on qui—'

'I tell you what, Ginny. How about you butt out of my life and try sorting out your own. It's not like you've exactly got everything together, is it?'

I feel like I've been slapped.

'Sorry.' She suddenly looks so small.

'S'okay.' I say, and then we lapse into silence for a few

moments. I glance around the kitchen, which looks kind of grimy. Dishes teeter in the sink, the water cold and greasy. 'Carmen coming today?' I say more to make conversation than anything else.

'I fired her.'

'Oh.' Carmen has been Cassie's cleaner for five years. Cassie has joked to me she couldn't live without her. And, despite the fact that Carmen speaks little English and Cassie even less Spanish, there seemed to have been a genuine warmth between them. 'I get on brilliantly with people who can't understand a word I'm saying,' Cassie once said, winking when I commented on this. And now she's fired her.

'She kept trying to clean the bloody bedroom when I was in bed. She works for me, right? So if I don't want her to clean the bedroom, she should just leave me the fuck alone.'

I say nothing, but I am wondering two things: why is Cassie so angry with someone who just wanted to give her fresh sheets, and why was she in bed in the middle of the afternoon?

The taps drips.

Chapter Thirty-One

Nick and I are back on! (I finally plucked up the courage to call him again and, despite my learned tendency to assume the worst when it comes to blokes, even I couldn't ignore just how pleased he sounded to hear my voice.)

We are watching *Café de Flore* at the Swiss Cottage Odeon, and I'm so happy that I don't care that they've run out of Twirl Bites, or that I've forgotten my glasses and wouldn't really know if it was Vanessa Paradis or Joan Collins on screen. I exaggerate about the eyesight of course . . . but not the happiness.

Nick reaches out and takes my hand. He has nice hands – long, elegant fingers.

After a while, I am regretting the large bottle of water I gulped down before the film started and decide to nip to the loo. Bright eyes and flushed cheeks stare back at me from the mirror. I look happy.

I make my way back into the dark auditorium, trying to be as undisruptive as possible. I sit down and reach out and take Nick's hand. I don't want him to think I've gone back to being the old Ginny again. Well, technically, the new Ginny, but you know what I mean.

The hand recoils at my touch. I look over and see I am sitting next to a complete stranger.

★　★　★

Nick is still laughing. 'That bloke must have thought it was his lucky night!'

'Stop it,' I say, poking him in the ribs. 'I've never been so mortified in my whole life.'

We walk out of the cinema.

'Do you fancy Chinese?' he says.

'Mmmm. We HAVE to have salt and pepper squid though.' I suddenly catch myself. 'Sorry, did that sound really bossy?'

He laughs. 'I grew up with two sisters. That doesn't even rate one on the bossy-ometer! Anyway, I love salt and pepper squid.'

'Julia told me you once burst into tears saying that it wasn't fair that even the family dog was female!'

He grins. 'Glad she's been sharing all my best stories! Anyway, be fair, I was pretty young at the time. About twenty-two, tops!'

We walk past the hotch-potch of battered shops. 'So, what was it like then – growing up in a female-dominated household?'

'It was good . . . once my sisters grew out of the phase of playing hairdressers with me. I was three before I discovered that, despite everything I had been told, it simply wasn't true that all superheroes wore a top knot.'

'I bet you looked lovely.'

'Oh yeah, very macho. Especially when they completed the look with a ribbon. As we got older, there were different challenges. I learned, for example, that there is always someone else in the bathroom. And that "do I look fat in this?" is actually a trick question.'

A number eighty-two bus stops next to us. A couple of teenagers with American accents and huge backpacks cross-examine the driver as to whether it will take them to Victoria. The driver wordlessly gestures towards the huge sign on the front of the bus saying 'Victoria'.

'My sisters are ace though – I try very hard not to let them realize that of course – but they are. When Mel and I split up, I wanted to handle it in the traditional blokey way. Y'know, hole up in my flat with only a bottle of Jack Daniels for company. Keep conversation to a basic "extra pepperoni with that" minimum. But Sarah and Julia kept turning up. Making me do pointless stuff like wash and eat. They made me talk too, although Christ knows why given it was just a one long "I thought Mel and I were forever" monologue on a loop. Any of my mates would have run out of the door screaming. Well, either that or just start talking about what a bad season Spurs were having. But my sisters just soaked it all up and made endless lasagnes.'

My brain has seized on the 'I thought Mel and I were forever' part of what Nick said, and even though we are moments away from salt and pepper squid and sea spice aubergine, and I haven't eaten much all day, the butterflies in my stomach suddenly feel more like fully grown pterodactyls.

'So what happened with you and Mel?' I try to make my voice sound oh-so casual. 'I mean, if you don't mind talking about it.'

'Mel really wanted to have a baby. And it just wasn't happening. So we went for all the tests – which were a lot tougher on her than me – and Mel was diagnosed with unexplained subfertility. Which is a real bummer, because you think doctors are always going to know the answers, and if they don't know what the problem is, then how the hell can they find the solution?' I look at his face. The pain etched across it is so palpable, it hurts just to look at him. 'We started having IVF, and by some miracle Mel got pregnant on our first try. We were ecstatic, painting the nursery – we lived in a one bedroom flat actually, but you know what I mean – arguing over names. Then she miscarried. It was awful. Obviously. But the worst thing about it was that it seemed to just rip us apart. Everything I said to her was wrong. When I said, "We'll try again," she heard, "I don't care about the baby we've lost." When I told her, "As long as I have you nothing else matters," she heard, "It doesn't matter." He looks across at me, and gives me a sad half-smile. 'Sorry. That was probably a little more information than you wanted.'

'Don't be silly,' I say, struck by the fact that he left out the one bit of information I already knew (provided to me by Julia): that he'd actually come home from work one day to find Mel in bed with someone she worked with.

'Mel ended up having an affair. But the truth is we were over before that started.'

I reach out and squeeze his hand. He could talk about her so differently, but it says so much about him that he doesn't.

We carry on walking. No London tourist guide ever put Finchley Road down as a must-see. Indeed, it would be hard to imagine the copy which eulogized about how you absolutely had to take some time out to marvel at the dingy shop fronts of Hair By Nora, or William Hill Betting, or Quickster Mini-mart. But, suddenly, walking along hand-in-hand with Nick, Finchley Road suddenly feels lovelier than I would have ever have thought possible.

Chapter Thirty-Two

The first few weeks of any relationship are good, I know that – you have yet to pee in front of each other or argue over who should take out the bin – but these are *really* good.

On the day I have a big pitch for a new account, I wake up feeling almost as nervous as I did on my first day in the job, and once again Nick is the person who builds me up and tells me I can do it.

We have tickets to the theatre that night, but at 7 p.m. I feel so tired, I can't imagine keeping my head upright for the next four hours, let alone trying to appreciate the finer points of *Torch Song Trilogy*. 'I'm really sorry,' I say on the phone. 'Can you go with Steve maybe?'

'Don't be silly. I want to hear about your day.'

The thing is, I know he really does. He'll want to know all about how the pitch went and, even though I'll tease him about pumping me for information because he works for another PR company, what I'll really be thinking is how nice it is to be with someone who not only asks me what's going on in my life but really listens. He's not just waiting for his turn.

By some miracle, Jarielle have decided to stay at his flat tonight, so Nick and I have the place to ourselves. He makes me take a hot bath while he cooks dinner, and I lie in the bubbles worrying that the bigger bubble is going to burst.

And then he brings me a glass of wine and kisses the end of my nose, and I forget about bubbles bursting and he forgets about dinner.

Later, when we've abandoned plans of Nick's slow-cooked ragu and are tucking into toast and Marmite, we chat about a girl at MediaMaster who's just told everyone she's pregnant. Nick says he'd be scared to ever go down the baby route again after what it did to him and Mel. And I see it: the big sharp pin that's going to burst my bubble. But then we carry on talking about other stuff, and I push it to the back of my mind.

Nick is excited because he's managed to get us a table at Dinner. I am excited because I can't believe I have a boyfriend who has enough faith in our relationship to have made a reservation two weeks in advance. (Jack didn't do 'in advance'. Asking him to sign up to a plan for the evening any time before 6 p.m. represented scary commitment. Who knew whether we'd still be together in six hours?)

'I'm definitely having meat fruit,' Nick says on the phone. He had a reservation at Dinner once before and was going to take clients but then they cancelled last minute.

I stand in the office loos where I'm due to perform the day to evening transformation so beloved of magazines. (Heels, red lipstick and a jewelled clutch take this dress from work-wear to partywear in three easy strokes!) They don't mention that the eye make-up you applied that morning has worked its way down your cheeks. Or that your tights have somehow acquired a ladder.

I am dealing with the smudges when Fiona, my super-posh boss, walks in. 'Orff out?'

'I'm going to the Heston Blumenthal restaurant.'

'Oh how lovely. But not in those tights I hope?'

'I thought I'd managed to pull them high enough that the ladder wasn't visible.'

Fiona lets out a braying laugh and starts rummaging in her large navy tote. She pulls out a packet of black tights. 'You'd be amazed what I've got in here. Stain remover, headache tablets, sewing kit . . .' She hands me the tights.

'Are you sure? I could always just go without tights?'

She waves her hand in the air. 'Oh no, you'll be frightfully cold. I don't know what's happened to "flaming June" in the last couple of days. Very exciting that you're going to Dinner.' She disappears into a cubicle. 'Rupes is desperate to go there. Keeps going on about the meat fruit. It's frightfully hard to get a table though . . .'

She reappears and washes her hands. 'Good job with Des Jacobs today by the way. I wonder if that dress needs a necklace . . .' She looks at me in the mirror and then takes off the necklace she's wearing. 'Here, try this.'

The necklace is a silver chain with little diamonds about an inch apart all the way round. Knowing Fiona, the diamonds will be real.

'Oh, I couldn't . . .'

'Just try it,' she insists.

I put the necklace on.

'Perfect.' And I've got to say, it does look perfect. Terrifyingly perfect.

'But what if I lose it or something?'

Fiona shrugs. 'It's insured.'

I sit on the tube in a little bubble of smugness. Fiona seems to like me (she still intimidates the hell out of me, but I think that's my issue). Better still, things have been going so well with Nick. We had our first row the other day, which you wouldn't think is any cause for celebration, but it was a revelation to me because I discovered Nick can have an argument without turning into a completely horrible person. So many of the guys I've gone out with have been of the 'all's fair in love and war' variety. No blow too low. As is so often the case with rows, I can't even really remember how it started – something to do with him insisting I hadn't told him I was out with clients that night and me being adamant I had. But it doesn't matter. (And I don't just mean it doesn't matter about who was right, which never really matters.) When we're not having civilized rows, everything is pretty bloody perfect. And I'm sorry if that sounds smug, but hell I've kissed enough frogs to deserve one prince.

I flick through the paper skimming an article about a new hole in the ozone. I read an article on whether a new pill could really reverse the signs of ageing and a review of this week's new movies. I look at the column entitled 'Your Birthday Today'. Top of the list is Cassie. I had no idea today was her birthday. I feel awful not to have got her a present or even a card.

The girl opposite me has the volume up loud on her iPhone and it's filling the whole carriage with a metallic screeching.

I hope Cassie's doing something nice for her birthday. She's seemed so flat recently.

The tube disgorges me at Knightsbridge and I immediately get out my mobile to call Cassie. 'Happy Birthday!' I chirp down the phone.

'Thanks.' Her voice sounds flat, lifeless.

'Why didn't you tell me?'

'It's not exactly something to celebrate, is it?'

'Are you doing anything nice?' There's a note that creeps into my voice that makes me squirm. I'm talking to Cassie like my mum used to talk to me when I first started secondary school and I didn't know anyone. 'Who did you sit with at lunch today?' She tried to make it sound casual.

'I'm just waiting for Brad and Angelina. Apparently, Coldplay can't sing "Happy Birthday" but what are you going to do?'

I put down the phone and wander into Harvey Nichols where a woman in heavy make-up tries to spritz me with something. I am meeting Nick for a drink before Dinner but am early. Normally I'd be delighted by the prospect of half an hour to myself in the shops, but I can't shake my unease about Cassie. My mum brought us up to think that birthdays are a big deal. She used to put tinsel around our chair at the breakfast table. There was a fanfare of trumpets (metaphorical – she's not crazy!). So the idea of Cassie having a bloomless, cardless, presentless birthday doesn't sit well.

My mobile rings and Nick's name flashes up. He tells me he's just about to jump on the tube and how he can't wait to see me. I mention the Cassie thing.

'That's not good. I don't like the idea of anyone sitting on their own on their birthday.'

My heart does a little flip. He gets birthdays. He's not one of those 'I got a lone box of Roses for my twenty-first and it did me no harm whatsoever' types.

'We could ask her out with us. I'm sure the restaurant would squeeze another chair at the table.'

'She wouldn't come. There would be jokes about whether she should wear a green, furry suit.'

Spritzy lady is coming towards me purposefully. She sees my defences are weakened by being on the phone and is ready for a nutmeg and ginger strike. I dodge behind a pillar.

'Take her instead of me,' Nick says.

'What? I can't do that. You're the one who really wants to go there.'

'We can go another time.'

'Bu—'

'Look, if you don't even try to get Cassie out, you'll just sit there worrying about her.'

'Bu—'

'Tell me that's not true.' It is true.

'But what would you do?' I ask.

'Go home and prepare a meat fruit of my own. Just kidding. Sob into my pillow. Kidding again. Miss you but feel like we've done the right thing. Mean that one.'

A lump rises in my throat. Nick doesn't even know Cassie. 'You're okay, y'know.'

He laughs. 'You're okay yourself.'

I hang up the phone and stand there behind my pillar with a big grin on my face. I must look kind of insane, so much so that spritzy lady sees me but backs away. I can't help grinning though. Don't worry, I'm not out-and-out smug. There's still the baby thing, which keeps popping into my mind like one of those annoying bouncing icons that tells you you need to install software updates on your computer. I haven't brought the subject up – even the old Ginny knew you can't really have the Baby Conversation very early on in a relationship. There's no way of making that sound casual. So I'm pushing that to the back of my mind for now. And smiling rather a lot.

At work the next day, I am thinking about how much of a struggle it was to persuade Cassie to join me at Dinner (even though I pretended Nick had a work emergency and needed to cancel last minute), and how subdued she was all evening. I pick up a magic marker and have just started daubing at a scuff on my shoe when Fiona appears at my desk. 'Ginny, I wanted to talk to you about the press release you wrote for Vintage Linens.'

My heart sinks. I actually thought I'd done pretty well on that one. I spent ages describing how the woman who owns the company scours rural France looking for vintage fabrics, and how these fabrics are then given a new lease of life as cushion covers, linens, upholstery covers and throws.

'Fiona,' shouts Antonia. 'I've got Rupert on the phone.'

Saved by the bell.

'Tell him I'll call him back.'

Or maybe not. I brace myself ready for my dressing-down. Antonia's little face is crumpled. 'He says it's very urgent.'

Fiona sighs. 'Probably can't work out how to switch on the kettle or something. I'll catch you later on, Ginny.' She turns on her immaculate heel (I am certain Fiona has never – NEVER – taken a magic marker to her shoe) and heads towards her office.

Antonia turns her attention to me and tells me there's a new shortlist of potential Tinder dates for my perusal. I force a smile but am too worried about what Fiona is planning to say to enjoy playing matchmaker right now.

For the rest of the morning, I can't concentrate on anything I'm supposed be doing. Which means that when I'm talking to a journalist about Pasta La Vista, all I can actually think about is how I thought I was doing okay at Impact but maybe Annabel was right about me all along.

By lunchtime, I am so miserable, I am forced to buy myself a double chocolate fudge brownie. I have just stuffed a large piece into my mouth, when Fiona reappears. (Bosses should be made to wear bells round their necks so you can hear them coming at all times, no? Like cats.)

'Why don't you pop into my office when you've finished your lunch?' she says.

Her office? It's going to be worse than I thought, too-brutal-for-open-plan bad.

I stand up and swallow hard. The brownie seems to be lodged in my throat.

'Take a seat,' Fiona says.

I sit down and try, once again, to force down the wodge of brownie.

'You okay, Ginny?' she asks.

I nod my head. Fine, fine. Never better. Nothing like knowing you're barely six weeks into your new job and you've screwed up completely.

'I thought your press release for Vintage Linens was frightfully good. Really captured the brand beautifully. I can see all the magazine spreads now.'

'Oh—'

'I've noticed a few other things you've written too actually. You've got a very engaging style.'

Would it be uncool to burst into tears and throw myself at her feet right now. A little?

Fiona is smoothing her skirt. 'I wondered if you might like to write the Impact blog? I've always done it all myself – you know, being a control freak and all that – but I really haven't got the time, and anyway, I know it'd be in safe hands if I handed it over to you.'

My mouth opens and closes but no words come out. I came in expecting a detention and am leaving with a shiny gold star.

Chapter Thirty-Three

I am baking Cassie a cake to cheer her up. Admittedly, Cassie is not on the surface a very 'cakey' sort of a person, but I once overheard her reminiscing with Meg about their mother's Madeira Cake. How it looked so plain and unshowy and then you started eating it and found it just ambrosial.

I'm thinking of it as a kind of belated birthday cake. Everyone should have a birthday cake.

I cream the butter and the sugar. I remember doing this with my mother. I'm not sure how old I was at the time, but small enough to have to stand on a chair to reach the kitchen worktops. I add an egg with a tablespoon of flour.

I've decided I am going to try to talk to Nick about the baby thing. Maybe I'm making too much of him saying he would be frightened to go down that road again? After all, someone who went through IVF can't be totally anti-kids. Although, I'm pretty sure that when he talked to me about him and Mel, he said Mel really wanted a baby, not we really wanted a baby. And maybe, even if he was on board to start with, the IVF experience was enough to put him off completely? Aaargh, I need to ask him. When I can pluck up the courage.

My mind goes back to Cassie. She seems so down at the moment. Yesterday, I bought her *Heat* and *Hello!* magazines and she didn't even make one bitchy but hysterical jibe. 'Look, you can see her pants,' I prompted, but Cassie just stared straight ahead.

I sprinkle the cake with caster sugar and pop it into the oven. Even someone who isn't very 'cakey' would be cheered up by someone bothering to bake one especially for them.

My cake is moulding in its Tupperware. The cheerful golden-yellow slab is now grey. 'Cassie,' I say, 'I'm worried about you. You seem very down recently.'

'Well, no shit, Sherlock.'

The tap drips.

'I've been thinking, and I could talk to my boss and ask if we could represent you at Impact. I may even be able to get you mates rates.'

Cassie shakes her head. 'I think I'll give up on the whole PR thing.'

I think back to how insistent she was about me working for her a few months ago. How excited she got when the two of us talked about ideas. 'Are you sure? They're a really good firm. I'm sure Fi—'

She cuts me off. 'I feel no hope whatsoever for me or the world.'

She looks tiny and grey and tired. I put my hand across the table and try to place it on top of hers, but she pulls away.

'Don't say that. Look, I know how you feel. What it's like to feel completely fed up. But things could be worse. You're in great health. You've got lots of friends . . .' I pause, not sure if what I've just said is true. Cassie knows lots of people. 'You're financially stable. You've got a lovely home.'

Cassie puts her head in her hands. 'Yeah, yeah. I'm very lucky.'

The tap drips.

'We all are.'

She lifts up her head. Her eyes are flashing. 'Really?

People like you make me sick, Ginny! The world's going to hell in a handcart and you can't even take off your blinkers for a moment to see it. Do you know what I'd be doing if I were you? Stocking up on tinned food and bottled water for when some terrorist plants a fucking dirty bomb on London. The only reason I'm not bothering is I couldn't care less if I live or die.'

'Don't say that!'

'Why not? It's what I bloody think!'

'You're just sad right now.'

The tap drips.

Cassie rakes her hair back off her face. It looks slightly greasy. 'I think you'd better go.'

'I don't want to leave you on your own when you're like this.'

'What's it to you? You're not my publicist anymore.'

'I'm still your friend.'

'Just go.'

'We could go for a walk or something. It's a lovely evening and it would do you good to get some fresh air.'

'Go and live your own life. For this brief moment in time when you've actually got one.' She turns away.

The words sting but I steel myself to ignore them. 'We could go to Hampstead Heath. It's an absolutely gorgeous day out there.'

The tap drips.

'Just leave me alone, Ginny. I'm not your little project.'

The shouting comes through my open window. I look out to see Cassie hanging out of her sitting-room window. She's in her dressing gown and holding what looks like a giant platter.

'I don't want your fucking bagels or salmon. Don't you understand, you're supposed to be my bloody agent, not meals on bloody wheels?'

In the back garden, there is a perplexed-looking man who I surmise must be Barry. Cassie described him to me as short, chubby and bald, which indeed he is. She also said that in his own mind he's Robert Pattinson, but it's harder to tell if that bit's true. I certainly hope he does have a robust sense of self-esteem because at this moment he definitely needs it.

Cassie lobs the giant platter and Barry ducks. Bagels pirouette through the air.

'Cass,' he says pleading with her.

Cassie has a large blue bowl now. 'And latkes? Do I look like a woman who eats fried food? Really?' The bowl of latkes gets hurled at Barry. It smashes on the steps sending shards of blue china and potato flying like shrapnel through the air.

'Cassie! Don't do this. Let me come in and we can talk.'

'What about?' Cassie is shrieking at the top of her voice now and Mr Holden has poked his head out of his back door.

'Talk about what? Honey cake? Roast beef?' She disappears from the window and then returns with a large framed photograph. Clearly, she has run out of foodstuffs but not motivation. The picture flies through the air narrowly missing Barry's bald pate.

'Okay,' Barry says. 'Enough already. You're behaving like a meshuggeneh. I'll call you later.' He turns and heads out the gate.

I ring and ring on Cassie's doorbell. I know she's in there. I heard footsteps and the loo flushing a minute ago.

Eventually the door opens a fraction. 'What?' Cassie says. Her breath smells stale.

The phone starts to ring and I hear Shane's voice talking to the answerphone. 'Call me back, Cass.'

'I haven't seen you in a couple of days—'

'I'm not feeling very well.' She tries to close the door on me but I barge my way in. Her hair is all sticking on end and for the first time since I've known her she isn't wearing a scrap of make-up. All the curtains and blinds are drawn and there is a sour smell, which I'm not sure is from Cassie or the flat.

'Cassie. I think you're depressed.'

She gives a hollow, mirthless laugh and a sarcastic clap. 'You don't say.'

'I mean properly depressed. Not just sad. I don't know why I didn't see it before.'

'No, I'm not. I'm just fed up because I've fucked up my life.'

'I think it's more than that.'

'I'd like you to go away.'

I stare at her child-sized feet. When we went to a yoga class together she was immaculately pedicured. Now the remnants of red polish are chipped and dusty-looking. 'I'm not going to go away. I want to help you.'

'No one can help me.'

'Yes, they can. I've been reading up on depression on the internet and there's lots of different kinds of help and support available. I've read about people who had their lives given back to them by the right medication. Or CBT. Or homeopathy. There's even a woman in Kentish Town who uses yoga to treat depression. People say she's amazing.'

Cassie sinks down to the floor and curls herself up into a ball with her eyes closed. I sit down next to her. 'There are things you can do. We can do.'

We sit in silence. The tap in the kitchen drips in the distance.

'What have I got to look forward to except slowly rotting like a piece of fruit? I've ballsed up my career and ruined my relationships with anyone I've ever cared about.'

'The people I read about all felt like you—'

'How do you know what I fucking feel?'

I swallow. I must not take the anger personally. Not let it

stop me in my course. 'Will you just let me make an appointment for you to see your GP?'

'What's he going to do? Pump me full of a load of drugs which make me feel even more deadened than I feel already?'

'Well you can't just sit in a darkened flat day after day.'

'Why the fuck not?'

Chapter Thirty-Four

My hand cramps and I shake it impatiently before going back to writing again. It's nearly three in the morning and I'm still a scene or two away from finishing my homework for my course tomorrow evening. The brief was to write a story around the theme of comfort. Mine is about a mother singing to her child, and I'm really excited about it. Judy will tell me I've really found my voice. That I have a strong thesis and neatly woven threads.

I cancelled a date with Nick to finish this. He was gracious and supportive.

'Maybe he just didn't want to see me that much?' I said to Nancy when I told her about it on FaceTime.

She rolled her eyes. 'Or maybe he's just a nice guy? God knows, you're due one.'

A screaming sound punctures the silence and I look out to see a fox going through the rubbish in the front garden.

This wasn't the first idea I had for this story. That came, after much angst in the middle of the night last week. I got up and scrawled down a few notes. In the morning, I couldn't wait to read them, and was amazed to find that the idea had turned from brilliant to embarrassing during the course of the night. There were several false starts after that too, and I was starting to panic that, for the first time in my life, I wasn't going to be able to turn in my homework.

My hand moves across the paper, struggling to keep up with my brain. The last two hours have been easy; the words flowing out of my pen as freely as the ink. It's as if the Writing Fairy is doing it all for me. Of course, she won't be able to get up and go to work for me at 6.45 a.m. It won't be her who'll be bleary-eyed in the status meeting or struggling to think of creative ways to generate excitement around a new whitening toothpaste. But that, to misquote Scarlet O'Hara, is something I'll think about tomorrow. For now, I'm just enjoying having a story I can't wait to show people.

My story gets slammed.

'Some touching stuff between the mother and the child,' Judy says (she always starts with a positive – probably still would do if you'd copied out 'Humpty Dumpty'). 'But too much exposition. You're giving us lots of backstory and not an awful lot is happening in the present moment. You need to flip this around so that the backstory is minimal and the action in the present is centre stage.'

'I'm not sure I engaged with the child,' says Katia.

Or your husband, I think meanly.

Mr Published agrees that 'too much exposition is the problem'. I hope he's more original in his writing than his critiquing.

Mr Travelogue calls it 'a bit flat'. And this coming from him!

Even Tupperware Lady can't think of anything nice to say about the story itself. 'I just think you're so disciplined to have got it done in just a week.'

I dig my nails into my palms. The fluorescent lighting is harsh and unforgiving. Everyone looks horrible.

I manage not to cry until I am right at the end of the road. 'Not coming to the pub?' whined Mr Travelogue. *Oh yes, because that would be lovely. So you could tell me a bit more about why I am the boring one!*

My heels click clack angrily along the pavement. I was so excited on my way to the group tonight, I was already spending the advance from my first novel in my head, clinking champagne glasses with Nick Hornby . . .

Anyway, that's it now. I gave the writing thing a shot, and it's got me nowhere. I will give it up and have much more time for nice things. Perhaps the group are wrong though? Everyone knows it took Ian McEwan ages to get published and the people rejecting him were a lot more qualified to judge than that lot. What do the amateurs in my group know? Not one of them is published. Well, except Judy and Mr Published. But they're hardly household names, are they?

A red Fiesta pulls up beside me and a middle-aged woman with a bubble perm and too much rouge asks me if I could give her directions to Euston Station. Her husband, who is in the literal driver's seat but not the metaphorical one, stares straight ahead, mute and murderous looking.

If I'm being honest with myself, the criticisms are all completely fair. I'm not a writer, I'm just someone who wrote the odd good story at school. They weren't even that amazing. A lot of Miss Pinchbeck's praise was probably down to the fact I always handed in my homework on time and never messed around in lessons. Hot, fat tears start to roll down my cheeks.

By the time I walk through my front door, I have decided to cancel my date with Nick tonight. Instead, I will wallow in self-pity, moving from fridge to sofa and back again. I will wear food-stained tracksuit bottoms and watch the Real Housewives of Wherever. I get his voicemail and hang up without leaving a message. I glance in the fridge and see I have a bottle of white wine. So far, so good. Unfortunately, there is little else. No matter. Supper, in the shape of a large tub of Ben & Jerry's Chunky Monkey, is in the freezer.

The doorbell rings.

'Sorry I'm a bit early,' Nick says kissing me on the cheek. 'I tried to call you . . .'

'I'm out of battery. What did you need?'

'I . . . I . . . doesn't matter.' Well, I can hardly ask him to go away, can I? I'm clearly not going to derive any happiness from the professional part of my life, may as well not mess up the personal side. I just hope he doesn't remember I've been at my course.

'How did your story go down?' His eyes are shining and full of expectation.

'They panned it.'

His face falls. 'No?'

'Yes.'

He tries to put his arms around me but I stiffen. I suddenly have an image of my sister trying to get the twins to go in their double-buggy the other day and them making their little bodies completely rigid. 'That's so disappointing for you,' he says into my hair. 'When you worked so hard on it.'

'I didn't work that hard on it.' At least give me the out of thinking that it wasn't my best effort. Don't make me feel like a total loser. 'Anyway, I'm going to stop with the whole writing thing. It's ridiculous trying to fit it in now with a new job and you and everything. No one wants books or real writing any more anyway. We live in a world of blogs and tweets and Facebook updates.'

'You can't just give up.'

'Give me one good reason why not?'

'No.' He pulls away from me. 'I'll give you lots of reasons: Winston Churchill lost every election for public office until he became Prime Minister at the age of sixty-two; Walt Disney went bankrupt several times; Einstein's teacher dismissed him as "mentally slow"; Michael Caine's headmaster said he'd be "nothing more than a labourer"; Thomas Edison took one thousand attempts to invent the lightbulb. When a reporter asked him how it felt to fail a thousand times, he replied, "I didn't fail a thousand times. The lightbulb was invented with a thousand steps." Beethoven's teacher sa—'

I hold up my hands. 'I get the point! What are you – some sort of failure nerd?'

He laughs. 'I got it all from some training course they sent me on at work.'

My mind flashes back to trying to get over the huge inflatable wall on the training course Splash sent me on. Annabel's disgusted face as I slithered down to the bottom yet again. 'I always thought training courses were a waste of time.'

'The course was a week long. I've given you the best minute and a half.' I lean into him and he strokes my hair. 'Not quite actually. I forgot to mention the notes an MGM exec wrote after Fred Astaire's first screen test: "Can't act, can't sing. Slightly bald." Oh, and did you know that James Joyce's *The Dubliners* got rejected by twenty-two publishers? Or that Jack London got six hundred rejections before he got a short story published?'

I groan. 'Perhaps steer clear of the writing ones?'

'Fair enough,' he says, laughing. He kisses the tip of my nose. 'As long as you promise me you won't give up. You know what Confucius said, don't you?'

'Okay, now you're just scaring me!'

He laughs. 'Okay, I'll stop.' He kisses my neck. 'And we'll just have to find another way to cheer you up.'

'I thought I'd have to get you something from Tiffany to get that kind of reaction. Not Ryman!' Nick says, laughing.

I look down at the three Moleskine writer's notepads on my lap. Their pages are blank, and yet they say so much. I put my arms around his neck, pull him close and bury my face in his chest. 'Thank you, thank you, thank you.'

Chapter Thirty-Five

Nick's status as Boyfriend of the Year lasts less than twenty-four hours.

'Have I got a hottie to show you,' Antonia says, waving her phone around.

'The girl does not lie,' Ben pipes up. 'I have seen this one and he is absolutely gorgeous!'

I decide the press release I urgently need to get out can wait and get up from my desk. But just then Fiona emerges from her office and asks Antonia if she has a minute. Antonia rolls her eyes at me and mouths 'later'.

For the rest of the morning, very annoyingly, work keeps getting in the way. Whenever I seem to have a spare second, Antonia is away from her desk. Finally, just before lunch, we get our opportunity. 'He'd better be worth the wait!' I say.

Antonia laughs and tells me he definitely is.

And then she shows me a photo of Nick.

I am sitting in a dingy greasy spoon crying into a truly disgusting cup of coffee.

Nick is a cheating, lying scumbag just like the rest of them! He may have a nice line in pep talks and notebooks but he's no better than Jack.

I pull the tissue I'm holding into shreds. How could I have been so stupid AGAIN? How can I have wasted time – time

I don't have – with another cheat? What makes it even worse is once when the subject of Tinder came up, Nick claimed he had hardly any experience of it and had never thought it was the place he'd meet his Tinderella.

'Want anything else, love?' the waitress asks.

A boyfriend who can keep it in his pants?

'What the hell?' Antonia says, bursting into the café and plonking herself down opposite me. I suppose if you're trying to hide from your workmates, you probably shouldn't pick the café nearest the office. 'Why did you just run out like that?'

I take a deep breath, pick at the skin around my nails. I'm embarrassed to have this conversation with Antonia. I may not be that much older than her but I feel very much like her work mum. I should have all this stuff sorted out by now. 'That guy on Tinder – he's my boyfriend. Or rather, he was.'

Antonia stares at me for a second and then she does something I really don't expect because she bursts out laughing. 'How long have the two of you been dating?'

I bristle at being the object of her entertainment. 'We are exclusive if that's what you're getting at.'

She shakes her head. 'You don't have to be an active Tinder user to come up as a possible match. Us seeing him on there only means he had Tinder at one point.'

'Is that true?'

'Yes, you stay on there even if you delete the app.'

'You're kidding! So I'll still be on there?'

'Did you delete your profile?'

'I deleted the app.'

'Doesn't matter. If you didn't delete your profile, you'll still be on there.'

I take a big mouthful of the vile coffee and shake my head. 'Bloody hell! So Nick isn't a lying, cheating scumbag?'

She laughs. 'Well, not necessarily.'

★   ★   ★

That afternoon, I am quite the laughing stock of the office. Would you like a cup of tea, Ginny? Or don't you *trust* me to make you one?

How's that press release going? I *trust* you'll have it done in no time.

I *trust* you're on your way to our meeting now.

'Oh, leave her alone,' Ben says, laughing. 'If I was going out with that, I'd be a little nervy too!'

Which of course makes Georgia and Jacqui desperate to see photos. Everyone clusters around Antonia's phone and makes admiring noises and I feel yet another huge surge of relief about having got things so wrong.

'Oooh, that's a nice one on the beach,' Jacqui says.

Given that I only saw Nick's initial photo before running out this morning, curiosity gets the better of me and I get up from my desk and go over to have a look.

However, it's not the beach photo that catches my eye but Nick's bio: Works in media – but not a tosser! Wants dogs not babies!

And I feel the blood pounding around my head. Because Nick might not be a lying, cheating scumbag. But neither is he a man who wants kids.

Chapter Thirty-Six

I have managed to get Cassie to the GP – just to shut me up apparently. I sit in the waiting room hoping the doctor will be a sympathetic one rather than a pull–yourself-together type. GPs get something of a bad rap on a lot of the depression blogs I've read. To be fair though, if you're looking for an upbeat view of anything, a depressive's blog probably shouldn't be your starting point.

A tall woman with a shiny red face pokes her head round the door and calls for Janine. A pregnant woman gets up and waddles towards her. The woman with the red face apologizes for the delay to anyone else waiting for the midwife and says she's running a bit behind. I don't know if it's my imagination, but she seems to look directly at me, and I suddenly feel acutely conscious that I'm not pregnant.

Wants dogs not babies! That's a pretty unambiguous statement. And while I may have been able to fool myself into thinking I'd somehow misconstrued Nick's comments about being frightened to go down the baby route again, there's only one way to interpret this. The less clear thing is what I'm going to do about it, but right now I push it to the back of my mind so I can concentrate on Cassie (and, let's be honest, avoid thinking about it).

Apparently, one in five people suffer from depression. I look around the waiting room wondering if that's why anyone else is here. The guy with the Mr Bump socks and a suit? The woman with the hard face and all the gold jewellery? The harassed-looking mother with the child who has a hacking cough?

There are notices up about out of hours services and repeat prescriptions. Posters from the Eczema Education Trust and Priory Hospital. The latter has three pictures of a tumbler of whisky each one fuller than the last. Under the first it says, 'Unwinding', the second, 'Being Social' and the third, 'Call Priory Hospitals'. I know Cassie has been drinking a lot recently and wonder if her problem with booze is just a symptom of her depression or more than that. Not for the first time, I feel out of my depth.

I scroll through my Instagram feed which seems to be nothing but baby bumps and babies. Sarah Raffety is having baby number two! I feel like she's only just had the first one.

Wants dogs not babies!

Stop it!

The blue plastic chairs are very uncomfortable. I glance at my watch. Cassie has been in there well over twenty minutes. I don't know if that's a good or a bad thing. The woman with the gold jewellery is updating her Facebook profile on her mobile.

I get a text from the plumber I've found to fix Cassie's kitchen tap. He will be there at 9.30 tomorrow morning. Should be a quick fix.

Cassie emerges and gives me a shadow of a smile.

'How did it go? Was he sympathetic?'

She shrugs and hands me a prescription. 'He's prescribed me some antidepressants.'

'Okay. Well at least we're getting some help.'

The following evening, I pop into the supermarket on my way home from work hoping to find some things that might tempt Cassie to eat (not easy at the best of times). I am just wondering whether I could make the hideous courgette noodles she seems to like so much at the Triyoga café, when I notice Katia from my writing course.

She pretends not to see me. She picks up a melon and starts examining it very carefully.

My instinct is to keep up the pretence, but I find my trolley propelling itself towards her. 'Katia, hi! Haven't seen you the last couple of times at Writers' School.'

She pokes at the cantaloupe, not meeting my eye. 'I've been really busy.'

I think of the conversation I had with Nick. Me telling him I didn't really have time to write anymore now I had a job again. His voice was unusually firm. 'Make time.' I burble to Katia about how I could email her this week's homework if she wanted. Out of the corner of my eye, I see Chanelle, the assistant I had my 'bratisode' with about the wonky trolley. I hope she doesn't remember me. 'Will you be there this week?'

She sniffs the cantaloupe. 'Probably not.'

'But you're the best out of all of us, Katia. That piece you wrote about the empty sofa, your story about the baby's blanket . . .'

She gives me a small smile and puts the melon back on the shelf. I don't think she was ever going to buy it. 'It was nice to see you, Ginny, but I'd better get going.'

'Katia,' I say, as she turns to go.

She looks irritated and I am suddenly at a loss for what it was I wanted to say. 'I was going to say . . . well, ask . . . umm . . .'

She sighs. 'What? You want to know why I've stopped coming? Is that it?'

I shrug. Katia doesn't owe me an explanation. Maybe she's back with her husband, maybe she's too busy at work. It's none of my business.

'I sent out the first three chapters of my novel recently,' she says. 'I'd worked so hard on them. Got them just right. I was excited. I submitted to ten agents and got ten rejections. Standard rejection letters too, the kind you know are probably sent by the office intern.' She stares down at the floor, shakes her head slightly. 'I've just been dumped by my husband, why would I want to rip out my already battered heart and send it out to complete strangers so they can trample on it?'

I want to say something, anything, but I can't find the words.

'It's just too hard,' Katia whispers to the floor.

She looks up, her expression closed. 'So now you know. I'll see you around.'

I stare after her as she disappears in the direction of the tea and coffee.

It's just too hard.

Cassie won't take the antidepressants. 'Can cause side-effects,' she says reading the information leaflet. 'Slow heartbeat, nausea, diarrhoea, disturbed sleep – I'm already awake at 3.15 every morning. Thinning of the hair, mood changes, confusion, sexual dysfunction, psychoses or hallucinations . . . dizziness particularly when standing up.'

The tap drips insistently. The plumber came this morning but Cassie wouldn't let him in. He called me at work, and I thought about trying to explain the situation to him, but then imagined that conversation in my head and just ended up promising to pay the call out charge.

'All drugs have side-effects.'

Cassie never opens the curtains or blinds anymore, and protests if I try to.

'I'm not taking them.'

Cassie's mobile starts ringing and I see 'Shane' flash up on the screen. She punches 'decline'. It reminds me that I've missed a few calls from Jack recently. I guess I should call him back and find out what computer game or bottle of aftershave he's suddenly realized he left here, but frankly, what with thinking about Cassie and trying *not* to think about how Nick doesn't want a child, I feel like I can't deal with Jack right now.

The tap drips and drips. It seems to be getting worse.

'Look, if you don't want to take the antidepressants, there are other things we can do. Go back to the GP for a start. Maybe he'll refer you for counselling—'

'I don't want to talk about my sodding childhood! My childhood was fine. My early life was fine. Great even. It's now I can't stand. Now I'm a nobody.' Her face crumples and she starts to sob. 'I don't see the point in carrying on.'

I get up from my chair, crouch down beside her convulsing body and put my arms around her. The noise she's making is terrible – desperate – and it's all I can do not to cry myself. I want to help her but I don't know how. The two of us sit in the darkness.

'There are other things. Meditation, self-help groups run by people who have experienced depression and come out the other side, hypnotherapy . . .'

Drip, drip, drip.

Cassie lifts her head. Even in the gloomy light, her eyes are red and puffy. 'I just want to be left alone.'

★   ★   ★

- Cassie is not my mother, sister or even my best friend. (I grew up in London so am familiar with the idea of neighbours not even knowing each other, let alone helping each other.)
- I've got enough on my own plate (still pushing the Nick bombshell to the back of my mind but know I'm going to have to deal with it soon) without adding a hefty helping of depression on the side.

- You can't help someone who doesn't want to help themselves.

These are all the things I tell myself. And for a few days now, I have, as requested, left Cassie alone. I can't help myself listening out for her though. Or looking out of the window desperately hoping she might have made it out to a yoga class or just for a walk to the shops. I can't help continuing to interrogate the internet for answers too, reading account after account of people's struggles with the Black Dog. One guy gives a 'what not to do' section, and I realize to my shame I've done several of the things on it, from checklisting the reasons why Cassie's life could be worse to telling her I've found the answers. Which means I can tell myself that my help wasn't helping and that she is better off without me.

And yet it still doesn't feel right.

Chapter Thirty-Seven

I am coming home from work, wondering whether to flout Cassie's instructions and knock on her door later, when I look up to see Jack sitting on my front steps. 'What are you doing here? Picking up more of your toys?'

'I've been trying to get hold of you. I need to talk to you.'

'We've got nothing to discuss.'

'Please.'

I stare at him. I am with Nick now. And happy (well, apart from the fundamental gap between what we want from life). But something – closure maybe? – makes me want to hear what Jack has to say. 'You'd better come in.'

The flat feels oppressively hot, and I throw open the windows.

'I love you, Ginny.'

I spin round to meet his eye. 'Don't you think it's a bit late for that?'

'It doesn't have to be. What we had was amazing. Why just chuck it away? It's going to be hard work winning back your trust, I kn—'

'I've met someone else.'

'Oh. Oh.'

'Well, don't look so stunned! Did you think no one else would have me?'

'No. Of course not.' He sinks down on the sofa. 'May I have a glass of water?'

209

This could just be an affectation of shock. On the other hand, it is very hot. I go into the kitchen and fill two glasses of water. I feel like putting my head under the cold tap. Why does Jack have to do this now? For two years, I was desperate for him to commit to me. Even after he slept with Annabel, I would have taken him back the day he came for his sodding Xbox.

I hand him the glass of water, and he drains it in one greedy gulp.

The couple upstairs are rowing. A stream of expletives seep through the ceiling. 'I see they're getting on as well as ever.'

I ignore this casual reference. This reminder that he's on familiar territory.

'Do you love him?'

'It's none of your business.'

'I want you and I to be forever Ginny. I'm not going to propose now . . .'

My heart lurches.

'I thought about it, but I don't want to ask you to marry me when you're hurt and angry. I want it to be a beautiful, special moment that we remember forever. A moment to tell our grandchildren about.'

I feel as though I've had all of the air knocked out of my lungs. I have to hand it to Jack – he's good. I sit down, suddenly overcome with exhaustion. 'Please just go away.'

'Okay. But will you think about things?'

'There's nothing to think ab—'

'If it's me you want, you'll make me the happiest man in the world. Or at least England and the Home Counties. If it's him . . . well, if it's him, then he's a very lucky guy.'

It's a no-brainer, right? On the one hand, we have Nick, who, in the two and half months we've been together, has barely put a size ten wrong. On the other, Jack, who's dilly-dallied over what he wants (with dilly-dallied implying a kind of sweetness that definitely wasn't there), and finally betrayed and humiliated me.

And yet.

Nick calls to see if I want to grab a pizza, but I pretend to have a presentation to write up. 'Okay. But make sure you don't forget to eat,' he says, making me feel slightly lower in the nice-person pecking order than, say, Hitler or Gaddafi.

I pace around the living room. The key word in Jack's speech was 'grandchildren'. Because you can't have grand-children without having children first. And I really want to have children. A fleet of them. Too many for a normal car.

I open the fridge and stand in front of it enjoying the blast of cool air.

I still haven't talked to Nick about him not wanting kids, though what's to say really? I want them, he doesn't.

I take a carton of orange juice out of the fridge and pour some into a glass. Jack always liked the 'no bits' kind whereas Nick prefers the other type. Does this mean Nick is more grown up and evolved? Or does it just mean they like different types of orange juice?

I flop down on the sofa. Jarielle swoop in dressed in what looks like almost identical gym gear (#matchingoutfits). I think about Nick and the last few weeks. I think about what a catch he is. So much so that I almost call him and ask if he can still come over after all.

Almost.

Chapter Thirty-Eight

We are on location at Chiswick House shooting the lookbook for Vintage Linens. The stylist lays a red check tablecloth on a huge table and begins 'theming' a half-eaten breakfast (which, of course, doesn't look anything like a half-eaten breakfast in real life. No egg stains here. No cereal that has bloated in the milk to resemble wallpaper paste.)

I have just met Luc the photographer. Luc is a big enough name to eschew a surname. He has something of a reputation. Jacqui is the only person at Impact who's ever worked with him before, and the mention of him prompted a string of expletives and the admission that she'd 'rather do time' than have to repeat the experience. (Bear in mind that Jacqui dots the 'i' in her name with a heart and has pictures of her kitten all over her cubicle.) First impressions of Luc did not provide any sort of a counterpoint to Jacqui's opinion. He greeted me with a monosyllabic grunt and there was a distinct whiff of alcohol even though it was only 8 a.m. I'm telling myself that this MUST be mouthwash.

I get my phone out of my bag and type a message to Cassie. *Hey, how are things?* No, that's not right – too casual. What can I say though? *Do you still feel like there's no hope whatsoever?*

I close WhatsApp and open Instagram to be confronted by a picture of Janey Hicks brandishing her left hand at the camera.

So, so in love with this man! Can't wait to be your wifey!
Can't wait to have your kids! #engaged #Ilovehim #fiance.

I swallow down the football-sized lump in my throat, the visceral jealousy that makes me ashamed of myself.

The stylist places the final artisan loaf and invites Luc to approve the vignette (a.k.a. the half-eaten breakfast). He responds with a sneer. It's going to be a long day.

We have yet to take a single photograph. Apparently though, we are waiting for the right light. I am just hoping this arrives before the client does.

I use my phone to take a snap of a distressed armoire stuffed with linens. I am just about to brave Instagram again to post my picture when Luc appears behind me.

'Why are you taking pictures on your phone? Can't you see the light's TERRIBLE?'

He really does smell of alcohol. Maybe it's extra-strong mouthwash?

'Do we need individual shots of all these cushions?' the stylist asks.

'Yes,' I say.

'No,' Luc says, 'they're horrible.'

'Err, they're the product,' I say.

Luc lets out a small belch. The smell is not mouthwash. Not unless Jack Daniels have started making one. 'They're horrible.'

Oh, marvellous.

'If I laid them out over in that window seat, I think I could make them look rather pretty,' the stylist offers.

Luc shrugs, and I make a mental note to book the stylist for every shoot I ever do from now on.

At this point Rosie Pryce-Lloyd arrives. Rosie is Fiona's goddaughter and is doing work experience at Impact this week. I say 'work experience' but actually just 'experience' would be more accurate. Her first day was yesterday. She arrived at 11 a.m., proclaiming herself 'done in from an epic night out'. Her first task was to help Jacqui pack some goody bags for a launch party but she finished one to Jacqui's six. She then took a two-hour lunch before returning to tell Ben she 'wasn't very good at things like that' when he asked her if she could do some photocopying.

Luc is eyeing up Rosie appreciatively, and is making his way towards her. Great. Now my job description includes protecting my boss's goddaughter from an old lech of a photographer.

'Rosie,' I say. 'Would you give me a hand unpacking the grain sacks?'

Rosie looks at me blankly. I put my hand on the small of her back and steer her towards the bags of grain.

It's nearly lunchtime before Luc deems the light acceptable. One of the models, who is wearing pyjamas and cashmere bed socks, is positioned in the big bay window with a steaming mug of hot chocolate. Luc instructs her to look wistful.

'Why is she in her PJs?' Rosie asks me.

'The story we're trying to create is all about the relaxed home.'

Rosie's brow crumples.

Luc has started looking down the lens. I feel a surge of relief as I realize we're actually going to take a photograph.

'No good,' Luc says, before storming out of the room. His assistant, a wiry boy with a mop of dirty blond hair, follows in his wake.

At this moment Sophie, the client, arrives. We've never actually met in person before now, despite talking on the phone and emailing several times a day. She has always seemed very pleasant if a little nervy. In the flesh, she's smaller and younger-looking than I imagined. 'Hi,' she says introducing herself. 'You must be Ginny. How's it all going?'

'Great.' *Apart from the fact we haven't taken a single photograph.* 'Can we get you a cup of tea or coffee?'

'I'd love a cup of tea.'

'Rosie,' I say.

'Yeah,' Rosie says. 'Coffee would be lovely.'

Luc reappears. I try to introduce him to Sophie but he waves me away. Who cares about the person who's actually paying for all this?

He takes a few shots of the model in the bay window and then proclaims he is ready for the next set-up.

'I really hope today goes well,' Sophie says to me. 'Vintage Linen's first lookbook is always going to be very important and I've got such a strong idea in my head of how I want it to come across. I can see the Pinterest page now!'

'Luc's work is beautiful,' I say.

Sophie nods. 'I know. And the stylist has done a super job. It's just hard when it's your own business. All those hours I've spent flogging around French markets looking for stuff, decisions about websites and branding.' She laughs. 'Not to mention that my kids don't recognize me and we've had to re-mortgage our house!'

Rosie puffs out her cheeks. 'Whoa! Pity the photographer's wasted then.'

'What?' Sophie says.

'Rosie is such a little comedian!' I say. 'Now let's see what you think of the table set-up.'

The rest of the afternoon passes reasonably smoothly. There's a bit of a moment when Luc starts telling Rosie she should come and do work experience with him, but I'm confident I can privately persuade her that it wouldn't be a good idea (I'll just tell her it's long hours). We cover lots of shots.

Then it's time to photograph the bed (made up with bedding from Vintage Linens and accessorized by a model reading the newspaper). Luc looks down the lens and winces.

I look outside. The light looks fine. Very much like it did five minutes ago when he took the photographs of the grain sacks filled with 'laundry'. Luc looks down the lens again, but the shutter doesn't click. The whole room seems to hold its breath. 'Tell her,' Luc says, his voice sounding distinctly slurry, 'to take that look off her face! SHE LOOKS LIKE MY BLOODY EX WIFE!'

There is a horrible moment of silence. Everyone is frozen. And then Luc storms out of the room.

I smile weakly at Sophie. 'Photographers!' I say, trying to sound like this is completely normal. 'I'll go and have a quick word.' Breezy. Breezy, breezy.

Luc has locked himself in the props room. His assistant is standing outside. 'He won't come out,' he says to me.

'He has to come out,' I hiss.

The assistant shrugs.

I knock on the door. 'Luc. Can I have a minute?'

Nothing.

'Please,' I say.

'Fuck off, suit.'

'I'm not a suit,' I say. 'I've got jeans on.'

The assistant gives me a funny look and I scowl back at him. My jokes might be lame but at least I'm trying. 'Luc, I really need to talk to you.'

Silence.

'If that particular model is a problem, we can get another one,' I say. (And, yes, I know the poor girl has done nothing wrong, and I'm selling my soul to the devil, but she'll get paid no matter what, and right now all I care about is getting some photographs.) 'Luc. This is a very important shoot for us.'

Silence. I glance at the assistant and wonder if he could take the photographs. Then I realize that even if I could persuade him to, and even if they were fabulous, no one would think

217

they're fabulous because the assistant has a surname but no name. (Oh yes, in my world, the emperor is alive and well and constantly refreshing his wardrobe.) 'Luc. Your work is so special. We didn't consider any other photographers for this shoot because we knew that you and only you could deliver the images we were looking for.'

Silence.

Rosie emerges into the hallway. Her face looks blank and dreamy, as if she has just woken up and isn't quite sure where she is.

'Rosie,' I say, grabbing her by the arm, 'your one job right now is keeping the client away from here.'

She looks confused. 'Sophie?'

'Yes, Sophie!'

'Keep her away?'

'YES. Keep her chatting. Make her tea. Show her the next set-up. Anything. JUST KEEP HER AWAY FROM HERE.'

'Got it.'

I sigh. 'Good girl.'

Rosie drifts back into the main room and I turn my attentions back to the locked door. 'Luc, please just open the door so we can talk.'

'Fuck off, suit.'

I slide down the door and rest on my haunches. 'Luc. I haven't been in this job very long and, before I got it, I was out of work for a long time. A really long time. I need this job, Luc. And I need this shoot to go well. Please help me out.'

Silence.

I put my head in my hands. The door from the main room opens and Sophie appears. 'What on earth is going on? Rosie just told me whatever I did, I mustn't come out here.'

Really, Rosie? Really? I jump to my feet, suddenly aware that resting on your haunches with your head in your hands

218

doesn't exactly scream in control. 'Nothing to worry about. Luc is just having a little rest.'

'A rest?' Sophie says. There's a flush of pink rising up her chest.

I make a face which I hope conveys 'look, I know it's ridiculous, but don't worry, I've got it'. It's a lot to ask of one facial expression though and Sophie doesn't look remotely reassured.

'Ginny,' she says, her voice low and serious.

The assistant gives us both a sheepish smile. 'Think I'll go and change the bulb on that flash head . . .'

'I'm paying this guy goodness knows how much for today,' Sophie says, 'and he's not even taking any photographs. I've just looked at the shot list. We haven't even covered half of it!'

'I know,' I say, 'but I'm not worried.' *More like terrified.* 'We'll get the photographs, and they'll be beautiful.'

Sophie looks at me doubtfully. 'Do you want me to talk to him?'

'No. I've got it.'

She rubs her temples. 'I hope so.' She goes back into the other room. It's just me and Luc. With only a locked door between us.

I rub my forehead and try to think of what I can say to coax him out. I have tried flattery and found nothing I say can compete with his opinion of himself. I attempted to appeal to his better nature and discovered he doesn't have one.

I hammer on the door. 'Luc. That's enough now. You're getting paid a lot of money for today and this is completely unprofessional.'

'Fuck off, suit.'

'I mean it, Luc. You may not care about pissing me off, but PR is a very small business. You cannot afford to be seen as flaky. Look at Jonny Garner and Axel Heath. They were big-name photographers a few years ago. Now they can't get a job taking pack shots.'

Silence.

'You know I said we didn't consider anyone else for this shoot? Well, I was lying. There are lots of great photographers out there, Luc. And you're one of them, but if you start getting a reputation for being unreliable . . .' I think I hear movement on the other side of the door. *Please*, I think, *please*. The door stays shut. 'We could have used Roman Griffiths today. Or Jodie Mellor.'

The door opens and there, in a fug of whisky fumes, is Luc. He does not meet my eye. 'Roman is shit,' he says. 'You fucking suit.'

The rest of the shot list is covered off without incident. We look at the images on screen and everyone agrees that they're really special.

The stylist starts to pack her props and the assistant starts dismantling the lighting. I fold the linen bedding and begin piling it into bags. Sophie helps me but Rosie continues to text in the corner. I should say something to her but truthfully I just don't have the energy. Today has been so all-consuming I've barely even thought about the conversation with Jack (maybe not a bad thing).

'Do you think we should have got a close-up of that sofa?' Sophie asks me. 'I know it wasn't on our shot list but it's a great example of how something contemporary can look when it's got our loose linen covers on it.'

I look over at Luc who is reeling around the room with a large glass of red wine in his hand (because now he can drink publicly). 'I'll ask.'

Sophie nods gratefully.

I approach Luc, my stomach churning. I steel myself to be screamed at.

I explain the request. Luc narrows his eyes and stares at me. 'You want me to take another photograph? Now that all the lights have been packed away. One that was not on the shot list? Or included in the budget?'

'Yes.' My voice sounds squeaky.

'Are you sure you don't want Roman to take the photograph?'

I don't know if I'm imagining it but I fancy I see the merest flicker of a smile. 'No.'

The assistant sets up the shot.

'Thank you,' Sophie says to me.

'No problem.'

Luc goes towards the sofa. 'Where's the stylist?' he shouts. 'The cushions look horrible.'

'She's left,' the assistant says.

Luc tssks. He starts to rearrange the cushions. He is reeling around quite a bit now and the red wine is sploshing around his glass.

'Watch the wine,' I shout. But it is too late. A large patch of red wine spreads out over the seat of the sofa.

He starts laughing hysterically.

Sophie is less amused. 'Well, I guess we won't be covering this extra shot after all.'

'I'm sure there's something we can do to get the stain out,' I say.

She shakes her head. 'It'll come out when the covers are washed at sixty degrees. Until then, we're stuffed.'

'We can put a cushion on it.'

'No,' she says. 'Not in the middle of the seat. It'll look ridiculous.'

Luc is still cackling. I feel like punching him. 'A throw then?' I say to Sophie.

'Where are we going to get one of those from?'

I consider offering to go to buy one but the chances of

keeping Luc waiting around while I scour the shops are not good. I sigh. 'I'm sorry, Sophie.'

She puts her hand on my arm. 'It's not your fault.'

We go back to putting away the last of the bedlinen.

'I have got a grey blanket in the back of my car,' Sophie suddenly says to me. 'We use it for the dog when we've been for walks. It's normally really muddy but as luck would have it, I washed it the other day.'

'It's worth a go,' I say.

Sophie gets the blanket, she and I arrange it on the sofa, and Luc condescends to click the shutter a few times. And then it's finally time to go home.

I sit on the tube, my shoulders still somewhere around my ears, my bones aching with exhaustion, and I realize that I did okay today. I had a nervous client, a drunk and unco-operative photographer, and a flaky work experience girl (but no micro-managing, I-can't-say-it-wows-me Annabel). And I did okay.

Chapter Thirty-Nine

I wake up very early on Saturday morning after a restless night. It should be so simple, right? I just call Jack and tell him to take a hike. Of course, he says he's changed, but then hasn't he said that before?

The obvious thing to do is stay with Nick.

But Nick doesn't want a baby.

I pull my duvet over my head and let out a small scream. I need to talk this through with someone. I've been avoiding doing so because I'm all too well aware that Jack is hardly Mr Popular amongst my friends and family. Last night, when I saw *Nancy would like to FaceTime* flash up on my phone screen I found myself pressing *Sorry, I can't talk right now.*

But I know I have to speak to someone. I look at the clock and see that it's nearly 6 a.m., which means that Nancy will be fast asleep but my sister will have already been up for some time. I reach for the phone.

'Auntie Yinnie! Auntie Yinnie!' my nephews say, hurling themselves at my feet. I know they realize I'm good for a couple of Thomas the Tank Engine magazines and some chocolate buttons, but it's still flattering to get a welcome like that.

Rachel kisses me on the cheek. We go into the kitchen and it looks as if there's been a small nuclear explosion in there. Rachel is fixing one of the hinges on the kitchen cupboards.

She has a proper toolbox and everything. How did she grow up to be the competent one who owns things like a toolbox? I'm not sure I even have a screwdriver. 'So you said on the phone there was something you wanted to talk about?' she says. 'Me too, actually.'

'Well, you go first.'

'No. It's o . . .' She doesn't get to the 'kay' before bursting into tears.

'Rach,' I say putting my arm around her heaving shoulders. 'Whatever is the matter?'

'It's George and the biting. I know Mum said it was just a phase but it's happening all the time now. I got called into nursery yesterday to have a "chat". I've started avoided going to coffee mornings and soft play places and parks because I just can't face him sinking his teeth into some other kid and their mother treating me like I'm some kind of pariah.' A tear rolls off the end of her nose.

'Well, that's just crazy. He's so little still – he probably doesn't even understand what he's doing.'

'Try telling that to the mother whose kid is nursing a big bruise punctuated with little teeth marks. I got into a terrible row with this woman at Tumbletots the other day when I tried to tell her that her little angel had been provoking George. The worst thing was I was listening to myself and thinking that I've turned into exactly the sort of mother that I hate! The ones I've always been so rude about – the defensive type who comes to parents' evenings and tells you their kid is "just tired" when you're thinking he's on fast-track to Borstal.'

'Rach,' I say, stroking her arm. 'Come on – you need to get this in perspective. He's a lovely little boy. They both are. What does Paul think you should do?'

Her eyes flash with fury. 'Oh, don't talk to me about him! He thinks we ought to bite George back.'

'Really?'

She nods. 'Show him what it feels like.' She blows her nose on a Mr Men tissue. 'I thought I'd be a better mother than I am, Gin. I'm a teacher, for goodness' sake. I get paid to know how to look after kids.'

'You're a great mum.'

She shrugs. 'I'm okay. But I'm never as good as I want to be. I wake up thinking I'll be like Mum. I hardly ever remember her getting cross with us. Then within thirty-five seconds of the boys being out of bed, I've turned into Grumpy Impatient Mummy.'

'Rach. Stop it. You're brilliant. And George will grow out of this. You never hear of anyone getting kicked out of university for biting, do you?'

She laughs. 'S'pose not. I'll just have drugs and alcohol to worry about by then.' She pours some boiling water into the two mugs. 'Now, your turn . . .'

'Mumeeee, mumeee. Is we going to get the paddling pool out?'

'In a minute, sweetheart. I'm just going to make Auntie Ginny a cup of tea. Perhaps you'd like to watch a *Thomas* DVD?'

'No,' George and Felix chorus, 'we is hot!'

Rachel looks apologetically at me. 'It's fine,' I say, 'we'll talk later.'

But of course there is no later. First we have to blow up the paddling pool, then fill it with endless buckets of water (Rachel's neighbours are just the sort to report anyone who breaks the hosepipe ban), then help the boys change into swimshorts. Then get them out and dry them again, because we forgot suncream. Then distract them because they have to wait until the suncream soaks in a bit but they want to get back in the pool NOW.

★   ★   ★

Later, I am reading their bedtime story and George and Felix's warm pyjama-clad bodies are snuggled up against mine on the bed. George has started to rub his blanket under his nose and Felix's eyes keep closing for a second before he wrenches them open again. The smell of Johnson's baby shampoo and tiny boys is intoxicating.

'. . . And they all stood in the middle of the page and said, "Z is for Zebra."'

Rachel comes into the room. 'Time for—' She sees the boys have both fallen asleep on me and lowers her voice, 'Gosh! How did you do that?'

'I slipped some Ritalin into their milk.'

She grins. 'Let's get them tucked in and we can talk.'

I kiss George's sweaty mussed hair and stroke Felix's hot little cheek. 'No need. The boys have already answered my question.'

For something I've told myself countless times is the right decision, this is excruciating. The expression on Nick's face will be etched on my mind for a long time to come. He looks like I've punched him. Actually, he looks like someone much bigger and stronger than me has punched him, but you get the (not very pretty) picture.

'Sometimes I think people can be right for each other, but at the wrong time.'

He snorts derisively and gives me a look that makes me feel a lot smaller than five foot five. 'What the fuck does that mean?'

'Please . . .' I want to say 'don't be like that'. But how the hell do I expect him to be?

We are sitting side-by-side on the sofa. I say side-by-side; we are actually further apart than you'd imagine two people on a small sofa could possibly be. He gets up to leave. 'Right. Well, I'll be off then.'

'Nick—'

'What, Ginny? What more is there possibly to say? Let's be friends? No hard feelings? I don't think so.'

Suddenly I am desperate to explain myself. To tell him that it wasn't just Jack versus him and that I *need* to have a baby. But I promised myself beforehand that I wouldn't mention that. It just seems too cruel really after what happened with him and Mel. Yup, having children, or rather not having children, has wrecked yet another relationship for you!

He's heading for the door, and I have this urge to throw myself at his feet and say that I didn't mean it. And to come back, and never go away again. 'Nick—'

He turns around and looks at me. 'What?'

'I'm sorry.'

He shakes his head. 'Great.'

Chapter Forty

Weddings used to bring Jack out in hives. (Literally in the case of Brendan and Jenny's.) Now he talks about ours non-stop.

'Do you think that a hundred is a reasonable number? I mean once both sets of parents invite their list, that'll probably only leave us with about sixty. And, bearing in mind that everyone comes as a two. . . .'

I look at the super-shiny ring glinting on my left hand. The pear-shaped diamond with a streamlined platinum bezel setting. Quite the envy of the girls in the office. Even Fiona pronounced it 'frightfully pretty'. Jack is staring at me expectantly. 'I'm sure a hundred is fine.'

He scratches his head. 'You're probably right. Maybe we could invite more people for the evening do?'

'Maybe.' I stare at the ring. Telling my family and friends that I had not only got back together with Jack but was marrying him was not easy. 'Oh!' my parents said before pausing for what seemed like forever. 'Congratulations.'

Rachel and Nancy were less restrained. 'Are you sure?' 'After everything?'

Now everyone is acting pleased. I just wish I didn't know they were acting.

Jack's phone pings. 'Oh, bloody hell,' he says reading a text. 'Simon did his half-marathon in 1:42.'

This means nothing to me, except that I know it will have annoyed Jack greatly. Even though he and his best mate never actually run together, they're always in a race. He puts the phone down. 'I don't think we should go for a traditional cake. No one really likes fruitcake, do they?'

'Umm . . .' I am struggling to reconcile the words with the mouth they are coming out of. I never knew Jack cared about such things. And surely he's going to obsess a little more about Simon's half-marathon time?

'By the way, my mother wants to know if we're free three weeks on Saturday for an engagement dinner – the 20th of August.'

Jack used to have a problem making an arrangement more than about thirty seconds in advance.

'Oh no, wait,' he says. 'We can't make it on Saturday 20th August because that's the night Simon's pencilled for his engagement party.'

'Simon's getting married?'

'Yeah. Didn't I tell you?'

A little thought bobs into my mind: was peer pressure a factor in Jack's new-found commitment to commitment? No, the thought is preposterous. That would take Simon Says to a whole new level.

Jack kisses the tip of my nose. 'I love you, Ginny.'

I trace his jaw with my fingertips. I can't believe after all these years of pain, I've finally got my fairy-tale ending. I just wish I could relax and let myself enjoy it.

'I can't wait for you to be Mrs Powell.'

'Me neither.'

Jack and I are rowing about another couple's break-up. And not even a couple we know.

'I just think it's horrible washing your dirty linen in public like that,' I say. We are talking about an MP and his wife who have split up and are involved in a very public spat on Twitter.

'Oh, come on. It's the way things are. At least they both get to put forward their own sides of the story. He says she's been unfaithful, she says he's pushed her around. There's no such thing as a seemly silence nowadays.'

'You don't have to say "nowadays". I'm thirty-four, not ninety!'

Jack tssks. 'You're being silly. I'm just saying you can see why people would be tempted.'

'Yes. Well, you don't always have to give in to temptation do you?'

'What the hell's that supposed to mean?'

It was a cheap, childish snipe and I suddenly feel a rush of guilt because I promised not to keep mentioning 'it' if we were really going to move on. 'Sorry.'

He puts his arms around me. I bury my head in his chest and will myself to stop making trouble. Going back to Jack felt like a powerful reflex, so why isn't being back with him coming more naturally? 'Just promise me if we ever get divorced, you won't tweet about me.'

He kisses the top of my head. 'We're not going to get divorced.'

One of the strangest things about being back with Jack is that it feels both familiar and new at the same time. The frisson of a new relationship coupled with the familiarity of an old one.

Today, we're making Sunday brunch together and it's like a well-choreographed routine in which we both know our parts. He starts laying bacon on the grill pan, I get the eggs out of the fridge. I lay the table, he pours the orange juice.

'You know what's really making me worry about the wedding,' he suddenly says.

I start whisking the eggs. *Surely, we're not going to have the fruitcake conversation again?*

'My mum. It's going to be so hard for her having to be in seen in public with my dad after all these years. Particularly as he'll be there with my stepmother and my mum is on her own.'

I instantly feel guilty. Here's me thinking Jack was going to bang on about something trivial, when in fact he's just looking out for his mum.

I put down the bowl of eggs and put my arms around him.

'I'm actually considering not inviting him. I mean, my mum is the one who brought me and Tom up. She's the one who put calamine on our chicken pox scabs, made us do our homework, nursed us through exams and break-ups. My dad was nowhere really, even before he actually left. Too busy shagging around.'

I stroke his cheek, feeling a rush of sympathy for both the nine-year-old Jack his dad abandoned and the Jack who is standing in front of me right now.

He breaks away from me to take the bacon out from under the grill and flips it over.

I take this as my unspoken signal to start cooking the scrambled eggs.

'But he is my dad.'

I get the plates out of the cupboard, thinking how grateful I am that my parents are still together and I don't have any of this to deal with. How grateful that they've given me a template for what a good marriage looks like. 'It's really hard.'

'I think I'll talk to my mum. Make it clear that it might be our day but that I want her to be happy. That I know I owe her big time and if seeing him is going to be too hard for her, well then he doesn't get to come.'

I squeeze his hand and he kisses the top of my head. 'The bacon is ready. How are the eggs?'

'Ready.'

He smiles. 'We make a great team.'

'Babe,' Jack says, 'can you just get your head out of that note-book for one minute? We really need to make a decision on what canapes we want. If the wedding is at four, people are going to be hungry by that stage and they'll need something to soak up the booze . . . On the other hand, we don't want them filling up too much before the proper meal. Babe?' His voice is wheedling and irritated now.

'Sorry,' I say, forcing myself to look up. 'I just had an idea for a short story. I have to scribble it down before it goes out of my head.' I run my fingers over the pages of the notebook. It's one of the ones Nick bought me. I like the way the paper feels under my skin.

Jack has a wearied expression; one that tells you he is exhib-iting great patience. 'You know I'm very supportive of your writing, babe. It's just there's so much to do at the moment.'

'I know,' I say, trying to sound conciliatory. When am I going to tell Cassie I'm marrying Jack? It's ages since I last saw her. This evening I hovered outside her door for several minutes wondering whether I should knock. But then I walked away telling myself I was respecting her wishes and not just taking the easy option.

'Perhaps you could put the writing on a back burner for now?' Jack says. 'Go back to it once we've got the wedding out of the way?'

I snap the notebook shut. 'I was just jotting down a couple of sentences, Jack. Not writing the next *War and Peace*!'

'Well if you're going to be like that,' he says flouncing off into the bathroom and slamming the door behind him. Jack is a six-foot-four rugby-loving, beer-drinking, guys type of guy, yet I swear this wedding is turning him into Bridezilla.

Chapter Forty-One

The lift doors are just about to close when Fiona's cut-crystal vowels instruct me to hold the doors. She steps in. 'What a day!' she says, rolling her eyes. 'New client at Chocolicious. Dreadful little man who's decided he hates us without even giving us a bloody chance. Putting the business up for review.'

My stomach lurches. Chocolicious is one of the agency's biggest accounts. If it goes, there will definitely be redundancies. I've been finding myself checking Hootsuite before I even get out of bed every morning to see if there have been any news stories about my clients overnight, thinking of pitches in the shower, humming Dolly Parton's 'Nine To Five' to myself as I walk to work (yes, I know, embarrassing). I've been enjoying my job. Really enjoying it. And now I'm about to lose it. I'm going back to the days of being too scared to open the post.

The lift doors open.

Fiona's clear blue eyes fix on mine. 'Don't—' Her mobile starts ringing from inside her expensive-looking handbag. 'Hullo. No, not under the grill, in the oven. For an hour. Well, no, it won't be ready by the time you want to go to hockey. Because I didn't know you were going to bloody hockey. Put it in the microwave. Yes. But don't forget to prick it with a fork.'

I stand there shuffling from foot to foot. What is the correct etiquette here? Listen to your boss's personal conversation or leave when they were in the middle of talking to you?

Fiona sighs. 'In the fridge. Really, Rupes, you manage millions of pounds of other people's money, this . . .'

I decide to beat a retreat and give Fiona a little wave. She smiles and rolls her eyes heavenwards as she starts to explain that you have to press the big circular button right in the middle of the microwave to set the time.

It's late enough for rush hour to have been and gone so I get a seat on the tube and sink into it gratefully. I had been planning to check in on Cassie tonight. Decided that she may well have told me to leave her alone but the least I can do – the *least* – is check in on her occasionally. Now though, all I can think about is the prospect of losing my job. Since I've been at Impact, I haven't googled other jobs once. When I was a Splash that used to be an almost daily activity. And not just PR jobs either. When my friend Hannah told me they were hiring at the management consultancy she works at, I spent a whole morning thinking that maybe management consultancy would be for me. Then I remembered Hannah telling me about a clothing guidelines email she received when she joined which stipulated that women must wear tights at all times. At that point, I'd known that the corporate environment just wasn't for me. Not because of some dark childhood experience with hosiery, you understand, just because it would bug the hell out of me being TOLD I had to wear tights when it was ninety degrees outside.

By the time I come out at Camden Town, I feel sick with worry. All around me, people are chatting and laughing. It's all right for you, I want to shout.

What was Fiona going to say to me? *Don't worry, I think we can keep the business? Don't say a word about this to anyone?*

I walk up Parkway with leaden limbs. Summer, so good up until this point, has suddenly got bored and disappeared and now it's grey and chilly. My mobile rings and Jack's name flashes up. Great. I can't wait to get the whole Chocolicious thing off my chest.

'Simon's having fireworks,' Jack says, skipping the 'hello, how are you' part of the conversation.

'What?' I say.

'He's having fireworks at his engagement party. I've seen them lots of times at weddings but never at an engagement party.'

I am struggling to see why this information should be in any way important.

'Do you think we're going too low-key with ours?' Jack says. 'I'm going to talk to Mum and se—'

'We don't have to have bloody fireworks just because Simon is.'

Jack tssks. 'No, of course not. In fact, we definitely wouldn't want fireworks now because that's what they're having. I just wonder if we should up the ante a little.'

I grip the phone a little tighter. 'Jack, I haven't had a very good day.'

'Oh. Why?'

'Chocolicious is up for review. It's one of our biggest accounts. If it goes there are bound to be redundancies, and if there are redundancies, I'm bound to be a casualty. I've been really enjoying it there. More than I ever would have imagined actually. And the thought of being out of work again is horrible.'

'You might not lose the account,' Jack says. 'And even if you do, you might not lose your job. So, there's no point worrying. Now, do you think it's a mistake having the party at Mum's house? Would booking an outside venue give it more wow factor?'

A burger packet swirls up in the wind and wraps itself around my ankle. Jack's right that there is no point worrying

237

about Chocolicious. But I just wish he hadn't changed the subject quite so quickly.

The next morning, everyone at work seems to be particularly chipper. Ben is telling everyone a story about his ill-fated 'booze and cruise' night out. Don't you know we're all dead men walking, I feel like saying as he reaches his crescendo and peals of laughter bounce around the cubicles.

Jacqui has bought Danish pastries from the deli on the corner 'just because she loves us all'. I cram a corner of one in my mouth and chew it joylessly. A death row breakfast.

Georgia gets off the phone. 'I can't believe I've just booked a circus troupe and a string quartet. That's what I love about this job, it's completely bloody bonkers!'

At morning conference, I wonder if Fiona looks paler than usual or whether that's just my imagination. She tells everyone about the review. She is confident we can keep the business. She has a meeting with Darren Grant (the 'dreadful little man', I assume) in two weeks' time and we have until then to come up with something really fantastic.

We talk about other things on other accounts but everyone now has the air of those blokes you see at wedding receptions who are pretending to listen to the speeches whilst checking the football score on their phones.

We file out of the room. One lone pastry is left in the open box. 'Anyone want this Danish?' Jacqui says. 'It's a custard one.'

No one wants it.

We are brainstorming ideas for Chocolicious and I am considerably less than storming. In fact, I seem to have no ideas whatsoever. My mind is one big blank page (just as it was last night when I was trying to do my writing course homework). I pop a Chocolicious truffle in my mouth hoping for inspiration. It fails to provide any. As did the orange cream and the praline.

Jacqui suggests getting a celebrity as a brand ambassador (PR speak for someone who's paid to say they like the product).

Fiona scrunches her brow. 'The trouble is, with these budgets, we'd probably only get a Z-lister.'

More ideas are suggested and discarded.

I will my brain to kick into action but all I can think about is having to go back to job-hunting again. So, why were you in your last job such a short time? Oh, it was nothing to do with me. I was doing well there. REALLY.

The meeting shudders to a conclusion.

'Ginny,' Fiona says.

This is it. The 'last in, first out, it's nothing personal' speech.

'Gemma from Pasta La Vista was singing your praises to me the other day. She's thrilled with the way you've got their SEO up and she loves that whole Twitter thing you've got going.'

'Really?' I say. Gemma is the senior client at Pasta La Vista. I thought she was barely even aware of my existence.

'Yah.'

A spark of pride rises up inside me.

'So jolly well done.'

And then I realize. Fiona is being extra kind because she knows I'm going to be joining the dole queue any minute now. The spark is snuffed out.

Chapter Forty-Two

It's the slippers I recognize first. Gold, Moroccan sequinned slippers. So Cassie. Except when she's wearing them in Londis. I have popped in to grab myself something for supper, when I spot the slippers across the frozen foods aisle. I look up to see Cassie. She has bare legs, blotchy from the cold, and a crumpled raincoat, at the bottom of which you can see two inches of nightie. She doesn't see me. She is in the mode where she doesn't really see anything. She is crying. The tears are streaming down her face like her eyes have sprung a leak.

I put my hand on her arm. 'Cass.' The fluorescent lighting buzzes overhead. It's too harsh and unforgiving for such raw misery.

She looks at me and her mouth struggles to find words.

A middle-aged woman with a pale, pinched face and a thin mouth is staring at us. Staring in the same way that George and Felix stared at the one-armed man in the park the other day. Except the woman is not three years old. It's all I can do not to start screaming at her. Wanna watch crazy? I'll show you crazy!

I get Cassie home and put her to bed. Sit with her while she continues to weep. I feel helpless. And so, so angry with myself. Because I just abandoned her when she needed me most. And I can tell myself that I was doing what she wanted

241

me to do, but the truth is it was all too easy to walk away from something so scary, to wrap myself up in my own life and say there was nothing I could do. Hell, if I'm being 100 per cent honest, part of me was avoiding the tongue-lashing I'd have got for going back to Jack. What kind of a shabby reason is that?

I stare at the tiny gold slippers that lie discarded in the corner. They are soaked through from the rain and splattered with mud. I remember teasing her about how only she could look so glamorous in slippers.

She had gone out to buy cigarettes. The only thing powerful enough to drive her from her refuge today was her need for nicotine. She didn't even have her purse with her.

Her body convulses with misery. I stroke her back. I ask her if something has happened and she shakes her head.

Eventually she stops crying and goes to sleep. I creep out of her dark apartment and go up to my own. I do not turn on the lights. I lie on my bed.

Now it's my turn to cry and cry.

They say the best ideas are obvious ones and for the life of me I don't know why I didn't think of enlisting Meg's help with her sister before. She lives in one of the big houses on Chalcot Crescent with the huge bay windows that seem to beg for a Christmas tree. I stand outside and take a deep breath going over what I need to say in my mind. The front door is pillar-box red and has a lion door knocker.

Meg opens the door wearing a worn expression and a big slubby greeny-brown smock. I suddenly remember Cassie's jibe about her thinking she was deep because she has a bad haircut and a penchant for dodgy clothes. How I long to hear that catty humour again.

'Ginny,' she says, giving me a not-quite smile. 'This is a surprise.'

We go into the kitchen and she offers me a choice of camomile, green or nettle tea, the latter of which is apparently home-brewed. My mind flashes back to my uni days when the boys in our house used to make beer in the bath. How simple life seemed then.

While the kettle boils I ask Meg how she and the kids are.

'The kids are good. Bouncing off the walls and killing each other basically. So, normal! David and I have just told them he's working away at the moment . . .' Her voice trails off. She rubs at her temples. 'You didn't come here to hear about my problems though, did you?'

'No. Well, I'm sorry to hear things aren't easier. I wanted to talk to you about Cassie.'

'Cassie?'

'I think she's depressed. By which I mean suffering from depression rather than just sad.' One thing that's struck me recently is how misused the word 'depressed' is – people talk of being depressed about the weather or the rubbish that's on TV.

Meg takes a sip of her camomile tea but says nothing.

'I found her in the corner shop last night. She was a bit . . . upset. She's stopped going out, even to her yoga. She doesn't see anyone. And I think she often just stays in bed all day.'

Meg still says nothing. I guess this is a lot to take in.

'Also – and I don't want to frighten you – she's even talked about not seeing the point of carrying on. Of ending it all.'

Meg snorts. 'Yes, well, she's always been an attention-seeker. She ran away from home aged six because my mother refused to buy her white patent party shoes.'

I stare at her, utterly lost for words.

'Look, Ginny, I'll speak frankly. You seem like a nice girl.

Why you've got yourself mixed up with my sister confounds me, and if you want my advice, you'll stay well away from her.'

My mouth opens and closes but no words come out. The tears that were threatening to leak out of Meg's eyes when she was talking about her children have been sucked back in and her pale grey eyes are flinty once more. 'She helped you when you needed her recently.'

Meg snorts. 'Well that was a first, I can tell you.'

'Look, I'm telling you your sister has been threatening to commit suicide.'

She swats the air. 'She's a DRAMA QUEEN! Why do you think she became an actress?'

I stare into my camomile tea, which is even less appetizing than it was in the first place.

'Don't you worry about Cassie,' Meg says, as she closes the door. 'She can look after herself.'

I am left standing on the doorstep wishing I could believe that.

'I thought I told you to leave me alone.' I think there's the tiniest flicker of being pleased to see me in Cassie's eyes but I might be imagining it.

'I got you a present.' I hand her the brown paper bag containing the box of St John's Wort. 'Lots of people on the internet claim it works wonders.' Lots of people said it was completely useless too but I don't mention that.

'What's wrong with flowers or chocolates?' she asks, and I'm so relieved to see the hint of a smile at the corner of her lips. 'Do you want a coffee?'

'Yeah, but not one of your disgusting ones,' I say. 'Let's go down to The Tea Room. We can walk through the park.'

'So you can tick "fresh air" and "exercise" off your list too?'

I laugh. 'Maybe.'

'Do I have to get dressed?'

'I think it might be an idea. Unless you want people to think you're the local loony.'

'I *am* the local loony.'

I sit on the sofa waiting for her to get dressed. The curtains are still drawn and I itch to open them. On the side there's a note Shane must have pushed under the door.

Called round but you were out. Give me a ring. Shane x

When Cassie comes back, she is wearing kneed leggings and a big jumper. Her hair is still unbrushed and she's devoid of make-up. In her hands are a pair of huge sunglasses. Cassie having her sunglasses permanently welded to her face inside and out used to get on my nerves – it seemed diva-like and rude – but now I'm just grateful she still cares enough to reach for them.

'It looks like it might rain,' she says, pulling back the curtain a little.

'It's lovely out there.' This is not entirely true. The hot weather we've had so much of recently now feels like a distant memory and, this afternoon, the sky is the colour of a bruise. Which sort of sucks because I'm on the verge of getting Cassie to leave the house. If anyone needs sunshine right now it's her.

'I'm actually kind of tired.' She looks as if she's on the verge of tears.

'Just to The Tea Room.'

She sighs and pulls on a pair of boots. 'You're so bossy.'

As we walk through Regent's Park, I tell her, 'I took my nephews out for a walk the other day. It took us about an hour to get to the end of the road because we had to stop and inspect minutely every cigarette butt, used tissue, spat-out piece of gum and dead insect.'

'So taking the depressive out is a breeze.'

'A walk in the park.'

She doesn't laugh. 'I should have brought a jacket.'

I think back to the walk with George and Felix. Getting out of the door seemed to be a gargantuan effort and then when we'd finally done it and got as far as the front gate, George remembered he'd forgotten Diver Man. Apparently, we could not go for a walk without Diver Man. 'Here, take my cardigan. I'm too hot anyway.'

The old Cassie would probably refuse my cardigan on the grounds that it didn't go with what she was wearing. The new Cassie puts it on.

Cassie's mobile rings and she fishes it out of her pocket, sees Shane's name flash up and presses decline.

'Don't you want to talk to him?'

She sighs. 'I've told you, Ginny, I don't want to talk to anyone.'

I ignore the unspoken 'you included'. 'Have you thought about CBT? Or self-help groups—'

'Please, Ginny.'

We walk along in silence, me hoping that the sun will magically appear and seep through Cassie's skin.

I try to cheer Cassie up with a reference to her arch-nemesis. 'I saw Marina in the street the other day. She looked like she's put on more weight.' It's a cheap trick and not even true. Marina didn't look an ounce heavier. But I'm desperate to goad Cassie into saying the former Bond girl wouldn't get the famous red bikini past her knees now. I never thought I'd long for her bitchy jokes. Some small sign that the personality files haven't been wiped. Or that something might be funny.

A spaniel puppy darts in front of us. One woman on an online support group said her husband who had battled severe depression had really been helped by them getting a puppy. That said, it's hard to imagine Cassie with a pooper-scooper.

I fiddle with the button on my shirt. One of the things that was keeping me away from Cassie was not wanting to get into any sort of conversation about me being back with Jack. Now I realize that was crazy, because Cassie doesn't care about anything at the moment. Including herself.

Chapter Forty-Three

There are many things I like better about Impact than Splash. Let's start with the big one – there's no Annabel. People here seem to rate me (see point one). I've been given a wide variety of accounts to work on (see point one). There's a Friday chocolate cart here where they hand out free chocolate (the lack of free confectionery at Splash was probably nothing to do with Annabel, but let's blame her anyway).

This Friday, as Antonia edges into view with the chocolate cart, I feel even more pleased to see it than usual. I have spent the afternoon trying and failing to come up with great ideas for Chocolicious and am in desperate need of sugary comfort. (And, yes, I am aware of the irony!)

Ben makes a dive for the last packet of Maltos but I'm quicker to the grab.

He raises his hands in surrender. 'I know better than to fight a woman for chocolate!' He glances at the shots from the Vintage Linens shoot which are laid out on my desk. 'They look good.'

I smile. 'Yup. No one would believe that the photographer was murderous and half cut.' Sophie phoned me this morning to say how delighted she was with the photos. She laughed as she told me how her assistant had admired the beautiful throw.

'Do you want a coffee?' Ben says, taking a bite of his Nutz bar.

'I can't believe I stole the last packet of Maltos and now you're offering to make me coffee!'

He laughs. 'Neither can I. The chocolate cart must have put me in a good mood!'

Something drops into place in my brain. 'Ben,' I say, kissing him on the cheek. 'I think I love you.'

'It's genius,' Fiona says.

'Well, not really . . .'

'Ginny.' The voice is Head Girl Firm. 'It's frightfully dull when people can't take a compliment.' She places her chin on her hands and I am momentarily distracted by her engagement ring. I told Nancy the diamonds were the size of broad beans, but now I wonder if that was conservative. 'I'd like you to come to the meeting with me.'

'Me?'

Fiona laughs. 'Yah, you. It's your idea, isn't it?'

Chapter Forty-Four

Does it matter that we don't have a song? A track for our first dance that was always going to be.

Jack is in the bathroom humming 'Let's Stay Together', which is one of the ones he suggested earlier, and I am lying on the bed thinking that, although I have no problem with Al Green, it isn't 'our song'. And why don't we have one?

'I took a couple of photos of The Orangery on my phone. It's incredible! Simon wanted it for his wedding, but it's booked up that weekend, haha. Anyway, have a look and see what you think, and then maybe we can check it out together.' I hear the sound of his electric toothbrush, but then he switches it off again. 'We ought to book a venue as soon as we can. The good ones get very booked up . . .'

I roll over and pick up Jack's iPhone. The Orangery is pure wedding photographer portfolio fodder. 'It's lovely.'

Jack's reply sounds positive in tone although it's largely unintelligible through a mouthful of toothpaste.

I'm just about to put the phone back on the bedside table when, without really thinking about it, I scroll up through the images. Right at the top is one that nearly makes me drop the phone. It's a teeny tiny thumbnail, but it's also unmistakably Annabel. And even at this size, I can see she's wearing very little and that it's a video. My breath catches in my throat. I am just about to press the little arrow to start

251

playing it when I hear the shower being switched off. I quickly email the video to myself instead, and then scrabble to put Jack's phone back on the bedside table. I want to watch this on my own before confronting him.

When he comes out of the bathroom, he's talking about The Orangery's garden and how spectacular it looks with all the different coloured lights at night.

I go into the bathroom, locking the door behind me. I sit on the edge of the bath feeling sick. I can hardly bear to press the play arrow, but I do. And there is Annabel – stripping slowly and then masturbating whilst telling Jack what she would like him to do to her. I watch in horrified fascination, my brain flooded with about three thousand different thoughts at once. When did she send this to Jack? Why has he kept it? Why does she have to look porn-star hot, damn her? (Sort of olive-green underwear this time, for the brief period of time it's on. I really must review my black, white and nude only policy.)

When I asked Jack when it had ended between him and Annabel, he told me there had been nothing to end. That it had been 'just sex'. As if 'just sex' was like 'just a cup of tea'.

I don't know how long I stay in the bathroom. When I come out, Jack is sitting on the bed wearing just a towel, looking at more photos of The Orangery on his phone. 'The purple light on the water looks amazing doesn—'

'Not watching your videos of Annabel?'

His brows scrunch.

'Oh, don't give me your innocent face! I may have been fooled by it in the past but not now.' He is still wearing a cartoonish expression of non-comprehension. 'I found the video of Annabel on your phone, idiot! The one of her . . . pleasuring herself!' I'm not sure where that phrase came from. The last thing I want at the moment is to sound like some elderly nun. 'Kept it for posterity, did you?' I am shouting now. Jarielle will be able to hear every word but I'm too angry to care.

Jack tries to put his arms around me but I shake him off. 'I'm so sorry you had to see that, Ginny. I thought I'd deleted it ages ago.'

'Oh yeah?'

'Yes.'

'I think you kept it because you like watching it! For all I know, you could even still be seeing her in your spare time.'

'How can you say that?'

My whole body is shaking now. 'Oh no! You do NOT get to play the wounded party here!'

He has the decency to look slightly chastened. 'I really am so sorry you had to see that video. But, do you think if I had anything to hide, I'd have told you to look at my phone? I've said it before and I'll say it again: Annabel is nothing to me. She never was. It's *you* I want to spend the rest of my life with, *you* I want to have my babies.'

Hot tears start to prick the back of my eyes.

He reaches out and pulls me towards him. 'Trust me.'

Chapter Forty-Five

'This is the garden centre where I was arrested.'

It's not a good start really. I turn the ignition on, deciding to go somewhere else. It's not very likely that anyone at the garden centre will remember Cassie's statue-throwing days, but I can do without any curve balls.

Sunlight streams through the car windows. Cassie is having a 'good day' today, by which I mean she is not crying and has agreed – with a little bit of nagging – to leave the house. My time on the internet has taught me that Cassie has moderate depression. I never want to see severe.

'Remind me why we're doing this?'

She never wants to do anything nowadays. I imagine Triyoga's profits have plummeted. 'You'll enjoy it when we get there.' (This is almost certainly a lie. I've become a regular little Pinocchio recently.) I read a very inspiring book by a woman who suffered from severe depression and found gardening to be massively therapeutic. She talked movingly about the connection with nature, the simple comfort of your hands in the earth, the joy of nurturing something. I thought about Cassie's garden, which used to be immaculate when it was tended by Carmen's husband but now looks sad and neglected.

Jack wasn't too pleased with me spending the whole Saturday with Cassie when we have a wedding plan.

'She needs me,' I explained.

'*I* need you.' His voice sounded whiney, and I had to remind myself those are the words I spent years longing to hear.

We pull up outside West Hampstead garden centre. As far as I know, Cassie has never left here in handcuffs.

'I'm not interested in gardening. It's for old people, and I don't admit to being old.'

A hint of humour. My heart soars. 'Just think how nice it will be to transform that tangled mass of weeds and brambles into something lovely. We can plant jasmine, lavender, peonies . . .' I trail off, suddenly unable to think of any other plants. Truth is, as my history with houseplants proves, I'm not exactly Mrs Green Fingers myself.

We are in 'Patio Favourites' when I notice Cassie is standing frozen to the spot staring at a very young, very beautiful girl with a walking stick and a prosthetic leg.

'I have no right to be depressed.'

I put my hand on her arm. 'It doesn't work like that.' We're standing by a bank of vibrant purple-blue hydrangeas with almost indecent amounts of fat blooms. I run my fingers across one plant's smooth green leaves. 'I love hydrangeas, don't you?' Cassie shrugs.

'Can I help you?' says a weather-beaten man in a green sweatshirt. His sparkly eyes are surrounded by deeply etched lines.

'We're new to gardening. We need to buy some plants we can't kill.' That's rule number one: I want to help brighten Cassie's outlook, and it can't be very uplifting to look out onto reproachful brown corpses.

'Hydrangeas are good. So are buddleia. Hostas. As long as you stop the slugs getting to them.'

I don't want to think about the slugs. I have enough obstacles in my way without adding slimy creatures into the equation.

'Are you cooks? Mint grows like a weed.'

I suddenly have a vision of a beautifully tended vegetable plot. Neat little rows of carrots and potatoes. Runner beans snaking up their canes. (Can't believe I know they have canes!) We can nourish our bodies as well as our souls.

Or maybe we could plant spring bulbs? I used to do that with my mum when I was little. Spring flowers would be great for Cassie. Little green heads bursting through the cold hard soil to announce the arrival of spring and its longer, light-filled days. New life, new hope! Sunny trumpet-shaped daffodils. Fragrant hyacinths. Bluebells to make our very own little woodland patch!

'Ah,' the man says, when I ask him about spring bulbs. 'It's still a bit early for them. That's something to do come autumn.'

Cassie has wandered off. It's a good job I've been taking my nephews out a lot recently as it's provided excellent training for looking after Cassie. She even asks me if we're nearly there yet two minutes after getting into the car.

'I've got to find my friend. Thanks for the advice.'

Cassie is looking at the orange, yellow and green dreadlocks of an ornamental pepper plant.

'Like that one?' I pick it up and put it into my trolley.

'How's horrible Jack?'

'I do wish you wouldn't call him that, Cass. I am marrying him.' For a second, the words 'marrying him' make me feel like a little kid playing at being a grown-up. But I'm sure everyone feels like that occasionally when they're first engaged. And Jack has been nicer than ever since our row about the Annabel video. I just wish I could convince Cassie of how much he's changed. 'You should have seen how sweet and considerate he was worrying about how his mum was going to deal with seeing his dad at the wedding.'

'Hmm. Allegedly, Hitler was kind to animals.'

'Cassie!' I have to cut her some slack because she's depressed, and I suspect she knows this. I also suspect she'd say exactly the same thing if she wasn't depressed.

'Nick sounded lovely.'

'You never even met Nick. How about some lavender?' I pick up a pot.

Cassie shrugs. She is part toddler and part teenager at the moment. 'Smells of old ladies' knicker drawers.'

I put the pot in my trolley. 'Maybe that's what I'm aiming for. Oooh look, jasmine. You love jasmine, don't you?'

The shoulders lift again. She doesn't love anything right now. I put the jasmine in my trolley. I imagine Cassie and I out in her garden next summer, glass of white wine in one hand, watering can in the other. Butterflies fluttering all around. Her depression a distant memory. Because people do get better. Except the ones . . . best not to go there.

I have to say the £72.50 bill doesn't do much to lift my mood but I remind myself of the rewards and hand over my credit card.

Cassie is quiet in the car. I force myself not to fill the gaps with chatter. Apparently, one mustn't always try to cheer someone up even though the need to do so feels as if it's ingrained. I flick the radio on and the car is filled with Lady Gaga. Cassie makes a face so I switch to Classic FM but the piece they're playing is like a funeral dirge. I switch it off.

I give Cassie a couple of very light bags to carry. She was never robust at the best of the times, and now looks as if she might snap in half if you hugged her too tightly. I worry that she doesn't eat and try to take her food that will tempt her. Usually it just festers in the fridge until I throw it out.

She says she's too tired to garden now, that she needs to lie down. I feel a prickle of irritation. I have got myself into trouble with my fiancé (truly a horrible word) over this. Spent £72.50 on plants that need to be planted. But then you wouldn't complain if someone with flu said they couldn't weed and prune, so I start work alone. I will do the preparation and then, when Cassie has had a rest, she can do the nice bits. There is a thick tangle of weeds and brambles. I pull at some weeds, which come out fairly easily, but the brambles offer more resistance and I shred my arms to pieces on them. I should have bought some gardening gloves but we were in the queue by the time I thought of those. I struggle to get my spade into the soil, which is like concrete.

By the time Cassie comes out, my back is stiff and sore and my fingers are covered in cuts, yet I have only cleared the tiniest patch. 'It's going to take a bit longer than I thought. Still, it'll be a project.' Cassie looks at me blankly. The flicker of light that was in her eyes this morning seems to have been extinguished. On the other hand, she is out here, not curled in a ball in her dark bedroom. 'Would you like to plant the hydrangea?'

'No.'

'Well, pass it to me, then, would you?'

Cassie's eyes flit to the plant and then slowly, as if she's moving through treacle, she picks it up and starts coming towards me. Then, suddenly, her movements go from languid to fast as she trips on the edge of a loose paving stone, flies through the air and lands flat on her face on the ground. The plastic plant pot splits in half with the impact, and the hydrangea lands on the ground where it breaks in two.

Now it is me that is in slow motion. I see Cassie on the ground and will her not to be hurt badly. I kneel on the floor beside her. She is whimpering like an animal. There is a thick gash on her forehead and dark red blood is oozing into her eye. I try to remind myself that head wounds bleed a lot, look worse than they are. Her leggings are ripped on one knee and she has a big graze which is encrusted with dirt and gravel. 'My shoulder,' she says, amidst short, tiny sobs.

I get her inside and dab at her head with some antiseptic.

For a doctor's daughter, I'm pretty squeamish. Cotton wool pad after cotton wool pad turn from white to crimson. 'I think I need to get you to a hospital. I don't think I can do this on my own.'

The next morning, I try to rescue what's left of the hydrangea. I pick up the two sorry-looking halves and start to dig a hole.

Cassie's shoulder was just badly bruised and she got away with a few butterfly stitches in her forehead. 'Don't worry, it shouldn't leave a scar,' the doctor said. Cassie just stared at her blankly and I had to look away because suddenly the realization that Cassie didn't care about scarring – Cassie! – was just too much to bear.

The soil is hard and resistant and the hole barely seems to be getting any bigger.

I was crazy to start with this gardening stuff. I don't know when is the right time to plant things; I haven't tested the pH of my soil; I don't know a hibiscus from a hellebore. Jack says I shouldn't worry about it, that if I really want to sort out Cassie's garden for her, we'll tackle it together next summer. We'll be married by then, have more free time. I can't imagine Jack picking up a pair of secateurs. I know he'd like me to give up on Cassie too. 'Hasn't she got family?'

I pull my jacket tighter around me. Some days I want to give up on her. The days when she's mean and spiteful and tells me I'm an idiot to marry Jack and that I'll never write a book or do anything with him because men like that take up all the oxygen in the room and suddenly your dreams have been stolen from you. 'You don't mean that,' I say. She rolls her eyes. 'There is no "nice Cassie" underneath,' she says.

Some days she's almost like she was when I first knew her and she makes me laugh until my stomach hurts. Those are the days I think I could never walk away from her. On those days, we talk about the depression as if it's happening to someone else – logically and calmly. I ask her why she thinks she was okay when the whole social media storm was at its peak and then crashed months later, seemingly for no reason. She shrugs. Depression defies such neatness. One person could go through all manner of life-shaking traumas and never become depressed, another could seem to have it all and need to be sectioned to prevent them taking their own life.

Cassie has mentioned 'ending it all' less recently. I try to take some comfort in this. She still has bad days though. On Tuesday, I was a heartbeat away from sending the Jehovah's Witnesses who came to my door to see her. Maybe her answers were in *The Watchtower*? Then the voice of old Cassie rang in my ears. 'Why go to heaven when hell is where all the fun guys hang out?'

I reach out and touch the broken hydrangea. *Please*, I think, *get better*.

Chapter Forty-Six

An hour from now is the meeting with Darren Grant at Chocolicious. I have burned my ear with my hair straighteners, squirted foundation over my white shirt and discovered that the shoes I wanted to wear are still at the re-heelers which is in the opposite direction to the one I'm going in. Things can only get better, I tell myself.

Then Fiona calls. Her car has broken down on the way home from the 'cun-tree'. Rupes is calling the breakdown people now but there is no way she will be back in London in time for our meeting. Would I start without her?

Start without you? I want to scream. *ARE YOU TOTALLY MAD?* 'Wouldn't it be better to re-schedule?' I suggest, trying desperately to sound calmer than I feel.

'No, no,' Fiona, says briskly. 'Darren Grant is not a man you re-schedule on. Hold on a minute, can you, Ginny? Rupert, there's really no point in losing your temper like that. The breakdown people aren't going to pull out all the stops for a ranting, foul-mouthed lunatic.'

I rub my singed ear feeling desolate.

'I've got to go,' Fiona says. 'I'll be there as soon as I can. And, in the meantime, don't worry. You'll be fine.'

'You want me to give away my product for free? Every Friday? At train stations all around the country?'

A muscle is pulsing in Darren Grant's cheek. 'That's your big idea?'

A wave of nausea wells up inside me.

He laughs. It's not a laugh of amusement. He takes a sip of tea from his Chelsea FC mug and makes a kind of smacking sound with his lips.

'We thought we'd get the people giving out the free chocolate dressed up almost like old fashioned cigarette girls,' I say. 'A sort of 1940s, vintage type look. Only we'd have cigarette boys as well as girls. Wouldn't want to be sexist!' I glance up, suddenly acutely aware that sexism is probably not a big concern of Darren Grant's. And that I am babbling. 'Anyway, a 1940s feel.'

'What, so my brand looks really old-fashioned? Is that what they teach you girls at PR school nowadays.'

There's a sneer in his voice I really don't like, a heavy emphasis on the way he says 'girls' as if I'm not actually a grown woman.

I take a deep breath. 'No . . .' I feel like I might be sick. 'Umm . . . umm . . .' Everything I wanted to say seems to have deserted me. I dig my nails into my palms and think of something Cassie once said to me about difficult people: *Darling, if you can deal with me, you can deal with anyone.* I look at Darren. He has a very shiny head. 'It would get people to try the brand, create a warm feeling towards it and generate a lot of coverage.'

'It's going to cost me a pretty packet. Giving away my product for free.'

I think of getting Cassie to make the practice meal for *Celebrity Come Dine With Me* all those months ago. Remember how I wondered if I had overstepped the mark when I told her to stop whining. 'Oh, come on. I'm asking you to give away some of your own product. We're not talking about a big cost here in PR terms.' Darren Grant's eyes bulge alarmingly.

'Plus, you wouldn't have to do it for that long. Six months of Free Chocolate Fri-yays should be quite enough.'

Darren says nothing. He scratches his neck, revealing a flash of a tattoo beneath his collar.

I take a sip of water to help free my tongue from where it is sticking to the roof of my mouth. 'We thought we could build large models of a chocolate truffle to be central hubs.'

Darren looks at me. 'Aren't they just going to look like giant turds?'

Maybe job-hunting will be easier this time round? Let's face it, my CV hasn't had a chance to get too out-of-date. And I think Fiona will give me a good reference.

She bursts into the room now. She looks, by Fiona standards, slightly frazzled (so, like me on a good day).

'Four by four break down taking the kids to school?' Darren says.

Fiona smiles. 'I'm so sorry to be late. I'm sure Ginny has been looking after you—'

Darren laughs. 'You make 'er sound like a hooker.'

Fiona starts to take off her coat.

'Don't bother,' Darren says, raising his hand.

I stare at a stain on the horrible grey carpet tiles, willing myself not to cry.

'I'll give it a go.' Darren says. 'Your free chocolate idea. It sounds a bit like bollocks to me, but who knows? Make sure the hubs don't look like turds though.'

As soon as we get outside, Fiona hugs me. 'Well done!'

'I thought he was going to fire us,' I say.

'Me too,' Fiona says, laughing. 'Bloody well done!'

Chapter Forty-Seven

Marnie, the woman in the wedding shop, must think I'm a hideous brat. I am standing in front of the mirror wearing a couple of grands' worth of organza and I look like a sulky teenager who has been made to wear the dodgy jumper their granny knitted them for Christmas.

'I love this one,' she says through a mouthful of pins. 'The way it drapes, the slight train . . . Just wait until your mother and sister see you.'

I try to smile. And remind myself that this is what I wanted. And that I should be happy.

'Lots of brides get the jitters before the big day,' she says.

That's what this is – pre-wedding jitters!

'Just a couple more pins.'

I can hear my mum and Rachel chattering outside the changing room. They have had a month to come to terms with the idea of this wedding and are doing their very best to be excited about it. Nancy is just the same. When we FaceTime now, she even tells me to say 'hi' to Jack, although I can't help noticing her voice lacks conviction.

Marnie opens the door of the changing room and out I step.

My mum gasps. 'Oh, Gin, you look beautiful!'

My sister who can't believe her luck, because not only has she got a child-free Saturday afternoon, but she gets to play with sparkly things. She puts down the tiara she's fiddling with. 'You really do.'

It's a very smart wedding shop. One where you have to make a prior appointment just to look around.

Rachel pushes a diamante slide into my hair.

'Ouch!'

'Are you wearing a veil?' my mum asks.

'I don't know.' Should I know? Is not knowing if you're wearing a veil like not having a song?

'I love that one,' Rachel says, 'but I'd like to see you in the oyster-coloured one with the lace.'

'The Cecilia,' Marnie says, picking it off the rail. 'Yes, that's also a wonderful dress.'

Marnie and I disappear back into the changing room. I like her. She has an aura of calm and a way of acting like you're the first bride-to-be she's ever seen in the dress even though you know the girl before you tried on exactly the same one. She talks about trains you can bustle, and inter-locking ruffles and interior corsets and all manner of things that don't ever get talked about outside of wedding boutiques.

The Cecilia is strapless and dotted with teeny Swarovski crystals.

Marnie smiles at me in the mirror. 'Do you think it's your dress?'

I look and her and I look at my reflection. The dress is pretty. Very pretty. But something is stopping me from saying I do.

Nobody has the heart to order champagne even though that's what we'd planned. Lunch after a visit to a bridal boutique equals a glass of champagne. Except when the bride bursts into tears. (Poor Marnie. She was trying to be sympathetic, but I could tell she was more than a little worried about me getting mascara over The Cecilia. As I mentioned earlier, I don't do small crying.)

'I don't want you to go ahead with this wedding just because you feel the wheels are already in motion,' my mum says.

I fiddle with my napkin.

'Is it because you just know that he'll be unfaithful again?' Rachel says.

'No!'

My mother – who is not a woman given to drama – looks a little pale. 'Ginny. Being married is not easy. If you're not sure now, then don't do it.'

I pull a shred off the napkin. 'Maybe it's just pre-wedding jitters?'

My mum shakes her head sadly. 'I think it might be a little bit more than that.'

'We don't have a song!'

My mum and Rachel look at me as if I've gone mad. Which maybe I have.

'And I don't care whether we have cupcakes or fruitcake! I should care about that, shouldn't I?'

'Well—'

'And sometimes when Jack talks about how we've got to book up the band quickly, I feel like screaming! Even though I know he's right. And that, anyway, that should be a nice thing to do.'

My mum takes my hand in hers.

'Jack is all the things I've ever wanted him to be . . .' I say.

My mum looks at me, her small rough hand stroking the back of mine. 'Do what makes you happy.'

And that's when I realize. Jack is all the things I ever wanted him to be. But Jack is not Nick.

Jack has a delicious-smelling meal in the oven, soft music playing and enough candles lit to power the National Grid.

In different circumstances it would be wonderful. But it's not particularly helpful given I'm about to dump him.

'Hi, sweetheart,' he says, drying his hands on a tea towel. 'How was your day? Did you find your dress? Want a glass of wine?'

'I'm okay. I think . . .' I pause because, despite rehearsing my lines over and over again on the tube journey home, I suddenly have no idea what to say. I know some people might think of me finishing with Jack as the ultimate 'getting your own back' moment but there's not even the tiniest part of me that gets any pleasure out of this.

'I've made us roast chicken.'

Damn you!

'Roast potatoes, gravy, veggies.' He starts chopping carrots. 'I hope you're hungry!'

Stop being so cheerful! 'Jack, we need to talk.'

He puts the knife down. 'That doesn't sound good.'

Suddenly I feel all the resolve draining out of me. It doesn't help that my mind keeps flashing back to my break-up with Nick (it seems I'm becoming something of a serial dumper). 'This isn't right. We're not right.'

His face is a mask of confusion. 'You're breaking up with me?'

'Yes. I'm so sorry.'

'But I'm giving you all the things you ever wanted: commitment, marriage, babies.'

'Yes, I know,' I say, starting to cry.

He sits down on the sofa. I look at him, squashing down the thought that he would make beautiful babies.

'We'll have to cancel the venue and the caterers,' he says.

'I'm sorry.'

He nods. 'At least Simon will be happy I'm not going to outdo him on the engagement party front.'

I don't really know what to do with that comment so I say nothing.

The oven timer starts bleeping.

'That'll be the chicken,' Jack says, not moving from the sofa.

I get the chicken out of the oven. 'I really am sorry.'

Jack doesn't look up.

Is it weird that we eat the roast chicken, do the dishes together and even climb into the same bed?

'I'll start to pack,' Jack says to me after supper.

'Do it in the morning,' I say.

He has his back to me and I think he's asleep.

I listen to his breathing. Although I am exhausted, so many thoughts are swirling around my head.

This morning, I was going out to choose my wedding dress. Now, well, now things are very different.

I feel sad, scared and alone.

But deep down, I also feel relieved.

Chapter Forty-Eight

Of course, there's still the baby thing. And whilst I knew I absolutely couldn't marry Jack, that's still quite a big barrier to me being with Nick. (Another issue would obviously be telling him, I can't really just call up all easy-breezy and say, *Do you know, I think I've changed my mind*. But I guess there must be a way past that.)

I am sitting on a bench at the top of Primrose Hill. Everybody has a baby or child. Seriously, everybody. All around me, women are dispensing organic breadsticks and imploring people to play nicely and share. I manage to spot one woman of about my age who doesn't have a Poppy or an Alfie. But then the wind caught her dress and I saw a small but unmistakable bump. The foetus inside looked me straight in the eye, splayed hand on nose and went, 'Nah, nah, nah, nah nah!'

I try to concentrate on the view picking out Canary Wharf and the London Eye.

Some days I think I can live without a baby. Just because I count the smell of a baby's head amongst my favourite smells in the world, that doesn't mean I have to have one. I'll just be the best auntie in the world to George and Felix, the best godmother to all my friends' kids. I'll be able to really concentrate on my career, take my annual leave outside of the school holiday period, not worry about stretch marks. I will have lots of time to write (hmmm). Also, I will never have to scrape poo out of a cowhide rug or apologize profusely because my child has sunk their teeth into someone else's darling.

September seems to be making the weather do some very strange things. Right now it's glorious, but this morning it was distinctly chilly. It's like the universe has decided to play a giant game of cat and mouse.

A woman walking up the hill has a baby in a sling whose hat has slipped over his eyes. Poor little mite can't see a thing, let alone take advantage of the fact he is surrounded by some of the best views in London. A little girl in a pink leotard and georgette wraparound dance skirt is just ahead of them. She is pushing a miniature Maclaren buggy with a doll in it. (Even the three-year-olds have babies!) She has long flaxen hair like her mum but, whereas her mum's is perfectly groomed, the little girl's is matted and unbrushed. If I had children, I would move their hats when they slipped over their eyes. I would brush their hair.

The little girl stops to adjust the blanket covering her doll's legs. She speaks to her softly and solicitously. I remember my Tiny Tears and how I loved her. I was always bathing her, feeding her, cuddling her. Rachel had a Tiny Tears too, but she didn't care much for it — her doll was definitely an it. She never changed its nappy and once left it in the flowerbeds.

Two tweenage boys are fighting over a Frisbee. Their father is a few feet away on a red and white checked picnic rug reading a book. The boys hit and kick and punch and he looks up for a nanosecond to suggest they stop. Then he goes back to his book.

A group of women with assorted babies and toddlers — buy one, get one free! — are laughing and gossiping whilst the children run wild. One woman is spooning slop into her baby's mouth without ever looking at him. I wonder if Primrose Hill babies eat the same kind of food as other babies or if their purées come with jus and foams and micro cress?

I look north towards Hampstead. I can do this. Give up the idea of having a baby to be with Nick.

The woman on the bench opposite me starts tickling her baby's feet. And the baby is laughing like it's the funniest thing in the whole world. And I have to look away.

Chapter Forty-Nine

The healer is not what I was expecting. He wears an 'account-ant's' grey pin-striped suit, wire-framed round glasses, and has teeth so tiny they look almost like milk teeth. 'Welcome, welcome,' he says showing off the tiny teeth and pumping Cassie's and my hands enthusiastically. 'I'm Dermot.' His Irish accent is soft and lilting.

Cassie insists I go into the treatment room with her. Again, my expectations are confounded. There is no incense, no rose quartz crystals, no chakra symbols. Just a bright white room with a bed and a sink. It looks like a doctor's surgery.

Dermot asks Cassie to lie on the bed. The old Cassie would have had a quip here – *I thought you'd never ask* – but the new one just lies down mutely. 'Bio Energy Healing is about dealing with what's under the surface. Working with your energy field to draw blocked energy out. All living things are made up of energy. You may have heard this described as aura or chi energy . . .'

Cassie is staring out of the window. Her mind is elsewhere and it's not somewhere good. I am worrying about whether I've fed the parking meter enough coins to last the whole time we're in here. It makes me feel sorry for Dermot.

'It's a gentle, non-invasive treatment. I'll just use a series of hand movements to work into your energy field to draw the blocked energy out.'

He starts moving his hands in circular movements across Cassie's chest. He looks like one of the guys at airport security except he has no hand scanner. I'd worried about getting Cassie here today. One of the few things that endeared her to viewers on *I'm a Celebrity* was her fearlessness – whether she had to walk across high wires 150-foot up or swim in crocodile-infested waters you couldn't help but be impressed by how gutsy she was. Now she is often afraid to leave her flat. Today, she refused to get out of her dressing gown until right up to the last minute and kept saying it was all 'a load of New Age bollocks' and 'what was the fucking point'. The trickiest thing here was that I sort of agreed with her. I've brought her to Dermot out of desperation rather than confidence. Now – and maybe this is childish or maybe it's the comedown after the effort of getting her here – I feel suppressed giggles bubbling up. It's like trying not to laugh in church. (One woman wrote movingly about how re-discovering her Catholic faith helped her beat depression, but God knows how you'd get Cassie to go to a church. Or rather, He doesn't.)

Dermot is making circular movements above Cassie's head. 'We lose a lot of energy to pain. Physical pain, emotional pain. We don't want to feel pain so we use energy to keep it under the surface. I'm drawing blocked energy out now.' He seems to chuck something behind him and I imagine little blobs of pain on the floor like hair at the hairdressers.

When we'd finally got out of the door this morning – late but not irredeemably so – we bumped into Mr Holden who regaled us with news of his forthcoming hernia operation in all its grisly detail. I kept saying we were in a hurry, that I had borrowed my mum's car because we had an IMPORTANT appointment but we should really get going because the traffic was bound to be bad on a Saturday. On and on Mr Holden droned. I looked across at Cassie. I used to reprimand her for her impatience with Mr Holden. 'We'll all be old sometime.' She lacked contrition. 'Yes, I age ten years every time I have to suffer one of his "anecdotes".' This morning, I could have done with a little of that attitude but she just stood there with a glazed look that Mr Holden mistook for interest.

Dermot's flattened palms are hovering over Cassie's ankles. The traffic throbs outside. The room is warm and I close my eyes and before I know it, Cassie is shaking me awake. I hastily wipe a streak of drool from my cheek and try to look alert.

The reception is full of people waiting to be unblocked. A woman in a pink jacket guzzles a plastic cup of water next to the water cooler and then immediately pours herself another one. Perhaps she thinks it's like holy water.

'Let us know if you'd like another treatment,' Dermot says to Cassie. 'Or if there's anything I can help you with.' His gaze is fixed on mine. I put my head in my handbag, searching for the car keys and hiding any blockages or trapped pain from Dermot's prying blue eyes.

'How did you find it?' I ask Cassie as we emerge from the white Georgian terrace (you must have to release lots of blocked energy and pain to pay these central London rents).

Cassie shrugs. 'Waste of time.'

Excellent.

'I did feel very warm when his hands were above my head. I know the room was warm but that's not what I mean. It was like I was on one of those heated beds you get at beauty salons all of a sudden.' She shakes her head. 'Probably a hot flush.'

I smile. We are very far from the brethren-he-can-walk-again miracle I might have hoped for, but for Cassie to admit to even a warm feeling is really something. Maybe this will help a little? It might just have a placebo effect, but surely in terms of depression a placebo effect could said to be a real one?

The sun glints through the treetops dappling the grey pavements with light. I feel a squelch under my foot and look down to see I have stepped in something a dog owner has failed to bag and bin. It strikes me as cosmic karma that I step in dog shit just as I'm thinking I might have got one up on the Black Dog.

Chapter Fifty

Julia and Adam are getting married, which is fantastic, of course. It's just I'm not really in the mood for yet another always-the-bridesmaid engagement party. Or for seeing Nick there.

'Promise you won't try to wriggle out of coming?' Julia says to me on the phone.

'Course not,' I say, even though I have been wondering how I could do just that, ever since I received the save the date.

'No "work crisis" or "stomach bug".'

I love Julia to bits but she can be a bit scary. She's Global Head of Marketing for a big consumer goods company and has been known to fall out with friends because they use the other manufacturers' washing powder. I was bloody terrified about having to tell her I'd ditched her brother but by the time I called her, Nick had already told her that we'd split up and it was very much a mutual thing. Remembering the kindness of that act makes me feel as if I have something lodged in my chest.

I stand in front of my wardrobe hating everything inside it. Why can't I dress more like Fiona? She always wears bright colours so well and always has lots of fun accessories. Why can't I look like that chic girl I see on the tube every morning? Always in black, grey or navy, minimal accessories.

There's a knock at my door and I open it to see Cassie.

She is fully made-up and there's a light in her eyes I haven't seen in ages.

'You look fantastic!'

She takes in my grubby towelling dressing gown. 'Wish I could say the same for you! Isn't the party tonight?'

'I've got ages yet. Well, half an hour at least. Are you . . .' I hesitate.

'Having a good day? Yes.'

'That's wonderful.'

'It's only one day.'

'It's a start.'

'Yes, and talking of starts, let's get you ready, shall we?'

We go into the bedroom where she starts plucking things off hangers and making faces. She alights on a green dress I bought in the Zara sale and have never worn. 'Wear this,' she commands, as she passes me the hanger.

'Urgh, I can't. Too tight.'

'As in you can't zip it up?'

'No. Just a bit slutty.'

She bites off the plastic loop attaching the label and hands me the dress. 'You're thirty-four years old—'

'Nearly thirty-five.'

She gives me a look. 'You're thirty-four years old with a great figure. Wear the dress.'

'Really. It's . . .'

'Please put it on. For me?'

'Just my luck you choose today to be better!'

She laughs. It's a sound I've missed.

After I wiggle into the dress, I consider myself in the mirror. It actually looks better than I remembered, but I reach for a pashmina to cover myself up a bit.

'No,' Cassie commands from her chair. 'Now what necklace are you going to wear? Not that anyone will be looking at the necklace with that cleavage.'

I go for the pashmina again but Cassie is quicker than I am.

'Are you going to tell him how you feel?'

'It's not that simple.'

She raises an eyebrow.

I drive down the A3 wondering when I became the sort of person who hates weddings. I used to feel genuine excitement when one of those stiff envelopes plopped through my letterbox. But I've been to seven weddings in four years and it's getting not so much deja vu, as deja vu vu vu vu. One colleague of mine at Splash dragged ten of us all the way up to the Isle of Skye because we couldn't face the sulking in the stairwell if we didn't share her special day. My friend Rhona got married in France ('I've booked a special deal with the Chateau so it's only 150 euros per person. You'll have to share a room with my cousin Kaitlin – she's single too. Do make sure she doesn't sleepwalk'). I've bought four outfits I'll never wear anywhere else and put fascinators in my hair – my God, I hate fascinators! I've sipped glass after glass of warm Cava, eaten river-loads of cold salmon and chit-chatted with endless sour-breathed old uncles who nobody dares leave alone with children. I've been a bridesmaid twice, proving that peach really isn't my colour and the Little Bo Peep look isn't great on the over-thirties.

A man in a red Mondeo undertakes me in the left-hand lane, gesticulating wildly. I slink back into the slow lane.

But I love Julia and Adam, and I'm happy for them. Not long ago, I was wedding planning myself, choosing sets of towels for my very own John Lewis gift register. I should have matching towels by now, husband or not. I really must become a proper grown-up.

*   *   *

The engagement party is being held at Julia's parents' house in Surrey. Julia's parents are of course Nick's parents too and I'm praying they know nothing about me and Nick.

As soon as Julia introduces me to her mum, I see those prayers have not been answered. Her hand goes rigid in mine and the smile stays on her lips but immediately leaves her eyes. Can't say I blame her really. If I was her, I wouldn't be very pleased with me either.

I grab a glass of orange juice and immediately regret my decision to borrow my mum's car so I could drive myself here. The logic was not being beholden to trains or lifts meant I could escape at any moment but of course it also means I have to stay sober.

The party is much more full-on than I'd expected with a jazz band, caterers and a photographer. It's a mini-wedding, in fact.

'You look great,' I say to Julia.

'You too. Fab dress! What do you think of the colour scheme? It's the one we'll be using for the Big Day itself.'

I stare at her. Julia is not the type of girl who has been planning her wedding since she was five – she would have been too busy climbing trees or playing football – so it's weird that being engaged has suddenly turned her so 'bridey'.

There's a family photo on the wall. Nick, who must have been about thirteen at the time, is unrecognizable.

Julia notices me staring at it and laughs. 'That was when Nick was going through his spotty, chubby phase. Unfortunately, it coincided with Mum deciding she cut our hair just as well as any hairdresser. He was a real ugly duckling, wasn't he? Don't think he has ever noticed he's turned into a swan actually.' She rearranges a vase of hydrangeas as we walk past them. 'He's not here yet, by the way.'

I smile in what I hope is an insouciant manner. She introduces me to her sour-breathed uncle and leaves me chatting to him. Best get my practice in for the Big Day.

'Nice dress,' he says, leering at my cleavage.

He's busy telling me about his love of classic cars when Nick walks in. My heart seems to speed up in my chest and my mouth goes dry.

'. . . Austin Healey "Frogeye" Sprite. Maximum fun with minimal power . . .'

Nick looks at me and then looks away again.

'. . . how it set the template for the entire future . . .'

He has a girl with him. A beautiful stick-thin blonde in an orange silk shift dress that looks expensive and understated and immediately makes me feel like a fifty-dollar hooker. She is holding his hand.

'. . . Lamborghini Miura. The supercar king . . .'

I wonder if Julia would notice if I slipped away?

During the speeches – did I mention this was a mini-wedding? – I catch Nick looking at me out of the corner of his eye. I try to look like I'm having a really good time. I also try not to cry.

I am standing at the buffet table when he speaks to me. 'Mum and Julia have gone all out, haven't they? Not sure what we'll do for the actual wedding.' I smile. 'So how are you?'

'Fine.' The word hangs in the air in all its naked meaninglessness. 'You?'

'Fine.'

We both laugh.

'You still writing?'

'Yeah. I'm sure I'll never get anywhere with it bu—'

'Well, you certainly won't get anywhere with it if you don't try. How's Cassie?'

'A little better, I think. She has good days and bad days, but I think she's on the up.'

'That's good.'

I think about how Jack resented every second I spent with Cassie. Always told me she wasn't my problem.

Nick turns as if to walk away.

'I'm not getting married. To Jack, I mean. I hope I will get married someday.' Oh God, why do I babble like this?

He looks at me but I can't read what's going on behind his eyes. 'I'd better get back to Amanda. Just thought I'd say hello.'

A-man-da! 'Sure. See you around.'

I stand looking at the poached salmon and choking back the tears. It's nearly a respectable time for me to go home.

A guy in a loud shirt and a slightly too-tight pair of jeans appears. 'Hi.' It takes me a few seconds to remember who he is. Boring Phil. The guy I tried to make myself like because there was nothing actually wrong with him. And then he didn't even call.

Nick is on his hands and knees on the dancefloor giving horse-rides to a couple of kids. They are shrieking with delight and whipping him to go faster. How can a man who doesn't want children be so good with them? Nick is like Mary bloody Poppins.

Phil is telling me some story about when he and Adam got caught smoking at school; I'm pretending to listen, but my eyes keep flicking over to Nick, who is dancing with A-man-da now. The band are playing 'It Had To Be You'. Maybe she's just a friend? They are laughing. She reaches up and strokes his cheek. It's all I can do not to go over and punch her, scream that he's mine. Except, of course, he's not.

'I have to go,' I say to Phil, cutting him off mid-sentence. 'Bit tired. Long drive back.'

'Oh. Well, nice to see you again, Jenny.'

'Ginny.' Boring Phil doesn't even remember my name. It's the final bloody indignity.

Chapter Fifty-One

Cassie is seeing a therapist.

Cassie hates the therapist.

Why is it that with depression everything seems to be one step forward, two steps back?

'She wears crepe-soled red Mary Janes with big round toes,' Cassie recounts. 'Like toddler shoes.'

'I'm not sure how much her shoes matter here.'

'And awful skirts that gather at the waist – or what she has of a waist – in colours like royal blue or purple. Mother-of-the-bride colours.'

'Again, maybe not so relevant to her professional skills.'

Cassie snorts. 'It's a horrible little room too. Pale green walls – who paints anywhere pale green? – pine furniture and dusty fake flowers. You'd think for a hundred quid an hour she could shell out for a bunch of tulips! Oh, and there's always a huge box of tissues on the coffee table shouting, *Cry, why don't you?*'

'I think tissues are a reasonable thing for a therapist to have in her office.'

'Hmm.'

We are sitting outside in the back garden having a cup of tea. I've given up on the gardening as therapy, but even though the garden is overgrown and full of weeds it's still a nice place to sit, particularly since nature has thrown us an unseasonably warm day considering it's nearly October.

It's a joy to see Cassie today too. She seems almost like her old self. Not that I think she's completely out of the woods yet. If I've learned one thing about depression in these last few months it's that there are good and bad days. But Cassie has started to have more good days. And whether that's down to the healer or the therapist – neither of whom Cassie would like to give a scrap of credit – I have no idea. I just hope it continues.

'It's great that you've dumped Horrible Jack. Men like that never really change.'

'Stop calling him Horrible Jack.'

'Well sorry, but if the boot fi—' I scowl at her and she raises an eyebrow. 'I still think you should have said something to Nick at the party.'

'He was there with someone else.' I think about adding that Nick doesn't want a child but I can't face the conversation where Cassie tells me that it shouldn't matter. Cassie would not understand if I tried to explain to her that yesterday at work when I was getting everything ready for Lauren's baby shower, I had to choke back tears as I was putting up the 'about to pop' banner. She wouldn't understand that I'm dreading my imminent birthday because everyone knows that thirty-five is the age when your fertility drops off a cliff. She'd think I was mad if I told her that when Ben joked we ought to get a discount on the pitter patter confetti because we have so many baby showers, it felt like someone had punched me.

Cassie takes a sip of tea. 'She's got these whiskers that look like pubic hair coming out of her chin too. I mean, I get that she has a rich inner life but would it kill her to use a pair of tweezers now and then?'

I laugh. 'You're a terrible person, you know that, right?'

'I've never pretended otherwise.'

I turn my face up to the sun enjoying its warmth. 'You

don't have to be bessie mates with the therapist. All that matters is that she's helping you.'

'I don't know if she is. I don't think she gets me. I imagine it's beyond her comprehension to have once had your name in lights in cinemas all round Leicester Square, to have been romanced by Hollywood legends and cabinet ministers. I don't suppose anyone has ever romanced her. The other day, I was trying to explain to her my mindset when I first landed a big movie role. How I went from "thank you, thank you, I am not worthy" to "where's my fucking latte" in the space of about thirty seconds. I don't think she understood at all. She just sat there looking bovine. Not that she ever says much. Just sits there with her smug little hands folded in her lap going "hmm" and "ahh". I thought an actress's job was pretty easy but at least we have lines!'

'I think the point is, it's more about what you say.'

'But she doesn't like what I say! I'm not allowed to make jokes. When she was talking about my inner child – which she's obsessed with, by the way – I said I've never been that keen on kids, and she got all grumpy and said I use humour as a denial of my real feelings. She gets hung up on the craziest stuff too. I happened to tell her a story in which my mother told me not to upset myself and her eyes lit up like she'd just seen Brad Pitt. "Not to upset yourself? That's a very interesting phrase. It denies the emotion of being upset and suggests that the hurt was self-inflicted." And I tried to explain that it's just a turn of phrase, but she wasn't having any of it. "No, no," she insisted, "that's why you have difficulty getting your needs met." Difficulty getting my needs met?' Cassie guffaws. 'Hello! Has she met me?'

'Poor woman!'

'Hey, it's me you're supposed to feel sorry for!'

'You seem good. I mean—'

'I am good. Today. And today is a start.'

Chapter Fifty-Two

On my birthday, I wake up with a pounding head and the knowledge that opening my eyes is going to be painful. But I don't realize just how painful because, when I do, I have absolutely no idea where I am. I do not have a brown duvet on my bed. I do not have a Spurs calendar hanging on my wall.

A guy in a slightly grubby looking dressing gown appears. Dear God, it's boring Phil! Did I? A wave of nausea washes over me. 'Thought you might need these,' he says handing me two paracetamol and a mug of coffee.

I attempt to sit up and immediately regret it. I wince as I try to recall the details of last night, but can't really remember much.

Dear God, please tell me we didn't have sex.

What I do know is that I went out for drinks after work with Jacqui, Antonia and Ben. I remember I was telling Antonia that she should fire me as her dating advisor because I was officially crap at dating – that not only had I screwed things up with Nick and Jack, but I'd seen Boring Phil at a party recently and he hadn't even remembered my name.

I think Fiona turned up at the bar at one point? Yes, I was telling her how she was the best boss I've ever had. Mortifying!

'I'm going to jump in the shower,' BP says.

I am desperate to ask him if we slept together but it's not a question that trips neatly off the tongue, so I just nod. How on earth do people do one-night-stands? This is my first and DEFINITELY my last.

At some point in the evening we went on to a club. I think Ben may have suggested it. I remember dancing and saying I was having a fantastic time and then – oh, God! – crying and telling Ben that I was going to be thirty-five and I needed a baby daddy. Did he want to do it? We wouldn't actually have to have sex as I knew that would be horrible for him.

I gingerly lever myself up onto my elbow and try to take the painkillers, making myself gag in the process.

I'd know if I'd had sex. Also, although I have a big grey Guns N' Roses T shirt on (presumably BP's), I am still wearing my bra and pants. That's a good sign, right?

Shards of memory pierce my brain: me buying everyone shots; me telling random strangers that it was nearly my birthday; Antonia trying to confiscate my phone, telling me she wasn't going to let me drunk dial; me getting aggressive, saying I was an adult and could do what I want because it was my birthday . . .

I was loaded into an Uber, the driver reassured by the others that I wasn't going to be sick, me thinking *don't bet on it*. I don't remember coming here though. I mean, why BP? It's hardly like the two of us have this great connection.

He's back now, doing up his tie and telling me he has to leave for work. I don't even know what he does. (Yes, Ginny, *that's* the issue!) 'Oh,' he says, 'happy birthday by the way.'

'How did you know?'

He laughs. 'You told me last night. Repeatedly. Don't you remember?'

I don't . . . And then I see myself standing on BP's doorstep. The total shock on his face. Me saying it was my birthday tomorrow and I didn't want to wake up alone.

I think I even said: let's get it on (*who* says that?). The memory makes me want to hide under the brown duvet. Or, better still, curl up and die.

'Take your time and leave when you're ready,' BP says. 'If you're a friend of Julia and Adam's, I don't think you're going to rob me!' He laughs to signal this was a joke. 'There's probably enough hot water if you want a shower.'

Do I need a shower? If we had sex, I definitely need a shower . . .

BP is just about to disappear out of the door.

'B . . . Phil,' I say. 'Did we?'

A look of incomprehension crosses his face and then he grimaces. 'Christ, no! What do you take me for? You were completely off your face. There's absolutely no way.'

'Oh right, good. Just checking.' Thank you, God!

At lunchtime, I pretend to be meeting a friend for lunch so that my workmates don't feel they need to take me for some sort of birthday celebration. I have to say, apart from some light teasing about how someone might be feeling a little delicate, they've been pretty restrained – all things considered. There aren't even that many comments about me wearing the same clothes as the day before, even though my 'story' (locking myself out and having to stay at my sister's) isn't particularly convincing.

I head for Golden Square and sit on a bench, grateful it's a warm day and that the little man who's hammering away inside my skull seems to be calming down a little.

I spend what feels like three hours in Pret trying to decide on what sandwich I could possibly stomach and now taking the tuna and cucumber out of the bag, a wave of nausea tells me I haven't picked well. I stuff it back in the bag and take a swig of water.

So the day I've been dreading is here. I'm officially thirty-five – yay!

And what a great start my 'special day' got off to! I shudder at the memory of BP's face when I asked him if we'd had sex. Him saying goodbye, that he supposed we wouldn't see each other again until Julia and Adam's wedding. You know, just in case I'd got the impression that the two of us were an item now.

A man on the next bench is having the world's loudest row on his mobile. He bloody well did not say that! Stop twisting things! I wish he'd turn the volume down a little.

I scroll through my birthday messages on Facebook. There isn't one from Nick, but then what did I expect really?

My ex colleague Jess has posted a picture of the two of us at the Splash Christmas party. I've been thinking about Jess a lot recently. She's adamant she never wants kids and I always used to tease her when people brought their new babies into the office. *Shall I say you're desperate to hold him?* Now it feels like the joke is on me. Jess is going to be thirty-five next month and she's not feeling sick about it. There's no frantic googling sessions about fertility for Jess, no relationship maths every time she meets someone.

'Well fuck you very much!' the guy on the next bench shouts.

I switch to Instagram. Robert and James have posted a picture of two glasses of champagne sitting on top of the packing crates in their new kitchen.

Our home, our castle! #newhome #happy

I am happy for them but also a bit jealous. I know jealousy is an ugly emotion and one we rarely admit to, but I can't help it. Because it's not that I don't want Robert and James to have their perfect kitchen (they will definitely have napkins at their dinner parties), it's just I'm wondering if I'll *ever* have my own home. Maybe I'll still be living with Jarielle when I'm celebrating my fifty-fifth birthday.

Nancy would like to FaceTime flashes up.

'Happy birthday!' she says appearing on my phone screen. As ever she's clutching a can of Diet Coke.

'Thanks. And you've really got to sort out that coke habit, Nance.'

'Laughing at your own jokes is not cool, Ginny. Particularly when they're the same jokes you've been making for years.'

I poke my tongue out at her.

I tell her about last night and she can't stop laughing. 'Why him of all people?'

'I know,' I say. 'At least I didn't have sex with him.'

'You don't know what you missed!' she says.

'Stop it! Anyway, I'm worried now that thirty-five has hit me. Do you think I'm officially too old to buy anything in Topshop now?' *Or have a baby?*

'Yup. It's elasticated waists and comfy shoes all the way now. In griege.'

I groan.

'I'm meeting Will Powell for a drink tonight,' she says. 'Do you remember him?'

'His parents are friends with your parents? You had a snog once when you were about sixteen?'

'Yes, him. He's just moved over to New York.'

'Maybe he's The One?'

She laughs. 'Ginny, this is real life, not a rom-com! We haven't seen each other in over ten years. Anyway, it's not like the two of us had some kind of special bond. We were just teenagers awash with hormones and lager.'

I glance at my watch and tell her I'd better get back to work.

I watch a heavily pregnant woman who's coming towards me on Dean Street. She's got a 'Baby on Board' badge on her lapel although goodness knows why – I think the space-hopper-sized bump would be a clue.

I seem to see so many of those wretched badges nowadays (no wonder the world is overcrowded!), and every time I do I feel a sort of dull ache.

Perhaps I can use it as material for this week's writing homework, the theme of which is pain. Then again, if I want to draw on real life, there are so many other things I could use. The knife-twist in my stomach as I watched Nick and A-man-da. Finding Cassie that night in Londis. (She called me earlier to say happy birthday and, I don't know if it was my imagination, but her voice sounded a little flat. I'm probably overthinking it though. She seemed almost like her old self when we had a drink in the garden the other day.)

The pregnant woman and I cross paths and I see that she looks quite a lot older than me. Late thirties, or even early forties. See, I tell myself, women do have babies at that age. No need to panic.

But as I blow out the candles on my Colin the Caterpillar cake, panic I do. Every last egg is shrivelling up and dying inside me.

Well, at least that's what's going on in my imagination.

Georgia cuts the cake, hands me a piece saying the birthday girl should get the first slice.

I try to smile. I've always been someone who likes birthdays. This one, not so much.

'What are you doing tonight?' Fiona asks.

Mourning the loss of the eggs. 'I'm having dinner with my family.'

'Ahh, lovely,' Jacqui says.

I wish I shared her enthusiasm. It's not like I don't like my family, and Mum will undoubtedly have gone to a huge effort, it's just part of me feels that 'family' shouldn't just mean the family I was born into by now. Also, given my hangover, my absolute dream evening would be getting home early, finding that Jarielle are out, having a long, hot shower (BP's was tepid for about forty seconds and then turned icy cold) and then falling into bed. Rock 'n' roll!

'Mmm,' Antonia says, licking her fingers. 'I love a bit of Colin the Caterpillar. I hope you weren't too mortified by the embarrassing singing?'

'How very dare you?' Ben says. 'I have the voice of an angel!'

We all laugh.

'Want a bit more cake, Ginny?' Georgia asks. 'It's the ultimate hangover cure!'

I smile and decline. I thank them all for the cake and the card, for making an effort.

Now I just need to make an effort not to be such a miserable old cow.

The next day I feel knackered, although goodness knows why since I was in bed by 10.30 having drunk less than half a glass of Prosecco. Perhaps two-day hangovers are a thing now I'm thirty-five? Along with being barren.

I am at my desk trying to stifle a yawn when *Nancy would like to FaceTime* flashes up on my phone.

'You okay?' I say. 'Isn't it the middle of the night there.'

'It's 4 a.m. and Will has just left!'

I lean closer to the screen.

'Oh my God, Ginny. He's amazing. We just didn't stop talking and laughing all night.'

'That's fantastic!'

Nancy looks like a kid on Christmas Eve. She can barely even sit still.

'I mean, I know I mustn't get too carried away. We've only spent one evening together. He could be the kind of guy who orders Hawaiian pizza for all I know.'

'Hmm, that would be a bit of a deal-breaker.'

'He might say he reads nothing but graphic novels. He might like jazz. Or – oh my God – the Red Hot Chilli Peppers.'

'Or he could be The One?'

'Let's not get ahead of ourselves,' Nancy says, even though her face tells me she's thinking exactly the same thing.

I hang up the call, still smiling.

'Ginny,' Fiona says appearing out of nowhere. 'Have you seen the email from Darren Grant?'

My stomach lurches. Darren Grant may have agreed to leave the Chocolicious account with Impact for now but that doesn't mean he appears to have any confidence in the Fri-yay Giveaway idea, or us as an agency. Every day there seems to be another complaint from him. He was disappointed with the copy for the press release. Our ROI figures look questionable . . .

'Don't panic,' Fiona says (clearly my acting skills could do with improvement). 'It's not one of his rants. But he's saying he wants to move the time of today's status call from 4 p.m. to 9 p.m.' She makes a face. 'Apparently, it's the only time he can do.'

'That's okay,' I say, stifling a yawn. I was hoping to be in my PJs by 9 p.m., not talking to Darren Bloody Grant.

'You're a superstar,' Fiona says. 'Now obviously don't hang about here until then. If you have to speak to the frightful little man, then at least do it from the comfort of your own home. Leave early too – that way at least you can relax a bit before you have to call him. You look tired actually. You okay?'

'Fine.'

I just need coffee. Lots of coffee.

Chapter Fifty-Three

'The ambulance will be there soon,' the operator says.

How did this happen? Cassie has been going to her yoga class again, making me wear low-cut dresses. She even went to a showbiz party with Shane.

And now this.

'Where is the ambulance?'

'Coming.'

Make it come quicker.

'Is the patient breathing?'

I bend down and put my ear against Cassie's mouth. 'Yes.' My voice sounds weird and strangled.

'Good. Now I need you to get her in the recovery position for me.'

'I . . . I . . .'

'Don't worry I'll talk you through it. Is the patient on her back?'

'Yes.'

'Okay. Now kneel beside her and place the arm nearest you at a right angle to her body with her hand upwards, towards her head.'

I feel a stab of pure panic. Why don't I know how to do this? Where is the ambulance?

'Have you done that?' The operator's voice is steady,

emollient. I squeak a yes. 'Now tuck her other hand under the side of her head . . .'

At Fiona's insistence I left the office early. It was the least she owed me for having to talk to Darren Grant in my own time, she said. As soon as I walked up the stairs, I knew something was wrong. Cassie's front door was swinging open and I could see a handbag and a coat that had been thrown to the floor.

I have to keep asking the operator to repeat the instructions. Cassie's tiny body is heavy and disobedient in my trembling hands. Lifeless. 'Where is the ambulance?'

'It's coming. It'll be there any minute.'

Carmen was on her hands and knees next to Cassie's inert form, shaking her wildly. 'Miss Cassie! Miss Cassie!'

'Okay. I think I've done it.'

'Now gently tilt her head back and lift her chin. Check there is nothing blocking her airway.'

Airway? We need someone who knows what they are doing. 'Where is the ambulance?'

'Coming. Is there anything blocking her airway?'

'No, I don't think so. No. Now what?'

Now what?

'Just stay with the patient until help arrives. I'll stay on the phone the whole time. You're doing really well, Ginny.'

Doing really well? I could have stopped this, *should* have stopped this.

Tears are coursing down Carmen's cheeks. She is mumbling some kind of prayer in Spanish.

Stop it! Stop it!

The low battery warning flashes up on my phone.

'The ambulance is on Camden Parkway, Ginny. Just hold on.'

I stroke Cassie's hair.

I thought you were getting better.

Chapter Fifty-Four

At the hospital it's all questions and no answers.

'What exactly has she taken?'

'Will she be okay?'

'How long has she been unconscious?'

'Will she be okay?'

'You didn't find anything else apart from the vodka bottle?'

'Will she be okay?'

'But she had antidepressants and sleeping pills in the house?'

'WILL SHE BE OKAY?'

Chapter Fifty-Five

Cassie looks tiny in the hospital bed. Frail and broken. The tube they've pushed down her throat to help her breathe looks huge against her grey face.

The next few hours would be critical, the doctor told me. I could see her beeper vibrating, her trying to pretend she hadn't noticed, that all her attention was focused on me. Did I have any questions?

Why?

Bleep, bleep go the machines.

'I know it looks scary,' the nurse said. 'Hooked up to loads of machines and all.'

Looks scary?

I squeeze Cassie's small, bony hand in mine.

'Cassie,' I whisper. 'You need to wake up.'

I wipe away a tear that is rolling down my cheek. I asked the nurse if Cassie could hear me and she nodded and smiled.

'You need to wake up.'

What if Carmen hadn't chosen today to look in on Cassie? Got on two trains to go to see a woman who had fired her. 'I was worry for her,' she explained to me.

What if she'd left when she rung the bell and didn't get an answer? Just assumed Cassie was out.

'You need to wake up, Cass. Please.'

I stare at the swirly green lino. On my way home, I was

irritated by a woman on the bus because she was talking too loudly on her mobile. Feeling grumpy because I'd seen a post about Kieron getting engaged. Hoping Jarielle would have decided to stay at his flat tonight and wondering what I'd make for supper.

Now, I am in Intensive Care, willing my friend to live.

You could have talked to me.

I glance at my watch – 11 p.m. Shit, I completely forgot to call Darren Grant. It's okay, he'll understand. He's not a monster. I reach for my phone to send him a text. But my phone is dead.

Never mind. A few hours ago, forgetting to call Darren Grant would have been a big deal.

Not now.

A big purply bruise has bloomed on the back of Cassie's hand. The junior doctor couldn't get the cannula in. *Can't find a vein,* he explained to me, his voice going up an octave and his hand shaking wildly. I was sorry for him and irritated in equal measure. *Get someone who knows what they're doing.*

It's oppressively hot and the smell of disinfectant and stale bodies is making me feel sick.

I stroke Cassie's lifeless-looking arm. 'I need you to be okay. I need you.'

I rest my forehead on the edge of the bed, still holding her arm. 'Do you remember you told me once I was getting more and more like you every single day? And it was a joke because I was being kind of a bitch. But the thing is I am more like you now. I'm less afraid of stuff – arsehole photographers and clients, dumping Jack, doing stuff I might suck at like writing.'

I bite the inside of my cheek, lift my head from the bed. 'What I'm saying . . . trying to say is . . . you've taught me so much. And my God I know that would make you laugh in my face. But it's true. Because you are so bloody fearless, Cassie. Such a badass.'

Alarms start going off from the next bed. Rubber-soled shoes pound the floor, curtains are pulled, instructions barked.

'You think you're a mess, but the irony is you're one of the strongest people I know. And I know that sounds weird right now. But . . . all this is only because you're not well.'

I grip her arm tightly. 'You are going to get well again. And until you do, I'm going to be strong enough for the both of us. But first, you need to wake up.'

Chapter Fifty-Six

It's seven the next morning when I get home from the hospital. My hand shakes as I try to get my key in the door, undo the buttons of my coat, plug my phone onto the charger.

I lie on my bed staring at the ceiling, too tired to even cry.

The phone rings. Jack. What does he want? 'Hello.'

'Hi. I was just wondering if you've found my green tie at your place? The Reiss one. I can't find it anywhere and I'll be driving past in about twenty minutes so I thought if you did have it, I could pick it up.'

I feel a surge of irritation. He's worrying about a fucking tie! I have to remind myself that he doesn't know.

'I haven't seen it.'

'Oh. That's annoying. Are you okay? You sound a bit odd.'

'I'm fine,' I say, dissolving into uncontrollable sobs.

Eighteen minutes later Jack is at my door. He puts his arms around me and holds me tightly while I cry all over his freshly pressed white shirt.

'Sorry about the mascara,' I say when I finally stop.

'It's okay.'

My head is pounding. 'You know this doesn't change anything between us?'

He raises his eyebrows. 'What, you're not going to marry me because I let you ruin a good shirt?'

'Sorry. Listen, I'd better get ready for work.'

'You're not going to work, Ginny. You're in no fit state.'

'But I have to. I can't risk losing my job again.'

'You're not going to lose your job. Do you want me to phone Fiona and explain what's happened?'

I shake my head. 'I'll do it. I have to tell her I forgot to call Darren Grant too. Oh, bloody fuck – Darren Grant!'

'Who?'

'A client,' I say vaguely, already punching out a message on my phone. *So sorry to have missed you last night.* No, that's not right. *So sorry I didn't call last night. My friend . . .*

Now what? How do you explain this in a text message?

I type several different messages, none of which I'm happy with. In the end, I decide there is no good way of saying this and just press send. 'Fuck,' I say as the message goes. 'I put a kiss on the end by mistake.'

Jack smiles. 'Now call Fiona while I run you a hot bath.'

When I get out of the bath, Jack has made me tea and toast.

'I'm not hungry,' I say before gobbling it all down.

A message appears from Darren Grant. *Sorry to hear about your friend. I'm free to talk anytime between two and four today. Or tomorrow?*

He sounds okay. And he didn't mention the kiss.

'I'd better get to work,' Jack says. 'Are you going to be okay?'

No. 'Yes.'

He puts his jacket on. 'I'm sorry about Cassie.'

My eyes fill with tears and I nod.

Jack strokes my face and then turns to go.

'Jack,' I say calling after him. 'Thank you.'

He shrugs his shoulders. 'Least I could do.'

Chapter Fifty-Seven

When Cassie was in Intensive Care, I made a deal with God (a God I'm not sure I believe in but still found myself talking to).

Let her live and I will never ask for anything else.

He's kept his part of the bargain, I've welshed.

I am in Cassie's flat ostensibly packing clothes for her to come home in but actually freaking the hell out. How can I make sure she doesn't do it again? Should I throw out all the booze? What about kitchen knives?

Which is when I ask God for more people. Namely, someone who knows what they're doing.

Carmen has been incredible. She's been to the hospital every single day. When I got there yesterday evening, she had somehow persuaded Cassie to walk up and down the ward, which is more than I've managed.

She has also worked her magic in Cassie's flat, fixing the dripping tap and giving the place a thorough clean so that surfaces gleam, fresh sheets are on the bed and the sour, sad smell has gone. When I discovered her on her hands and knees scrubbing the kitchen floor, I offered to help but she shook her head and shooed me away, just as she did when I tried to pay her.

But however wonderful Carmen is, the language barrier means I can't share the endless questions that jostle for position in my mind. Should I stay in Cassie's spare room for a few days because upstairs is too far away? Do I need to get someone to sit with Cassie (aka guard her) when I'm at work? How do we make sure she takes the medicine she's been prescribed?

You might think Meg would be the person to talk to about such things but she's been worse than useless. When she finally turned up at the hospital, she didn't even bother to conceal her anger. 'How could you do a thing like this?' she spat at the tiny pale grey husk of a figure huddling under the blanket. In the next breath, she was telling me that Cassie 'didn't really want to kill herself', that this was all 'just for the attention'.

I stare at the spot in the middle of the floor where Cassie was lying and the memories flood my brain so that my breath catches in my throat. Cassie's splayed limbs, Carmen's quiet sobbing, my panic as the ambulance controller spoke to me in what seemed like a foreign language.

In the bedroom, I scoop up some of Cassie's make-up from her dressing table and put it in her washbag. Is it ridiculous to take make-up to someone who recently tried to take their own life? Even if that person is Cassie?

I am about to put a compact into the bag when I hesitate. Cassie could break the mirror and use it to slit her wrists. Is thinking like that paranoid or responsible?

I would have called Barry because I know that, as well as being Cassie's agent, he's also been her friend for many years. Everything she has ever told me about him convinces me that, despite having bagels, latkes and insults hurled at him, Barry would be here now. But Barry is on a cruise somewhere in the middle of the Atlantic Ocean. Mind you, it can't be that long before he finds out, the news made the papers today. I hated the way it was reported. The salacious interest in the gory details, the pointless speculation about whether Cassie left a note.

So Barry will find out soon enough. But for now, apart

from Carmen, I'm on my own. Well, that's rubbish – there are all the incredible people at the hospital. The doctor who jokes with Cassie about how she's a doctor too (even though he was probably about twelve when Cassie was Dr Lisa on *Casualty*). The red-haired nurse who told me Cassie could definitely hear me that first night, and the volunteer who, when I was feeling particularly desolate, just seemed to know and put a cup of tea in my hand even though she absolutely isn't allowed to make tea for visitors.

And, of course, I have the people who always look out for me. My mum who has filled Cassie's freezer with soup and gently nagged me not to forget about looking after myself, Nancy who listened for an hour last night while I sobbed about how I keep saying the wrong things. ('You should have told me' was supposed to sound caring, instead it came off as flippant. 'With the right meds, you'll be yourself again in no time' was meant to be positive, but actually it minimized her pain.)

But I still wish I had more 'Cassie people'.

I zip up the holdall and take a deep breath. I got my miracle and I need to be grateful. I am grateful. It's just I'm also drained, stressed and exhausted.

And scared. So bloody scared.

I close the door to Cassie's flat, take a deep breath.

And there, coming up the stairs, is Shane.

'Ginny,' he says, the concern etched all over his face. 'I've only just seen the news. Is she okay?'

'She's alive.' It's not the same and we both know it.

He shakes his head and puts his hand on my arm. 'We can take care of her.'

We.

Chapter Fifty-Eight

Cassie's good days stretch into good weeks. The bad days aren't as bad. She keeps seeing the therapist and keeps bitching about her. 'Did I tell you she's got the most annoying voice? Breathy and little-girly?' She starts having regular blow dries with Bruno again and getting her nails done. 'At least if I do actually manage to top myself next time, I'll be an immaculate corpse.'

'Too soon,' I tell her reprovingly, but she just laughs.

She told me the other day that more often than not she wakes up feeling 'normal' now. 'You know how precious that is when you've had a stomach bug or the flu. Well this is like that, times a *million*.'

I try to be normal around her too – to not feel awash with panic if she doesn't immediately answer one of my messages, and refrain from constantly asking how she's feeling. I tell myself that she's okay and ignore the voice inside my head that screams, *But you thought that before.*

And then Cassie gets a job. We are walking on Primrose Hill when she gets the call. Shane is about to do a tour, and Kate O'Flynn dropped out at the last minute. He mentioned Cassie to the producers and they agreed to see her. Now she has been offered the part.

'I'm Miss Ffoliot-Ffoulkes!' she shouts. A woman steers her toddler's Easy Rider a bit further away from us.

'That's fantastic! Who?'

'Miss Ffoliot–Ffoulkes. *Murder on the Nile.*'

'I thought it was *Death on the Nile.*'

'That's the book. I start rehearsing tomorrow! And the play starts next week. We go all over the place. Some godforsaken parts on the country, but who cares? I'm working. And it's a fabulous part. She's self-obsessed and cantankerous . . . so hardly a stretch!'

I am so delighted for her. I envelop her in a hug.

'Ginny,' she says into my shoulder, 'can I do this?'

My eyes fill with tears. 'Standing on your head.'

Chapter Fifty-Nine

I am in the book shop staring at the book in my hand, not quite knowing how it got there.

Life Goals: How to Set Them, How to Achieve Them

It's the sort of thing I would have sneered at in the past. My life goals are eating pizza in front of Netflix in my PJs.

Hahaha.

Cassie has been away on her tour for a week and, without tempting fate, it feels like we're out of crisis mode. Which is great, although if there's one good thing about crisis mode, it's that it doesn't give you much time to worry about anything else.

Like your own life.

For weeks after Cassie's suicide attempt, I went to work and did all the things I normally do. But it was like I was on a kind of autopilot.

Now she is in recovery.

Which leaves me standing in Camden Books reading that Bill Gates, Richard Branson and Elon Musk all regularly set life goals.

And it's not just a flirtation with a glossy red hardback either. I feel like I'm suddenly all about this kind of stuff. It's as if while I've been busy looking after Cassie, my brain has gone behind my back and come up with all these subconscious ideas.

When the first Chocolicious Fri-yay went well, I went to the pub with the others but then after one drink I found myself saying I had to get home and do my writing home-work for the next day. It's like there was this bossy little voice inside my head.

It's the same voice that tells me, however much I miss Nick, even if it doesn't work out between him and A-man-da, I have to forget about him because I want a baby.

I guess I have already been thinking of life goals.

And it's a massive pain in the bum.

'I can really recommend that,' the guy behind the counter says.

He doesn't look old enough to shave, let alone have life goals.

'It's a technique the US military use called backward planning. You just make your goal the final step and then work backwards to create the small steps that will help you achieve it.'

'So you go backwards to go forwards?' That's it, Ginny, stay glib.

'Haha, yes, I suppose you do! It's better than treading water though, isn't it?'

I buy the book.

Chapter Sixty

From: Cassie Frost
Subject: Greetings from sunny Cambridge
Date: 15 November 2016 15:35:49GMT +1:00
To: Ginny Taylor

At the Arts Theatre Cambridge this week. Gemma has got the sulks. First, she got dreadful reviews – well-deserved I'm afraid, but I didn't tell her that – then a fan snapped a photo of her coming out of the stage door looking rough and posted it online. Everyone is running around saying 'poor you' while I try to bite my lip and refrain from saying she shouldn't go out in public with no make-up and greasy hair. (I do realize I speak as a woman who was recently in her local corner store in her slippers but that was different.) In my day – I know, I know! – we were taught it was part of our job to be camera-ready at any time. And that was before the internet!

Lots of boring interviews with local press and radio this morning. One cheeky DJ referred to me as the Jungle Diva. Like he was being so original! Anyway, he can call me what he likes as long as we get full houses!

Funny thing happened last night. Shane and I were

leaving the theatre and there were loads of fans waiting at the stage door. Shane is always brilliant with them all – signing autographs, having his picture taken with them, generally making them feel as if he has all the time in the world and they've made HIS day. There was this one woman, who seemed to have what my dad would refer to as the eyes on. She started telling Shane *he* had sold her this musical jewellery box on QVC, and how it was quite pricey, but it looked like a good quality item, so she'd splashed out and bought it for her granddaughter. Apparently, the ballerina that is supposed to dance when you open the box had stopped dancing after a couple of weeks. She seemed to think this was Shane's responsibility! It was all I could do not to step in and tell her that Shane didn't make the wretched jewellery boxes, he was just a presenter, for goodness' sake! Shane asked her – very politely – if she'd contacted QVC, and she said she had but they just sent her a letter saying they were sorry she was disappointed, but it was an issue she should take up directly with the manufacturer. You said it was a 'quality piece', she told Shane. By this time, I was getting quite irritable. We'd done two shows yesterday, it was eleven o'clock at night and now I had to stand there in the cold listening to this lunatic rant about ballerinas that didn't pirouette. Shane kept his patience though. Told the old bat he didn't work at QVC anymore, but he'd give someone he knows there a call (which he actually will). Then he took her phone number and promised to let her know what the guy says. She looked almost smiley by the time we left. Honestly, the great British public!

I have to say Shane has been brilliant with me too.

Now, don't Mills & Boonify that in your mind! I mean AS A FRIEND! He's been driving me from place to place, booking up digs, even making sure I eat regularly. He's almost as bossy as you when it comes to my 'recovery'! The only problem is everyone insists on acting as if we're an item.

  C x

Chapter Sixty-One

It's like the last day of school except instead of hitting Pizza Express, we go to the pub.

Judy takes a large glug of red wine. Little gold bird cages complete with tiny yellow canaries on perches swing from her beleaguered earlobes. She's been a great teacher, Judy. I may even sign up for her 'Understanding Character' workshop.

I sip at my gin and tonic. Tupperware Lady is telling a story about her pet lizard, Raptor. Who'd have thought she'd keep a lizard? She's full of surprises is Tupperware Lady. She read out a story last week that was so raunchy it made my cheeks flame. She probably has a big Tupperware box for all her sex toys. And to think I was worried for her when Mr Travelogue read a piece about the things Thai nightclub girls could do with ping pong balls! (A story which only he could make dull.)

The pub is full of people from nearby offices. Jackets have been discarded and ties and tongues loosened. A girl in a tight red skirt takes off her high black patent shoe and rubs the ball of her foot. The gesture reminds me of Cassie (who always has unsuitable shoes) and I feel a stab of anxiety. I tell myself this time she really is better.

Mr Published didn't turn up this week. I wasn't there but apparently in the pub after last week's class, he got very drunk and admitted the only thing he'd ever had published was the Warhammer newsletter he writes every month.

One of the noisier groups are obviously estate agents. They are competing loudly for who has managed to shift the 'crappest property' that month. I take a sip of my gin and tonic noting how, despite the fact I'm thirty-five, getting so much as a toe on the property ladder is yet another box I've failed to tick. I will probably still be renting when I'm sixty. Jarielle will be long gone and I'll be living with new strangers.

Annabel's souless-sister taps away on her Blackberry. Apparently, it's already 6 a.m. in China.

Telephone numbers and promises to keep in touch are exchanged.

I think about Katia. The day I bumped into her in the supermarket, I wanted to tell her that she shouldn't give up. That she was too good and that the next agent would probably snap her up.

But maybe Katia was right and it is just too hard?

'Don't forget to kill those adverbs!' Mrs Tupperware says.

'Remember to show, not tell!' Judy adds.

And then we all head off into the night. All of us dreaming that we will be the one who beats the odds.

Chapter Sixty-Two

From: Cassie Frost
Subject: Heeeeelp!
Date: 18 November 2016 10:00:30GMT +1:00
To: Ginny Taylor

I have done something so silly! AAAAAARRRR-GGGHHH! Shane and I ended up in bed together last night! What have I done?
  Cx

From: Ginny Taylor
Subject: Heeeeelp!
Date: 18 November 2016 10:02:14GMT +1:00
To: Cassie Frost

Why is that bad news? Every time I have spoken to you in the last few weeks, you've been 'Shane this and Shane that'. Clearly you're keen on him and he's potty about you! I'm opening champagne!
  Gx

From: Cassie Frost
Subject: Heeeeelp!
Date: 18 November 2016 10:05:40GMT +1:00
To: Ginny Taylor

Might have known that would be your reaction! Am going to yoga before he wakes up. Will call you later. Try to think of some sensible/non-Ginnyish advice before then!

   Cx

Chapter Sixty-Three

I wish there were more people in the crematorium.

How can empty pews pay respect? Celebrate a life? A life that might not have been led perfectly (whose life is?) but was full of hope and possibility and struggle.

People are busy. They have commitments. Plus, it's a week day. Not everyone can get time off work.

But still it feels wrong.

A funeral has its own shape and pattern just as a birthday has cake and candles.

And this one is wrong.

There won't be enough voices to carry the hymns.

Enough heads to bow and shoulders to sag.

Not enough people. Not enough fuss.

The weather outside is glorious. Blue skies, sunshine. It's done its bit.

But in here it's a different story.

'Do you think we'll have to say he was a lovely guy?'

'Cassie!' I whisper through gritted teeth.

'What? I hate it when people talk differently about someone just because they're dead. Mr Holden used to call the two guys who own your flat "those homos". It made him doubly unhappy that Tim is what he described as "coloured". When I said once how lovely all the blossom looked in spring, he snorted and said it made such a mess of the pavements. Mr Holden was a lovely guy is a non-sequitur.'

'Keep your voice down!'

'What, because all the other seven people here cared about him so deeply?'

'His sister looked very tearful when she greeted us.'

'How often did you see her come to visit him?'

There's a rustling coming from where the organist is waiting behind his curtain. It sounds as if he might be eating a packet of crisps.

'Last time I was at Golders Green Crematorium, it was for Mandy Copeman's funeral. Now there was a classic example of what I was talking about. When she topped herself, no one had a bad word to say. Oh, Mandy was so kind and compassionate. No, she wasn't. If you saw her giving money to a blind man begging in the street, you knew she was really just snaffling his day's takings. So, yes, it was sad she'd killed herself, but, no, I wasn't going to say she was ever in the queue for canonization.'

The preacher is a Humanist called Rory. Apparently, Mr Holden was vehemently anti-religion ('Maybe we had something in common after all,' Cassie said when she heard this). Rory has floppy hair and a booming voice.

'Someone missed their vocation as an actor. Bet if you told him he reminds you a bit of Hugh Grant, he'd do a fake modest laugh and say everybody says that.'

'Sssshh.' I elbow Cassie.

Rory intones about how although he never had the pleasure of meeting John, his sister, Mary, had told him lots about the kind of man he was.

'Like she'd know.' Cassie's stage whisper isn't quite as quiet as it might be and the woman in front turns around and glares.

Rory is talking about a life well lived. What does that

even mean though? To be kind, happy, successful? All of those things?

We listen to a recording of Susan Boyle singing 'I Dreamed A Dream'. I wonder what Mr Holden's dreams were and how many of them he fulfilled? I know he never wrote his book but what other disappointments did he take to his grave? Maybe he desperately wanted to swim with dolphins or always pictured himself running a marathon?

'I feel bad I knew so little about him,' I had said to Cassie in the car on the way here.

'Relax – you've already won Neighbour of The Year looking after me. Plus, we're going to the funeral, aren't we? I must say it's very convenient that it fell during my week's break from the tour.'

'Convenient?'

Cassie looks unabashed.

I think about what I do know about Mr Holden. That he worked for the civil service, never married and didn't have kids. He told me once when we were putting out the rubbish at the same time that he'd nearly married a girl he worked with. I wonder what happened with her? What went wrong? Whether she married someone else and he spent the rest of his life pining for her? Perhaps, to this day, his flat is hiding reams of love letters that have yellowed with age.

After the service, Mary says that she and Martin would like Cassie and me to go back to their house for a sherry. 'Everyone is.'

'"Everyone" seems like a strange choice of word when there were only nine of us there, don't you think?' Cassie says to me in the car.

They live in Kentish Town.

'Five minutes away from us and we never saw her,' Cassie whispers. 'Those tears were either for show or guilt.'

Mary's house is already decked out for Christmas.

327

'She must be very organized – having decorations up before the end of November,' I say to Cassie.

Cassie rolls her eyes. 'She's the type to put them up in August.'

'Do all help yourselves to the spread,' Mary says. 'There are cold cuts and all sorts.'

I look at the sideboard on which there are cold meats, sausage rolls and coleslaw, all of which look as though they have been sitting under their clingfilm shrouds for quite some time.

'Bet that food has been sitting out for hours,' Cassie whispers. 'Look how the ham is curling up at the edges.'

I look at the heavily laden fake Christmas tree. I cannot believe it's nearly December. This time last year, I'd only recently discovered Jack and Annabel together.

Two sullen and lumpy teenage boys are sitting on what Mary refers to as the three-piece. She explains that they are her grandsons and while they couldn't attend the funeral itself, she thought they ought to be here as 'a mark of respect'. They have been forcibly unplugged from *Call of Duty* and are looking most put out to be expected to make nice with the old people.

'Poor sods,' Cassie whispers. 'You can see them wondering what the hell they're doing here given they only met the old bloke about three times in their whole lives. I hope they're getting something in the will.'

Martin tops up our glasses whilst Mary appears at my feet to remove an imperceptible bit of mud that has apparently come off the bottom of my boot. 'So,' Martin says to Cassie, 'have you retired from the television and theatre now?'

'No. No. I'm doing a tour at the moment actually. *Murder on the Nile.*'

He stares at her with such open scepticism that I feel tempted to shove a French stick down his throat.

'My son is in the City,' the plump lady with the varicose veins suddenly pipes up apropos of nothing. 'He's doing ever so well.'

'A grand fromage,' Martin says, tittering to himself. I should introduce him to my brother-in-law.

'You should see his car!'

'So how did you know John?' says a hard-faced woman with a helmet of grey hair and a bunched-up mouth.

'Neighbours. We both are. Were. You?'

'We worked together in the civil service.'

I wonder if she is The One. It's hard to imagine the face in front of me ever having loved but maybe it has just loved and lost.

Mary is coming around with a bowl of baked potatoes. 'Anyone want a jacket with their meal? I've just warmed them through in the micro.'

'You were on that jungle show,' the woman says to Cassie.

My shoulders stiffen. Please, I want to say, I know she seems okay, but she's been suffering from depression. I think of the 'Baby on Board' badges people wear. I want a 'Be Kind' badge for Cassie.

'I never watched it. I can't bear reality television. But I gather you made a bit of a show of yourself.'

Cassie laughs. 'A bit of a show of myself? Imagine that, on a show.'

The women pats the back of her helmet. 'According to the newspapers, it wasn't your finest hour.'

'Hmm. Well, I did eat a kangaroo's arsehole. That's a pretty fine hour, wouldn't you say?'

The room has gone quiet and Helmet Hair's mouth bunches to a close. We leave soon after.

★　★　★

'Well, that was fun!'

We both start laughing and, before I know it, I have tears coursing down my cheeks. 'Her face!'

'Yeah, don't think we've made a friend there. Not with any of them really. I thought Mary was going to sweep you up and put you in the bin when you deposited a bit of mud on her purple carpet. And did you hear her telling me I look different to how I look on the telly? I don't think the "different" was a compliment!'

I unlock the car. 'It didn't upset you, did it?' Her wellness is still new and fragile.

'Nah!' says Cassie sliding into the passenger seat. 'How can you take any opinion seriously when it's provided by a woman who has a pink toilet roll doll in her bathroom?'

'She did not! I haven't seen one of those for years.' I start the car.

'Do you think he had a life? Before he got old and boring?'

'I hope so. Not everyone needs to be a movie star to be happy though.'

'Hmm, I think it kinda helps, but that's not what I meant. It's not about him being "someone". Just about him being someone to someone.'

'Talking of which, how are things going with Shane?'

She shrugs. 'We had a bit of a domestic earlier. He'd assumed I'd take him to that premiere with me. Just because we're together, doesn't mean we're joined at the hip! Not every couple is Jean and Marielle.'

'Can't you take him?'

She puffs out her cheeks. 'Maybe. Anyway, we weren't talking about me and Shane, we were talking about our dearly departed neighbour.'

'He told me once he'd nearly married someone at work. I wondered if it was Susan.'

Cassie raises her eyebrows. 'Helmet-hair? Can't imagine her

being in love with anyone.' She takes a lip gloss out of her bag and applies it while looking in the passenger mirror. 'I hope there are more than nine people at my funeral.'

'Too soon! But when you do die of natural causes after a long and happy life, the place will be packed.'

'Good. And no carnations please.'

Chapter Sixty-Four

When the landline rings, it's always a sales call. And I feel sorry for these people, I really do – they're only trying to earn a living like the rest of us – but they are SO annoying. 'Ginny Taylor?' a voice says.

'Yes,' I say wearily, preparing all the polite ways of saying 'go away and don't ring back'.

'My name is Bella Davies.'

I really don't care.

'I'm from *Nuovo* magazine.'

Or maybe I do.

'And I'm calling to tell you that your short story has won third place in our competition.'

I let out a tiny squeal – slightly pig-like – and ask her if she's sure. That it's not some other Ginny Taylor?

She laughs. 'The story's called "A Walk in the Park", right?'

I nod which is kind of useless since we're on the phone, but Bella Davies goes on talking about the prize giving ceremony and how I'll have the opportunity to get some detailed feedback and advice from the panel of judges. One of them is a literary agent, she says, so you never know. I try to take in what she's saying but all I can think of is that I've won something (well come third, but still), and I haven't done that since the Kindness Cup.

'Would you like me to read you the judge's quote that will go by your winning entry in the magazine?' Bella Davies asks.

'Ummm . . . yeah.' With natural eloquence like this, she must be seeing why I've chosen to try to write.

'An emotive, descriptive and insightful story . . .'

I really want to tell Nick, because he's the one who found out about this competition and suggested I enter it. And he, Nancy and Cassie are the ones who've been my biggest writing cheerleaders.

'Ginny Taylor has a real lightness of style.'

I didn't know I had a style at all, let alone a lightness of one! I love that! I suddenly feel that I'm on the path writing wise. That it will be bumpy and littered with rejection slips but I'm on it.

'She does the relationship stuff brilliantly.'

At this point, I start to guffaw. Does the relationship stuff brilliantly? Only on the page, Bella Davies. Only on the page.

Chapter Sixty-Five

I am wedding dress shopping again.

'How about this one?' I suggest to Cassie.

She wrinkles her nose. 'Muttony.'

'This one?'

'Matronly.'

Our sales assistant is not at all like the lovely Marnie who was so patient when I was trying on dresses. This woman has the air of someone who has been around the block a few times and is bored, bored, bored. She is wearing unsmudged black eyeliner in two harsh black lines and has dirty bleached-blonde hair with black roots. She got off to a terrible start with Cassie when she assumed I was the bride. (Small mercy, she didn't assume Cassie was my mother.) 'Some of our more mature brides want to cover up their arms or camouflage a not-so-trim tum.'

Cassie, whose abs are more toned than mine will ever be, gives her a steely look.

We manage to find a few dresses Cassie considers worth trying on and I settle myself on the white chaise lounge. 'Promise me,' Cassie said when she told me the news, 'you'll help me find a dress that doesn't make me look like Miss Havisham.'

She comes out in an empire-line satin column dress. Her face betrays the fact she's not happy.

'Can I even wear white? Is it ridiculous? Shane says it's fine but then he's a bloke. And wouldn't care if I turned up in a bin bag.'

'It's your Big Day, you can wear whatever you want,' the assistant says, her voice toneless. She looks like a prison warden in civvies. The sort who spits at the inmates.

'I think white is fine,' I say. 'I don't think all the virginal connotations are important now. I'm not sure about that shape though. Try one of the others.'

She disappears into the changing room and the assistant offers me tea or champagne in a way that makes it clear she'd like me to have neither. I ask if we may have a couple of glasses of water and she stomps off.

Nancy phoned me last night and said that she and Will had been having 'if we get married' conversations. And I am ecstatic for her, of course I am. But I can't help also feeling a little left behind. Nancy managed to meet someone in a city where there are no single, straight men. She and Will have been together less than two months.

Cassie comes out from the changing room in a dress that has a sixties feel to it. 'You know the old rule about if you wore it the first time . . .' she says before I can say a word.

She goes back into the changing room and I am left staring at the rows of wedding dresses lined up like a crocodile of school children. I really loved that last dress I tried on when I was going to marry Jack. I miss that dress. Not him though. Even though he was so kind the day I got back from the hospital, I just know the two of us aren't right.

'Perhaps I need to be a bit more Ironic Bride,' Cassie says, swirling out in a cloud of tulle.

'What? Scarlet? Leather and studs?'

She gives her trademark throaty chuckle. 'You're right. Hideous.'

'What about a great suit?'

'I don't want to look like I'm going to the f-ing office!'

I laugh. 'Try the Caroline Herrera on. I bet that will look great on you.'

'Really? You don't think I need a little more coverage? I mean, I know that's a bit rich from a woman whose left tit was recently splashed all over the national newspapers but that was just an unfortunate wardrobe malfunction.'

'Just try it.'

She disappears dutifully back to the changing room. I wonder whether Nick is with A-man-da right now? Perhaps he's making her brunch? He makes excellent scrambled eggs.

Cassie comes out, looks at herself in the big baroque mirror and makes a face. 'You know what? I think we're looking in the wrong place. We shouldn't be in a bridal boutique at all.'

'Okay . . .' I'm not sure quite what she has in mind, but I do know a wedding dress shop is pretty much the last place I want to be right now.

Chapter Sixty-Six

Fiona appears and asks me if I've got a minute. I have to get past this feeling that I've been summoned to the headmistress's office, and that I've been very, very naughty. I must try to see Fiona as someone who has rescued me from hosiery crises and credits me with single-handedly saving the Chocolicious account.

She has been asked to make a speech at this year's PR Person of The Year event, but it's the night of Oscar's parents' evening and she can't possibly send Rupes – he upset the Head terribly last time with his comments about a good buggering and beating never doing him a jot of harm. She'd like me to go and make the speech in her place.

My mouth turns to cotton-wool (just at the thought – imagine what I'll be like when I'm actually there). I look at the silver-framed photos on Fiona's desk, which all look like something out of a Boden catalogue.

'Something the matter?'

I look at her and, for a moment, consider telling her the truth. But then I realize that nerves will be something that Fiona has heard of as a concept but never actually experienced – a bit like state education. If there's one really great thing about PR it's that, contrary to what you might expect, it's allowed me to completely avoid public speaking. You only so much as have to utter, 'Do you want to lead this presentation?'

for others to leap like you've just said, 'Do you want a whopping great pay rise?' Which I suppose in a way you have.

'I thought you'd be pleased.'

'I am pleased,' I croak. Pleased like I was when I reversed into a skip doing the three-point-turn in my driving test. As delighted as I was the day I came home to find Annabel sucking on Jack's cock like a popsicle. 'Thrilled.'

Fiona smiles. 'Excellent.'

I turn to go. My heart is thudding in my chest (to repeat – just at the thought).

'You'll need a good frock.'

I arrange my face into a smile. Like that's my biggest worry.

Chapter Sixty-Seven

I spend the next week veering between moderate panic and total freak out.

On Wednesday, I am in a meeting with Fiona when I realize that I haven't been listening to a word she's been saying because I've been too busy visualizing myself getting up on stage and being physically sick in front of six hundred people.

Then I forget to reply to an email from Darren Grant. A few hours later he sends another. *Can I have an answer on this, please?*

Ouch.

Or do you need me to sign off with à kiss?

I google advice on how to overcome your fear of public speaking and watch endless YouTube videos of upbeat Americans. I put my faith in Brad because the first thing he says is that being afraid of public speaking is perfectly rational.

Thank you, Brad.

Think of our ancestors, he tells me. Standing alone in an open place with nowhere to hide facing a large group of creatures. They would have been eaten alive!

'I don't think I can do this,' I say to Nancy on FaceTime. 'I know I'm being pathetic but . . .'

'You're not being pathetic. Public speaking is the number one fear. It's in front of death. As the Jerry Seinfeld joke goes, if the average person has to go to a funeral, they'd rather be in the casket than doing the eulogy.'

I laugh. 'Well, that's made me feel loads better.'

The time I dread most is 4 a.m. At 4 a.m. the fear is HUGE. Luckily Brad is there for me. He tells me I need to reframe the questions I ask myself in my head. Replace positive ones with negative ones. Not what will happen if I screw up but what will happen if I smash it?

Hmm, easier said than done, Brad.

Cassie tries her best to be sympathetic but I can tell she's struggling. Being the centre of attention is her oxygen. 'Have you got something fabulous to wear?' she says.

I cheat on Brad and watch a YouTube video by another – a woman who tells me to try power posing. I am to stand for two minutes with my legs spread wide and my hands on my hips.

I feel like an absolute idiot.

By Friday, I am ready to tell Fiona that I absolutely can't do it. That I'm flattered she asked me but it's just not my thing. That thinking about it makes my heart race and my chest hurt and that sometimes I can't even breathe.

And then she is all upbeat and perfect and Fiona-ish and I can't tell that I am hyperventilating at the thought of what is essentially just talking. Not skiing down a black run or throwing myself out of an aeroplane for a sky dive – talking.

The fear doesn't go away though. When I'm trying to write a press release, the blank page on my computer screen is like a projector screen for the horrible images my mind conjures up. Me tripping as I walk up the stairs, my mouth so dry I can't speak, me fainting and wetting myself in front of six hundred people.

'What's the worst thing that could happen?' my mum said.

Fainting and wetting myself in front of six hundred people. That's fairly bad.

My 'proper' writing is out of the question. Since being placed in the writing competition, I have been determined to prioritize my writing, and every day I have been getting up at 6 a.m. so I can do an hour before getting ready for work. Now that's shot to pieces. Firstly, after restless sleep that's punctuated by stressy dreams, I'm too tired, but secondly my imagination seems to only be able to flex its muscles in one area. The only story arc I can think up at the moment is me screwing up this awards night.

I can't even self-medicate with my trusty favourite Twirl Bites because the near constant nausea gets in the way.

I can do this, I tell myself repeatedly.

Now I just have to make myself believe it.

Chapter Sixty-Eight

My head is so full of having to get up there on stage at the awards dinner that I manage to get on the wrong bus. I am coming home from lunch at my parents' house. It was just me and my mum because my dad had been called into the hospital for an emergency.

I am just about to get off the bus and go back on myself when I realize that I'm only two stops away from said hospital. I decide on a whim that I will pop in and see my dad. He will have finished his surgery by now, so may be free for a quick cup of coffee. It's worth a try. He might even be able to give me some advice about getting through the speech. He speaks at big conferences all the time. Better still, he might even be able to give me some kind of magic sedative that will still leave me with my wits about me.

I walk into the main entrance. I came here once when I was little and I'd got an orange pip stuck in my ear. As soon as the people in A&E realized who my dad was, I was quite the celebrity. Years later he told me how his colleagues teased him about the important surgery they'd performed on me (basically sticking a vacuum cleaner-like pipe down my ear).

A young girl with lots of piercings is sitting on a bench sobbing. I ask if she's okay, which is kind of a pointless question really. She nods and I head for the lift.

One of the first people I see in Cardiology is someone I

know. Anthea is a stout, resolutely cheerful nurse. The it's-just-a-little-bit-terminal sort. 'Hullo, Ginny. You look lovely! Changed your hair! What are you doing here?' I explain I'm hoping to catch Dad. 'He's not here today. It's his day off.'

'He was called in.'

Her brow creases. 'No. I don't think so. I've been here all day.'

My heart feels like it's going to burst out of my chest and my mouth feels dry. Anthea must be wrong. My dad must be in the hospital and yet somehow they've missed each other. Except Anthea isn't the sort of person to miss anything. So my dad isn't at the hospital.

The girl on the bench is still there and still crying. I wonder what has made her so sad. Who she has been to see and what's wrong with them. A mother with cancer? A grandad who's dying? A brother in a coma? People have worse problems than a dad who isn't in the hospital.

But where is he? And why did he lie to my mother?

I dial my parents' number knowing that all the nonsense I've been filling my head with will soon be put out of my mind. My mother will answer with the same sing-songy voice she always does: 'Hell-o-o.' I will sound casual, thank her for lunch. She will tell me that the strangest thing happened. There was a mix-up and Dad wasn't needed at the hospital after all. That I only just missed him.

But she doesn't say that.

Instead she tells me he's asleep in front of the TV. 'Poor thing! Apparently, he had quite a day of it at the hospital!'

My stomach lurches like I've just dropped down a massive dip on a rollercoaster. 'Oh.'

'Ginny, love, are you okay?'

'I'm fine, Mum.'

'Just you sound a little weird. I know you're really nervous about making that speech but you're going to be fine. And I know this break-up with Jack has been hard on you too but, for what it's worth, I think you made the right choice. You can't go into a marriage unless you're 100 per cent sure.'

I try to swallow the lump in my throat long enough to make an excuse to get off the phone.

I sit there for ages after hanging up, unable to move or think straight.

Jarielle come in laden with shopping bags and start asking about how my Saturday has been. *Oh, just wonderful!* I make my excuses and disappear to my bedroom.

I desperately want to call Nancy but she and Will are going to Florida today. Their first ever holiday together. I know Nancy would pick up my call anyway because, well, she's Nancy, but I can't be that selfish.

My stomach feels like someone is turning cartwheels inside it. And for a change that's nothing to do with the awards dinner.

Chapter Sixty-Nine

I walk along Regent's Park Road trying to get my head together. Fairy lights twinkle from every window. Perfect homes for perfect families. But then that's what my parents' house looks like from the outside too.

My mobile goes. It's Cassie returning my call from earlier. She's sorry she didn't call back as soon as the matinee was over but Shane was insistent she had to eat first. He's so bossy. Is everything okay?

The story tumbles out, words tripping over each other.

Cassie listens, saying nothing.

And then, when I finally finish, the first thing she says is, 'Whatever you do, don't say anything to your mother.'

I am stunned. 'You're joking, right?'

'No. My best advice is to forget about everything you know. Or rather, think you know.'

I stand in the middle of the street, my heart pounding. A couple walk past me hand in hand. She is laughing like he's just said the funniest thing in the whole world. 'What I know for sure is that my father lied to my mother about where he was that day.'

'Maybe he was organizing a surprise for her.'

I snort.

'Look, maybe he was doing exactly what you think he was doing, but it doesn't matter—'

'Doesn't matter?' I say, my voice going up an octave.

'Doesn't matter in terms of you getting involved.'

I stare at a Christmas tree that's filling a huge bay window. It's decked out in turquoise and gold. It's almost too perfect. There's probably another tree in the playroom the kids are allowed to decorate with coloured lights and clashing baubles.

What will Christmas with my family be like this year? Will I flinch when my dad hugs me? Blurt something out to Rachel when she's fussing about tinsel or stuffing? Cry when my mum says she's worrying the roast potatoes aren't crisping up? Sod the potatoes!

I dig my nails into my palms. 'If someone close to me had known about Jack and Annabel, I'd have wanted them to tell me.'

'Hmm.'

'What does "hmm" mean? You're saying I should keep quiet? Protect my father?'

'It's your mother I'm asking you to protect.'

'What, by living with a man who . . .' I can't bring myself to finish the sentence. This is my father we're talking about. The man I've always looked up to. 'She's put up with a lot over the years. Giving up her career and ambitions, bringing up my sister and I almost single-handedly, always having to be the cheerful one no matter how she was feeling because if you think she's had a bad day, well think about Dad's. He'd lost a child on the operating table, devastated a family. His bad day trumped everyone's.'

'There are all kinds of marriages, Ginny. Hang on a moment, there's someone at the dressing-room door. Honestly, you can't get an ounce of peace around here.' Her voice softens as soon as she realizes it's Shane. A cup of tea would be lovely. No, she hasn't forgotten she said she would have a nap.

I wrap my scarf a little tighter against the cold. I am thinking about a time when I was eleven years old and I picked up

350

the phone upstairs and heard my father talking to someone on the other end of the line. He was talking to them in a soft, croony voice. 'I will if I can darling.' Blood rushed to my head and I put the receiver down. He must have heard the click because seconds later he came upstairs and said he'd just been talking to a very upset mother whose child was terminally ill. I wanted to ask him why he called her 'darling', but I said nothing.

Cassie's attention is back with me now. Shane says hi. She sounds girlish. Like a loved-up teenager. And to think she has always billed herself as a cynic when it comes to men, cast me as the incurable romantic. 'Listen, Ginny, what I'm saying is this. Not everything in life is black and white . . .'

I cut her off before she can continue with this drivel. 'My father is screwing around on my mother. It all seems fairly clear cut to me.'

Cassie sighs. 'I know it's hard for you.'

I feel so angry with Cassie. Her reaction is so different to the one I'd expected from her. Irritation fizzes inside me making my skin prickle and my teeth clench. My boots pound the pavement.

'And how are you feeling about next Wednesday? Any better?'

For God's sake. Why would I be feeling better?

Cassie doesn't understand.

On either count.

Chapter Seventy

The day of the PR awards dinner dawns and I wake up at
4.30 feeling lousy. Last night I woke up screaming after having
a dream that I went up on stage and the audience was made
up of multiple versions of my father all with different women.

I throw my evening dress into my work bag not really
knowing if I'm going to be able to muster the courage to need
it later. If I thought I was losing the plot before my unsched-
uled visit to St Mary's, I've been a hundred times worse since.

The morning drags past and I keep looking to Brad for
advice when I'm supposed to be working. Remember to
pause, he says. Keep breathing.

At eleven, my mum calls and says she's going to be in the
area at lunchtime and can she buy me lunch. I know this is
a geographical convenience she's contrived; she wants to give
me a pep talk in advance of tonight, keep my spirits up and
tell me I can do it.

Of course, she doesn't know that seeing her isn't easy right
now.

I umm and err before saying that would be lovely. We don't
have to talk about Dad. I can put that out of my head.

We sit opposite each other in Manny's, order chicken and
avocado sandwiches on white bread. Your sister would not
approve, my mother jokes. She would remind us white bread
is as bad for us as a doughnut.

The urge to tell my mother rises like vomit in my throat.

She looks so relaxed today. Happy. Can I bear to shatter that?

She starts to burble about the birds she saw on the feeding table this morning and how George and Felix are coming over later and she's going to make salt playdough with them and do I remember how I loved that so much?

'How are you feeling about tonight?' she says, her eyes filled with concern.

'Okay,' I lie.

She reaches across the table and squeezes my hand. 'You're going to be fine, my sweetheart. Just take deep breaths and tell yourself I'm the only person in the audience.'

I nod.

'I don't think it helps that you've had such a rough time of it lately. Starting a new job, supporting Cassie when she was ill, breaking it off with Jack. I know you did the right thing there but it can't be easy. One minute you're planning a wedding, the next . . .'

'I don't think I was ever really planning the wedding.'

My mother squeezes my hand harder. Hers feels warm and rough. For a second I want to tell her how I feel about Nick.

'Was calling off the wedding anything to do with Nick?'

'How do you do that?'

She smiles, her pale blue eyes twinkling. 'You never were very hard to read. I could tell as soon as you were let out of the school gates what kind of day you'd had. If you'd got a sticker for good work or had been told off for talking.'

'I wasn't told off much.'

She laughs. 'No. You were a good little thing. Anyway, Nick?'

'I didn't leave Jack *for* Nick. It wasn't right between us. That said . . .' I just can't have this conversation now. 'Please can we not talk about it?'

'Sure.'

I imagine a lot of mothers would push, but not mine.

The urge to tell her about my father rises up to the surface again. My grandma lived until she was ninety-two. If Mum does the same, she's got thirty years left. She could leave my feckless father and do anything she wants. Travel the world. Set up a business. Fall in love with a man who deserves her.

'I need to tell you something,' I blurt with no grace whatsoever.

'Oh?' She reaches up to brush away a stray piece of hair and I stare at the wedding band on her left hand which looks old and worn.

'The day I came over to have lunch and Dad told you he was at the hospital.' I pause, my courage deserting me.

My mother says nothing. Her head is bowed and I can't see her expression. A car alarm starts up outside. Then suddenly she speaks. 'Stop.'

'I don't und—'

'I said stop.' Her voice has an unfamiliar edge to it.

My brain is struggling to process. I look at my mother. Blood red blotches have appeared on her cheeks and her normally kind eyes are steely and cold.

We sit there in silence for what seems like forever.

'I'm sorry. I just thou—'

She silences me with a look and throws some cash down on the table. 'I think I'd better go.'

Chapter Seventy-One

I am sitting in the toilet cubicle at work shaking.

It simply hadn't occurred to me that Mum knew what was going on (and she must know. It's the only explanation for why she closed the conversation down like that). I wasn't prepared for her to be angry with me either. My mother has hardly ever been angry with me, not *really* angry. The only times I remember were when I ran out in front of a car aged five, and when I was a teenager and she saw me coming home on the back of a motorbike without a helmet. And now.

How the hell am I going to get through tonight? When Brad talked about 'getting yourself in the zone' I'm pretty sure this isn't what he had in mind.

I called Cassie as soon as I left the café. I expected her to say I told you so, but she didn't. She told me my mother wouldn't stay cross with me for long. That she wasn't really cross anyway; just sad I knew something it would've been better for all of us if I didn't.

'How can she stay with him?' I wailed, crying like a small child.

'He's her life.'

That was the expression my mother had always used: Your father is my life. I'd always thought it was such a lovely, romantic thing to say. Now I understand a different meaning entirely. Our lives are enmeshed, too complicated to pick apart.

'I wish I could be there with you instead of in bloody Darlington.'

'I'm okay,' I say through the sobs. 'Do you think she just stayed with him because of Rachel and me? Because I would never have thought she'd put up with this. Him working all the hours God sends, yes. Her having to give up her career, I guess. Even reconciling herself to the fact that that "Lovely Doctor Taylor" isn't always so charming at home. But this?'

'Don't be so hard on her Ginny. A marriage is a big complicated messy thing with good bits and bad bits. Maybe your mother has just weighed up the pluses and minuses and decided the sums work for her.'

'Or maybe she's just settled for something she shouldn't have.'

'Maybe. But whatever the choices are, they're her choices.'

I stare at the toilet floor. How am I ever going to face my father again? How am I going to get through tonight?

Growing up, I always thought my parents' marriage a happy one but then it takes a hell of a lot of broken china before any kid ever considers any other possibility.

They rowed, of course, but my mother always reassured me that anybody who lives together rows. It didn't mean anything. Look at me and my sister: laying into each other like savages sometimes. Didn't mean we didn't love each other.

I have to go back to my desk. People will be wondering where I am.

I want to tell Rachel, but at the same time, I'm frightened to. She's such a daddy's girl; this would crush her.

I stand up and take a deep breath. Once, when I was a child, I thought my parents were going to get divorced. It was after a row on a drive to Toulouse. I'd never seen my mother so angry. Also, divorce was at the forefront of my mind because Claudia Newman's parents had split up. Claudia kept telling me she was pleased because it meant she would have twice as many presents at Christmas but I knew she wasn't really happy.

I stand at the sink and splash my face with cold water.

I think about my parents' wedding anniversary dinner at Mon Plaisir. 'If you knew thirty-five years ago what you know now, would you still marry me?' my father said.

'Are you kidding!' she replied.

I remember us all roaring with laughter.

Now it doesn't seem quite so funny.

Chapter Seventy-Two

It's just under an hour until the awards dinner. I am about to call Fiona and tell her I must have eaten something dodgy at lunch. I know I'm letting her down, that even if she was prepared to miss parents' evening, she couldn't get to the awards dinner in time now. I know with Jacqui and Ben both away, there's no one else on the team that could fill my shoes.

But surely I'm letting Fiona down more by completely screwing this up. And if I couldn't do it before, then how the hell can I do it now? I can barely manage to stop crying.

Fiona picks up on the first ring. 'Ginny. Everything okay?'

She'll be nice about this, tell me it can't be helped.

But it can be helped.

'Umm . . . err. Just wanted to say I hope the parents' evening goes well.'

I grab my dress and head for the office loos, where I've spent most of the afternoon.

I need to put the discovery about my dad and the row with my mum to the back of my mind.

It's glaringly obvious that she stayed with him for the children. Me and Rachel. Of course, any woman who puts so much effort into creating the perfect home – from sewing curtains to restoring furniture – wants the perfect family to go in it. What good would my beloved Lundby dolls house have been to me without a mummy and a daddy? The thing

I can't work out is why she stayed when we'd grown up? Was it just too late by then? Or does she love my dad so much she'd rather have part of him than none of him? (And, shouldn't I – of all people – understand that?)

Back of your mind, Ginny.

Fifty-five minutes until the awards dinner. I put on the dress, struggling to do up the zip at the back. I try to make my red golf-ball eyes look slightly better with a ton of concealer but end up giving up and just put on lots of lipstick.

My heart is racing and I am sweating.

Forty-eight minutes.

You can do this.

In the lift Rob tells me I look nice and wishes me luck. Just hope I don't trip on my dress going up on stage, I joke.

Oh Christ!

Outside, the wind blows the rain into my face and turns my umbrella inside out.

Delays on the central line. It's a sign. I can't go through with this.

Yes. You. Can.

Get an Uber.

Finding your ride. Surge pricing. Whatever. The nearest driver is sixteen minutes away. Too long.

It's not my fault if I can't get there . . .

Stop it!

I will get a black cab.

No yellow lights.

I stand on the street corner getting buffeted by the wind and rain. *Set yourself up to succeed*, Brad said.

Finally, a cab with its light on. As I throw myself into it, my phone rings. I fumble to answer. It's Julia.

'I just wanted to wish you good luck for tonight.'

I am sweating now.

'Also, look I don't know exactly what happened between

you and Nick but I just wanted to give you a heads-up that he'll be there tonight. And it looked as if it was slightly awkward between the two of you at the engagement party so I thought I'd better warn you.'

'Thanks,' I manage.

Tears prick the back of my eyes. Just when tonight couldn't get any worse.

The traffic is horrendous, and I keep looking at my watch as if that will somehow slow down time.

Finally, the cab pulls up outside.

Now I just have to make myself go in.

Chapter Seventy-Three

I force myself through the door and the first person I see is Annabel.

'Ginny. No sombrero tonight?' She smirks.

In the loos, I try to rescue my appearance. Brad says it's important to look your best for that extra boost in confidence. I look at the mud splatters up the back of my cream dress, my puffy red eyes and my fringe that has frizzed halfway up my forehead, Henry VIII style.

Fail number one.

On my way to my seat, I see Nick and A–man–da. She is wearing a very simple navy dress. The type that looks like nothing on the rails. It also does not have any mud splatters up the back. And her hair is not frizzy. (Perhaps it doesn't rain on A–man–da? Perhaps she not only gets Nick but a rain-free pass through life?)

At the table, people are saying things to me but it feels like they're speaking underwater.

I keep looking at the stage and my heartbeat starts to get faster and faster.

I can't do this.

A waiter puts noisettes of lamb in front of me, and it's all I can do not to be sick there and then.

I can't do this.

People talking. Waah, waah, waah. So many people in the room.

So many people who will be looking at me.

I can't do this.

My fingers and hands are starting to go numb and I suddenly feel light-headed, as if I'm struggling to get air into my lungs.

I can't do this.

I'm having a heart attack.

I force myself to breathe.

Eventually, my heart rate slows down a little and the pins and needles in my hands subside. I think of Brad telling me to visualize success like elite athletes do, but I couldn't feel less like an elite athlete right now.

It's time for me to go on stage.

My legs feel gelatinous.

I can't get up.

I can see Annabel out of the corner of my eye, her face a sneer of a smile.

And that's when it hits me. All the things that have happened in the last year. All the things I have coped with. I am stronger than I think.

And I can do this.

Chapter Seventy-Four

Epiphany moments should happen somewhere extraordinary, a place where one is in awe of nature or overcome with spirituality. On a beach at sunset, the golden light dancing and shimmering across the waves. In a silent retreat surrounded by kind-eyed Tibetan monks.

Mine happens on a night bus that smells strongly of vomit. Instead of Tibetan monks, the cast is the drunk and the knackered: a man who shovels fried chicken into his mouth as if he's in one of those speed-eating competitions, two teenage boys who talk in low intense tones, a few grey-faced workers in suits who sit with stooped shoulders, looking like they've had the life sucked out of them.

A middle-aged woman is careering down the length of the bus addressing everyone like a crazed tour guide who's gone off script. She used to live in that block of flats when she was a kid. She was clever at school. Could have got into the grammar if the bastards had let her take the exam.

Amidst all this my mind snaps into focus. Suddenly, I know exactly what I have to do.

The teenage boy is moaning to his friend about his little sister. Spoilt rotten, she is. His parents were NEVER like that with the rest of them. She wants a new iPhone now. A new iPhone!

Why didn't I think of this before? It seems so obvious now.

367

He can't believe his dad! His mum has always been soft, but his dad?

My mind races with possibility. After the initial high of getting through my speech, I had been feeling utterly exhausted, but now my whole body is alive, nerves and synapses firing.

A man gets on with no way to pay. His wallet has been stolen, he tells the bus driver. The bus driver looks unconvinced but waves him on.

Now I come to think of it, realizing I COULD get up and make that speech was an epiphany moment too. You wait forever for them and then two come along at once. Like buses, haha.

The boy behind me is getting increasingly agitated. They let her do whatever she wants! She's their little princess who can do no wrong!

I know this won't be easy, but nothing that's worth having comes easily. And this is definitely worth having.

Tour guide woman is approaching. All around me people bury their faces in their newspapers or stare more intently at their phones. She is broadcasting about how she used to be a performer, seemingly not minding that she has a less than attentive audience now.

My mind turns inward again. My whole body is fizzing with excitement. I am surrounded by grime, discarded chewing gum and fast food packets, but suddenly the world looks good.

'Christ,' Cassie says. 'You get over your fear of public speaking and it unleashes a monster.'

I laugh. 'I wasn't expecting you to call me a monster! Crazy, maybe, but not a monster!'

'Oh, you're definitely crazy too.'

Marielle drifts out of her bedroom at this point and I am

sure she must have overheard Cassie calling me 'crazy' because the greetings and small talk seem to take longer than they should. After what seems like ages, she goes off to make coffee.

'She's alone!' Cassie mouths at me.

I shake my head and point at the bedroom. Wherever you see Marielle, you know Jean can't be more than a few metres away. It's like they've got some kind of reverse restraining order on them.

'So,' Cassie says, 'I was just telling you you're batshit crazy.'

I laugh. 'Yes, thanks. Although to be fair you think people having babies at all is mad!'

'Touché! But surely having one alone is next level mad?'

I know although Cassie's tone is light, she's not really joking. But I also know I can do this. 'When I think about my life in ten years, I don't want to imagine myself without a child. And when I was sitting on that bus last night, I was suddenly struck by the revelation that I could have a baby on my own, that I didn't need Jack, or Nick, or any man.' Cassie makes a face. 'Okay, I know I still kind of need a man. I'm not expecting the stork to bring me an infant!'

Marielle walks back through the living room with two steaming mugs of coffee. I don't know if I'm imagining it but she seems to linger a little before going back into the bedroom. I suppose the snippets of conversation she's over-hearing would be kind of intriguing.

I stifle a yawn. I was so wired I stayed up most of the night googling. I read and read until the words on the screen turned to jiggling maggots before my eyes, and I felt a surge of excitement because there were suddenly all these choices I hadn't even realized I had.

Cassie is shaking her head. 'It will just be so hard.'

'I know it won't be easy. From getting pregnant in the first place, to giving birth, to bringing up a child on my own without anyone else to contribute to the cost. Plus, no one to swear at during labour, and no one to give me a break when the baby won't stop screaming at 4 a.m. . . .'

Cassie's face is a mask of horror. I imagine myself telling other people: my parents, my sister, Nancy. Even though none of them are child-averse like Cassie, and will of course be there to support me when they can, I don't doubt they'll all feel pretty much the same as her, all look at me like people were looking at tour guide woman on the bus. It doesn't matter though – I will be telling people, not asking them.

'I still think you should talk to Nick,' Cassie says.

I shake my head. 'It's not the kind of thing you try to talk someone into. Anyway, he's with someone else now.'

Cassie shrugs. 'And you've already made an appointment with the fertility clinic?'

I nod. 'I want to see what my options are. Find out what sort of timeframe we're looking at.'

'Yeah, you still seem quite young to be thinking about all this.'

I shrug. 'Not if you believe what you read in the papers. But maybe I can afford to wait a bit. It doesn't hurt to have a plan in place though. I want to talk to the clinic about everything from just freezing my eggs to artificial insemination.'

'Couldn't you ask one of your gay friends? Turkey baster style?'

'Too messy.' I say, and Cassie pulls a face. '*Emotionally* messy!' I elaborate, laughing.

Cassie grins and takes a sip of her tea. 'You seem very sure about this.'

'I think maybe it's been in the back of my mind for some time and I just didn't dare let it surface. It feels good to have a plan. Empowering, if you like, even though I hate that word. Mind you, I'll probably feel considerably less empowered when I'm lying there with my knickers off and my legs in stirrups!'

Cassie laughs. 'Public speaking, having a baby on your own . . . what next? Running for Prime Minister?'

'Anything is possible!'

Chapter Seventy-Five

Three months later

For everything I've said about being weddinged out, I can't fail to be excited about Cassie and Shane's. If, when Cassie was ill, you'd told me she'd be where she is now, I wouldn't have believed it was possible.

She has insisted I help her get ready but when I get down to her flat there is already a small team doing just that (old habits die hard). Bruno – resplendent in a tight hot-pink suit and black shirt – is on hair, Linda is on make-up, and someone who calls herself Twinkle is in an undefined role that appears to involve making coffee and being bossed around. She's a little too old, both for the role and the name (and don't get me started on her little plastic tiara).

Cassie jumps up from her chair to greet me. She has big curlers in her hair and is wearing the same white towelling dressing gown I saw rather too much of when she was ill.

'You decided to wear white after all!'

Cassie grins. 'Have you seen the *Mail on Sunday* today?'

'Course. You know I get it delivered.'

She pokes me in the ribs. 'You're supposed to be nice. This is MY Big Day.'

Bruno rolls his eyes. 'Heaven help us!'

Twinkle – who is apparently really called Anne Marie – shoves a copy of the paper into my hands.

'Oh, my goodness! Look at this photo of you and Shane together on *Top of the Pops*. How much blue eyeshadow are you wearing? And talk about big hair! I love the recent photo of you though.'

'I don't. People are always going on about too much airbrushing but I'd have liked more! Look at my crows feet!'

'You look great, darling,' Bruno says, adjusting one of the curlers. 'Rrradiant.'

I read the article out loud. 'Be My Baby . . . Again. Today, after a whirlwind romance, Cassie Frost will tie the knot – or should we say re-tie the knot – with Shane O'Connor. The two will be joined by showbiz friends at Westminster Register Office and then for lavish celebrations at trendy media haunt Shoreditch House.'

Linda dabs at Cassie's nose with a powder brush. 'There is something very romantic about marrying the same man twice.'

'I just think it's greedy having soooo many weddings when some of us can't even find one guy,' Bruno says.

'Tell me about it.' I agree.

'Oh, you've found him,' Cassie says. 'You've just mislaid him.'

I may be the very embodiment of Ms I Don't Need a Man now, but I still like the thought of having only mislaid Nick. He's like the jewellery you hide in a safe place when you go on holiday. Maybe he'll turn up in my cornflakes packet one morning (minus A-man-da. Don't want her with my cereal).

I go back to reading out the article. 'Fate played its hand when the pair bumped into each other in London's Soho. Shane says, "I couldn't believe it when I saw Cassie. She didn't look any different."'

'His eyesight is not what it was,' Cassie says.

'"My heart was going like the clappers and all the old feelings came flooding back."'

'Ahhhhh!' Linda says, reaching for the mascara. 'Did you feel the same?'

'Err, no.'

'Well I hope you're not going to say that in your speech!' I say. 'Not unless you want to join me in the worst wedding speech hall of shame.'

Cassie pokes her tongue out at me.

Bruno feels the curlers. 'Right. These are ready to come out.'

'Now you're not going to get too jealous when you see me with another man, are you darling?'

He laughs. 'All depends if there are any leftovers on offer.'

I was with Cassie when she chose the pale grey Vivienne Westwood dress but that doesn't stop me gasping when I first see her all ready. Her hair is swept up and she is wearing simple diamond earrings and shoes that would make me walk like Les Dawson but she wears as if they're trainers. 'You look beautiful.'

'Thank you. It's only taken three and a half hours too!'

The cab driver recognizes her, and for a second my stomach clenches as I think we're going to get the you-were-a-night-mare-on-the-jungle-show rant. 'I remember you in that movie with Sean Connery. Used to have posters of you all over my bedroom wall. You're still gorgeous!'

I thank the god of taxi drivers in my head.

We drive past Dermot the healer's office. It seems a lifetime ago Cassie was lying on his table staring out of the window with a deadened expression on her face. 'I wonder who Dermot's unblocking now.'

Cassie smiles. 'Hopefully his receptionist. She wasn't a very good advert for his healing powers, was she? I thought she was going to have a cardiac arrest when that woman next to me ripped the lentil bake recipe out of *Body & Soul*.'

'Ah, yes. But the "cobbler's children". You nervous? I don't mean about Shane, but about the day?'

'Are you kidding? I love the attention! And, anyway, being famous is like being a bride every day of your life.'

The sun glints off the stone pillars outside the register office. Shane is waiting on the steps flanked by four chubby women who look like him in drag.

'Oh, my goodness,' Cassie says. 'The O'Connors are out in force! You should make notes, Ginny. Today will be perfect material for a writer.'

I am about to correct her and say would-be writer, but then I swallow the words. Writer sounds just fine.

We pull up and Cassie reaches for her bag to pay the driver.

He waves his hand. 'This one is on me, darling. I consider it an honour to have taken my screen goddess to her wedding.'

Cassie's eyes fill with tears. 'Thank you.'

The cab driver gives us a little wave and pulls away. 'Have a wonderful day.'

At the wedding reception, my mind drifts to the state of my parents' marriage, and I wonder, as I have so many times over the last few months, if they're happy together.

I take a sip of my champagne.

As Cassie predicted, my mum didn't stay cross with me for long. She phoned me the night of the awards dinner, asking how it was, saying she'd known I could do it and she was so proud of me. 'I'm sorry we had cross words earlier,' she said. 'Mum, can I ask you . . .' But she cut me off before I could even finish the sentence. The message was unspoken but crystal clear: We are not going to discuss this. Not now, not ever.

'That's a very sad face,' a man says extending his hand towards mine. 'I'm Barry. Cassie's agent.'

I shake his hand, and quickly plaster a smile onto my face. 'I've heard a lot about you.'

'What, like I'm bloody useless and never get her any work?'

I laugh. 'That sort of thing.'

'She's meshuggeneh, that one! But I'm used to women busting my balls. My wife Shirley over there makes Cassie look like a pussycat.' I look across the room where a tiny white-headed lady is chatting to one of Shane's aunties. It's hard to imagine her out-diva-ing Cassie. 'And I've got three daughters. My rabbi said to me the other day it's great I've been coming to synagogue so much. He doesn't realize it's only because they keep the women separate!' I laugh. 'So, why the sad face?'

For a split second, I almost feel tempted to tell Barry the truth. He looks kind. 'I'm fine.' Cassie told me her therapist doesn't allow her to use the word fine. Apparently, it's a blocking word. 'It's good to see Cassie like this, isn't it?'

'It is.' We both look across the room. Cassie and Shane are standing together talking to a group of people. Both of them have the sort of Ready-Brek glow you see in the adverts.

A waiter comes past with a tray of cocktails. I'm somewhat surprised to see I've already drunk all my champagne. I take one of the cocktails. I'm not sure what's in it – pear maybe, definitely mint – but it's delicious.

Barry and I are joined by Rod and Ian who were introduced to me earlier as the Panto Boys. It's an interesting title – neither of them have been boys for at least thirty years, and I assume they must do something other than appear in pantomimes. (Surely an occupation just a tad too seasonal?)

'Wasn't it just soooooo moving at the register office?' Ian says.

He is sporting an orange and pink flowery shirt that might have looked good on a man ten years younger and ten pounds lighter. Rod, who is tall and thin with little round glasses, is by contrast dressed like an undertaker, although thankfully minus the hat. It's extremely hard to imagine him donning fake boobs and a thirty-inch purple wig and shouting 'Oh no you couldn't'.

'And doesn't Cassie just look fab-u-lous!'

Meg walks past and gives me a tight little smile. I haven't been able to bring myself to talk to her yet. Rachel and I might get on each other's nerves sometimes but there is no question we'd be there for each other if either of us ever needed help. I nearly punched Beth Wilson when she told a seven-year-old Rachel that Father Christmas was really just your mum. Meg orders herself a gin and tonic. She is wearing a shapeless cheesecloth dress in what I can only describe as camouflage green. 'At least no one can accuse her of trying to steal my thunder,' Cassie said when she saw her.

'We're still coming down from the high of our last panto,' Ian says, even though it's March. 'We were the Uglies in *Cinderella*. It was our eighth time! We've got all our own costumes and wigs. You should see our ball gowns! *Big Fat Gypsy Weddings* has got nothing on us!'

'We do also love playing the robbers in *Babes in the Wood*,' Rod says.

'He's the bad boy, as if you couldn't tell!' Ian says, giving me and Barry a wink.

'But the Uglies was like coming home for us.'

I start to laugh before realizing he is deadly serious and could just as well be talking about reprising the role of Lear at the National.

378

'And I love Bromley,' Rod says, much like one would say I love Paris or The Maldives. Ian nods. 'We've done some of our best shows there. *Snow White* with Linda Lusardi and Sam Kane. Lovely couple! *Aladdin . . .*' He has tears in his eyes now. '. . . *Peter Pan, Dick Whittington.* All Bromley.'

'Has Cassie ever done a panto?' Ian asks Barry.

'Only one.'

Ian and Rod gasp in unison as if this is the most horrible thing they've ever heard. I wouldn't be surprised to find out they live in a primary-coloured house where seven dwarves scuttle around singing 'hi ho, hi ho' as they do the dusting.

'I think she would make a brilliant Wicked Queen!' Ian says without a trace of irony.

Barry chuckles. 'Tell me about it.'

Waiters start coming round with miniature bowls of delicious things like pork belly and mash, and fish and chips. I smile as I watch Meg's two boys make the waiter with the tray full of bowls of fish and chips stand there for ages whilst they deliberate over which ones have the most chips in them. As the waiter finally gets away, Thomas is moaning Matthew has three more.

'This soooo beats canapes!' Rod says. 'We're definitely having bowl food for our wedding. Even the name of it sounds chic.'

'Do you think so?' Barry says. 'Bowl food? Sounds a bit Oliver Twist to me. Tasty though.'

Last time I came to Shoreditch House, I was with Nick. It's one of his favourite places. It was a warm evening and we sat on the roof terrace drinking very cold Chablis and eating burgers. I remember him wiping a tiny bit of ketchup off my chin and then kissing me.

Shane's relatives, who are abundant in number and what one would politely describe as larger than life, are making the most of a free bar. One of his brothers-in-law, who spilt the beetroot risotto down his shirt, has now removed it and is performing 'Do You Think I'm Sexy' on the dancefloor, topless. This would be better if the band were playing 'Do You Think I'm Sexy'. The beetroot has left stains all down his chest. From a distance, it looks like blood.

A well-known breakfast TV host comes up and gives Barry a big hug. He's even more orange in real life than on screen.

'You've got Penny as your co-host now,' Barry says.

The breakfast TV host – whose name I've completely forgotten – nods. 'What a bitch! Shags everything that moves too.'

Shane's speech is brilliant. From his starting line of 'I first met Cassie thirty years ago. Clearly, I've swept her off her feet', he has the whole room – except perhaps the now napping Do You Think I'm Sexy brother-in-law – captivated. By the time we raise our glasses many of us have a tear in our eye. Ian is practically hiccupping he's crying so much.

I have another glass of champagne. Must slow down after this one.

I'm on my way to the loo when Cassie grabs my arm. 'You having a good time?'

'Absolutely, it's a great party.'

'Yeah. Pity my husband's family insist on behaving like they're in an episode of *Shameless*!'

'Your husband!' I smile.

'I know. Now, get your sick bucket to the ready, because here's where I go all sentimental and mawkish on you.'

'Uh-oh,' I mock, but she grabs my hand. 'I just want to say thank you for being there. Even when I told you not to be. My God, you have a problem with listening sometimes! Thank you for getting me through those dark days. Keeping me going. Rescuing me from Londis in my slippers. And paying for my fags. For making me wash my dressing gown

380

occasionally. Nagging me to eat. Believing in me when I couldn't believe in myself. Making me feel like I wasn't alone. Oh, and – teeny detail – saving my life.' Her voice cracks. 'You know I don't like to make a habit of saying nice things, but I'll make an exception to say you are one of the strongest, most generous, kind and loving people I've ever known. I couldn't have got through the depression without you.' She gently dabs under her eye, 'Don't you start crying! I bet you're not even wearing waterproof mascara,' she says, but she's too late. I have tears rolling down my cheeks.

'Is it bad?' I say, sniffing.

'If I'm honest, you're channelling Marilyn Manson more than Marilyn Monroe right now.'

I laugh. 'I'll go and fix myself in the loos.'

'Do you want me to send Linda?'

'You're such a prima donna.'

'Always.' She smiles.

I walk out of the room where the reception is and straight into Nick. He gives me a very strange look and then I realize I am sporting what Cassie described as a Marilyn Manson look. Of course I am. Because that's just what you want when you bump into your ex. *The* ex. 'What are you doing here?' I ask.

'Having dinner.'

With A-man-da, I bet. 'Oh.' He, of course, looks great. He's wearing jeans and the blue shirt I always loved on him. 'I'm at Cassie's wedding.'

'I saw in the papers she was getting married. That's fabulous news.'

I nod.

We both just stand there.

'So, I'd better go and fix my face,' I say.

'Yeah.' He heads for the Gents. 'Enjoy the rest of the wedding.'

'Nick . . .' I don't know if it's all the cocktails and the champagne but I suddenly have an almost unbearable urge to tell him how I feel. Perhaps I could talk him round on the baby thing? Or we could compromise? I could make do with just one baby. A little one. 'I . . . I . . .' My mouth goes dry and I suddenly feel like I did when I was standing on the high diving board on holiday in Gozo when I was eleven. 'Go on, Gin,' my father shouted, 'you can do it.' Nick is looking at me, waiting. 'I . . . I hope you have a nice evening.' He stares at me for a second and then disappears into the Gents. I never did dive off that high diving board.

I go into the Ladies, lock myself in a cubicle and burst into tears. Nick is going to marry A-man-da. She will be Julia's sister-in-law and I will have to put up with having her casually dropped into conversation – Nick and Amanda (Julia will not say A-man-da like me) came for supper the other night, Amanda told me this funny story on Saturday. Julia will like her, suggest I would too if I got to know her.

People come in and out of the ladies to pee, reapply lipstick, and gossip. One of Shane's sisters asks the others if they have got any thrush cream on them. I bite the sleeve of my dress so that no one will hear me crying. I am in no mood to be comforted.

I cry and I cry. My eyes will be as puffy as they are smudgy.

Suddenly there's a knock on the cubicle door. I didn't hear anyone come in.

'You okay in there?' I recognize the voice; it's Twinkle.

'Yes, fine,' I chirp, trying to make my voice sound like someone else's.

'Ginny?'

'I'm fin . . . fine . . . than . . . thanks.'

'Open the door.'

I say nothing.

'Open the door or I'll get Cassie.'

I open the door.

'You look terrible.'

'Thanks.'

'Is it about a bloke?'

I nod.

'What happened?'

'It's complicated . . .' I suddenly realize I am on the verge of seeking relationship advice from someone I barely know who goes by the name of Twinkle, which is surely a low-point even for me. 'I'm okay. Really.'

She nods. 'You might want to touch up your make-up.'

I laugh at her power of understatement.

'Are you sure you're okay?'

'Course,' I say, wiping the mascara trails off my cheeks.

We go back up the stairs and a waiter appears with a tray of drinks. I pick up a glass of champagne and take a hefty swig. I told Twinkle I was ready to go back and join the party, but the truth is, I may need a little help.

When we get back to the reception, Finola, Shane's eldest sister, has just started a conga. This is mostly populated by O'Connors, although Thomas and Matthew are part of it (from the look on their faces they've never seen grown-ups behave like this), and Ian joins on at the back. 'Come on,' he shouts to me. 'We can't let the English contingent look like party poopers.'

'You're not going to, are you?' Twinkle says. For someone who's sporting a plastic tiara, she seems remarkably nervous about the idea of making a fool of herself in public.

'Course not.'

Finola wheels past us, her round pink face flushed with excitement. 'Come on and do the Conga . . .' they sing. Their voices are clear and perfectly in tune – years of singing in church no doubt. They're also loud enough to completely drown out the band's light jazz.

Ian sashays at the back. 'Come on, darling. You know it makes sense.'

One of the uber-cool young waitresses comes over with a tray of cocktails. I think they must have two rules when they hire people here: they must be very young, and they must be the sort of people who would never *ever* conga. I drain my drink in one, put the glass back on the tray, and put my hands on Ian's chubby backside.

'Ginny!' Twinkle shouts, her face flaming on my behalf.

Really though, what have I got to lose?

'Choo-choo-choo . . .'

I kick out my leg. I don't need Dermot to unblock my pain, I need a giant human crocodile.

'. . . And as you do the conga, you make the party stronger . . .'

We circle the room and then suddenly I look up and see Nick. Just standing there watching me. Terrific. Surely though, if I immediately stop conga-ing now, I look even more uncool? So I carry on, although my kicks are a little half-hearted.

'What are you doing here?' I say, once I have uncoupled myself from Ian.

'I heard there was a very sophisticated party going on in here and couldn't resist joining it.' I guess he can read the confusion plastered on my face. 'I'm joking, Ginny. I came to talk to you.'

My head spins. That last cocktail really wasn't a good idea.

'What were you going to say to me earlier? You didn't just want to wish me a nice evening.'

'Err . . .' I feel really light-headed.

He puts his hand on my elbow. 'Are you okay?'

Meg laughs. 'I'm starting to see you and my sister have more in common than I thought.'

The waitress appears again. She really is very good at her job. I put my empty glass on the tray and take a full one.

'Are you sure that's a good idea?' Nick whispers.

'Absolutely.' I take a sip and miss my mouth but luckily I don't think anyone notices.

Cassie has been out of the room having her hair touched up by Bruno, but as soon as she swoops back in, her eyes alight on Nick like a heat-seeking missile.

'Hullo,' she says appearing beside us.

Nick extends his hand. 'I'm Nick. Sorry, I'm not a wedding crasher. I just happened to be having supper nex—'

'You couldn't be more welcome,' Cassie says. 'Really, I've heard so much about you.'

Okay, she's going a little over the top now. I don't need any help when it comes to being totally uncool.

'I was just talking about the problem with binge-drinking amongst the young in this country,' Meg says.

Cassie gives her a withering smile. Her eyes flicker towards the dancefloor where one of Shane's sisters has just fallen over and is now lying flat on her back laughing hysterically and showing the world her pants. They're the sort of heavy-duty control pants that you just know she probably wouldn't have been able to stomach catching a glimpse of in the mirror a few hours earlier, yet now she is in no rush to pull her dress back down. 'Not just the young it seems. Anyway, Meg, may I borrow you for a second? There's someone I'd like you to meet.'

Meg's face scrunches. The idea of there being someone Cassie wants her to meet seems improbable to say the least, but before she can open her mouth to protest, Cassie puts a vice-like hand on her arm. 'Ginny, Nick,' she says, 'I'm sure you've got LOTS to talk about.'

Bloody hell!

As Nick and I are left standing alone, it strikes me that I've suddenly sobered up, and not in a good way. I don't think I could feel more nervous if Cassie had asked me to stand up and make a speech.

'What did you want to say to me outside the loos?' he says.

'There's really no point. You're with A-man . . . Amanda.'

He is looking at me intently. 'Amanda and I had three dates.'

'Oh. Oh. I thought you were going to marry her. And Julia was going to talk about her all the time, an . . .' I trail off realizing I sound like a complete loon. My heart is threatening to jump right out of my chest and land on the floor. I suppose that's one way of falling at his feet. I take a deep breath. 'When I left you for Jack . . .' Not sure that was the most elegant start, but luckily I am interrupted by a loud hiss of feedback from the microphone. Do You Think I'm Sexy has woken up from his stupor, ripped the mic away from the singer and is poised for an important announcement. 'Hello everybody,' he slurs.

Shane is making his way across the room but is held back by two of his sisters.

'I'd like to make a very special toast to the happy couple!'

'Looks like you've had one too many toasts already,' another man heckles from the dancefloor.

Do You Think I'm Sexy ignores this. He is a Rock God after all. 'I also want to announce a special surprise – legendary at every O'Connor wedding.' He pauses for dramatic effect. 'Karaoke!'

His words divide the room with most people visibly appalled but the O'Connor clan (with the notable exceptions of Shane and the new Mrs O'Connor) erupting into whoops and cheers.

Finola is making her way up to the stage. 'Bags I sing "I Will Survive".'

Niamh, the sister recently flashing her prosthetic coloured Spanx, is at her heels. 'That's my number, Finola, and you know it!'

Finola spins round, her face pink. 'You know you can't hit those high notes.'

'Hit 'em better than you, you ol' bitch! I'm sick of it being the bloody Finola show. We ALL are.'

Finola and the whole room freezes. Then she raises her hand and slaps Niamh hard across the face.

Niamh's jaw drops and then she hurls herself at her sister grabbing a handful of her hair and throwing her to the floor. Several family members join the fray, but rather than break up the fighting pair, they seem to become embroiled until the dancefloor is a sea of kicking, slapping, punching O'Connors. Shane and a couple of waiters are doing their best to bring calm but they are just too outnumbered.

'I'd better lend a hand,' Nick says.

He wrestles his way through the bodies and gets his arms around Niamh who he manages to pull away from the throng despite her wild thrashing.

At this point, Do You Think I'm Sexy hurls himself down from the stage screaming 'Get your hands off my wife!'

Nick turns to raise his hands in a gesture of supplication but Do You Think I'm Sexy's fist is already flying through the air to land on Nick's nose.

'For a drunk guy, he's got a pretty good aim,' I say, dabbing at Nick's bloody nose with a ball of cotton wool.

He laughs.

'Does it really hurt?' I ask.

'Nah. He punches like a girl. Well, when I say a girl, I don't mean Niamh or Finola.'

I smile. I am standing so close to him I can feel his

breath on my cheek. We are outside the loos. Our special place.

'Okay, good. Right. What I wanted to tell you earlier . . .' I say.

Coleen emerges from the ladies. 'Y'all right?' she says to Nick. 'Sorry about my family, sure I am. I've tied Niamh up with me tights.'

She disappears, taking my courage with her. 'We can talk later. Let's go back in.'

Nick shakes his head. 'Tell me what you were going to say.'

'It doesn—'

'Ginny!'

'I want a baby.' I blurt out. 'Not this minute, but I do want one. Well, more than one. And I've tried not to, I really have, but I can't help it. So I'm going to have a baby, even if that means doing it on my own. Even if that means not being with you.' I can't meet his eye as I'm telling him this, but when I finish speaking I lift up my head and see that he looks like he's just been told he is terminally ill. I didn't realize I was still holding onto a teeny flicker of hope that he might change his mind about wanting kids, but I must have been, because it's extinguished now.

Do You Think I'm Sexy reels out of the party room. 'Mate,' he says to Nick. 'I just came to say I'm so sorry. Don't know what came over me.'

Maybe it was those fourteen cocktails, I think somewhat hypocritically.

He is shaking Nick's hand vigorously. 'No hard feelings?'

'Course not,' Nick says.

'Can I buy you a beer then?' Do You Think I'm Sexy says. The generous offer of a man who knows it's a free bar.

'Maybe later.'

He staggers back into the party and I go to follow him. I just want to get away from Nick now. It was a mistake to try to have this conversation and being around him is just like picking at a scab.

'Ginny,' he says. 'You're not making sense.'

'I want a baby.'

'Yes.'

Cassie emerges from the party room with Linda and Twinkle. 'Oh sorry,' she says. 'Didn't know you two were out here. Are you okay, Nick?'

'I'm fine – all good.' He gives Cassie a big smile.

'I'm so sorry about the family I've married into. Tell you what, forget the bloody Priory, if there was one thing in the world that would make me give up drinking, it's watching this lot.'

Cassie hurries Linda and Twinkle away. She's clearly trying to leave Nick and I alone and it's all I can do not to tell her she's wasting her energy.

Nick is rubbing his temples with his thumb and forefinger. 'Okay. Let's start again. You want a baby?'

'Yes. And you don't.'

'What?'

'So we can't be together – even if you wanted to be, which you probably don't – because a few years down the line, I'll be hating you every time another friend of ours gets pregnant. I'll be the kind of woman who cries over the teeny socks in Baby Gap. Hang on, did you just say "what"?'

'Yes.'

'When I said you don't want a baby?'

'Yes.'

My turn to rub my temples now. 'But you don't want a baby.'

'What do you mean?'

'You said after what happened to you and Mel, you'd be frightened to ever try for a baby again.'

391

'Yeah, I am. I'm scared shitless if I'm honest. But it doesn't mean I wouldn't do it. I love kids.'

'But what about your Tinder profile?'

His face scrunches. 'What?'

'Your Tinder profile says: Wants dogs not kids!'

'Does it?' He shakes his head. 'Alex wrote it. A whole bunch of us were out one night shortly after I'd split up from Mel. They were all going on at me about "getting back in the saddle". Alex made me give him my phone so he could get me on some dating apps there and then. I was so pissed I forgot all about it, to be honest. Christ knows why he wrote that though. I suppose he just assumed. Well, either that or it was the Budweiser talking.'

'Oh.' My brain is struggling to catch up, and before it does so, Nick takes my face in his hands. He traces my cheekbone with his fingertip. The cacophony of music and chatter and laughing from next door seem to fade away.

I put my arms around his neck, breathing him in. 'I'm sorry I got it all so wrong. I don't know what to say . . .'

He puts his finger gently on my lips. 'Nothing.' And for once in my life, I listen, and shut up as he leans towards me, making me feel as though my whole world has just, finally, clicked into place.

Behind us, the door rocks on its hinges as it is flung open. Matthew runs out closely followed by his brother, who is brandishing a bright yellow Nerf gun. 'Die, suckerrr!' he shouts. A hail of orange bullets fly between me and Nick, preventing what was about to be the most romantic kiss of my entire life.

As a foam bullet ricochets off my forehead, Nick laughs.

'Maybe a little girl?' he says.

Charlie's Eye

Dorothy Horgan

PUFFIN BOOKS

PUFFIN BOOKS

Published by the Penguin Group
Penguin Books Ltd, 80 Strand, London WC2R 0RL, England
Penguin Putnam Inc., 375 Hudson Street, New York, New York 10014, USA
Penguin Books Australia Ltd, Ringwood, Victoria, Australia
Penguin Books Canada Ltd, 10 Alcorn Avenue, Toronto, Ontario, Canada M4V 3B2
Penguin Books India (P) Ltd, 11 Community Centre, Panchsheel Park, New Delhi – 110 017, India
Penguin Books (NZ) Ltd, Cnr Rosedale and Airborne Roads, Albany, Auckland, New Zealand
Penguin Books (South Africa) (Pty) Ltd, 24 Sturdee Avenue, Rosebank 2196 South Africa

Penguin Books Ltd, Registered Offices: 80 Strand, London WC2R 0RL, England

www.penguin.com

First published by Hamish Hamilton Ltd 1997
Published in Puffin Books 1998
6

Set in Palatino

Made and printed in England by Clays Ltd, St Ives plc

British Library Cataloguing in Publication Data
A CIP catalogue record for this book is available from the British Library

ISBN 0–140–38237–2

Chapter One

'Mum, tell Charlie to get it out. Go on, Mum, say something. If our dad was here . . . just wait till our dad gets back.'

'Now, Sally,' Mrs Morris said, absentmindedly smoothing the toast crumbs off the table into her apron, 'you know quite well Dad won't be back for a bit yet, driving those big lorries all over France.'

'It's not France, it's Belgium. And he's going to take me one day.'

'Shut up, big-head,' Sally snapped.

1

'Charlie doesn't mean any harm.' Mrs Morris went on with her tidying up. 'After all, you're three years older than Charlie, Sally. And what's got to get out of where?' Mrs Morris stuck a grip in her fly-away ginger hair and looked anxiously at Charlie with her cornflower blue eyes.

'Mum, it's in the lav. That silly Sam of Charlie's is in the lav,' Sally said. 'It was there when I went just now. Looking up at me like a bloomin' dead fish.'

Charlie put on a very reasonable expression as Mrs Morris patted down the tight ginger curls on the little round head which bobbed up and down as the words came rushing out.

'It was an experiment. You said that if I put Sam in your birthday trifle, you'd flush him down the lav. Well, he doesn't flush down. He just stays there. He's still there now, if you want to know. So if I can't flush him down, you can't either. Big fat pig. Ginger rat's-tails. Just because it was your birthday. Loads of silly girls all talking about make-up and stupid boyfriends.'

'I'd rather be fat than a skinny little runt like you,' Sally shouted. 'And I don't have rat's-tails. It's the fashion, that's what,' and she tossed her hair back. 'All you can think of is football, football, football. You're weird, you are. Do you have to live in a track-suit? Weird!'

'I was wondering why you were wearing your patch, Charlie,' Mrs Morris said, and she went upstairs to fish Charlie's glass eye out of the lav. It was lying there in the water, all blue and sparkling. She went to disinfect it.

'And you should have been nicer to your big sister yesterday,' she said, coming back with Charlie's eye. 'On her birthday. With all her friends. Fancy putting your glass eye into the trifle.'

'Ruined my birthday, that's what,'

Sally screeched. 'That was my twelfth birthday. I'll never have another one. My only one, ruined!'

Mrs Morris tried to interrupt, but Sally wasn't going to stop.

'It's Charlie's fault. Everything is always Charlie's fault. My friends won't come here any more. It's like having the plague or something, having Charlie. Whose fault is it anyway that Charlie got a glass eye in the first place?'

And finally Sally stormed out, aiming a kick at Charlie's ankles with her Doc Marten boots, but Charlie dodged. Sally hit the chair.

'Mind the furniture, dear,' Mrs Morris said.

Charlie smirked triumphantly at Sally. When Sally was a safe distance ahead, Charlie, with her glass eye where it was supposed to be, went to get the school bus. Before the door closed, Mrs Morris called out.

'Charlotte . . .'

Charlie paused. You had to listen

when Mum said Charlotte, instead of Charlie.

'Charlotte, you just try to behave yourself. Or else. You just wait till your father gets home . . .'

And Charlie left.

Charlie was something of a hero on the school bus, because of the tricks she did with her glass eye. She had to go to school in Ashby, four miles away, because the nearest school was full. So they said. Sally said it was because they'd already heard about Charlie.

'Never,' Mrs Morris said, but Mr Morris (who happened to be at home at that time) was inclined to agree with Sally.

All the people in Danton (where the Morrises lived) knew how Charlie had lost her first eye, the one she was born with, on the way to the play group.

She'd made a grab for Billy Herbert's new bow and arrow which he'd got at the fair. The arrow shot straight up and then straight down, and hit poor Charlie in the eye. Miss Roberts, the play-group lady, rushed forward to help Charlie and Mrs Morris, while Mrs Brown, the other play-group lady, dialled 999. All the children cheered and shouted with relief and joy as the ambulance arrived, with its lights flashing and its siren sounding. They all tried to press forward to watch Charlie being carried into the ambulance. Miss Roberts and Mrs Brown had to come and shoo them all into the hall. There they all crowded round the window to watch the ambulance disappear down the road.

After all that excitement, the children never settled down again, and Mrs Brown had to telephone for them all to be taken home early.

The play group was never the same after that. Some mothers kept their children at home, some children said it was too boring at the play group without Charlie Morris, and they didn't want to go if she wasn't there. They all wanted the ambulance to come every day, or better still, the fire engine, and when they didn't come, some of them began to lie down on the floor and howl, and pretend to be hurt, just to get the ambulance to come back. It was the beginning of the end for the Danton play group.

Everybody was very concerned about poor Charlie, lying there in the children's ward in the local hospital. She got lots of presents – sweets, chocolates, toys, tapes to listen to, videos to watch. She was making a very good recovery; she talked to all the doctors and nurses and wandered all over the hospital, chatting to other patients and exploring all sorts of exciting rooms; she never moaned about losing an eye, and chose the brightest patch that she could find.

Then a nurse drew Mrs Morris aside, and asked her if she would kindly take Charlie home.

'But she's not due home till next week,' Mrs Morris protested, and she sighed. Of course it would be lovely to have Charlie home again, but the peace and quiet had been quite nice too, especially when they'd known that she was really doing very well, and that one eye was almost as good as two. But the staff nurse explained that they couldn't spare a whole nurse just to be Charlie's minder. It was people like Charlie, she said, who were bankrupting the National Health Service.

The play group didn't open again. Miss Roberts went to New Zealand. Mr Morris said that Charlie'd done more damage to nursery education in Danton than any government ever could. Then he drove off again in his big lorry to Brussels.

Charlie took to her glass eye very quickly. All the grown-ups were amazed. They said 'ooh' and 'aah' and 'how brave' and they shook their heads and hurried off quickly. But

8

Charlie said her new eye was her best friend, and she called it Sam.

Charlie used to put Sam on the breakfast table and talk to it – until Sam got banned. Mr Morris, on one of his brief visits home, was reaching out for more sugar lumps at breakfast time, and reading the sports page at the same time. His hand fell upon Sam, and Sam plopped into Mr Morris's cup of tea.

'What the . . .' he shouted, as Sam went down with a great splash – Mr Morris always had a very full cup.

'That glass eye's banned. As from now,' he shouted, as Mrs Morris rescued Sam and poured out a fresh cup of tea.

Sally sniggered. 'Serve her right,' she said.

Some of Charlie's tricks went a bit wrong. It was Charlie and Sam who put an end to the school swimming lessons. Charlie put Sam on the floor of the pool, and invited the other children to dive in for it.

Unfortunately Miss Nixon (known as Knickers) leaned too far over the edge of the pool to investigate and fell in. The lifeguard had to come and rescue her. To the disappointment of the children, he didn't have to dive in because the water was so shallow. He just paddled down the steps and hauled her out.

Charlie and the others thought that was a bit of a let-down. Then some of the children kept on scrambling for Sam, and it got stuck in the filtering mechanism. As a result of that, the pool had to be drained, and Sam got battered and scratched.

Charlie had to be kitted out with a new eye.

'No, you can't have a brown one this time,' Mrs Morris said, putting her foot down.

At school, Miss Nixon was standing in front of the children with two new boys. Charlie knew at once that she didn't like the big one.

'Now today,' Knickers said, 'we have two new boys in our group. This is Jason Jones,' and she pushed the big one forward, the one Charlie didn't like. He was tall and hefty, with spiky black hair. 'And this is Brian Holmes. Brian has come all the way from Yorkshire.'

'Did he walk, miss?' Charlie asked, because Ashby School was in Lancashire. Charlie didn't mind the look of this one, skinny and small. A lot smaller than Jason Jones. A bit smaller than she was.

'Don't be silly, Charlie. Now, everybody must make these new boys feel at home.'

Charlie moved up a bit to let the skinny boy sit at her table. She only moved a little bit, so that Jason Jones couldn't fit in as well.

At playtime, all the children rushed into the playground. A group of them ran to get the football that always stayed outside the door of the shed where the games kit was kept.

Jason Jones was the quickest and got to the football first. Charlie thought he wasn't acting like a new boy ought to act.

Jason Jones grabbed the football, elbowing the rest aside. 'Right,' he shouted. 'I've got the ball. I'm the captain. Come on. Let's have a game. Follow me.'

'Hey, Charlie shouted, grabbing his arm. 'I'm always the captain. I always get the ball first. I'm the captain, aren't I?' she shouted to the other children. But they didn't answer, and some of them began to shuffle nearer to Jason Jones.

'Hey. You lot. I'm always the captain. I'm the best. Look at me . . . 'and she whirled round and round, challenging them. The other children watched her, then they looked at Jason Jones, then back at Charlie. They didn't move.

'Tough,' Jason Jones said, and he kicked the football to the other end of the playground and turned to the other children. 'Right,' he said. 'I'm the fastest runner. Nobody gets that ball before I do.'

And they all knew it was true – even Charlie knew it was true. Jason Jones was bigger and stronger and faster than they were. They all knew it, even though he'd just come that day to the school. Nobody moved.

'So I'm captain, right?' he demanded 'Anyway,' and he turned to Charlie and stuck his face right up to Charlie's face. He peered at her closely, although he'd been told not to stare at the girl with the glass eye. 'You can't be captain. You're . . .' and he struggled to find the right word. 'You're handicapped. That's what you are. Handicapped,' and he ran off to get the football, followed by most of the other children.

Charlie and the skinny new boy stayed put.

Charlie sat back on her haunches. This was something she didn't understand. How could they all desert her like that? She felt betrayed and alone. She shivered.

'Art frozzen?' the skinny boy asked her. The other children near by laughed and shouted, 'Art frozzen? Art frozzen? Is that your name? Art Frozzen?'

Charlie focused her mind on the skinny new boy. 'What?' she asked.

'Wi' cold. Frozzen-like.'

'Oh, frozen!'

'Like I said.'

Charlie's mind was full of very confused thoughts. 'What's "handi-capped" mean?' she asked.

'Nay. Ask your mam,' the skinny boy answered. 'Come on. Let's have a game of conkers.'

Charlie straightened up. Who was this new boy? He talked a bit funny. He didn't sound like the rest of them.

'Here's a big 'un,' he said. 'Bet you can't find a bigger 'un than this 'un.'

Charlie was still trying to work

14

things out. Why had the gang deserted her? They shouldn't have let that big new boy with the spiky hair get away with the football. And what was this skinny new boy called?

'Art Frozzen? I thought Knickers said you were called Brian Something.'

'Brian Holmes,' the skinny boy said. 'Art frozzen's talking broad. I only said it to make you laugh. My gran talks broad all the time. I don't. Our mam won't have it.'

'Art Frozzen's a good name,' Charlie said, feeling a bit better. 'Suits you.'

'You can call me Art Frozzen if you want to.'

And they started to hunt for conkers together.

'Did you have a nice day?' Mrs Morris asked when Charlie got home.

'I got a new friend. Called Art Frozzen.'

'That's nice.'

'From Yorkshire.' Charlie paused. 'And what's "handicapped" mean?'

CHAPTER TWO

Mrs Morris pretended not to hear Charlie's question. She switched on the TV and gave Charlie a big bag of crisps to keep her quiet.

But the question didn't go away.

'What's "handicapped" mean, Grandad?' Charlie asked her grandfather when he came round at teatime.

Grandad Morris looked thoughtful. 'Handicapped? That's what they done to my horses. Handicapped – footicapped, too, if you ask me.'

'Don't pester your grandfather, dear,' Mrs Morris said, and Grandad Morris disappeared behind his newspaper.

Charlie didn't think Grandad Morris had been very much help anyway, as she wasn't a horse – she was a person.

'It's . . .' Sally opened her mouth to speak, but Mrs Morris pushed a jam tart into it, so Sally couldn't go on.

'Have one of these, dear,' Mrs Morris said. 'Straight from the oven.'

Sally's eyes grew round and filled with tears as the hot jam stung her mouth. But she got the message, and didn't say anything more on the subject. She contented herself with 'Who's Mummy's little darling, then?'

Charlie looked at them all in disgust. 'You don't know anything, you lot. I'm going out to play.'

The next day, Charlie thought she'd try Miss Nixon.

'How d'you find out what a word means when you don't know, miss?' she asked.

'If you can spell it, you look it up in the dictionary,' Miss Nixon said, and she took Charlie over to the shelf where the dictionaries were. 'Go on. Look it up for yourself.'

Charlie looked at the dictionaries. She never bothered with this bookshelf. These were all the boring books: all hard words and no good stories. But she knew Knickers wasn't going to let her off.

'Go on,' the teacher said.

So Charlie took a smallish dictionary off the shelf and put it on her table.

'Look at her,' Jason Jones said in a loud voice. 'Going to look up some dirty words.'

'That is a school dictionary,' Miss Nixon said. 'And there are no dirty words in it, unless you mean words like "work" or "be quiet".'

Suddenly Charlie didn't want to

look up this word 'handicapped' in front of Knickers and the rest of the class. She didn't know why. So she looked up 'football' instead, because it was the only other word she could think of just then. In fact, she always thought of 'football' when she saw – or heard – Jason Jones.

'Now, Charlie,' Miss Nixon said, looking over her shoulder. 'Why have you put your finger on the word "football"? You should know the meaning of the word "football" by now. You, the keenest footballer in the class!'

Charlie went hot all over.

'Just checking, miss,' she said, very glad that she hadn't got her finger on the word 'handicapped'. Knickers would have shouted it out in front of everybody, and then they'd all know she was 'it'. Suppose some of them knew what it meant when she didn't? Even though she was 'it' and they weren't? That wouldn't be fair either.

Charlie waited until dinner-time.

She pretended to be putting the book back on the shelf.

'Come straight out when you've put that book back,' Miss Nixon said, and shooed everybody else out into the playground.

Charlie quickly flipped through the pages of the dictionary until she came to 'hand'. That was easy to spell, but then it took ages to look at all the 'hand' words until she got to 'handicap, handicapped'.

Suffering from some disability or disadvantage, she read.

'Stupid book,' she muttered, putting it back on the shelf. Now, instead of one word she didn't know, there were lots. Maybe she could ask Art Frozzen again? Art Frozzen was a bit different from all the others. Not such a big mouth. At least Art would listen and not let on.

'Hurry up, Charlie,' Miss Nixon called. 'No need to take all day,' and she hustled Charlie out into the playground.

Charlie didn't like the playground any more. She could see that Jason Jones had got the football again and was being captain, shouting and bossing everybody about. Except for Art Frozzen, who was leaning against a wall, swinging his best conker round and round. It went so fast that it made a whirring sound. And it kept people like Jason Jones away.

'Give you a game?' Art said to Charlie. Art burst Charlie's two best conkers. Charlie decided she wouldn't ask Art Frozzen again after all.

'Can I have some brown bread?' Charlie asked after tea, the same day.

'You going to see Old Meg again?' Mrs Morris asked.

'She pongs,' Sally said. 'And I bet she's got fleas. She's a witch, that's what.'

'No harm in Old Meg,' Mrs Morris said. 'Poor thing. Oldest inhabitant, she is. Everybody knows Old Meg. She's a bit wanting, that's all.'

'She likes brown bread. And she's my friend,' Charlie said.

'What's her real name, then? If she's your friend?' Sally jeered.

'Her name's Old Meg. She told me. So there,' and Charlie went off with a bag of brown bread.

Charlie decided that Old Meg was her best chance. Old Meg must know lots of words if she was the Oldest Inhabitant. And Knickers never went near her. Neither did Jason Jones or any of the others, because they nearly all lived in Ashby where the school was. Charlie decided it would be quite safe to ask Old Meg.

Charlie found Old Meg in her usual place, sitting on a bench among huge piles of empty boxes at the back of the closed-down supermarket. When Old Meg saw Charlie, she quickly put the top on the bottle she was drinking from and hid it under the boxes. She wiped her torn sleeve across her mouth and grinned toothlessly.

''Allo, Charlie, me old love. Got some brown bread for Old Meg? Brown bread for tea afore I goes back home to me little house?'

Charlie pounded her way through the boxes and gave the bag to Old Meg. Old Meg stuffed great chunks of brown bread into her mouth, letting the crumbs fly everywhere. Her wrinkled face hung in folds and, to Charlie, she looked like a ragged, friendly, battered old teddy bear. She didn't look a bit like a witch, but she did pong. Charlie didn't mind the pong, but she kept a safe distance away because of the fleas.

'Now all I needs is a nice swig of my ... er ... medicine,' and Old Meg took a long drink from her bottle. Charlie wondered why she needed so much medicine.

'You know lots of words, don't you?' Charlie asked.

'More than most, I'd say,' Old

Meg grinned and rubbed her hands together. 'Got a good lot of words on the tip of me tongue.'

'What's "handicapped" mean?'

A change came over Old Meg, as if her muscles were tensing up with effort. She stopped grinning and her forehead creased as if she was trying to remember something, something hidden very deeply in her mind.

'I knows about that . . . let's see . . . now listen . . .' and she searched through her jumbled memories. 'It wuz when I was a lass. A little lass, like you, in this orphanage. They wuz going to sort us out, she said. Sister Clare, lovely she was, but strict. She said them as were *this* – what you said – would be took away, and put in a place, and they'd throw away the key. "Now, Margaret Mary O'Shea," she said . . .' Old Meg stopped, as if she was surprised to remember her name after so long.

'Yes, that was it. That was my name

then. "Margaret Mary O'Shea, you gotta learn this poem," she said, that angel. "Learn this poem, and say it to them." And did she rap my knuckles until I learned that poem. Red raw, they wuz, my knuckles. But it worked, see? Every day, with a ruler. Until I knowed it.'

She looked closely at Charlie. 'It worked, see. When them guardians came, "Stand up, Margaret Mary O'Shea," she says – that was my name then – and I stood up and says this poem, right through. "Nothing wrong with that girl," they says, and went off and left us alone. Just like she said, that Sister Clare of the Angels. Sister Clare of the Ruler, more like.'

'Learn a poem?' Charlie asked in amazement. 'Did that make you *not* handicapped? And you didn't get put away?'

Old Meg had relaxed again. 'Well, I didn't get put away. But if you was "it", I don't swear as it would cure you.' She tried to sort out her thoughts again.

'But it proved I wasn't "it". What I'm saying is, you proves yourself. That's how I proved myself, but different people got to do it different ways. You proves it to yourself and to everybody else. Like I said. You gotta prove yourself.' And she closed her eyes and began to snore straight away.

Charlie shook her by the arm. How could anybody fall asleep that fast? Whatever was she talking about?

'What poem? What poem?' she shouted down her ear. But she thought Old Meg had probably forgotten it by now. She forgot lots of things, like what day it was and what her real name was. Would she remember some old poem? And if it worked for Old Meg, would it work for her?

Old Meg groaned and opened her eyes, and looked blearily at Charlie.

'What poem?' Charlie asked again.

Old Meg struggled unsteadily to her feet. She put one hand over her heart and held her left arm out stiffly in front of her. Then she planted her feet more firmly apart, like a statue. She cleared her throat.

' "Old Meg she was a Gipsy . . ." ' She paused and smiled. 'That's me, see? Old Meg.' And then she started the poem all over again, and went on and on and on. Charlie didn't understand much of it. No wonder she had to have her knuckles rapped to force her to learn it. Charlie didn't wait for her to finish. She slipped away while old Meg was droning on and on. Old Meg didn't even notice that she'd gone.

Charlie tried to remember what Old Meg had said. She'd got to find this poem and learn it, even if she didn't understand it. She had to remember some of the words, to ask Knickers to find it for her.

'I want to find a poem, miss,' Charlie said next day to Miss Nixon.

First a dictionary, now a poem? Not like the Charlie Morris she was used to.

'What poem?' she asked.

'It's about Old Meg.'

' "Old Meg she was a Gipsy . . ."?'

'That's it. That's it,' Charlie shouted, very excited. 'Is it in a book? I need it, miss.'

'I can get a copy from the upper-school library.' Miss Nixon was being very careful now. 'Could you tell me why you want it?'

'To learn it . . .' Charlie stopped. She wasn't going to let Knickers know about Old Meg and how she – Charlie – had to prove herself, just like Old Meg. Prove that she wasn't 'it', that she wasn't handicapped.

'I'm afraid it's rather long, not really what we usually do in our group. It might be rather difficult.'

But she got the book for Charlie.

When Charlie got home and opened

the book and found the poem, her heart sank. There was miles and miles of it. She took it to her bedroom.

'That child's sickening for something,' Mrs Morris said.

'She's just sickening,' Sally said.

Charlie lay down on her bed. She felt like giving up – almost. That poem might have worked for Old Meg, but it wasn't going to work for her. And she still didn't know what 'handicapped' meant. And she had to get even with Jason Jones.

The next day Charlie gave the book back to Miss Nixon, who wasn't at all surprised. Poetry and Charlie Morris didn't seem to go together. But she was puzzled about Charlie Morris. Had she really decided to become a poetry freak – or was she trying to prove something? Her behaviour had been very odd recently. Something was the matter. *Was* Charlie Morris trying to prove something? And if so, what?

CHAPTER THREE

'Neat,' Art Frozzen whispered to Charlie at dinner-time the next day. 'Very neat.'

Jason Jones had just let out a howl of pain. He was spitting sandwich all over the dinner table. Along with some chewed-up bread and soggy corned beef, out came Charlie's glass eye.

Charlie trapped it quickly in an upturned plastic beaker.

'Spider,' she shouted, and ran to the window, pretending to throw it out. She threw out the gooey mixture of bread and corned beef, and dropped the sticky glass eye into her pocket.

'Jason Jones, haven't you got any manners at all?' Miss Nixon had come rushing up. 'And clean up all this disgusting mess.'

'But, miss,' Jason Jones spluttered, his mouth bubbling with bread-crumbs and corned beef. 'That was her glass eye in my sandwich.' And he pointed accusingly at Charlie. 'That wasn't no spider, miss. It was her glass eye.'

Miss Nixon looked at Charlie. She was wearing her best patch. Miss Nixon began to feel uncertain.

'Charlie . . .' she began.

'Spider, miss. Honest,' Charlie said.

'Big as this, miss.' Art Frozzen backed her up, waving his hands backwards and forwards, trying to decide how large he dared to make the imaginary spider.

It was the word of two against one.
And really, Miss Nixon thought. Not
even Charlie Morris would put her
glass eye into somebody's sandwich.
That was just too unlikely.

'My front tooth's gone all wobbly,
miss,' Jason Jones shouted furiously.
'You can't make a tooth go all wobbly
on a spider.'

'Very hard bread, miss,' Charlie
said. 'Spiders get into stale bread.'

Miss Nixon didn't intend to get
into an argument.

'Come with me to the medical
room,' she said to Jason Jones. 'We'll
wash your mouth and get you to a
dentist to check that tooth.'

Jason Jones had no choice but to do
as he was told. The rest of the class
looked at Charlie with admiration.
This was like the old Charlie Morris –
even if she wasn't the captain of the
football team.

The next day Jason Jones's mother
came storming up to the school to

complain. She charged into the room without even knocking. This was the first time the class had seen Jason Jones's mother, but they didn't need to be told who it was. She looked just like Jason Jones, multiplied by about ten. She was larger in all directions than anybody else's mother, and she even had spiked-up black hair. Her mouth was a bright red lipstick slash, and her teeth were long and brown, like a dog's. All the children sat up and looked interested.

'Where's that kid with the glass eye what made my Jason's tooth go all wobbly in his sandwich?' she shouted, getting a bit muddled up in her rage.

Miss Nixon steered her gently outside the door again, beckoning Jason Jones and Charlie to come as well.

The rest of the class let out a sigh of disappointment. Jason Jones's mother was clearly something of a heavyweight, and she looked as if she might be pretty free with her fists as well. So they all stayed very quiet to listen out for any interesting developments.

'I bet my tooth left loads of scratches on that rotten glass eye,' Jason Jones said. 'It was a good tooth, that was. One of my big teeth. I could open bottles with that tooth, and now it's all wobbly.' And he tried to get up very close to Charlie, to inspect her glass eye for scratches.

Miss Nixon managed to get in between them. She didn't want any unnecessary violence to break out. 'Now the dentist said the tooth will tighten up,' she said, trying to calm them all down.

'She can look, if she wants,' Charlie said, nodding in the direction of Jason Jones's mother, and looking very helpful. She'd managed to turn her back on Jason Jones. She went up to Mrs Jones and closed one eye, so that Mrs Jones could inspect the other one. She stared at her straight and without blinking.

Mrs Jones began to feel uncomfortable. A girl! And such a pretty little girl, with red curly hair and lovely blue eyes – it must be a very good glass eye, she thought, you really couldn't tell the difference. She'd always dreamt of having a beautiful, angelic little girl. And what had she got? Jason, that's what she'd got. This kid was so much smaller than Jason too. And handicapped as well.

Suddenly she swung round as if to clout Jason round the head. He ducked and she missed by miles.

'You great bully,' she shouted. 'Pick on somebody your own size. Poor little lass's handicapped an' all.' Then she stamped out of the school.

Charlie turned round with a smirk on her face.

'All right. Back to your work, everybody,' Miss Nixon said.

The children all sighed with disappointment. It had all been over much too quickly for them.

But Charlie and Jason Jones both

knew that Charlie had covered up her glass eye, and stared at Mrs Jones with her real eye, the one she was born with. As a matter of fact, Jason Jones's tooth *had* scratched her glass eye, and her mother had been very cross when she'd noticed it.

'You've had your ration of new eyes,' she said. 'Now you'll have to wait for your birthday. You can have a new one then. Instead of that electronic dinosaur you keep on about.'

Charlie thought she'd much rather have the electronic dinosaur, but she knew she'd better not say anything more. Not yet, anyway.

But the very next day the whole class looked with amazement as Jason Jones walked in. He scowled. They stared in silence. Jason Jones had a black eye, a cut lip – and a gap where the wobbly tooth had been.

The silent stares shifted round to Charlie Morris, but Charlie was staring too.

'Nothing to do with Charlie Morris,' Jason Jones snarled, determined that the enemy should get no credit for his injuries. 'Did a wheelie. Came off. Hit a lamp-post. But,' his voice rising to a shout, 'it was her fault it went wobbly. If it hadn't've went wobbly, it wouldn't've come out so easy!'

'Knickers said the dentist said it would tighten up,' Charlie stuttered.

'Didn't get the chance, then, did it?' Jason Jones growled back, and they all went to their places as Miss Nixon came in.

Jason Jones made the best of his front-tooth gap by learning to whistle through it very loudly. Charlie felt a bit disappointed. Jason Jones was still captain of the football team. But at least being 'handicapped' – whatever that was – did have some advantages, if it got Jason Jones clouted by Mrs Jones, instead of her!

Now Jason Jones really had it in for her. She knew this because every time

Jason Jones went past her, he didn't even look at her: he just let out this horrible screeching whistle. The other children looked round and backed away when they heard it.

'You want to watch him,' Art Frozzen said. 'He's really got it in for you. You want to watch your back now.'

Charlie gave him a withering look. As if she didn't know. As if everybody in the whole school didn't know. Now it wasn't just a case of getting even. It was a case of survival as well.

CHAPTER FOUR

At school, Charlie got more and more ingenious. Her glass eye turned up everywhere – like a new-laid egg in the bird's nest on the table for the Living Earth project; like a giant blue bean in the jar where the butter-beans were sprouting; like a small blue pool on the cress tray. She was determined to stay one step ahead of Jason Jones, if possible.

Charlie got so many letters sent home, complaining about her tricks with her glass eye, that even Mr

Morris moved out from behind his newspaper one tea-time and grunted, 'Get yourself expelled, you will.'

'Expelled!' Sally snorted scornfully. 'It's "excluded", not "expelled". And you've got to more or less murder somebody before you get excluded. Or you can get excluded if you've got super-nits. They give you that smelly stuff to put on until they go away.'

'Nits?' Mrs Morris said indignantly. 'We got rid of them, didn't we? You haven't got those back, I hope.'

'If we've got to use that stinking lotion again, I'm off to Belgium tomorrow.'

'Don't be so stupid,' Sally said. 'What I meant was, if she hasn't done a murder or got those super-nits, she won't get excluded.' Then she glared at Charlie and said, 'Well, have you?'

Mrs Morris interrupted quickly. 'Don't be so silly. Of course she hasn't. Hasn't done either, or got either. You'll just have to try to behave, Charlie, that's all.'

Charlie smiled. When she smiled, she looked really good. But only Mrs Morris seemed to be taken in. Sally put her tongue out at her, and Mr Morris got out his map and began to plan his route across Belgium.

In the end, Miss Nixon put an absolute ban on Charlie's eye being anywhere except where it was supposed to be. And she applied the ultimate sanction.

'Charlie Morris,' she said, 'if your glass eye goes wandering again while you are in school, you will be banned from taking part in the Big Match.'

It worked. To be in the Big Match meant everything to Charlie Morris. She wasn't going to miss being in the Big Match. Charlie's eye stayed put.

Miss Nixon couldn't help admiring Charlie's skill at football, and her enthusiasm for the game. That glass eye didn't hold her back at all. It had never seemed to be a handicap to young Charlie Morris.

But Charlie hadn't forgotten about this word 'handicapped'. She'd looked at the racing pages of Grandad Morris's newspaper, and it seemed to her that 'handicapped' meant that a horse had to carry more weight. That didn't seem fair, but as Jason Jones was a lot heavier than she was, that should mean that Jason Jones was handicapped, not her. She imagined Jason Jones getting bigger and bigger, like a giant balloon, then floating upwards and exploding into pieces on the ceiling. That made her smile, but the real problem still wasn't solved.

The Big Match was a tradition. It was played between Ashby and Arrowby Schools' under-tens, over two legs, on two consecutive Friday afternoons. Both schools had the afternoons off to cheer their sides on. These were the biggest days in the football calendar. Charlie Morris had already played once, and this was her last chance to play again, because next year she'd be too old. Next year she'd have to play for the under-elevens. But it was only the under-tens that had the Big Match. And Charlie knew that Knickers meant what she said.

Miss Nixon had noticed how the class had divided into two camps for the past few weeks: the Charlie Morris camp and the Jason Jones camp. Even tables and chairs seemed to be moved by unseen hands so that there was a distinct gap, a sort of no man's land between the two groups. One half of the class seemed to be hypnotized by Charlie Morris's glass eye, and the other half seemed to be under the control of Jason Jones's tooth-gap whistle, like a herd of sheep at a sheepdog trial. Between Charlie Morris's glass eye and Jason Jones's piercing whistle, Miss Nixon was beginning to think that enough was enough, and very soon something quite firm would have to be done.

Even though the tables and chairs had been put in their correct places the night before, by now they'd moved, propelled by shuffling feet and wriggling bottoms, into separate camps.

'Who moved the chairs and tables?' Miss Nixon asked, knowing quite well that she wasn't going to get any satisfaction from the answers the children would offer. The favourite explanation was magic or ghosts.

'Maybe the room's haunted,' Art Frozzen suggested. 'Like that place a pig haunted on the video.'

'What nonsense are you talking about? What pig on what video?'

Knickers knew at once that she'd asked the wrong question. Everybody started jumping up and down, waving their hands in the air, trying to retell the story of a pig-haunted house. They clearly all knew the story off by heart.

'It's a pig-ghost, miss,' one of them said.

'It comes and haunts. It does really gruesome things, miss, like . . .'

'Enough. That's enough. I don't want to hear any more of this nonsense. There are no such things as ghosts, or pig-ghosts, or any other sort of ghosts. It's all . . .'

Something flew through the air as Miss Nixon was trying to calm them all down, and there was a loud PLOP. Mavis Green, a small timid girl, screamed. The rest of the class gasped, staring at the fish tank which stood on a table under the window-sill. A small brown object with pointed ears and a long tail was sinking to the bottom. The startled fish were swirling in all directions.

'It's a frog-ghost, miss. I saw it. It flew right past me,' Mark Ellis said.

'It's going to eat the fish, miss,' Mavis Green squeaked.

'Can fishes drown, miss? They're

all coming up for air,' Trish Little said.

The fish seemed to be gasping for air. The strange brown creature had begun to dissolve into a dirty gluey gunge. The tank looked all muddy. Something else, small and white, seemed to have settled on the pebbles at the bottom of the tank.

'It's the ghost-frog,' Mark Ellis shouted, pointing to the white shape in the fish tank.

'Get the fish out, quick,' Miss Nixon said, handing out paper beakers. 'Ask Miss Hewitt if they can go in her tank,' and she pushed the grabbing hands away, trying to give the beakers to the calmer children who wouldn't spill the fish and the water on the way to Miss Hewitt's room. But the fish didn't co-operate. They panicked. They flipped and flapped, jumped and leapt, splashing water everywhere, pursued by the clutching hands of the children. Some ended up in the cress tray, one landed in the bird's nest, another fell into the paint tray and got dyed purple. In the end, they were all scooped up, although some seemed to be showing symptoms of heart failure. Once in the clean, quiet water of Miss Hewitt's fish tank, they all gradually revived.

'Hey, miss,' Jason Jones shouted, pushing his way right up to the fish tank. 'That's my clay squirrel, that is. My clay model. It's in the fish tank, see,' and he pointed to the muddy mess which was slowly dissolving in the water. 'It was up there, miss.' He pointed to the windowsill above the fish tank.

'And how did your clay squirrel end up in the fish tank?' Miss Nixon asked.

'The ghost-frog did it,' Mark Ellis said.

Jason Jones turned and pointed to Charlie Morris. 'It wasn't no ghost-frog, miss. I bet it was her. Charlie Morris. My clay squirrel was better than her clay rat, that's what.'

Charlie Morris covered up her good eye with her hand and stared unblinkingly at Jason Jones with her glass eye. She'd found this trick made Jason Jones quite nervous.

'Stand up, Charlie Morris. Look at me. Never mind Jason Jones,' Miss Nixon said. 'Explain.'

'It flew out of my hand, miss.'

'What flew out of your hand?'

'My rubber, miss. My best one. I was testing it—how far it could jump. And it went that far, it hit Jason Jones's clay squirrel, miss, and knocked it down into the fish tank. It's in the fish tank too. There, on the bottom.' She pointed to the small white shape on the pebbles.

Jason Jones was trying to rescue his dissolving squirrel from the fish tank. He rolled up his sleeves, put his hand in the water, and got hold of the gooey mess. It oozed between his fingers.

'Put it in this newspaper, Jason,' Miss Nixon said. 'And everybody else sit down.'

'Can we give it a funeral, miss?' Jason Jones asked, wrapping the newspaper round the remains of his clay squirrel.

'Clay squirrels don't have funerals,' Miss Nixon said. 'Put it in the bin.'

'That's not fair, miss. Our cat had a funeral,' Jason Jones said.

'That's different,' Miss Nixon said. 'That was a pet.'

'Yes, but we never found the body. It went missing and after a bit we had the funeral. But we didn't have the body,' Jason Jones explained.

Suddenly everybody wanted to have a funeral for Jason Jones's clay squirrel. At least there was a body – sort of.

Miss Nixon put her foot down. 'We are not going to have a funeral for a clay squirrel,' she said. 'Instead, we will all work on the topic of squirrels. Different people can do different things on squirrels.'

'A funeral would be better, miss,'

Jason Jones complained. 'Can I do something about a funeral?'

'Today we will all do something on *live* squirrels,' Miss Nixon insisted firmly.

'Can't I write a poem about a ghost-frog?' Mark Ellis asked.

'Squirrels,' Miss Nixon repeated, and she wrote SQUIRREL on the blackboard. In the end, everybody was working on squirrels.

'What about a play, miss? *The Ashby School Horror?* With Jason Jones's squirrel and Charlie Morris's rubber frog?' Mark Ellis was very keen on drama.

'Definitely not,' Miss Nixon said, and that was that.

Miss Nixon was pinning her hopes on the Big Match to heal the division in her class. She hoped it would unite them all against a common enemy: the Arrowby School under-tens. And it was only two weeks away.

She intended to make this match part of the healing process, to make

Jason Jones and Charlie Morris join together in a common cause, and to unite the two divisions in the class. Well, there was no harm in hoping, she thought.

CHAPTER FIVE

The day of the Big Match was getting nearer. Everybody in the class felt involved – even Art Frozzen, who couldn't care at all about football usually, and said there was only one game worth watching: Rugby League – even Art Frozzen began to feel the excitement mounting.

Ashby had won for the past two years, and Charlie Morris had played in last year's team, even though she'd been smaller than the rest. But she was quick and accurate and nobody could catch her when she got going.

If Ashby got the most goals in the two matches this time, they would keep the cup which a famous football manager, a friend of one of the school governors of Arrowby, was going to present.

Charlie spent a lot of time day-dreaming about that cup, imagining it, all silver and shining, standing on the windowsill of the school hall. She almost felt it was her cup – she'd be the only player to have been in the team two years on the run.

'Now,' Miss Nixon was saying, 'we're all waiting for the Big Match on Friday afternoon. It's time for the captain and vice-captain to put their heads together and make out the final list. And anybody who isn't in the team can be a substitute.'

Jason Jones rolled his eyes to the ceiling. Typical, he was thinking. It would be just his luck to have to use Art Frozzen as a substitute. Or worse,

Mavis Green. Suppose he had to use Mavis Green as a substitute? With her sparrow legs and squealing noises. It was too awful to think of.

'Miss,' he said. 'Miss, I don't think we'll need any subs. Or just one or two would do.'

'Everybody must get a chance,' Miss Nixon said.

'Please, miss,' Mavis Green squeaked, 'I don't want a chance.'

'Then you can be a spectator,' Miss Nixon said. She couldn't really imagine Mavis Green playing football, or anything more violent than tiddlywinks.

Jason Jones felt he'd had a lucky escape from Mavis Green, and he might be able to put up with Art Frozzen if he had to. After all, *he* was the captain. Miss Nixon didn't seem to know this.

'Now, who's captain?' she asked, smiling brightly at them all.

'Me,' Jason Jones said loudly.

Nobody else claimed to be captain,

so Miss Nixon said, 'And who's vice-captain?'

'Don't need a vice-captain,' Jason Jones said grumpily. He didn't like the idea of sharing being the boss with anybody else.

'Well. As Charlie Morris has played in this match before, I think she should be vice-captain,' Miss Nixon said.

So Charlie Morris became vice-captain. She didn't want to be bossed about by Jason Jones, and Jason Jones didn't want to share picking the team with Charlie. They glared at each other. Jason Jones began to let out a threatening whistle through his broken tooth.

'No whistling in school,' Miss Nixon said.

'He should be ref, miss,' Charlie said. 'All he can do is whistle.'

'Well, at least I've got two eyes to see the ball with,' Jason Jones snarled back. 'I'm not handicapped like some. One-eyed twit.'

'Two eyes?' Charlie snapped back. 'You couldn't see straight with four.' She'd noticed the word 'handicapped' again, but as she couldn't think of anything to say, she satisfied herself with a rude gesture.

'That's enough,' Miss Nixon said. 'You two come here and sit at my table and I'll watch while you make out the list.' She knew she was going to have to keep a close eye on the two of them. 'You can take it in turns to name a player,' she said quickly.

'Me first. I'm captain,' Jason Jones said. 'I get the first go.'

'All right, Jason. Name your Number One,' Miss Nixon said.

'Right. Number One – goalie – Joan Donovan.'

Charlie had to agree, although she didn't like to admit it. But Joan Donovan was bigger even than Jason Jones and played goalie in a league team. Nobody could argue with that choice. So Charlie just nodded. She wasn't going to say 'yes' out loud and let Knickers think she let Jason Jones boss her about.

'Your turn, Charlie,' Miss Nixon said.

'Me. At Number Nine,' Charlie said loudly.

'Me. At Number Eight,' Jason Jones shouted.

And they glared at each other.

'Well,' Miss Nixon said wearily, 'that's three. What about the rest?'

'Mark Ellis, at Number Three,' Charlie growled.

'Sharon Smith, at Number Ten,' Jason Jones spat out the name.

'Jim Walker, Number Four.'

'Phil Thompson, Number Five.'

'Tracy Robinson, Number Six.'

'Billy Briggs, Number Eleven.'

Suddenly Charlie realized it was her last turn to choose a player. There weren't many good ones left. Josh Turner was good, Roy Thomas wasn't bad, and there was mousy Mary Evans who sometimes played with a girls' team. But there was Art Frozzen too.

Art Frozzen was carefully doodling with a pencil on the table, making sure he didn't look up and catch anybody's eye. All sorts of thoughts were rushing through Art's head. He wasn't any good at football. Everybody knew that. But to play in the Big Match, even if it wasn't Rugby League, what would his dad think of that? Imagine what his dad would say if he got chosen . . . but he wouldn't get chosen. Nobody would ever choose him . . . not with Josh Turner still not picked.

Charlie could see Art Frozzen doodling with his pencil. She knew what he was thinking: Josh Turner or Art Frozzen? Charlie hesitated. Everybody wanted to play in the Big Match, even Art Frozzen. Charlie remembered how Art Frozzen had been the only one who hadn't run off after Jason Jones on the day when Jason Jones had made himself captain.

'Art Frozzen at Number Seven,' Charlie said very quietly, because she knew Jason Jones would have something smart to say.

'Load of rubbish,' Jason Jones jeered.

'Art Frozzen,' Charlie repeated, more loudly.

Art Frozzen couldn't believe his ears the first time – it must have been a mistake – but when he heard his name again, he knew Charlie Morris meant it. Charlie Morris had chosen him to play in the Big Match! Art Frozzen went pink with delight and nodded in Charlie's direction, without raising his eyes from his pencil. It was enough. They both knew that.

'Josh Turner, Number Two,' Jason Jones said.

And that was the team.

Miss Nixon wasn't too happy about the look of the team. It looked too much like Jason Jones's gang v. Charlie Morris's gang. She would have to remember to tell them they were supposed to be playing against Arrowby, not against each other. But she put the list up on the notice-board. She was going to be linesman and Arrowby were bringing the ref.

Charlie was so busy practising football and imagining herself scoring the winning goal that she didn't have time to keep on trying to find out what 'handicapped' meant. In fact, she forgot all about it for a while. Every moment was taken up with football, either playing football or thinking about football. She kept thinking about that lovely silver cup. It wasn't fair that Jason Jones was captain. *She* ought to be captain. *She* ought to be the one to walk up and receive the shining cup. Everybody would be clapping and cheering, the crowd of spectators would open up a path as she walked forward to receive the cup. She would hold it over her head and wave it about and everybody would cheer. They would shake up bottles of Coke and spray it everywhere . . .

But now it would be Jason Jones who got all the glory, not her. But she could still score the winning goal. She would be a hero, like Cantona or Ryan Giggs.

Charlie tried to imagine something very bad happening to Jason Jones, then she would be captain. Maybe he'd sprain his ankle or break his leg or get chickenpox. You had to stay in bed with chickenpox. She'd had chickenpox and had two weeks off school with it. But she knew it wasn't really going to happen like that, even though she looked very carefully every morning at Jason Jones to see if any spots were developing. And Jason Jones wasn't going to fall off a ladder just to suit Charlie Morris.

By the time Friday afternoon came, Jason Jones and the rest of the team were all fitter and stronger than ever, just waiting to get at Arrowby.

*

It was a tough match from the kick-off. Ashby supporters stood in a crowd on one side of the pitch and Arrowby supporters stood in a crowd on the other. Arrowby seemed to have brought the whole school to support their team in a couple of mini-buses, so the number of supporters was about equal. Even before the kick-off they'd all been shouting and whistling. As the teams ran out on to the field, there was a great cheer. First Arrowby came out in their blue and white strip, then Ashby in their all-red strip. The noise was deafening. Then there was silence, and the ref blew his whistle to start the match.

Both teams tore up and down the pitch. Their supporters stood at the sidelines and cheered every move. In the very first seconds of the game, Arrowby collected the ball off Ashby, who'd kicked off badly with a lob. Immediately Arrowby pushed forwards, pressing hard on the Ashby defence. A great pass wide down the left was picked up by the Arrowby Number Eleven right on the line. He lifted the ball into the centre, but Josh Turner rose into the air and headed it clear for Ashby. The Ashby supporters breathed a sigh of relief and the Arrowby supporters, who'd been cheering wildly, fell silent.

Jason Jones picked the ball up at his toes and carved through the Arrowby defence. He reached the penalty area and took a hefty kick at goal. But he misjudged it and lofted the ball high over the goal and into the spectators. The goal-kick was headed back by Jason Jones again. The Arrowby defence booted it for a corner.

Charlie Morris took the corner, centering to Sharon Smith, but her aim at goal was scooped up by the Arrowby goalie.

The goal-kick was a good one, right into the Ashby danger area. Josh Turner intercepted and chested the ball down and flashed it out to

Charlie Morris. She took the ball up and centered to Sharon Smith who buried it in Arrowby's net. All the Ashby supporters went wild. But their joy soon ended, as the linesman – Miss Nixon – was clearly indicating offside, and the goal was disallowed. The Ashby supporters groaned.

The game got hotter and hotter. Joan Donovan made a great save and all the Ashby supporters cheered. Jason Jones had two near misses and Charlie hit the woodwork. In spite of all Ashby's efforts the half-time whistle blew with the score nil-nil. All the spectators cheered as the two teams left the field.

Jason Jones was giving his team a pep talk.

'We gotta go for it,' he urged them. 'We gotta play the home advantage. Next leg is away. We gotta clinch it here and now.'

There were cheers again as the two teams ran out. The second half was just as hard, but both teams were beginning to feel the strain. Their legs got heavier and heavier. Arrowby kept threatening Ashby's goal, but Joan Donovan cleared every time and kept them in the game. Jason Jones shouted encouragement to Ashby. Again one of Arrowby's strikers pushed forward. Charlie Morris had fallen back to help the defence. Now she made a neat interception and deprived the Arrowby striker of the ball. She played a clever back-heel to Joan Donovan.

But Charlie hadn't seen that Joan Donovan's view was blocked by an Arrowby player.

The ball trickled slowly over the line. The whistle blew. The ref indicated 'goal' and pointed to the centre circle. All the Ashby supporters were silenced. The Arrowby supporters were jumping up and down with joy. Charlie couldn't believe it. An own goal! The Arrowby supporters began to shriek and shout and sing: 'One-nil, one-nil, one-nil, one-nil . . .'

'You blind or something?' Jason Jones snarled at Charlie as Joan Donovan slowly picked the ball out of the net, muttering something that the ref fortunately didn't hear. 'Got two glass eyes, have you? Handicapped? You're worse than handicapped. You're useless. That's what. Worse than useless.'

Charlie couldn't say anything. She played as hard as she could for the rest of the game, but she couldn't find an opening. When she came forward, the Arrowby defence stuck to her like glue. Time was running out for Ashby. All Arrowby had to do was to hold on to their one-goal lead.

Art Frozzen, Ashby's Number Seven, who'd been put out on the right wing where he could do the least damage, got a touch, but lost the ball instantly to the Arrowby defence. The game began to limp to its close. When the final whistle blew, Ashby had lost: one-nil.

Charlie ran straight off the field, grabbing her coat and bag from the sideline. She didn't go in for the tea, although it was always a very good spread and the rest of the players were glad to sit down and celebrate (Arrowby) or plan the return leg (Ashby). Charlie didn't wait for the school bus. She went out of the school grounds and began to half-run and half-walk back to her own village, even though her legs felt as heavy as lead. She ran past the Ashby Rugby Club where they were getting ready for their barbecue, and went straight to where nobody would find her – straight to the back of the empty supermarket and Old Meg's bench.

Charlie scrambled through the cardboard boxes but found Old Meg snugly curled up on the bench in a sort of cardboard tent. She was fast asleep, an empty bottle by her side. Charlie made a space for herself on the floor beside the bench. She put her head in her hands. Now she knew what 'handicapped' was – it was 'useless'. That was what Jason Jones had said. Worse than useless. And Jason Jones was right. She'd never, never go back to school again. She probably wouldn't even go home. She was finished. She sat and sat and sat. Now she knew what 'it' was. And she was 'it' – worse than useless. Charlie could feel the hot tears running down her face. She didn't even try *not* to cry. She really was finished.

CHAPTER SIX

Charlie coughed. That woke her up. There was a funny smell and her throat was stinging. She coughed again. Her throat and all her insides felt hot.

Where was she? Old Meg let out a sudden snort from the bench beside her, and Charlie remembered. She remembered in a flash all that misery, the own goal, running and running, hiding in the boxes beside Old Meg's bench. She coughed, more harshly this time. Her eye pricked. Old Meg was snorting like an angry bear.

Fog. Thick fog. Dark. Suddenly Charlie was wide awake. She had to get home. Late for tea. If Dad was back, she'd be in dead trouble. She coughed again. Bonfires. That was the smell. Bonfires. Not fog. Smoke. Thick smoke. The boxes were on fire. She couldn't stop coughing.

'Old Meg, Old Meg,' she screamed, gasping and coughing and kicking the snorting bundle of rags. 'Fire. Fire. The boxes are on fire.'

Little rivulets of blue flames were running along the edges of the cardboard. Smoke belched out as the boxes burst with the heat.

'Wake up. Wake up, Margaret Mary O'Shea,' Charlie shouted and kicked Old Meg hard. Old Meg stirred at the sound of her name – the name of her childhood. Charlie kicked and kicked, harder than she'd ever kicked a football. She kicked her on the ankles, on the feet, on the shins, anywhere she could reach. Old Meg grunted and staggered to her feet, gasping and retching. Charlie pushed her and shoved her until they stumbled together out over the burning boxes as the flames were taking hold. They both crumpled in a heap against the wall on the other side of the road, gasping for breath. A siren sounded in the distance and got louder.

Suddenly Charlie jumped up.

'I've got to get home,' she shouted to Old Meg who was lying slumped against the wall, and she ran off, still coughing and spluttering, with her face streaked with tears from her stinging eyes.

All Old Meg could say was 'Aargh, aargh.'

'Wherever have you been?' Sally demanded, angry and amazed, as Charlie burst into the kitchen, breathless and very dirty. 'Mum was going to call the police. Wait till she sees you. You're really for it. You stink, too

– bonfires, that's what. You look a real mess.'

'Shut up,' Charlie said automatically. 'Why don't you just shut up?'

'As if anybody'd want to kidnap you,' Sally jeered.

Mrs Morris came into the kitchen.

'I thought I heard . . .' she said, and stopped suddenly, taking in at a glance the mess Charlie was in as she stood there, grimy and breathless, and – for the moment – speechless. 'Bath, then bed,' was all Mrs Morris said, and pointed upstairs.

As Charlie went upstairs, she could hear Sally complaining. 'It's not fair, Mum. It's just not fair. You said you'd skin her alive. That's what you said. Being so late and everything. You said you'd murder her.'

'I'm just glad she's back in one piece,' Mrs Morris said. 'I can always murder her later.'

'Well, good job our dad's not here. He'd murder her *now*,' Sally shouted

73

furiously and ran out, slamming the door behind her.

Then Charlie didn't hear anything else because she closed the bathroom door and turned on both the bath taps full blast. After Charlie had had her bath, Mrs Morris brought her some cornflakes and milk to eat in bed and then she fell asleep straight away.

Next morning Charlie came downstairs very quietly, looking neat and clean in fresh clothes. Mrs Morris was making toast and Sally was eating it.

'Is Dad back?' Charlie asked nervously.

'Another lucky escape for you,' Sally jeered. 'Not home yet, is he? Just wait till he does get back.'

'How did the match go, dear?' Mrs Morris asked, trying to keep the peace.

The match! Charlie's heart sank. Just for a few hours she'd forgotten all about the match, what with the boxes getting on fire and thinking about the trouble she'd be in for getting home so late, and missing tea. That own goal! Wretchedness came back to her. But at least she didn't have to go to school if it was Saturday.

'We lost. One-nil,' she muttered, looking at her toast as if it was suddenly very interesting.

'Not such a clever-clogs, are you?' Sally saw her chance to put the boot in. 'Mary Evans's sister told me you scored an own goal.'

'Why don't you just shut up?' Charlie shouted, and she chewed her toast very loudly with her mouth open, leaning across the table and pushing her face right up to Sally's.

'Mum . . .' Sally was beginning to shriek with disgust. 'Mum, she's . . .'

But there was a knock at the door and Mrs Morris went to open it. Then she took a step back in surprise. There was a policewoman standing in the doorway.

'Mrs Morris?' the policewoman

asked. 'Can I come in for a moment? I don't want to stand talking to you on the doorstep. Not very nice for you, see? Neighbours watching, and all that.'

Mrs Morris stood back and let her in.

In the kitchen the policewoman looked keenly at Charlie who was still eating her toast.

'Ah,' she said thoughtfully. 'Is this your daughter, Mrs Morris? Is this young Charlotte, er, Charlie Morris?'

'Yes,' Mrs Morris said, feeling all hot and bothered. 'She's not in any sort of trouble, is she? She's a good girl.'

'They're all good to their mothers,' the policewoman said wearily.

Sally snorted and watched curiously.

'Well, Mrs Morris,' the police-woman said. 'Can I sit down? I think we should have a little talk. A small girl answering the description of your daughter was seen running

from the site of a fire beh[ind] [a] [su]permarket yesterday.'

The policewoman waited [care]fully.

'Oh no,' Mrs Morris said qu[ietly]. 'You must be mistaken.' But s[he re]membered what Charlie had lo[oked] like when she'd come in and [when] Sally said she smelt of bonfires.

The policewoman looked caref[ully] at Charlie and then back at [Mrs] Morris. 'I'm afraid there's no mist[ak]ing the description. A small girl [in a] football strip, with red curly hair.'

Sally caught her breath and looke[d] at Charlie, but she didn't say any[thing. After all, Charlie was her sister, and she wasn't going to grass on her whatever it was that she'd done. She quietly went out of the kitchen.

'Well, Charlotte, er, Charlie,' the policewoman said, turning to face her. 'Perhaps you could tell us something about it all?'

'About what?' Charlie asked, playing for time. Suddenly Charlie

ealized that the policewoman hought that she'd done it – set fire to he boxes behind the supermarket. She felt fear and indignation at the same time.

'It wasn't me,' she said, her voice shaking a little. Did they put girls of nine in prison, she wondered? Did they take them away from home and lock them up? She looked at her mother and went all cold and sweaty. Would they take her away from Mum? And what about Dad? Even Sally suddenly seemed nicer – after all, Sally was her sister.

'Of course it wasn't her,' Mrs Morris said fiercely.

'Let her tell us in her own words,' the policewoman said, and she took out her notebook. Charlie didn't like the look of that at all.

'I fell asleep. In the boxes. On the floor. By the bench . . .'

'Wait a minute,' Mrs Morris interrupted. 'What were you doing going to sleep in those old boxes? Why

didn't you come home on the school bus?'

'Let her tell it in her own words,' the policewoman said again. Charlie hadn't thought she'd ever feel like saying 'thanks' to the policewoman, but she did then. How could she ever explain to anybody how she'd felt, knowing she was 'worse than useless'? How could she explain the need to hide away from everybody, except the one person who really understood – Old Meg – because she'd been through it herself?

'I was asleep in the boxes. Behind the supermarket. Where Old Meg goes.'

'Old Meg?' the policewoman asked with her pencil held in the air.

But Charlie didn't take any notice. She just went on and on, talking faster and faster. 'Then I woke up. It was the smoke. I thought it was fog, but it was smoke. It made me cough. That's what woke me up, the smoke.'

'Tell me about this other person,' the policewoman said patiently.

'It was only Old Meg.' Then Charlie felt scared. Had she landed Old Meg in trouble? She didn't want Old Meg to be put in prison. 'She didn't have anything to do with it. She was asleep. She didn't start it.'

'Let me get her name right. What name did you say again?' The policewoman seemed to be having a lot of trouble with Old Meg's name. Her pencil was still in the air.

'Well,' Charlie slowed down a bit, 'her name's really Margaret Mary O'Shea. She remembered who she really is. She's remembered her real name. She told me. But everybody calls her Old Meg.'

The policewoman wrote down *Margaret Mary O'Shea* in her notebook. Charlie peered across at the notebook and saw the name written very clearly: *Margaret Mary O'Shea*. For some reason she didn't understand, she felt glad that Old Meg's real name had been written down, as if that really did make her Margaret Mary O'Shea again.

'Yes. Well,' the policewoman said, standing up again, 'I'd better track down this lady, Miss O'Shea, and get a statement from her. We have to follow up all lines of enquiry. I'll get back to you, Mrs Morris. Goodbye.'

After the policewoman had gone, Sally came back into the kitchen from behind the door where she'd been hiding, listening to what had been going on.

'I bet it was you,' she accused Charlie. 'I bet you got some fags and set the boxes on fire.'

'No, I never,' Charlie shouted in fury. 'I don't do fags. I'm in training.'

'Training to score own goals, I suppose?' Sally shouted back. 'You think you'll get away with this, just like everything else.'

Mrs Morris shooed Sally out of the room.

'Now let's have a few answers to

straight questions,' she said to Charlie. 'Whatever were you doing sleeping in cardboard boxes? And who's this Margaret Mary O'Shea? Not Old Meg? Is that Old Meg's real name? And I never knew. And what did happen in the match?'

But Charlie wasn't going to tell anybody how she'd cried and cried. Cried herself to sleep like a baby. If anybody ever found out, anybody at school, that would be even worse than scoring an own goal. But Old Meg would never let on, because she'd been through it herself – she'd had to prove herself. And that was what Charlie still had to do. There never seemed to be enough time to do it. Things kept happening to her.

But at least the policewoman had gone and Mum was still on her side, mostly, anyway. Sally was never on her side, but she was used to that. You couldn't tell with Dad, being away so much. When he was at home, he liked a quiet life.

Charlie turned things over in her mind. She'd survived being nearly roasted in a fire. She'd survived being nearly arrested for something she hadn't done. But the worse would be on Monday when she had to go back to school and everybody would be talking about the match and that own goal. She'd got to survive that as well.

Chapter Seven

But Monday morning at school didn't come. On Saturday evening Charlie was sick all over the bedroom carpet. She was all hot and sweaty and gasping for breath.

'Can't breathe properly,' she whispered hoarsely, feeling quite frightened.

Mrs Morris called the doctor and the doctor packed her off to the local hospital. Mrs Morris followed Charlie anxiously through Casualty, through the X-ray department, into the children's ward. The sister in the children's ward didn't seem too delighted to see her.

'Charlie Morris? Not *the* Charlie Morris, back again after all these years?' She made a mental note to warn the young nurses who were new on the ward about this patient.

Mrs Morris felt she ought to apologize for Charlie, even though she hadn't done anything to apologize about.

'What's the matter with her?' Mrs Morris asked the nurse. 'She can't get her breath properly.'

'She seems to be suffering from the after-effects of breathing hot smoke. We'll give her something to make her comfortable and we'll just keep an eye on her for a few days.'

Then the sister went off to warn the other nurses and tell them all the dreadful things Charlie had done when she was in the hospital before.

'You don't have to stay,' Charlie said to her mother. 'I've been here before.'

But Mrs Morris stayed until Charlie had fallen asleep and then she went home.

When Charlie woke up, it was Sunday. Sunday in hospital was very boring. Charlie couldn't understand why. Last time she'd been in hospital, it had been great fun, like one long party, as far as she could remember. Now there was nothing to do except have a bath and wait for the meals to come round.

Mrs Morris and Sally came on Sunday afternoon and brought her Walkman and a box of chocolates that Sally kept helping herself to.

Charlie said, 'It's really boring in here.'

'They haven't found that Old Meg,' Mrs Morris said.

'When can I come home?' Charlie asked. 'There's nothing to do in here.'

'The nurse says you'll have to wait until the doctor sees you tomorrow. Nothing happens on Sunday.'

'Too right,' Charlie grumbled.

'They won't let me do anything. And they follow me about all the time.'

'Who do?' Mrs Morris asked, puzzled.

'Those nurses. They even followed me to the bathroom when I was going to have a bath.' Charlie felt very insulted by this.

The nurses were keeping a very close eye on Charlie.

'Never mind, dear,' her mother said. 'They're just looking after you.'

'More likely the police asked them to keep an eye on you,' Sally said.

'Now, Sally, don't talk nonsense,' Mrs Morris said.

'What d'you mean, the police asked them?' Charlie shouted at Sally.

'Well, seeing that they still haven't found that Old Meg person. Maybe they think you'll try and make a get-away, so the nurses are trailing you.'

'But I haven't done anything,' Charlie shouted indignantly. 'They don't need to trail me.'

A nurse came up to the bed, she was never very far away. 'Now don't get so excited,' she said. 'You'll put your temperature up.'

After a while, when they'd run out of things to say, Mrs Morris and Sally went home, leaving another box of chocolates for Charlie, as Sally had gobbled up most of the first one.

Charlie didn't mind the idea of staying in hospital on Monday. That way she'd miss school, and by Tuesday they'd probably have forgotten about that own goal.

Monday came.

'Just a few days longer,' the doctor smiled at her.

'I've got to be out by Friday. I've got to play in a match,' Charlie said.

'What sort of match?'

'Football.'

The doctor looked surprised. 'Well, you might be out of here by Friday. I expect you'll be able to go home on Thursday. But there'll be no playing football, I'm afraid. Not this week.'

Charlie nearly jumped out of bed. 'I've got to play. I've just *got* to.' She was almost shouting at the doctor.

'No "got to" about it. No playing football this week,' and the doctor moved on.

For the rest of the day Charlie was silent with misery. She didn't even cheer up when Art Frozzen came to see her with some comics.

'Not all girls in here, is it?' he asked, looking round nervously.

'It's anybody, stupid. Anyway, I'm a girl, aren't I?'

'Yes. But you're different,' Art Frozzen answered, and he sat on the chair by the bed. 'They said you'd been put in prison.' Art helped himself to a chocolate. 'That you'd burned down the Town Hall or something.'

Charlie cheered up a little. 'Who said?' she asked.

'Everybody. Well, nearly everybody. And that you'd tried to burn an old witch, like in the olden days, but she got away. That's murder now, burning witches. The police are still looking for her. There's no body – just like Jason Jones's cat.'

'That's a load of lies,' Charlie said. 'Did you go to the prison first, to find me?'

'No. Knickers said you were in here. When are you getting out?'

'Thursday. But I can't play in the match.'

Art Frozzen couldn't believe it. 'You gotta play. Tell them. We'll end up playing with mousy Mary Evans. We won't have a chance.'

'What about Roy Thomas?'

'He's got the flu.'

They both fell silent, contemplating certain disaster, and finishing off the chocolates. When they'd all gone, Art got up.

'I've got to go now,' he said. 'Wait till Jason Jones hears we've got to play mousy Mary Evans. I don't envy you, when he finds that out.'

'Wait a bit,' Charlie said as Art was

moving off. 'Did they say anything like . . . I mean . . . you know . . . about the match last Friday?' She couldn't bring herself to speak the words 'own goal' again.

'Oh that,' Art said dismissively. 'No. They're all talking about the fire you started – and that old witch that's disappeared. Have you buried her somewhere? That witch? They still haven't found the body. Maybe the police'll come for you when they do find the body. Well, it'll be the police or Jason Jones. One or t'other,' and Art left.

Charlie thought about the choice between the police getting her first or Jason Jones getting her first. She decided she'd feel safer in the hands of the police than in the hands of Jason Jones.

On Tuesday the lady from the eye clinic came to see her.

'You've been through a lot of eyes,' she said, joking. But Charlie didn't even smile. 'What's the matter?' the eye lady asked.

Charlie tried to explain.

'Football? For girls? Goodness me. But it's only a game, isn't it?' she said brightly. 'Fancy getting upset about a game. I mean, it is only a game.'

Charlie could see that she'd never begin to understand what it was all about, so she decided not to say anything more about it. Only a game? It was the Big Match, and she was in double trouble over it.

'It doesn't seem like the Charlie Morris we used to know,' the sister said and the eye lady agreed.

'Girls playing football! Whatever next! And they forget it's only a game,' she said.

Charlie knew that some people would never understand.

On Wednesday afternoon Charlie spotted a policewoman talking to the sister. She rolled out of bed – on the side opposite to the one nearest the policewoman – and, squirming under the beds, she made her way to the toilet and sat there for nearly half an hour. The other children watched in amazement, but said nothing. They weren't going to grass on her if the police were after her.

'Are you all right in there?' a voice asked after what seemed like ages, and there was a knocking on the toilet door.

Charlie came out. The police-woman had gone and Art Frozzen was standing by her bed.

'Jason Jones's got a new tooth,' he said.

'You can't grow three lots of teeth. That one that broke was a second tooth. He told me. A big tooth,' Charlie answered.

'He hasn't grown it. It's a false one. A pot tooth. Like you've got a glass eye – he's got a pot tooth. He can stick it right out, like this.' And he stuck out his tongue. 'Well, almost,' he added. 'Like a vampire. Ace.'

'What about the match on Friday?

Did Jason Jones say anything about mousy Mary Evans?'

Art Frozzen looked round the ward. There were nurses everywhere.

'Can't say it in here,' he muttered. 'Murder's the nearest thing. You'd better stay out of his way.'

The thought of murder reminded Art Frozzen of something else. 'That old witch – the police found her. She isn't dead. I don't think she's a witch either. You said you'd murdered her.' Art Frozzen sounded quite disappointed.

'No, I didn't. *You* said that everybody said I'd murdered her. But I said I hadn't.'

'Well, she isn't a bit dead. She's down at the night shelter. Not dead at all.'

'I told you she wasn't dead.'

'I thought you said you'd murdered her,' Art Frozzen said. 'They haven't hung anybody for murder for years and years and years. I read a book about it. By the man who used to hang them. He used to have a pub when he wasn't hanging people.'

'Everybody knows that. He came from Oldham.'

'Who came from Oldham?' Art asked.

'The man who used to hang people.'

'Everybody knows that. What about the match? Are you coming to support?'

'Yeah, I'll come and watch. I'll be sick as a parrot, that's what. And that mousy Mary Evans isn't going to wear *my* Number Nine shirt either. She'll have to find a shirt of her own.'

Then Mrs Morris and Sally turned up and Art Frozzen sloped off. Mrs Morris was smiling all over her face. Even Sally looked almost pleasant. Charlie wondered why.

'The police came round again . . .' Mrs Morris began and Charlie's heart sank.

'But she isn't dead and I didn't murder her,' Charlie protested.

'Well, of course she isn't dead. Of course you didn't murder her. Saved her life. That's what she told the police, that Old Meg. They said you might get a certificate or something – for saving her life. That Old Meg told the police you'd rescued her from the fire.'

'It was some fireworks that started that fire,' Sally butted in.

'Fireworks?' Charlie asked, getting a bit confused with all their excited chattering.

'Set the boxes on fire. From the Rugby Club barbecue. It wasn't you.'

'I told you it wasn't me,' Charlie shouted.

'Now don't get excited,' a nurse said. 'You're going home tomorrow. Quite famous, you are. It's in the *Journal* about you,' and she unfolded a paper and showed them the page which was headed: *Margaret Mary O'Shea's Story*.

The nurse read out the bit with Charlie's name in it. 'Margaret Mary continued her story: "I was sleeping like an innocent new-born babe, worn-out after the heavy labours of the day . . ." ' Charlie remembered the empty medicine bottle – ' "when I was awakened by a young hero called Charlie Morris just as the flames closed around us." '

The nurse looked at Charlie. 'That's you, isn't it?' and she smiled. 'I bet your mum's real proud of you.'

'I always was real proud of her,' Mrs Morris said. 'She didn't have to prove anything to me.'

'A policewoman came in earlier to see Charlie and congratulate her for being so brave. We couldn't find you anywhere,' the nurse said, turning to Charlie.

Charlie didn't say anything. She'd been stuck in that toilet for ages – and for no reason at all! That police-woman hadn't come to arrest her after all. She wasn't to know that, was she? She'd thought the police were after her for something she hadn't done anyway. Now everybody was acting as if she was the greatest! Well, everybody except Jason Jones probably. Jason Jones probably thought that she'd done the team down twice now – first that own goal, and now not being allowed to play. That really was worse than useless, not playing at all, and having to sit on the sideline and watch mousy Mary Evans play in her place. Well, she wasn't going to wear *her* Number Nine shirt, no way.

Charlie decided it was quite nice being a hero, even though it seemed to have happened by accident. She hadn't planned to get Old Meg out of that fire, she'd just done it without thinking. Got them both out, because she was so frightened.

Then Charlie remembered what Old Meg had said about having to prove herself. Perhaps she had done that now, without meaning to, by getting Old Meg out of the fire. Maybe you could prove yourself without even knowing it. She'd heard quite a few people say that she'd proved herself a proper little hero, so maybe it was true. She seemed to have done it without meaning to at the time; it had been a lot easier than learning that long poem of Old Meg's. Most people didn't seem to think she was worse than useless. Most people seemed to think she was the greatest – or almost the greatest. Of course Sally kept on telling her not to be a big-head, but Sally would say something like that. She'd say something like that even if it was *her* she'd got out of the fire, not Old Meg.

And, of course, there was one other person she hadn't proved herself to. In fact, that person was probably thinking that now she was even *more* worse than useless. What would he think when he saw her sitting on the sideline, with mousy Mary Evans playing in her place in the team? Jason Jones wasn't going to think any better of her, not if she'd rescued ten people from a fire, single-handed.

And it was Jason Jones who'd started it all off, calling her handicapped and worse than useless. Suddenly Charlie realized that she'd proved herself to loads of people she didn't need to prove herself to – like the nurses and the policewoman. Who cared what they thought anyway? And Mum (who really did matter) was always saying that she didn't need to prove herself to her. Even Dad (when he was home) was always the same to her, whatever terrible things she did or didn't do. None of these people ever said she was handicapped or worse than useless, not even Sally on a bad day.

It was Jason Jones who was the one who counted. It was Jason Jones and what he had said that was bugging her all the time. Because Jason Jones was bigger and faster and just as good at football as she was. To Jason Jones she'd never be the greatest.

And it was Jason Jones she dreamed about all Thursday night.

Jason Jones getting bigger and fiercer, his hair getting spikier and blacker, and his big white pot teeth sticking out of his mouth like two rows of tusks as he chased after Charlie whose legs got so heavy that she couldn't run, and there she was, standing glued to the grass in the middle of the football pitch, in front of a huge jeering crowd, trying to kick the football – but her boots were nailed to the ground.

Chapter Eight

When Friday afternoon came, two coachloads of spectators were taken from Ashby School to Arrowby School. Everybody wanted to go to the match because word had got round that a famous manager was going to present the cup to the winning team.

Just my rotten luck, Charlie thought gloomily. Just my rotten luck not to play when I could have been talent-spotted by the number-one manager in the whole country. I could have got my great chance to play in league football.

She sat silently on the coach next to Mrs Morris.

Of course, the team had all gone off together, hadn't they, and she was left with a load of mothers and baby brothers and sisters. She could see Jason Jones's mother on the coach, with all her hair spiked up. There were a few fathers there too, but Mr Morris was still driving his lorry in Belgium, so he wasn't there. Charlie looked at the man sitting just in front of them in the coach. She could only see the back of him, but across his jacket, in huge white letters, were the words: BRADFORD BULLS RUGBY LEAGUE CLUB. Art Frozzen's dad – it had to be.

She nudged her mother. 'That's Art Frozzen's dad.'

Mrs Morris nodded cheerfully towards him. 'Hello, Mr Frozzen,' she called out. 'Nice day for the match.'

Art Frozzen's dad looked

surprised. 'The name's Holmes,' he said.

Mrs Morris turned to Charlie. 'I thought you said that was Art Frozzen's dad?' she said, puzzled.

All Charlie could say was 'Oh, Mum,' and she subsided into embarrassed silence. It would be too difficult to explain about Art Frozzen's name. Anyway, she didn't feel like talking. She wasn't even going to get a chance to make up for that own goal that put Ashby School one down already. Now they were playing away and she had to sit and watch.

The Arrowby supporters were already sitting on some benches along the sidelines when the Ashby coach arrived. All the Ashby supporters rushed to sit on the benches on the opposite side. Charlie dragged her mother down to the end bench, right by one of the goals.

'If we win the toss, we'll choose this end, to get the slope,' she said. They were closely followed by Art Frozzen's dad.

'Why don't we sit in the middle?' Mrs Morris asked.

'We've got to sit by the goal, that's why,' Charlie replied, and Art Frozzen's dad nodded his head in agreement.

Charlie took her jacket off to show her Number Nine shirt: bright red, spotlessly clean, carefully ironed. That was the best way of making sure that mousy Mary Evans didn't even get a chance of wearing it. Nobody was going to stop Charlie from wearing her Number Nine shirt, even if she wasn't allowed to play.

In another part of the ground, in front of the pavilion, there was a table and three chairs. The cup, all shining in the autumn sun, stood in the centre of the table. Charlie looked at the cup with longing. Even if Ashby won, she'd never get her hands on it now. She wouldn't even get a medal. If they lost, it would be her fault twice over – once for that own goal, and then for being out, injured. She wouldn't even get a loser's medal.

Mr Hughes from Arrowby School was sitting in one chair, and Miss Robertson from Ashby School was sitting in another. The chair in the middle was empty. That was the chair for the famous manager who hadn't arrived yet.

Mr Hughes looked anxiously at his watch and muttered something to Miss Robertson. The spectators on both sides of the pitch began to fidget and look round at the table with the cup on it.

'What's the time?' Charlie asked Mrs Morris.

'Nearly half-past two,' Mrs Morris answered.

'Kick-off's two-thirty. You don't think he's forgotten? He still hasn't come.'

'Of course he hasn't forgotten. He'll be here. Don't worry,' Mrs Morris said.

Art Frozzen's dad looked at Charlie. 'I've heard about you from my lad,' he said. 'Good player, he says. Ever thought of Rugby League when you grow up?'

Charlie said she hadn't.

Then the two teams came running out of the pavilion. They were going to start without the famous manager. A wave of disappointment went through the spectators, but they clapped and cheered as the players took up their positions on the field.

Charlie had guessed correctly. They were sitting by the Ashby goal. Jason Jones had won the toss and chosen the advantage of the slope.

Charlie sat hunched up in concentration as the ref blew for the Arrowby kick-off. Arrowby had already realized that Ashby were without one of their best players – Charlie – and they pushed hard from the start. Arrowby kicked off and immediately moved threateningly in the direction of the Ashby defence. An Arrowby mid-field player flashed the ball out to the right; it was picked up and centred just as another tall Arrowby striker moved forwards. He rose into the air, headed the ball towards the top left-hand corner of the goal, but skied it high over the wood.

'Wake up. Wake up, defence!' Charlie shouted, jumping up and down.

A hefty goal-kick from Joan Donovan gave Ashby a breathing space. Jason Jones took the ball up and thundered towards the goal. The Arrowby goalie sprang like a cat and deflected it for a corner. Charlie's heart sank. *She* always took the corners. Surely they weren't going to let Mary Evans take a corner? But that was what happened. And – predictably – the ball trickled pathetically forwards and was instantly cleared by a huge kick from one of the Arrowby defence.

Then three of Arrowby's front runners combined brilliantly to provide their striker with a simple shot at goal. Again, Joan Donovan saved the day for Ashby by coming out bravely and taking the ball from the feet of the Arrowby striker. All the Ashby supporters cheered and shouted and the Arrowby supporters clapped politely.

Jason Jones ran round his team, giving them instructions and urging them on to greater efforts, as the ball once more was cleared from the danger area. The Ashby team was trying to combine to cover for its weaknesses, but the Arrowby attack kept opening up the Ashby defence. Jason Jones covered the field from one end to the other in his attempt to hold the team together and put the brakes on the Arrowby attack.

Josh Turner was trying to tighten the defence, and more than once cleared the ball from the goal area. But Charlie could see the weakness at the other end, where Sharon Smith wasn't getting any help from Mary

Evans, and was being so under-used that the Arrowby team were hardly bothering to mark her at all.

Charlie breathed a sigh of relief when the whistle went for half-time with the score still nil-nil. She'd counted that Arrowby had had at least four shots at goal to Ashby's one. She just hoped that Jason Jones was going to be able to talk some sense and fight into the team.

'Isn't it lovely?' Mrs Morris said to her. 'What a nice sunny day.'

Charlie grunted. It didn't seem a very nice day so far, and it looked as if things might get worse. 'We've got to go and sit down at the other end,' she urged her mother.

Art Frozzen's dad had already made his way up to the far bench and Mrs Morris and Charlie caught up with him.

Then there was a buzz among the spectators as a large black car drew up by the pavilion. Charlie grabbed her mother's arm. 'It's him.

It's him. He didn't forget. Look, it's him.'

The famous manager got out of his car, put a newspaper in his pocket, and walked up to the table to shake hands with Mr Hughes and Miss Robertson. He talked to them for a few minutes, then he walked over to the benches and talked to the spectators.

'Traffic jam,' he said. 'But we made it in the end.'

Charlie held her breath as the famous manager came over to where she was sitting with Mrs Morris and Art Frozzen's dad.

'This is where the experts sit,' he said with a sharp nod of the head, and he went off to sit at the table behind the shining cup.

'He talked to us, Mum,' Charlie said. 'Didn't he?' She could hardly believe it had happened.

'Yes, dear,' Mrs Morris said. She didn't know very much about football, so Charlie wasn't surprised that she didn't have much to say about the famous manager. But wait till Dad got home. He'd listen.

Then the teams ran out on to the field for the second half. Jason Jones had clearly given Ashby a good roasting, because they came out like a different team. Charlie prayed that they wouldn't be put to shame in front of the famous manager.

Arrowby were taken by surprise at Ashby's new attacking game. They took the ball straight away into the Arrowby territory within seconds of the kick-off, with some incisive running and passing. The Arrowby defence was taken by storm and Sharon Smith aimed a shot at the far corner of the net. The Arrowby goalie managed to touch the ball with his fingertips and turn it aside for a corner.

'Not Mary Evans again. Please don't let Mary Evans take it,' Charlie prayed inwardly. Jason Jones had the same idea and signalled to Jim

Walker to take the corner. It was an improvement on Mary Evans's effort, but nerves got the better of Jim and the ball was easily cleared by a good header from the Arrowby defence.

Jason Jones was working overtime and getting good support from his team. They seemed inspired by the presence of the famous manager. But Arrowby were inspired as well, and began to get their game together. The supporters on both sides of the pitch were jumping up and down, cheering and shouting, as the players hurtled up and down the field, first towards the Arrowby goal, then back to the Ashby goal. Charlie could see that the famous manager was following it all with great interest.

But it seemed as if both nets were protected by some magic. The ball hit the woodwork, went over the top, went round the side, went everywhere except into the net.

'Come on. Come on. Score!' Charlie willed them on.

'Put it in the net,' Art Frozzen's dad shouted. 'Stop messing about!'

Art Frozzen had been running up and down the sideline, hoping the ball wouldn't come anywhere near him. So far he'd been lucky, because Sharon Smith was picking up everything that looked at all promising. All Art Frozzen had to do was to stay where Jason Jones told him to stay and run when Jason Jones told him to run.

Art Frozzen's dad looked at his watch. 'Less than five minutes to go,' he said.

Charlie couldn't sit still. She was shouting at the top of her voice, along with all the other supporters on both sides.

Art Frozzen had made his run down the sideline again, on Jason Jones's instructions, and he was standing just in front of Charlie. He looked as though he was thinking of having a little chat with his dad, when suddenly, out of the blue, the ball landed at his feet. He hadn't seen it coming and he looked at it in horror, glued to the spot. He felt as if somebody had dropped an unexploded bomb at his feet. His dad was standing speechless, with his mouth open, like a statue. The Arrowby defence were closing in. But Jason Jones outpaced them down the middle of the pitch.

'Centre it! Centre it!' Charlie screamed, seeing Jason Jones still unmarked in the front of the goalmouth.

'Art frozzen?' his dad yelled.

Suddenly the legs unfroze and Art booted the ball to Jason Jones's feet. Jason Jones welted the ball as hard as he could, into the top right-hand corner of the net. The goalie didn't have a chance.

'It's a goal! It's a goal!' Charlie screamed, along with all the other Ashby supporters.

Even the Arrowby supporters

clapped and said, 'Good goal,' and tried to sound as if they meant it.

A few seconds later the final whistle went. All the supporters clapped and cheered. A draw, one-all, over two legs, was an honourable result.

Charlie raced on to the pitch and clapped Jason Jones on the back.

'Ace goal! Ace goal!' she shouted and she thumped Art Frozzen and everybody thumped everybody else.

Then the famous manager stood up to present the cup. He made a short speech and said they'd have to share it – six months for each school. Then he handed out the medals. They all got the same sort of medal, because it was a draw.

Jason Jones and the Arrowby captain held the cup between them and ran round the field with it, followed by their teams. Everybody cheered again. Then they all came back and stood in excited groups. Miss Nixon rescued the cup. The match had certainly done what she'd hoped it would do. Jason Jones, Art Frozzen and Charlie Morris were acting more like best friends than old enemies.

The famous manager signalled them all to be quiet. 'I haven't finished yet,' he said, and he took the newspaper out of his pocket. It was the *Journal* with Old Meg's story in it.

'I picked up this paper at the garage,' he said. 'There's a young woman here, wearing a Number Nine shirt, who couldn't play today. So she doesn't get a medal. I bet she's very unhappy about that. Now I'd like you all to know why she couldn't play today. Now listen here . . .' and he read out the story about the fire. Everybody listened. When they thought that he'd finished, they clapped very loudly. But he hadn't finished. 'If that young woman would like to accompany me to the boot of my car, I've got something she might like to have. Seeing that she didn't get a medal.'

Charlie was too excited to speak.

With Mrs Morris and Art Frozzen and Art Frozzen's dad, and Jason Jones, she went to the shining black car with the manager. The manager opened the boot. It was full of football gear, all used, muddy and dirty. He pulled out a red shirt with Number Nine on it.

'This is my Number Nine shirt,' he said. 'My son. My Number Nine. It'll be a bit on the big side for you, but you'll grow into it, I don't doubt. Take a year or two yet.'

He handed the red Number Nine shirt to Charlie. Charlie couldn't believe it. She held the shirt as if it was something very precious and delicate, as if it might break. She looked at the famous manager.

'Yes. It's a bit niffy. His mother hasn't washed it yet. Sweat and mud,' the famous man said with a grin. 'That's football. And that was good football out there, good team-work. Football's a great game. It's *the* great game. Right?' He turned the question to Art Frozzen's dad.

Art Frozzen's dad thought for a bit. 'Aye,' he said. 'I reckon it might catch on.'

And they both laughed.

Charlie pulled the dirty red shirt over her own very clean one. It came down past her knees.

'You can't ever wash this, Mum,' she said, smoothing her hand carefully over the caked mud so as not to dislodge any of it.

'That's football,' the manager said again, and got into his car.

'Hey,' Jason Jones said to Charlie. 'Look at my new tooth,' and he fished it out of his screwed-up hanky. 'Not allowed to play football with it in. Watch this,' and he put the tooth in his mouth, pushed at it with his tongue, and made it stand out like a tusk.

'Ace,' Charlie said.

'We'd have won the cup outright if you'd been playing,' Jason Jones said.

'Right,' Art Frozzen agreed.

Charlie hesitated. Then she said, 'What about what you said before? Like that I was handi-thingy, whatever it is? Worse than useless. That's what you said. What about that?'

Jason Jones wiggled his false tooth backwards and forwards. 'Didn't *mean* it, did I? Daft ape, you. You're the best footballer we've got. After me, that is. What d'you think about my pot tooth?'

'Ace,' Charlie said. 'What d'you think about my glass eye?'

'Ace,' Jason Jones said, and he began to shout, 'We are the greatest. We are the greatest.'

The rest of the team gathered round and joined in the chanting. 'We are the greatest. We are the greatest,' and they began to run off together to the pavilion and tea, thumping the air and heading imaginary footballs into distant, invisible goals.

Except for Art Frozzen. He turned

to Charlie who was standing there uncertainly.

'Well, you coming or what?' he asked.

'Race you,' Charlie grinned back, and they ran off after the rest of the team and disappeared into the pavilion.

READ MORE IN PUFFIN